THE DEVIL TAINTED US

SHANJIDA NUSRATH ALI

Copyright © Shanjida Nusrath Ali, 2022

All Rights Reserved.
This book or any portion thereof may not be reproduced or used in any matter whatsoever without the express written permission of the authors except for the use of brief quotations in a book review. This is a work of fiction. All names, characters, business, events and places are either the product of the authors' imagination or used fictitiously.

ISBN: 9798403246880

Warning: The book contains intense sex scenes, drug abuse, physical abuse, suicidal scenes, molestation scenes, violence, religious references and explicit language. Readers discretion is advised.

PLAYLIST

Scare- Boy Epic

In Flames- Digital Daggers

Often (Kygo Remix)- The Weekend, Kygo

See You Bleed- Ramsey

Dirty Mind- Boy Epic

War of Heart- Ruelle

Monsters- Ruelle

Madness- Ruelle

Closing In- Ruelle

Wolves- Sam Tinnesz, Silverberg

Black Sea- Natasha Blume

Deep End- Ruelle

Bad Dream- Ruelle

Shadow Preachers- Zella Day

Wolf- Boy Epic

Sirens- Fleurie

Love and War- Fleurie

Heaven- Julia Micheals

Man or Monster- Sam Tinnesz, Zayde Wolf
Flames- Tedy
Glass Heart- Tommee Profitt, Sam Tinnesz
Walk Through the Fire- Zayde Wolf, Ruelle
Far from Home (The Raven)- Sam Tinnesz
The Other Side- Ruelle
You Belong to Me- Cat Pierce
Watch Your Back- Sam Tinnesz
Devil Devil- MILCK
Secrets and Lies- Ruelle
Don't Let Me Go- RAIGN
Even If It Hurts- Same Tinnesz
All Is Lost- Katie Garfield
Caught in the Fire- Klergy

PROLOGUE

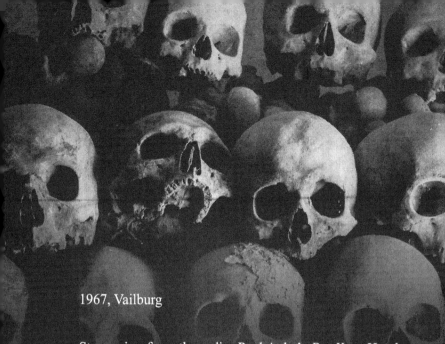

1967, Vailburg

Strumming from the radio, Paul Anka's *Put Your Head On My Shoulder* mingles with noise from the traffic my brother and I pass by. My head bobs with the beat of the music, vision blackening slightly by the shades resting over my nose. With one hand on the steering wheel and the other resting loosely on the door of my black Chevy Camaro Convertible as the wind brushes our cheeks like a gentle caress.

My brother takes a deep drag of his cigar, exhaling clouds of smoke with the air smelling like burnt tobacco. As we get closer to the street of our parents' house, I can feel the atmosphere turning tense and dark. But we both know that it has to be done.

For so many years, we have stayed quiet, baring every

ounce of shame and torture without any protest. Year after year have passed for us, suffering this unforgettable hell we lived and breathed in. I ease off the car's accelerator, before hitting the brakes at the closed iron gate. Malcolm, our fifty-year-old house guard, comes to the gate with a gentle smile on his face before he lets us pass without any questions. He doesn't need to interrogate us, he has been like an uncle to us since the day we were born.

"What brings you two here? I thought you went on your business trip," he asks, crossing his arms.

"Are mother and father home?" I query instead, taking off my shades.

He nods timidly in response. "They returned from the mall fifteen minutes ago."

I hear a rustling sound beside me as my brother takes out a huge wad of money and passes it to Malcolm. "Go home for good. We don't need you anymore."

His face constricts with pain, a frown appearing between his brows with hurt reflecting in his eyes. "But sir, what have I done? I do not understand that…after twenty years of my service I…I," he stutters.

"We're doing this for your own good, Malcolm. Everything is taken care of, you can leave now."

Without uttering another word to him I drive ahead, taking the circular turn around the fountain my mother has spent a large fortune on. Parking the car, we both open our doors in sync as I button up the front of my black tux and get the stuff we bought an hour ago before arriving here. Bursting open the wooden door that has an elegant design carved in, we enter the house, greeted by the sound of the TV echoing throughout the main room. We know the maids aren't home because they were informed about their jobs being terminated before we got here. Following the sound, our footsteps thud against the marble floor as we enter the living room.

Both our parents are relaxing on the plush, gray couch. Mother's head rests against father's chest while his back rests against the couch with one hand around mother's shoulder and the other resting on her thigh. Such a sight would be evident enough to tell they are just like any other normal couple who are enjoying each other's company as they watch a sitcom show, laughing loudly seeing other people make a fool out of themselves in front of millions. Mother is dressed in her favorite green dress with puffed sleeves. Her blond hair is styled perfectly with light makeup painted on her face. Perfectionist as always. Father isn't in his usual suit dress. Instead, he is wearing a casual blue polo shirt with off-white pants and polished black shoes.

The ideal picture of a rich, happy couple.

But none of it is real. Just a fucking fake reflection of the monsters that lurk behind them both.

We head to the opposite couch, standing behind it and

both our parents look up with their fake smiles faltering.

"Boys? When did you come back?" mother asks, leaving her husband's side as she stands, straightening her shoulders. Father also follows her motion putting his hands inside his pockets.

"I thought you two were supposed to come back next week. Did the meeting end early?" he asks with a frown, a serious expression shadowing his face.

We both remain silent, looking at them with a cold, heartless face. Sensing the uncomfortable silence, mother claps her hands gently offering that same bogus smile she has always given us since infancy.

"Well, how about some lunch in the backyard?" She looks from father to us, waiting for our response, "I will get the maids to prepare your favorite meals and it is perfect, bright weather for spending some quality time."

There is silence again except for the actors saying their dialogues on the TV. I look at my brother whose face mirrors the same emotions I am feeling at the moment.

Coldness. Rage. Emptiness.

The next minute, we both take out the guns hidden inside our suit pockets, pointing them at our parents. Horror instantly takes over their faces as their eyes widen and their breathing accelerates.

"W-What…What are you two doing? Put the guns down, right now," father stutters as he gives it all to sound brave even though he is failing miserably.

"You…you two don't have to do this. We are your parents…w-we are a family-"

I snicker under my breath while unlocking the safety button.

"Family?" my brother starts, "I don't think you both even fucking know what that word truly means."

"Listen, if you are doing it for the money then you know both of you are getting the business and wealth next month. You both are now adults, so, eventually, it's all yours-"

I shoot the vase watching our parents scream and tremble from fear. A sight that I have been waiting for years to witness. And dear God, it is a sight to behold.

I shake my head, followed by a sinister, dark grin.

"You both know the true reason."

"Y-you want us to apologize? Fine, we will do it. We both are so sorry," mother looks at father, nodding at him to follow her words.

"Yes. We are so sorry for what we did. Please, forgive us. We have forgiven every mistake you two have made, it's only fair you forgive us, too."

"You two are our own blood. Our sons. It's not like we are your stepfamily-"

"Just the thought of you being connected to us by blood is what makes this more unforgivable," I interrupt her. "You two have ruined the beginning and end of our lives. No matter what we do or where we go, our lives will always be tainted because of what you did."

"It's clear as daylight neither of you is sorry, so stop lying," my brother seethes through his clenched teeth, tightening his hold on the gun.

Mother starts to sob, shedding her crocodile tears, assuming that will change our minds. Sad news for her, we stopped caring the day they ruined my and my brother's lives.

"You won't get away with this. The police will get involved for sure." Always being the diplomatic man in the room.

"Any last words?" I ask, my index finger hovering over the trigger.

"Please, listen…w-we c-can make t-this work. Please don't-"

Father never gets to finish his final sentence as I pull the trigger. Watching the bullet pierce right through his forehead as his body instantly falls on the carpeted floor. Mother screams in terror and shock as she watches her husband's blood pooling around his head already.

We walk towards her, enjoying the sight of her body trembling like she is losing her mind like a lunatic. Hovering over her like the demons about to rip her wretched soul away forever, she looks up at us, begging for her life with her tears.

"Please…I'm sorry…I should have been a better mother. Please don't kill me…I won't tell anyone."

After a fleeting moment of silence, my brother pulls the trigger and ends our mother's meaningless life with blood from her head spraying our face and suit.

It is over. Our parents are dead and we killed them.

Maybe the police will see our actions as a sign of greed for our father's wealth but the truth will always be known to us only. And they deserved it. Not bothering to wipe away the blood, I head to the shelf where father's expensive cigars and drinks are stacked. Taking a cigar, I take the remote and walk towards the empty couch, sitting down and switching to a different channel. My brother sits beside me with my father's most expensive whiskey in hand, drinking straight from the bottle. He passes it to me as I let out a heavy smoke before taking a sip, letting the whiskey leave a soothing burn down my throat.

"Wasn't there supposed to be a match today?" my brother asks, drinking with his eyes straining on the screen.

I scowl, thinking about it for a few seconds. "I think it was canceled and moved to next week."

"Oh, didn't know that."

Selecting a comedy-drama sitcom show, I lean back with my legs crossed as my ankle rests on my opposite knee.

Any other person would simply run away and hide his tracks after committing such a crime, but neither I nor did my brother feel even an ounce of guilt and remorse for the sin we committed. We know they deserved it and that it was the right thing to do after suffering for so many years.

We both were introduced to darkness the day we opened our eyes. Innocence and joy were never a part of our lives. We predicted after today everything will be alright, darkness would no longer be our companion. But we were wrong because deep down we knew this darkness was sucking us into a black hole that we may never return from.

And killing our parents proved it.

There was no turning back. Not anymore.

It's all over.

We are ruined by the devil within us...the devil tainted us.

THE DEVIL TAINTED US

Chapter One

AGATHA

1983, Vailburg

I scream at the top of my lungs that I can feel my own ears ringing in pain. The group of strong and rough hands of the doctors and male nurses. The two female nurses who have come to do their job are standing at the corner with their wide, horror filled eyes meeting my black ones.

"Get the Velcro straps! Hurry!" the doctor orders the nurses in his loud, gruff voice. The nurses didn't waste a single second before dashing out of the room.

"Ah!" I scream again so that I nearly feel the nerves on my necks popping against my pale skin. Their fingertips now digging deeper into my skin, dark bruises will be left as a reminder for several days.

I writhe as hard as possible with all my might, not caring that my hair is a mess and the hospital gown is starting to ride up, exposing my bare legs.

Before I know it, I hear the faint snapping sound of the velcro as they start to tie me down to the bed. My legs are tightly bound against the bed posts, with no room for any movements. But the doctor, absentmindedly, let go of my hand, and using my chance I grab the nearest steel tray from the bedside table. Gripping it tightly, I hit as hard as possible against the side of the doctor's head.

"Fuck!" he grunts in pain, instantly holding his head before he crouches. I hit him again, witnessing him fall face down on the floor with the nurses helping him.

With my free hand, I snap open the velcro straps, freeing myself before I hop out of the bed and head towards the door.

"Don't let her get away!" I hear the doctor scream. Adrenaline fuels my fear and anxiety as I rush out of the room without a single glance over my shoulder. Breathing heavily, my wild eyes look around frantically for an exit…an escape. The corridor is empty like a desert with bright, plain lights brightening up the white walls and floors. The familiar smell of medicines and antiseptics fill my nostrils while I run down the hallway.

A vast door at the right side catches my sight. Ignoring my dry throat and thumping heart, I run towards the door. Heavy footsteps echo behind me, getting closer and closer.

Hope for freedom starts to rush through me but it is instantly crushed like an innocent ant when the door doesn't budge as I push it. I twist the handle frantically but it is pointless. Before I can think of another escape, those familiar strong hands engulf me back to be trapped where I escaped from.

I scream again, pulling away from their holds that I lose my footing and kneel on the floor. But it doesn't bother them as they drag me down, ignoring my pleas and cry for help.

"Please, no! Don't do this! No!" I yell with my voice echoing loudly in the hallway. I continue to writhe until we get back to the room. The doctor is slightly massaging his injured head when he glares at my return.

"Get her on the bed. Right now!" he barks at the nurses who carry me and lay me down with their vice grip.

But before I can even contemplate the situation, I feel the sting of the needle on my right arm. In the blink of an eye, my nerves start to turn weak, my body slackening as it feels weightless. My mind is losing control as everything around me starts to become blurry. The faint voices of the doctors and nurses reach my ears but I can't grasp a single word. Bit by bit I'm breaking connection with sanity as darkness engulfs me into its arms.

I can't move. My head, my chest…burning pain. Every

inch of my body feels trapped…bound to darkness. It is dark everywhere.

Where am I?

I will myself to open my eyes but my body is defying me. I try to speak but I can't feel my lips. Whispered voices reach my ears…listen to it. Listen. Damn it! Listen!

"She cannot be here anymore, Mr. Arthur." It's the doctor's voice. But what is Tristen doing here? He can't be here…he shouldn't…

"You know well she has already been through a lot after losing her sister. After my wife's death nothing has been the same for her. You have to help me, doctor, because this is my only option."

No. Do not talk about her. Do not mention her name from your lips!

"Mr. Arthur, I understand your concern. But she was on the verge of losing control today. I can't risk the reputation of my hospital and the safety of my employees because of your sister-in-law. I fear that what she is beyond us…perhaps she is…" his voice trails off.

"She is what?" Tristen asks.

"The nurses have heard her talk to herself about sins and demons in her room. She would look wildly every now and then at the walls. And some nights she would keep clawing her skin until it bleeds while she laughs hysterically. Her demeanor all points to the only conclusion that she may be possessed."

"What! Have you gone insane, doctor-"

"I am stating the facts, Mr. Arthur. We all pray to God for our loved ones to be safe and healthy. We believe in His existence, so why can't we believe in the existence of demons and the devil?"

There is silence for several seconds. "All I know is that Agatha cannot be in my hospital. I'm sorry, Mr. Arthur."

"What do you propose then?" he asks.

The doctor sighs shakily before muttering his response, "There is a place I know that treats people like her. But it is far away from the Vailburg Hill's range. No visitations are allowed until she is fully recovered. And there are nuns and priests who take care of the patients. And one of the priests there is a doctor who will be there twenty-four hours in case of emergencies."

"Are you suggesting…" Tristen doesn't finish his words and there is no other answer from the doctor as well, with the silence and suspense clawing within my heart.

"Oh, doctor. I will do everything in my power to make sure she is better. That is all I care for. Do not worry about the money or time, I will give them both."

"Very well then. I will send them a letter first thing in the morning. We should have a response from them soon."

The voices continue to whisper but they soon turn muted to my ears as darkness starts to shroud my soul again. But one thing I'm certain of is that the next time I open my eyes I won't be here anymore.

I will be in an unknown place with strangers and being treated like a devil possessed woman. But I'm well aware of the place they are referring to. The name itself is like those horror stories children hear about from their grandparents, that I don't want to think of. But I have no other choice… none.

The gates to this living hell will be opening for me.

I will soon be in the Magdalene.

THE DEVIL TAINTED US

CHAPTER TWO

AGATHA

"Times will come when men will try to tear you apart like a delicate flower. Teach you things like you will be an adolescent for the rest of your life," Helena mutters, combing my hair from behind. I sit in front, on the small stool, listening to her words.

"That doesn't mean they know more than you ever will. They will order and control you," I feel the wooden ends of the brush massaging my scalp, "but you just let them blow by and lift your face up with pride and power as you do whatever the hell you want to do."

I turn my head sideways, looking at her illuminated figure by the fireplace before asking, "But why? Won't you be there for me?"

She turns my face forward and gathers my long, black hair in her hands as she starts to braid it. "Someday you are going to be all alone. Nobody to look up to but yourself. So, you will have to find a way to take care of yourself without being a pawn to the world."

After finishing styling my hair like she does every night, I feel her soft hands cupping my shoulders.

"It's better to be alone, Agatha. That way you will feel safe around yourself because trusting someone else is like putting yourself into the dens of the devil."

I jolt awake from a sudden bump. I'm in the car with Tristen as we drive down the gravel road. His side is filled with the vast, uncountable trees of the forest, while my side faces the ocean. The atmosphere feels too suffocating so I roll down the window.

The cold breeze fans my cheeks, my hair running wild with it. I've missed this so much. We take many things in life for granted that are easily found in our daily lives. But we understand it's true value when it is taken away.

Why is that the case? Why can't we appreciate the things we don't even deserve, every now and then?

We are mortal fools indeed.

Tristen halts the car near the Vailburg shipping dock where the heavy crashing of the ocean waves surrounds us. The winter fog shrouds upon the ocean, blocking the beauty of it. Frowning, I look at him as he stares straight ahead of him at the empty road. His grip tightening on the steering wheel of his Chevrolet that his father gifted him on his wedding day.

I still remember that day as he whisked away my elder sister, Helena, in his arms, both of them laughing like the happy couple they were. She waved me a goodbye before they both headed for their honeymoon. But little did I know that was the last time I would see Helena smile.

Tristen's Adam's apple bobs as he gulps and lets out an exhausted sigh. "I don't want to do this to you, Agatha."

He is wearing a black suit with a gray tie. His hair perfectly styled back, as always. He has been a perfectionist since day one, but I guess marriage was the only thing he wasn't so good at.

"But I am doing it for your sister. She would want me to take care of you," he faces me with a pitiful frown and caresses my hair, "You need to get better for her."

I remain silent, watching a ship floating beside the wooden deck. But suddenly, I notice the place is nearly vacant unlike the usual crowded times. The fog is thick and heavy, but I can hear faint footsteps coming from the back.

Tristen cups my jaw to face him with a softening gaze.

"I'm sorry, Agatha. But there is no other option left."

Suddenly, I hear the door on my side open, sending an electric charge through my body. Before I can contemplate what is happening, two strong hands grip my arms, nearly digging into my skin, as I'm pulled out of the car.

Horror dawns at me and my eyes dart at Tristen to help

me. But the bastard is calmly sitting, staring forward. I open my mouth to scream for help but that chance is taken away by those same pair of hands as it clasps over my lips. I thrash against his hold when suddenly another man comes in and holds my legs, helping my captor.

The man in front of me wears a black coverall with his face being hidden by the white vendetta mask. We reach the dock side, where a boat behind the ship catches my sight. Another man in the same attire is already waiting as the men throw me to him. He catches me and I take that chance to scream at the top of my lungs for help. It is ear-piercing even to me and I almost plan to jump out of the boat to swim away.

"Help! Help me! Someone!" I scream.

The boat trembles when the one who held my arms jumps on it and grasps my jaw. Pulling out a huge, shiny knife he points the tip right at my throat.

My body turns still like a statue with fear clawing my nerves. His face is also hidden with the mask but yet I can feel his warmth close to my face.

"Done with screaming?" his muffled, gruff voice asks.

I remain silent.

He tilts his head sideways, digging the knife a bit more against my racing pulse. "One more word from that pretty little mouth and I'll stab the blade right through your throat."

The coldness and emptiness in his voice sent chills down my spine. It feels like it doesn't matter if I live or die before wherever he is taking me. He let go of my jaw before presenting his hand to the other man who passed him an injection.

The tears I have been holding back, leak from my eyes as the memories of being injected several times flash in front of me.

"Shedding tears won't save you, little girl," he mutters, bringing the needle close to my arms. My body starts to shiver from the cold and fear. Adrenaline rushing through my spine like never before.

He leans closer when I feel the light prickle of the needle against my skin as he presses the syringe. "The least you fight, the easier it will be for you. Trust me."

Trust him? Trust a man who is holding my life like a loose thread?

Never. And yet, something about those last two words of his holds a promise.

A promise that I'm unaware of and still wanted to believe deep down. Soon that same feeling of my numbing nerves return. My eyes start to become drowsy and I know I'm going to hit my head on the boat's plank as I will fall sideways, but I no longer have control over my body.

"Let's go. We don't have much time left," the man orders as the rest of his words start to fade away.

The world tilts around me as my body leans sideways but the hit on my head never comes. Instead, a hand cups my head, protecting me from getting hurt before gently guiding me down. But before I can see who it is, my vision turns black.

HIM

I gently place her head down while I question myself why I even bothered saving herself from hurting. I'm the one who will be hurting her and ruining her to the depths of her innocent soul.

"Is she out?" one of the new guys asks.

I simply nod my response. "Head straight to our destination."

Both of them get to work as we start to make our way back to the living hell our new guest will be welcomed in. I sit down, removing my mask and letting out a deep sigh, feeling my heart still pounding from the adrenaline rush I faced a few moments ago.

It never crossed my mind that this is what my life will be as a thirty-seven year old. But this life chose me, not the other way around. I am a slave to my own fate where darkness shackled my soul and heart.

I look towards the horizon with the breeze touching my scruffed cheeks. I run a hand through my hair as my gaze shifts towards the girl who is going to be imprisoned like me.

She already is as she is with you.

My eyes take upon her features, looking at her pale skin that I'm itching to touch just to feel the softness. Her black hair is dark as the night that is caressing her cheeks, with few strands touching her closed eyes. She looks beautiful…just like an angel. Just her beauty is making my nerves rush faster and my heart pound harder.

But that isn't going to save her or change her fate. I will be the devil who will rip off her wings and become her downfall.

Be prepared, angel. Be prepared.

CHAPTER THREE

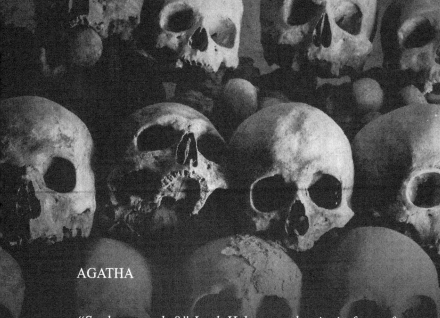

AGATHA

"So, how was he?" I ask Helena as she sits in front of the dressing table, removing her pearl ear-rings. I lean my hands and back against the table while facing her.

I notice her cheeks turning red as she smiles shyly, avoiding eye contact.

"He was okay."

My brows furrow together in confusion. Why is she lying?

"Just, okay? But you are blushing just hearing about him."

She rolls her eyes keeping up that coy smile and takes a tissue to remove her cherry-colored lipstick. I want that color too.

"Tell me, Helena," I whine, shaking her shoulder.

"Why are you so curious about him?" She chuckles.

I pout my lip, crossing my arms. "Because mommy didn't

let me see him. She said only the elders will be there and I should stay in my room."

"Ah. But I thought you had a peek from the bathroom window."

"No! I was trying to look from the library-" I press my lips together, feeling the tang of embarrassment from being caught. Mommy never said I couldn't go to the library to see the man who would soon marry my sister.

"So, you were snooping, huh?" Now Helena crosses her arms, narrowing her eyes as she bites down to her lip. "Weren't you the one to say the other day that it is bad to snoop into-"

"But I didn't have any bad intentions." I kick an imaginary rock as I keep my gaze cast down. "I just wanted to see him, that's all."

"Aww. Come here." She pulls me down her lap, hugging me from behind.

"He looked like Prince Charming."

My eyes widen in excitement. "The one from Cinderella?"

She nods with a gentle smile. "Exactly like him. He is sweet, polite and respectable."

"So, you will marry him?" I ask.

"I think I will."

"But he doesn't have your shoe. Cinderella got her prince when she lost her shoe."

Helena laughs heartily, kissing my cheek but I wipe it

away with my palm. "That was in the original story, maybe this one deserves a different twist, don't you think?"

"So, he won't give you a glass slipper?"

She chuckles again, hugging me tighter, as I relish in her warmth and love, praying that whether she gets the glass slipper or not, she will get her happily ever after.

I feel my body swaying. My consciousness returns to me as I blink my eyes open. The gloomy, gray sky is the first sight that greets me as the rain droplets fall on my skin. Swallowing deeply, I feel my dry throat clearing up slightly. I try to move my hands but then notice the thick ropes binding them. Frowning, I twist them but it's of no use.

Suddenly, reality hits me, memories of being kidnapped by three men fill my mind. Looking out the corner of my eyes, fret dawns at me as I find those three men with one of them rowing the boat. Their backs facing me. I carefully lift my head up to see our destination.

There is nothing but water surrounding us. Deep, clear and dark ocean water. I face the direction the men are looking to find a vast island. From afar it's hard to get a clear picture but it's surrounded by deep and dark forest. At the very top a castle-like monument rests.

We are close to our destination and the thought makes

me feel suffocated in this vast sea.

God. What am I going to do?

I have to escape one way or another.

I keep twisting my binds but there is little to no room for my hands to move. The only way I can think of escaping is attacking my captors. I look behind me to luckily find a knife, the same knife that man held against my throat.

I move ever so slowly, trying my best to move along with the boat to make no noise. I quickly push the handle of the knife with my mouth, pointing the blade to the rope and start moving it back and forth. In my head I keep praying that none of them turn around, while the knife starts to work its magic, loosening my restraints. But then I feel the boat slowly go down and realize we are now mere seconds away from the shore.

Fuck. No. No. No.

This can't be happening. Dear God. No, please.

I speed up my motion as my palms turn sweaty with panic rushing down my spine. When the rope goes loose and my hands are free, hope starts to shine upon my soul, but it is snatched away when the shadow of my captor falls upon me. Before I can look up, he grabs me by my hair, pulling my head back. I grip the knife tightly and make a move to plunge it right through his cold heart. But the hard bump of the boat as it stops at the shore makes my feet tremble, making me fall back with the knife dropping from my grip.

"Ah!" I groan in pain. But soon the agony gets doubled when my captor forces me up holding my hair. His friend joins in and they both carry me out like the way they got me in. The crashing of the waves and cawing of the crows are the only sound echoing around.

"Let me go! Help! Somebody help me!" I scream. I thrash against their hold. The one holding my arms has his skin exposed and I don't bother to think before I sink my teeth into his wrist, biting as hard as possible.

"Fuck!" he grunts, but doesn't let go of my arm. I bite harder that I can almost taste the metallic flavor of his blood on my tongue. Soon he loses his tolerance and pries his hand away from my mouth, losing my arms that his friend loses his balance and falls too.

The rope falls on the ground making me free from restraints. I instantly stand up and dash away from them, running towards the deep, dark forest. The men soon start to chase me, but I don't look back once as I run deeper and deeper. The more I get in, the colder it feels. I notice even my heavy breathing is coming out in the form of fog. With my bare feet, I feel the crunches of the fallen leaves with the wet soil dusting my sole.

My lungs are burning…begging for air but my mind keeps telling me to not stop for a second. Suddenly, I realize I don't hear their thudded footsteps anymore. It is pure silence.

Taking a chance, I look over my shoulder, finding

nobody. I stop beside a coastal redwood tree. I inhale and exhale heavily letting out a few coughs as I try to calm myself while my eyes look everywhere for any traces of my captors. I run a hand through my hair and continue to walk ahead with a steady pace this time.

I have to get out of here. And the only way to freedom is the shore where the boat is. But I can't risk going there now because one of them must be guarding it. Goosebumps prick my skin from coldness. I hug myself, rubbing my palms along my arms. My sleeve dress doesn't help to keep me warm.

But all of a sudden, I feel an electricity running through my spine. Before I can attempt to escape, I feel those familiar arms caging me with my back pressing tightly against his chest.

"Nowhere to run now, little girl," he rasps, his hot breath brushing my earlobe.

In one swift move he presses me against the tree, brings my wrists behind my back and binds them with ropes. I let out a gasp when he turns me around to face him and grabs my neck, applying slight pressure on my throat. He is still wearing his mask as he leans closer. "For that act you pulled, I will get you later."

"Please let me go. You don't understand-"

"Shhh," he shushes me and gestures with his index finger against the lips of his mask. "You may think you will escape from here or that somebody will help you. But get one thing straight through that useless brain of yours."

I can feel his fingers digging into my skin. "Not a single living soul in this place will help you. You are like a trapped bird. I am the hunter who brought you and this place will be your cage."

He is so close that his mask touches my nose. "Welcome to Mery Heights, little girl. Be prepared to breathe in a living nightmare. But most of all," he slightly moves his mask up, showing his lips and five o'clock shadow, "be prepared to be tainted by the devil."

His lips are touching my cheek, sending shivers down my spine. His words are a threat, his presence feels forbidden and his demeanor foretelling danger.

He retrieves a scarf from his back pocket and uses it to cover my eyes, depriving me from one of my senses. My breathing paces up with fear and vulnerability.

"The more you fight, the more you will lose yourself. My advice is that you bear it and try to live through it. Many have come with a brave spirit like yours but even the bravest ones yielded," he murmurs. Holding my arms, he drags me somewhere while I keep thinking of every possible way to escape. More footsteps come along, signaling the arrival of his other friends.

He pushes me forward before I bump onto a hard chest and feel two hands capturing me by my bound hands.

"Should I inject her again?" one of them asks.

"No, she already had a dose. Another might hamper with the treatments," he murmurs.

The hand keeps a vice grip on me, guiding me ahead, taking me to my so-called cage. The whole walk I remain silent, no longer fighting because I know now isn't the time. At this moment, I have no choice but to follow my unknown path.

Perhaps once I get to the place, I would know where to escape from. But the question is, for how long would I have to keep trying for my freedom?

The walk seems to be endless, and the only sounds piercing my ears are the flying crows above, along with the crashing waves. The further we head in, the colder it feels.

There is no snow here, that's for sure, but I even start to guess the sun didn't rise either. Few moments later, they stop, making me follow their lead.

Suddenly, I hear the screeching sound of an iron gate opening, followed by the crunching of the leaves.

Are we here?

I feel my throat burning with anxiety, my nerves shivering from fear, adrenaline running down my spine like cold water.

Shit.

We head in and I realize I can hear someone screaming. It is faint but it is still there, and that only amplifies my fear even more.

"You two wait here," he orders before passing by me and stalking forward. But he quickly returns back and this time I'm pushed towards him.

"Go and wait at your quarters. I will meet you two there," he says and takes me ahead. Another door opens, but this one feels like a regular door. I can feel my surroundings closing in, feeling less cold.

Hushed words and chatters echo around but he responds to none, continuing our journey. Few minutes later he stops and there is a soft rustling of keys with a door clicking open. We step in until he pauses again, this time standing right behind me. He is so close that I can feel his warm breath against the back of my neck.

"I'm going to untie you now." Is he?

"But I won't take the blindfold off. When you hear the door close, only then you are allowed to see. Understood?" his rasps in his deep voice. My sensation is highlighted just from his mere presence.

I simply nod.

In one swift move, my hands are finally free. I rotate my wrists to ease down the ache, but I can still feel him standing behind me, leaning more closer that his lips nearly touch my shoulder. But I move away from him, worried he will do something more terrifying than capturing me.

"Don't come near me," I warn him, even though the blindfolds don't let me see the monster who kept me captive.

He lets out a dark chuckle that only holds terror and darkness.

"If you think you will be the one making the demands here, then let me clear your doubts." His footsteps get closer while I take mine back until I feel like a wall against my back, blocking my escape.

I raise my hands to take off the blindfold but he holds my wrists.

"You are breaking the rules, little girl," he mutters with a husky tone, trapping my hands above my head.

"Just let me go. Don't-"

"Don't what? Hurt you? Rape you?" he mentions my ultimate fear, making my breathing turn ragged. My chest heaving up and down as I feel his other hand cupping my chin.

"You are nothing but a prisoner here. And prisoners don't order, they kneel," his breath feathering my cheek while his fingers tighten around my chin. His hands are so big and rough along with a cold skin.

"Break me how much you want, torture me with everything that is nightmares for others, but here is a news for you: I won't kneel. Ever," I threaten him through my clenched teeth, denying to be afraid of him.

He chuckles under his breath. "Tough one I see. Well, I will have fun breaking you bit by bit, each and every day."

I can feel him grinning before he lets go of my hands

and takes a step back. "Just remember, you brought it upon yourself, little girl."

With those last words he walks back furthermore before shutting the door. The moment the door closes I take off my blindfold, blinking rapidly to light dilating my pupils. I'm in a bedroom, a dusty and dark one.

The walls are made of gray bricks with cracks on them. No wallpapers or paints. There are no photos or any paintings hanging. Just a phrase written in long, rough strokes that says: *DON'T WORSHIP THE DEVIL WITHIN YOU. TRUST GOD AND ANGELS ONLY.*

The ceiling also has cracks and dust that it nearly feels like it will fall down on me anytime. A lantern sits on top of a small table beside the single bed, which is covered with nothing but a plain, white sheet and one pillow at the head. The cold wind gusting through the long thin window grasps my attention. There is no glass covering it except for the thin curtain swaying. I rush to get the view of the place that holds me captive, but I see nothing but the ocean and trees covering my sight.

Shit.

I stride towards the door only to find it locked from the outside. That fucker locked me in. I twist the handle again and again, nearly on the verge of ripping it off, but I don't carry the strength of a monster.

I take a step back, feeling my lungs burning with

suffocation of imprisonment and hopelessness. I can't do anything but wait. I don't know how long that will have to last but it is my only choice.

I have to be strong and patient.

I walk back to my now so-called bed, resting my back against the pillow with my knees against my chest.

Wait. Observe. Then strike.

My sister's words echoed in my mind, giving me the light at the end of the tunnel of darkness I am in. I will escape.

One way or another, until my last breath, I will give it all to escape.

THE DEVIL TAINTED US

Chapter Four

AGATHA

"Take out the small plates from the second shelf, Agatha," mommy tells me, pointing at the cupboard where she keeps most of the expensive plates and cups.

I do as told, bringing the utensils on the countertop. I help mommy fill the plates with pieces of key lime pie that she has made, before putting them on a tray and carrying it towards the garden area where everyone else is chatting.

"Ah, here she is," dad mutters with a gentle smile that he always offers me, helping me set the tray on the table before pulling me beside him to take a seat.

"We were just talking about you," he says. The other guests laugh in unison as if dad just cracked a joke. Today Tristen's family members have visited again to bond with our family more. He is sitting beside Helena, while his parents are on the side couch.

"Your father was telling us about your passion for art."

I blush, fidgeting with the colorful beads on my frock with my gaze cast down.

"How old are you now, dear?" Tristen's mom asks, placing her cup of tea on the table and taking a bite of the pie.

"Fourteen," I barely whisper from shyness.

"And you are pursuing art at such a young age? That is very impressive," she mutters.

"I want to be an artist when I grow up," I add, feeling my cheeks flushing.

"I would love to see them actually," Tristen says, leaning forward with his hands tangling together as they rest on his knees.

Dad caresses my shoulder and nods. "Why don't you show him, sweetheart? Tristen loves artworks too."

I nod back and stand up with Tristen following behind me as I guide him towards my room. Luckily, mom tidied my room beforehand so I won't have to be embarrassed with showing him my room.

It is just like any other normal room with a bed, table, wardrobe and a small shelf. But the right corner is my favorite as I paint there most of the time. My easel, brushes, paint tubes and a few art pieces are there, as Tristen walks towards it and looks at each and every work like he is analyzing them.

He simply watches the landscapes I painted, along with

a few rough sketches of trees and flowers, and nods with an appreciative look.

"These are very beautiful." *He wasn't lying.*

I let out a breath of relief, and look everywhere but at him as I whisper a thank you.

"You also have a sketchbook?" *he asks with a smirk.*

I nod and walk forward to pull out the thick sketchbook, filled with more sketches of landscapes and few still figures. I place it on the table and start showing him.

"I'm very curious to know what inspired your artworks. Will you tell me?"

I nod enthusiastically and start to picture stories after stories that inspired me to pursue art. He sits on the chair beside my aisle and keeps nodding like he is attentively listening to my words. I feel a sense of pride and happiness blooming within me.

But suddenly, I feel him caressing my elbow with the back of his knuckles and for a minute my words falter. A slight uneasiness starts to appear, but I keep talking.

"This one is...when me and mommy went to my grandparents house. They have a small greenhouse there and it has lots of flowers."

"Is that so?" *he asks, inching closer so that I can feel his warmth. I try to take a step back, feeling...wrong. But he grasps my elbow, pulling me closer lightly. My heart starts to hammer against my chest from a sudden fear as I look at him from the corner of my eyes.*

"Keep talking. I love listening to your stories," he whispers against my ear. There is something dark and demanding about his tone that made me afraid. Goosebumps scatter all over my skin, sweat beads starting to form on my forehead. This is wrong...it feels bad.

Why is he so close to me?

"I...I...We-" I stutter.

"I said, keep talking," he grunts. His hand crawls its way forward as he wraps it around my waist, my side crashing against his chest.

Now my whole body is shivering, I can feel tears of helplessness blurring my sight.

But then footsteps from the hallway echoes to my room, sending relief through my heart of getting safe. Tristen instantly pulls back and stands up, fixing his suit. But the warning look he sent me, makes me look away from the monster standing in front of me.

Helena comes to the doorway with a polite smile. "Your father is asking for you."

She looks at me and frowns. "What happened, Agatha?"

I open my mouth to answer but Tristen beats me through it and lies. "I think too many compliments about her talent made her emotional. She is having tears of happiness." He ruffles my hair and walks to my sister.

"Hope to see you again, Agatha," he mutters over his

shoulder before he puts a hand over Helena's shoulder and both exit my room, leaving me all alone in the midst of fear and shame.

I have no clue about how many hours passed as I stay in my room. There are no clocks to tell me the exact time. But the weather outside started to turn gloomier and darker with every passing hour, gesturing to the arrival of nightfall.

Suddenly, the rattling of the door makes me sit up in alert as I watch it opening. I expect those men to come back... expected *him*...but I'm taken aback with surprise when I see a woman dressed in a nun's attire standing at the doorway.

She seems to be in her mid-twenties with porcelain skin. Her lips and face look pale and cold, almost making her look like a lifeless soul. Her green eyes speculates me from top to bottom as if she is inspecting me like an object.

"You must be the new girl. Agatha, right?" she asks. But silence is my only response.

She offers a dark smirk and steps inside as she closes the door behind her, letting the tension and suspense build up in the room, along in my heart. A set of prayer beads with a rusted cross pendant is wrapped around her right hand. I have always thought the believers of God looked angelic and gentle, but in front of me is a complete opposite example.

She sits on the bed, in front of me, still offering me a

heartless smile. She leans her prayer bead wrapped hand forward and takes a loose strand of my dark hair, before caressing it between her thumb and index finger.

"Silence and disobedience won't lead you anywhere here," she murmurs in a shrill, detached voice that holds a hint of dark humor.

"Why am I here?" I ask, my hands fisting the bed sheet tightly.

"You are in a place to be treated. Your brother-in-law sent you to us to be cured," her knuckles brush back the side of my cheek, "-and to repent for your sins."

I frown in confusion. "Neither am I sick, nor did I commit a sin."

She chuckles darkly under her breath, looking me straight in the eye as if she can see through my soul.

"Defy how much you want, child. But it won't change the dark, shameful truth about you."

I shake my head, feeling anger and frustration simmering within me. "You know nothing about me. So, fucking stop with the lies and tell me the truth."

"You have learnt, haven't you? You have seen the outcomes of your sins and yet you keep adding them in your meaningless life. Why, child?"

Before I let her words make me lose control of the last thread of my anger, I grip her wrist and push it away from my face, glaring at her like she is my nemesis.

"You better tell me why the fuck I am here before I strangle you right here and now."

She shakes her head slowly while tsking. "Oh, Agatha. You need to be cured as soon as possible, before the devil himself swallows that innocent soul of yours.

She clasps her hand over mine. "But do not worry, by the time your departure arrives, you will be a better person." She stands abruptly, kneeling beside the bed and takes out a small luggage. I did see it before when I was looking around the room, but it was locked. She opens it by turning the numbers and grabs out a white long nightdress and passes it to me.

"You will be wearing this most of the time and when you are called for checkup, but during the prayers and confessions you will be wearing another dress that is inside this luggage. The clothes inside this bag will be your only clothes that you will wear during your stay here."

I skim my hands through the silk fabric and grasp it in a tight fist before throwing it across the room. I stand up instantly and grab the luggage before sending it to the same place as the dress.

Without thinking I push her away and dash to the door, opening it and striding to the hallway.

"You can't run away, child. The Magdalene won't let you pass until you are cured," I hear her voice calling out before I run along the path and find a long circular stair leading downwards. As I descend, I find a few other girls, dressed just like the nun. But I didn't stop to ask for help, not having an ounce of trust for them. Few distant screams and cries reach my ears but I ignore them.

Trust no one. No one at all.

I keep running until I reach what seems like the main hall-room, but it is more like a church room. Benches after benches reached up-to the altar, with Mary's and few other saints broken statues. But I don't care about any of those when I see the door that leads to my freedom. Sudden roaring of the thunder fills the surrounding, gesturing the arrival of the storm. I run out, feeling the cold wind engulfing me as I see the place that holds me captive.

It's the castle that I first saw and from afar its identity may have deceived anyone, because the closer you go to it, the darker it gets. I find the steel gate right away which is luckily open, but before I can make it there a hand right away grips me by my hair before another lands a sharp slap across my cheek, making my ears ring from the hit.

"You don't give up, do you bitch?" the man grunts with vexation painted on his face. His black hair rustles back with his pale skin making him look even more dangerous. Another slap lands on my other cheek, burning my skin fiercely. The grip on my hair tightens even more that I feel he might tear off my hair from the roots. The excruciating pain courses through my scalp, making my nerve cells thump.

"This is the third time, try again and I will cut you if

I need to," he warns through his clenched teeth. His tight muscles are straining against his black cassock.

Suddenly it dawns at me that he must be one of the men who brought me here. He holds my hand and drags me inside, not caring when I stumble down and claw his hands.

The girls I passed by previously start to gather at the doorway, but none of them make a move to save me from my punisher. I was right. None of them can be trusted.

He brings me inside and pushes me against one of the benches.

"There is no escaping. Your only ticket is the time you are cured."

"What is with this bullshit?" I scream, hearing the girls gasp from my words and behavior, "I'm not sick. You," I point a finger at him, "were one of the men who kidnapped me here. I know it!"

He slaps me again, this time I feel the bruise on my lips, tasting the metallic flavor of blood. "Silence. You were brought here under your brother-in-law's order. And you aren't going anywhere, so stop attempting."

Everyone around us just keeps staring at the charade that is happening in front of them. But I notice how their expressions are almost lifeless…absolutely cold. None of them react to a stranger being hit and abused, it nearly feels as if I'm surrounded by walls.

No emotions. No reactions. Pure emptiness.

Just then the nun who was in my room comes dashing towards us. The man glares at her as if he will skin her alive. She instantly looks down in fear and anxiety before she leans down to grab my arm.

"You had one job, Agnes. One. Job," he says sharply.

"I'm sorry, Father Geryon. It won't happen again," Agnes looks at me and leans close to my ear, "-we have to go, right now. You have created enough chaos for one day."

She helps me stand up and takes me back to my room. The minute we enter, she makes sure the door is locked and before I know it, she pushes me against my chest so hard that I fall on the ground, hurting my elbows.

"You little brat," she spews, pointing a finger at me, "because of you I will later be punished for my mistake."

"Like I give a single fuck about it," I retort back, trying to get up.

In a flash, she grabs my hair and pins me against the wall with my face pressed against the concrete. The discomfort only makes the bruise on my cheek throb more.

"You think your bratty mouth and nuisance behavior will save you. But it will be your downfall," she warns.

"The only way you will survive here is by giving in. The faster you do it the less painful it will be for you. Now get dressed like a good little girl." She pulls me back and forces me towards the area where I threw the dress.

She stands with her arms crossing. "Pick it up," she

orders.

I know I can't deny her as I will end up with more hits. And I can't risk myself being weak, so, I cave in and pick the dress, waiting for her to leave. But she stays rooted to her ground, giving me a stern look.

"There is something called privacy and I would like to have that," I mutter.

"I am sure you didn't need privacy when it came to committing sins, and your body isn't something special that needs worshiping. Change. Right. Now."

Swallowing the lump in my throat I take off my dress, with my back facing her. My entire body feels warm from uneasiness. I put on the new dress, feeling the fabric slightly itchy against my skin. It covers me from top to bottom, up-to my ankles, including my arms too, like a Victorian nightdress.

"Come with me," she orders in a strict tone before stalking towards the door while I follow her behind.

This time she takes a different route, taking a right turn, walking down a dimly lit hallway. But the further we walk, the more my nerves tenses up with caution and mist of fear. I look around, to memorize every inch of this place. Jotting down every way possible to plan for my escape in my mind.

The place looks elegant and well-built from outside, right away taken from a fantasy story. It is a vast castle that seems to have been built in medieval times. But from inside it is broken and eerie, as if it is a living nightmare. The place has four floors and we are on the third, following Agnes on the top floor. There are doors on either side and a double door at the very end of the hallway. The walls are mostly cracked as if they haven't been taken care of for several years. I can see mosses and molds between those cracks. Some even have deep nail marks and some have strange writings on the wall with a black paint, but it is hard to read them because of the cracks and mosses. Behind me there seems to be a balcony where the wind blew in, along with the cawing sounds of the crows.

Maybe from there I will find a route.

Reaching at the end of the hallway, she opens the double doors, gesturing to me to enter. Gulping, I try to calm down my racing heart as I step into a room which looks like a check-up room from a clinic or hospital.

The sight instantly brought those horrific memories that have been silent for a few days, but now are returning back to claw me with terror and anxiety.

My breathing paces up, my ears ringing with my pulsing nerves. I can feel my blood turning cold, filling my skin with goosebumps. Sweat starts to form on my forehead and at the back of my neck, as I feel lt adrenaline rushing down my spine.

I can't be here. No.
I don't want to be here.

I turn to run away but Agnes already locks the door.

"No! Let me out!" I yell, slapping my palms against the door. I hold onto the handles and give it all to open the door, not giving a fuck if I have to rip it open. I feel my knees weakening and tears burning my eyes.

I don't want to be here.

I don't want to be here.

"Please. I can't be here. I can't…."

My breathing turned deep and ragged that I can't help wrapping a hand around my throat. My skin crawls with anxiety as I kneel down on the floor with my forehead pressing against the door. I beg the memories to be buried.

But suddenly, I feel a hand brushing my hair back while my body shivers.

"Hey," a gruff voice gently whispers. "Hey, it's okay."

No. I'm not okay. I can't be…

The hand continues its motion and I feel his lips against my ear lobe. "Don't think about those. Don't let your nightmares haunt you." His tone is gentle and soothing like he truly wants me to calm down.

Don't trust anyone, Agatha. No one.

"Hush. It's okay. I got you," he murmurs. "Calm your nerves, take a deep breath."

And I do. For some unknown fucked up reason I do as he says, following his words and inhale and exhale gently, focusing on my breathing.

"That's it, deep breaths."

I feel my nerves taking a steady turn with every breath I take. His hand continues to touch my hair and even that is helping me. However, I can't help but feel this deep ache within me.

"That's good. I can feel every inch of your body relaxing finally. I got you."

He picks me up as I rest my head against his chest, feeling the steady rhythm of his heart. I want to be away from this room. I don't want to be here.

I can't be here.

I keep my eyes closed, not wanting to look at the room again that brings back horrors in my mind. I clutch onto the lapels of his shirt tightly, my body still shuddering from the aftermath of my trigger.

"Father-" I hear Agnes' voice but she doesn't get to complete it.

I don't know for how long I'm being carried but when I feel the soft bed sheets against my skin, I know I'm not in that checkup room anymore. My muscles turn lax and I finally let go off his hold, curling myself with my arms around me, shielding myself like I always did.

I still keep my eyes closed when I hear the soft click of the door, not bothering about what is happening anymore. Letting this darkness help me soothe my nightmare.

It's okay. You are safe now.
It's okay, it's…okay.

I keep chanting the mantra in my head again and again, until a tireless sleep consumes me, taking me away from my nightmares which I'm part of, for a few hours.

It's okay.
You are safe.
Safe.

CHAPTER FIVE

AGATHA

"This is a marvelous work, Agatha," Helena mutters with pride and happiness, kissing my cheek. "I'm so proud of you."

I smile, but it doesn't reach my eyes. I focus back on the landscape I'm working on when there is a light tap on the door.

It's Tristen.

My body instantly tenses up as I pretend his presence to be invisible. My hands tremble a little as I paint the trees with a light sap green color.

"Am I interrupting anything?" he asks in a gruff tone as he steps inside the room.

No go away!

"Not at all. I was just telling Agatha; how beautiful her painting is."

He walks ahead, standing beside me. Leaning close to look at my painting but I know it is just an excuse. He nods in admiration and places his hand on my shoulder, lightly caressing my exposed skin with his thumb.

"This is truly gorgeous. My little sister-in-law has a unique talent," he mutters with a smile, looking at me with a gentle look. Anybody would be easily fooled seeing that expression, that hides the lurking monster who comes out when nobody is around, to haunt me with its darkness.

I instantly stand up and go to the other table where I pretend to clean the paint off my brush as I whisper a thank you.

"She really should study art when she goes to college," Tristen suggests, standing beside Helena.

"I know some great teachers who can help her improve and practice more." He places one hand inside his suit pocket and the other rests on my sister's shoulder, while she looks at him with a bright smile filled with adoration.

"That is a great idea. She is usually free during the evenings so that would be perfect timing." She looks at me. "What do you think, Agatha?"

I simply nod with a half-hearted smile.

"Perfect. I will contact her and let her know. She is a marvelous teacher, trust me." Just then his phone rings and he excuses himself to pick up the call.

I keep my focus on cleaning my brush when Helena walks

towards me, caressing my hair. Just what I need.

"*Agatha?*"

"*Hmm?*"

"*Is everything okay?*"

"*Yes. Why wouldn't it be?*"

She shrugs. "*I don't know but something feels off. You can tell me you know. You can tell me anything you want without hesitating.*"

Can I?

I don't know how to even express through my words how dirty and wrong I feel whenever he is around me. How shame and guilt inks my heart and soul every time he touches me and there is nothing I can do about it.

How is he gaining everyone's trust and love like he has been a part of this family from the very start?

But most of all, how can I tell my sister the truth when she is in love with him?

How can I break her heart when I have no proof against him...how can I hurt her?

But deep down I feel Helena might listen to me and believe my words...my nightmares. She has always cared and loved me more than anyone else.

Maybe...just maybe she will help me.

I open my mouth, picking up my bravado to finally confess when Tristen walks inside the room again.

"*Sweetheart, the florist called. She is on her way.*"

Helena straightens up and nods, hesitating to leave. "Okay, I will go to the living room then."

She lightly cups my cheek offering me a soft smile before she walks away. Leaving me alone with the monster again.

When I wake up again, it is night time. A candelabra, holding three tall, white candles illuminates my room. I instantly sit up, finding myself in the same white attire.

Licking my lips, I look around. The shadow of the window falls on the floor by the moon. I let out a sigh of relief finding myself alone, but my mind starts to race with the events that happened today.

So much has happened.

I run a hand through my hair, going through the scenarios of today. It is not a puzzle anymore that I'm inside a church which has an asylum inside it. And the only place that has both is the Magdalene.

I have heard about this place a few times from the locals. And my mother even told me stories about it when I was a kid. It is described as a place to cure the ill or possessed ones, but it comes with a price. Some even say it's nothing but cursed by God, which is why it is always dark and raining mostly. But I never thought I would end up being a victim of this place.

Tomorrow I will have to try to escape again, and the mere thought of returning to that room makes my body shudder. As I think of that moment, I can't help but ponder about the man who is kind enough to guide me…to help me.

Who is he? Is he a member here?

Agnes called her father, which only hinted he is perhaps a priest here. But the question is, is he a savior or a villain?

I look at the door, feeling tempted to go out and escape right away, but something tells me it will be a foolish risk to take. But out of nowhere, I hear the lock rattling as if someone is coming in.

I quickly lie down and close my eyes, pretending to sleep, even though my heart starts to beat faster and faster when the door opens.

Calm down, Agatha. Calm your mind.

The heavy footsteps echo in, and I feel the person getting closer to my bed. Who is it?

Agnes?

I sense the person's presence right beside me…so close.

"Your body is betraying you." A familiar deep, gruff voice hushed close to my ears. It is the man from that room.

But I don't cave in. I remain as still as possible, evening out my breathing.

"Even when you are failing, you still don't give up," he continues. "But it won't last for long. You have been brought here for a reason and that must be fulfilled if you want to be free."

Silence is my answer.

"If you truly want to be free here, then you have to give up. You have to obey or else when you return back, you will have nothing left." He lightly brushes the back of his hand against my cheek, inhaling deep into my nose.

"It is said forbidden things are always tempting because they make you crave for it right through the core of your soul. Unfortunately for me, you are turning into a craving that even my soul can't resist," he whispers.

"But I have already sinned so much that I must control this too. Although, you won't escape this. You will have to cave in and you will, little girl."

It's...*him.*

I feel him wrap his hand around my throat, turning my head to face him. My eyes are about to flutter open, to see my captor before he stops me.

"Keep your eyes closed, little girl," he orders in a monotonous tone and without knowing I yield.

His nose runs along my jaw while my body turns paralyzed against his touch. His lips lightly brush against my cheek as they skate towards my lips, but never come in contact. My heartbeat paces up. A dark desire starts to bloom within me.

"I can feel your pulse racing," he presses his thumb against my pulse point on my neck, "your skin is flushed just from my touch. Your hands are grabbing the sheets tightly, controlling your urges."

I don't realize I'm clutching onto the sheets until he mentions it.

"You are breathing like you are craving for air." I am.

"But it's something more that you want, something forbidden…something sinful. Do you know how I know it?"

I don't respond. I can't as words vanish from my mind.

"Because I want it too. I always take until the person has nothing left, but since the moment I met your fierce soul, I've never yearned for something so badly. And something tells me, one taste won't be enough. I shouldn't break the rules, but I've never abided by the rules."

His words hold a dark promise that I should run away from, but my body unknowingly wants to rush towards its arms. His tone is filled with a desire that is pulling me closer and closer. I clench my thighs together, breathing heavily, syncing with his. He is dangerous and psychotic, something I should be scared of, but his actions and words send a thrill through my body.

"You want this, don't you?" he asks, lightly licking my bottom lip, making my body shudder just from that light touch.

"No," I rasp.

He chuckles under his breath, as I feel his chest rumble. "Lying is a sin too, little girl. Every soul is punished for it in this world and in after life." His grasp on my neck tightens as he presses on my windpipe, but not enough to suffocate me.

"Tell the truth, little girl and you will be rewarded," he whispers. "The truth. Do you want this?"

Say, no. Deny him.

My consciousness keeps demanding to push him away. But my heart goes against me as I whisper my answer.

"Yes...I want this."

I feel him smile wickedly and the next second his lips press against mine. His other hand covers my eyes as if he knows I will disobey him and get a peek at him. I have been kissed before and they were always gentle, slow and sweet. But this?

This is the absolute opposite.

He kisses me deeply, pressing my head into the pillow. His tongue peeks out, mingling with mine. A deep groan erupts from the back of his throat, sending goose-bumps all over my skin. He nibbles on my bottom lip, nearly making my skin ache from that sweet, sweet ache. My control starts to vanish, as my desire takes hold of the leash.

My neck arches to give him better access. I kiss him back, matching his deep, fast pace. My hands snake around his neck, grasping his thick hair at the back.

He muffles my moans with his electric kiss. My sensations heightening like never before with his lips working their magic. I feel my mind taking the route through this dark desire, even though it is wrong. It all feels wrong.

He captured me, nearly killed me but saved me when I was having a breakdown. I should steer clear away from him.

And yet, I can't get enough of his kiss.

It feels…hypnotic.

"So, much better than I imagined," he breathes against my lips. I can feel wetness pooling between my thighs, making my entire skin flush with my nerves rushing faster.

"Hide all you want, little girl, but it's a futile attempt when I can smell you from here. You are hungry for more, aren't you?"

"Yes, please. More," I murmur.

"Sometimes we don't get everything we want, do we, little girl?" he mutters and suddenly pulls back, but he keeps my eyes covered.

"For more you'll have to wait."

I make a move to get his hand away but as if he was anticipating it, he takes both my hands and presses them above my head.

"Don't do something you will regret later, little girl. Like I said, you will have to obey."

"I can tell you want to break me but no matter what you do I won't break so easily, you asshole."

He lets out that familiar dark sadistic chuckle that makes my nerves pulse faster. "I will truly enjoy breaking you. The more you fight, the more I will shatter you like a glass.

Before you know it, your soul will be crushed right in my palm. So, be careful what you wish for."

"Even a single pawn can defeat the king and gain victory."

"Time will tell who will be defeated, little girl. Have a good night, because your morning will be the start of your new nightmares"

He pulls his hand away and I instantly open my eyes, seeing him facing his back to me. Without giving a single glance over his shoulder, he walks out and locks the door.

I slump back into the bed, hiding my flushed face underneath my hands before letting them slide up into my hair. My eyes gaze upon the dark and cracked ceiling.

What the fuck happened?

How could I have even let him anywhere near me? Let my captor kiss me like I've never been kissed before. I could still feel his lips against mine and I traced my bottom lip where he nibbled me, the ache still imprinted.

His touch put me under his spell, that I didn't see coming. How could he affect me like this?

I have to get the fuck out of here quickly before he brainwashes me any further.

But his warning left me baffled about tomorrow.

What will happen in the morning?

But I know I won't be getting any answer until it's morning, so, I let out a deep sigh and try to give my mind some rest after the hours of chaos I've been having.

Cold water splashes over my face, jolting me awake as I choke and cough.

"Get up. That's enough sleep for one morning," Agnes mutters in a sharp tone, putting the bucket down.

"What the fuck is wrong with you?" I yell, still slightly coughing.

She grabs me by my arm, pulling me out of bed and passes me a dress that she must have taken from the luggage.

"Get dressed right away. Otherwise, you'll be late for the prayers," she orders, taking a step back and folding her arms.

"I'm not getting dressed again in your presence," I retort, pushing back my now wet hair.

She arches an eyebrow, not giving a damn about my protest. Clenching my jaw, I take off my wet dress and change into a new one but it was more like a maid's dress that was used to be worn around 1960 perhaps.

"Follow me," she mutters and I walk behind her until we reach the hallway where I was slapped yesterday. Everyone is already in their seats and hearing my approaching footsteps they all look over their shoulder.

Their blank, cold gazes nearly makes me shrink back but I continue following Agnes before we take our seat on the second bench. A girl is beside me, her hands tangled on her lap with her eyes cast down. She doesn't even acknowledge me when I sit beside her. There is not a single reaction. I'm not much of a religious person as my sister and our parents never visited church that much or prayed in general.

There is pin drop silence in the room. It nearly feels as if I'm the only one in the room. Heavy footsteps echo inside the room as I find Father Geryon standing at the altar with a small book in his hand. He looks around as if analyzing each and everyone here, before nodding in approval and opening his book.

He starts to recite verses and everyone around me starts to repeat his words, line by line, word to word. But it is the monotonous tone that sends chills down my spine. They don't even carry an ounce of emotion in their tones. It feels like they are all mechanical dolls and the priest's words are the key that is twisted to let them function.

Something is seriously wrong with this place, and that includes the people too. But except for Agnes and *him,* I didn't know whom else to find my way through.

My lips remain still while my eyes are busy looking around, searching for an escape.

"Repeat after him," the girl beside me whispers, but doesn't look at me. I frown.

"Do it before you cause another scene. At least pretend to be on the safe side."

Swallowing the lump in my throat, I follow her lead and repeat his words as much as possible. The girl now seems to be someone who could be able to help me.

A tapestry catches my sight which is right behind the altar, positioned at the center of the wall, hanging from the ceiling. The circular stained glass above the entrance door lets the light from outside shine upon it. It has a series of knitted pictures like it's telling a story. It begins with a girl falling down in a huge, dark hand with two people on top letting her go. Next it shows a man consoling a woman who looks broken and miserable. Then a black castle with a group of people facing front with a black shadow looming over them. The same girl who is being consoled looks nearly emotionless with the people surrounding her, with her hands looking red as if covered in blood, along with dark skies and crashing waves at the end corner of the tapestry.

Soon, Father Geryon's recitation ends and suddenly all of them stand up with a straight posture while looking ahead. I follow with a nervous glance around. Father Geryon leaves with a nod as everyone scrambles away, perhaps to do something important.

"Come with me," Agnes says and walks again, this time heading to the second floor to a room which is probably for washing clothes. A laundry-room. The condition of the walls and ceiling are the same as the ones in the hallway. There are three long columns of tubs till the end of the room with a mechanism used for twisting the clothes to rinse away the water. Huge piles of white clothes and bedsheets are set on the small table beside every tub. Few of the girls start to enter the room in a line, stopping by their designated spots and just stand there silently.

"Go to the corner and get to work," she says.

"What?" I ask in confusion.

"Clean those clothes and there better not be a spot left," she warns before dragging me to the empty tub area.

The tub looks like it hasn't been cleaned for ages with black marks and smudges covering it from outside. There is a wooden washing tray and a box of detergent inside the tub.

"Start cleaning," Agnes orders before she turns and walks ahead, standing at the wall beside the doorway. Everyone else around me starts to get on with their tasks right away, rubbing the clothes on the tray to get rid of any stains. The concentration painted on their faces was crystal clear, as if they were putting every ounce of their energy on this task.

I look forward and find the girl from earlier doing the same. Not knowing what to do, I lean the tray on the tub handle, pouring water over it to lather up the soap and place the wet clothes, moving them back and forth, washing them one after another.

The sounds of water splashing and snapping sounds of clothes when rinsing them.

It feels like hours passed but nobody complains about

anything. Though the skin on my hands is turning raw with visible cracking. I can barely feel my palms. I stop for a minute to try to soothe my hands when Agnes marches towards me with a glare.

"Who told you to stop?" she asks sharply.

"My hands are aching. They are cracking," I mutter, showing her the evidence even though she doesn't look at them.

"Those are bound to happen but that doesn't mean you have to stop. Others have no issues so you shouldn't complain either," she looks at the few clothes that are still untouched on my table, "Stop whining and finish your task."

"I said, I can't. My skin will peel off if I don't rest my hands."

She grinds her jaw and before I know it she goes to the back of the door and retrieves something from there. I can't see what it is until she stands in front of me and in the next second strikes my arms with a cane.

"Ah!" I scream

Instant pain courses through my body but she doesn't give a damn and continues to hit me back-to-back. I can feel my skin burning like an inferno from agony.

"Disobedience has penalties here," she seethes through her clenched teeth as she rains strike after strike over my body. My knees give away from weakness as I kneel on the ground while Agnes continues punishing me.

I even try to shield myself but nothing helps. My gaze looks around for someone to help me but none of them make a single approach. All of them continue washing clothes like that is the only important task to do while a woman is being abused in front of their eyes.

I scream and yelp in pain, feeling tears stinging my eyes while my entire arm starts to turn red, burning my nerves as if I've been set on fire. She stops to make me stand up by my hair, hauling me out of the laundry room before taking me back to my room. She pushes me down on the floor, pressing the side of my face onto the ground with her feet with the heel of her shoe digging into my temple.

"I have been telling you since yesterday, warning you again and again. But you are truly testing my patience like nobody else. When you are given a task, you do it. If not then prepare your mind and body to earn the consequences for it," she warns.

I try to push away her feet but the snap of the cane makes me pull back my hands. "Fuck, stop!" I cry out loud.

"No! You must be punished and learn your lesson," she bawls.

I assemble myself for the gut-wrenching pain again but a familiar voice stops it, saving me from the torment.

"That's enough, Agnes!"

Agnes right away steps back, dropping the cane and craning her head down. "She was not completing her task,

Father. She was complaining unnecessarily."

"And she seems to have been punished enough for it. Do not cross your limits, otherwise you will be the one in her place but much worse," he threatens.

"But Father Geryon said-"

"If you are looking to be punished then keep up this behavior and you will be whipped ten times."

She turns silent right away.

"Leave," he orders and without hesitating she rushes out of the room. I let out a breath of relief, trying to relax my aching nerves even though it is useless.

I hear his heavy footsteps thudding closer to me before he kneels and picks me up, depositing me on the bed. I wrap my arms around myself, protecting and comforting my own self, shying away with my back facing *him*.

He darkly chuckles. "You weren't moving away last night."

His words infuriates me, making me want to slap the fuck out of him, but I can barely feel my arms after the hits Anges landed.

"The least you can be is grateful that you were saved before you fainted."

I sit up and turn to hit him, but like he saw my movement coming he catches my wrist. And that's when I see *him*.

And he looks…mesmerizing. His deep brown hair, with few grey strands mingling along, is slightly pushed back as a few strands touch his forehead. His almond skin is highlighted by the light coming from the window, featuring his sharp jawline which had a five o' clock shadow. But his eyes...his deep black eyes are the most captivating sight. It seems to be holding intense and raw emotions that he isn't willing to reveal and masks it with an emotionless look. He is also wearing a black cassock with the sleeves folded, showing off his muscular, veiny arms that have thorn stems inking on his skin. He even has a white collar peeking out that completes his priest attire. I notice a silver chain with a small cross pendant hanging around his neck. He seems to be either in his late thirties or early forties.

My eyes then fall on the small bite mark on his wrist, reminding me it was the same mark I left on my captor before I tried to escape.

It's him.

A dark smirk crosses his lips, the same lips that took my breath away with a kiss. He knows what I'm thinking and there isn't a drop of remorse or guilt in his eyes for the cruel act he committed by kidnapping me here.

"Perhaps your brother-in-law forgot to mention that you can be a major pain in the ass too," he murmurs and leans towards the small table beside my bed to get a brown file that wasn't there before.

He opens it and starts to look through it. "I wanted to do some checkup yesterday but you had a panic attack all of a sudden," he looks at me above his lashes, "not a fan of hospital?"

"I'm not ill. Nothing is wrong with me," I state.

He simply shrugs. "But your reports say otherwise. It says last year when you turned nineteen, you started to have a mental breakdown. Your sister's death seems to be the trigger. But it even mentions you started having auditory-verbal hallucinations of your sister, where you saw and talked to her. You also attacked the staff members and doctors back at the previous hospital, nearly killing the doctor." He closes the report, and this time he is analyzing me.

"I'm not crazy."

"I didn't say you are crazy. There is a difference between craziness and illness. Mental illness is curable and a phase that everyone goes through because of how fucked up our lives are no matter how perfect you pretend it to be. Craziness is a stage when you don't know the difference between sanity and reality, a stage when you can't be healed," he murmurs, his gaze never leaving mine, "-but you have a chance to be better. Your medications will start tomorrow."

"And the chores? Cleaning clothes and getting beaten is part of your treatment?"

"We believe in curing our patients mentally and spiritually. And being disciplined is part of it. Like I told you before, if you want to survive here then learn to obey, little girl."

"Stop calling me that. I want to get out of here. You seem to be the doctor here so let me out."

He shakes his head. "I can't until you are fully recovered. Mr. Arthur has signed the papers and already paid for your treatment. So, you won't be stepping a single foot out until I say so."

"I don't care. You and your friends *kidnapped* me, holding me against my will. I won't hesitate to report *you* and your bullshit, fucked-up asylum-"

He leans close with a threatening look, sending shivers down my spine in sudden nervousness. "And then what? You think your single complaint will take me down? I will be ruined forever just from that one move? Here is the answer for you before disappointment hits you."

He holds my jaw, pressing his fingers into my cheeks.

"Not even God Himself can take me down. I hold that much power here. So, try your best but it will be a waste. Nobody will believe your words even if you bring all evidence. So, it's better you stop thinking of these hopeless things and focus on your curing process," he mutters before letting go of my jaw and standing up.

"Sister Agnes will show you where the patients go to take their meds. Be there on time and report to me or her. And do your given chores without complaining, next time I won't save you, knowing you were asking for it."

Taking the file with him, he walks out of the room

while my eyes are strained on his broad shoulders. When I'm finally alone, I look at my now bruised arms, hesitating to even touch them. My palms are still cracked from the laundry room.

I'm in pain. I'm hungry. I am tired.

But most of all I'm alone…nearly on the verge of losing my hope.

However, I'm not going to let this place or *him* break me. I will fight tooth and nail with him if I need to in order to survive. I will take thousands of hits but I will keep trying till my last breath.

I'm not going to be hopeless.
Never.

CHAPTER SIX

AGATHA

Five days have passed by and I was starting to understand the routine of this place.

Five days have passed since I last saw *him*. After he saved me again, he didn't come to see me or talk with me. I didn't even find him anywhere around the building when I followed Agnes from one room to another for doing my chores which was nothing but a pain in the ass.

Every morning starts with us waking up, washing our face and mouth before going for the prayers. Everyone would then be assigned to a certain chore and sent to their designated area to work without any arguments. Only two times a day a meal is served during lunch and dinner. Afterwards, we would go to the second floor to stand in the line where we are given tablets and medicines from a small counter to be taken on time after we are done eating.

And yesterday at the end of the day we were sent to a confession room that is on the second floor, with a vast confession box that looked more ancient than my grandparents times perhaps. Father Geryon was inside it and told us to confess our sins we may have thought of or did in the following days. We waited in line outside the door and only entered when our names were called. I didn't have anything to confess but my words weren't believed which only ended up me being punished by Agnes again when I was back in my room.

Most of the patients here seem to be lifeless but there are few ones who will suddenly scream or yell at a random situation. Crying like they are in constant agony, clawing the walls while kneeling on the floor. They are ignored most of the time by the nuns and priests but if it gets too much then they are taken to the checkup room where they will come out like nothing happened.

Everything is done in an order and in strict times that it nearly feels like I'm in a boarding school but a much worse place.

So far, Agnes seems to be second in-charge after the priests here. There are three more nuns too but even they dance to Agnes' tune.

I keep observing the place and the timetable to plan out my escape. I can't do anything in haste here knowing well I will be caught and punished severely for it. Every step I take has to be thought out and taken carefully. One wrong move and everything will be over.

I try to get to talk with the girl who seems to be the only one talking with me every now and then, guiding me with my chores secretly. She definitely knows something and perhaps a safe route to my freedom.

But it's tough to even get to talk with her privately with the nuns and priests keeping a watch on us for twenty-four hours. Like even now, we are standing in the line to take our medications with her right in front of me, but I can't talk with her while Agnes is keeping an eye on everyone.

With every patient passing by after they are done, we move one step forward. I look over my shoulder for a quick glance and when I'm sure Agnes is away from earshot, I lean a bit close to the girl.

"Don't say anything here," she barely whispers as if she knew I was going to approach her.

"Why not? She can't hear us," I keep my voice as low as possible.

"The other patients might report to her." We take a step forward. "And if you think I'm going to help you then you are wrong. I can't do anything." She keeps looking forward.

"Then why were you giving me guides all these times? Why me?"

"Because you reminded me of someone that I lost because I didn't help her even though I could have. But don't expect anything more from me. It's nearly impossible to leave this building even, Agatha."

"You know my name?"

"You have become quite the recent topic since you arrived."

"What is your name?"

"Bethany. But you can call me Beth," she murmurs in a hushed tone.

"Beth, we have to try. You said it's nearly impossible but not fully impossible. *We* can try and escape. Don't you want to go back and have your life with your family? Or on your own?" I ask.

"My family was the one who sent me just because they thought falling in love with a woman is a sin and illness."

I remain silent for a few seconds not knowing how to respond to that as we get closer to the small booth.

"You still have to help me-"

"Like I said, I can't. If I do then they will kill me. Hang me from the rooftop. I know that because I saw it happening."

My skin turns cold from her words in instant fear. My eyes automatically look up, thinking about the rooftop. I was cleaning the stone pavement at the front yesterday, noticing a concrete, broken and dark smudged statue of an angel at top. But now I can't stop thinking if that is the place from where the person was hung from.

"I said next!" the nun at the booth sneers, tapping on the

wooden table where she rested her hand. I blink my eyes, feeling my heart beat race faster as I nod at her. She passes me my usual white and red tablets and checks my name on the paper she usually uses for everyone. The woman is probably in her mid-sixties, looking like the eldest member of the Magdalene. She is even wearing the same nun dress like Agnes but she has glasses resting on her nose. She never talks much either and did her job with giving the medicines and checking that everyone takes it.

After I'm done for the day, Agnes follows me like a shadow until I reach my room and thankfully leaves me alone after I close the door. I quickly change my clothes wanting to get rid of the uneasiness I have been feeling since morning. As I lie on my bed, looking at the ceiling, Beth's words grip me to my core, taking bits of my hope and tearing into shreds slowly.

The more I look for a way, the more I find myself lost. I turn to my side, facing the window where nothing but the dark sky greets me with the cold wind howling in. As there is no blanket, I hug myself for comfort.

I have never felt so alone and deep down I blame Tristen for putting me in such a situation. Everything mentioned in that report is a lie, except for hurting the hospital staff but I had to do what I needed to do to save myself.

I'm being blamed for accusations that aren't true at all and yet everyone around me is trying to prove me wrong.

I have a hope that perhaps Beth will be able to help me but now even she has refused. The only person I can think of to rescue me from this dark place is none other than the devil who captured me. But I don't have faith in him.

Trusting a sinner can be dangerous.

Eventually, I close my eyes, drowning into a slumber with my mind running wild with thoughts.

I don't know what happens but my eyes snap open. I notice it is still night time. I sit up, frowning in confusion, feeling my body way too warm as if I have fever. I look around my room which is empty.

But I just feel something uncertain here. Like something is here but I have no clue about it. I gulp, licking my bottom lip before I take the candelabra walking towards the door which is surprisingly unlocked. I open it and step out in the hallway, looking left and right before taking the path down the stairs. My feet creak slightly with every step I take, when a scratching sound halts me at the second floor.

"Anybody out there?" I ask.

I look over my shoulder, feeling my heart drumming loudly, to see a pitch-black hallway. It is the floor of other patients where the laundry and library room are. I walk ahead, holding the candelabra forward, hearing the scratching sound turning louder. Shivers run down my spine with my throat clogging. When I reach the end, a white figure kneeling on the floor with her nails dragging along the wall comes into my sight. There is also something written on the wall with red paint as it drips on the floor.

THE DEVIL AND THE GOD ARE RAGING INSIDE US.

I inhale a shaky breath, feeling my palms turning sweaty and my hands trembling slightly. She keeps scratching the wall, leaving her nail marks on it, not caring that her fingers are already turning bloody.

Her black, wet hair curtains her face. She is wearing the same dress as me but some portions are torn. I slightly lean towards her, touching her shoulder, giving her a little shake.

But she suddenly stops clawing the wall and snaps her head towards me, her hair still shrouding her face from me. I take a step back cautiously, trying to normalize my breathing. She is still as a statue, and I feel she isn't probably breathing either.

"A-are you okay?" I whisper.

Suddenly, she catches my wrist and tugs me close to her, making me shriek. Her grip feels so tight that I feel she will break my hand into two. She is so close that her hair is touching my cheek.

"You are guilty. You are guilty," she rasps in a broken voice.

"W-what?' I barely whisper.

Suddenly she holds me by my hair and I let out a scream but it gets muffled when she presses my head against the wall tightly that I'm sure every inch of my face will be bruised with scars.

"You are guilty, Agatha. You did this to her," she murmurs close to my hair. She presses my head even more, making my whole skin ache in agony.

Luckily, thinking through for a second, I hold onto the candelabra tightly and hit it with her as she stumbles back. Without hesitating I hit her again with the candles falling on the ground and douses by turning the whole hallway dark now.

Shit.

Out of nowhere I feel her hands choking me, pushing me against the wall again.

"You killed her. She died because of you," she hisses. "*You* killed your sister. Guilty. Guilty. Guilty."

I give it all to pry off her hands but I can't find her hands. I can feel them nearly suffocating me but I can't find them.

"She died because of you. You will be punished. God will punish you."

I feel an excruciating pain travelling through my neck as her nails dug into my skin. I'm fearful that she will rip away my skin. My pulse is racing, my heart is beating at full speed. Terror is controlling my body as I feel the air being sucked away from my body while suffocating. She presses on my windipe more roughly, cutting off my breathing slowly.

My lungs start to burn as my eyelids start to close off bit by bit. My throat turns dry like sand.

"Agatha! Agatha!" a voice calls out loud, shaking my body. But it isn't the woman's voice anymore.

"Agatha! Can you hear me?" It is *him*.

I try to fight through the darkness, finding my way out by following his voice. But I feel she is forcing me furthermore.

Fight through it, Agatha. Fight.

"Fuck! Agatha!" he says, almost screams.

I feel like I'm suddenly pulled away from the darkness and into the light, no longer being tortured by an unknown woman. My entire body jolts followed by shivering, with my wide, wild eyes looking around. I take in a lungful of air, feeling relieved I can finally breathe.

He comes in my sight, lightly tapping my cheeks while his other arm wraps around my waist. I am on the floor, my head against his chest while I keep breathing steadily, trying to control my racing heart.

I search for the woman who nearly tried to kill me, haunting me to my soul.

"What are you looking for?" he asks, frowning in confusion.

"T-there was a woman. She tried to kill me by choking. I-I couldn't breathe," I stutter with a raspy voice.

"What are you talking about? Which woman?"

"She was here. I saw her at the wall," I point at the wall which no longer has the scratch marks or the writing. "S-she was here. I swear. She was scratching the wall and then suddenly she was holding me by my throat."

"There was no one here when I found you."

My brows furrow together. "What do you mean?"

"You were screaming for help. I found you writhing on the floor like someone was giving you an electric shock. Your entire body was trembling like that day at the checkup room. Perhaps you were having another anxiety attack or a seizure."

I shake my head, trying to stand up but he beats me to it and helps me. "I'm not lying. I saw someone here."

But the look on his face is evidence enough to tell me he doesn't believe me at all. The sight feels like a stab in my heart but I don't reflect it on my face.

"You know it's against the rules to roam around the halls after bedtime-"

"Take your rules and shove it up your ass," I sneer. "I know what I saw. You don't have to believe me but I'm telling the truth."

"Go back to your room, Agatha. You need rest after your medications."

I push him on the chest but he doesn't budge. "Fuck off."

I walk past him but suddenly he grasps my wrist and turns me around, bringing our bodies close with my breasts pressing against his chest and my hand positions behind my back.

"Your reluctance will be your downfall, little girl. I'm trying my best to control myself around you, because trust me," he leans closer that his breath is tickling my cheeks, "-you don't want to get yourself haunted with my cruel side. So, think carefully about your words before you speak them."

My eyes never leave his intense ones, feeling my heart thumping faster. Even in the dimly lit hallway by the moonlight, I can see the flicker of a forbidden and dark emotion painted on his face. His touch sends a shiver through my body, making my blood rush.

"Go back. Right now." He lets go of my hand and I don't hesitate to turn around and walk back to my room. By the time I reach my room, I close the door and instantly reach for my neck to feel the scars she left. But there is nothing but smooth skin. I don't feel any burning either like I sense from a bruise.

I frown in confusion and move my hand to touch my face where I'm sure I will feel a cut or aching from being pressed to that wall. But again, I'm proven wrong.

What the...

How is this...it's impossible.

I know it to my core that what happened is real. None of it is a dream or nightmare.

It. Is. Real.

But what is the conclusion for my missing bruises and scars that I felt every second in that moment. How can this even happen?

I run a hand through my hair and sit on the bed. Sleep vanishes from my eyes and when I look at the window it seems like dawn is arriving.

The woman's words keep ringing in my ears and mind like a curse. How did she know I have a sister?

Why was she blaming me?

Who was she even?

So many questions and yet I have answers to none. There is no way in hell I'm going to console myself with false words, telling myself that it was perhaps a nightmare and I was sleepwalking. The moment felt real, the pain felt real.

I know the difference between a dream and reality, and she is nowhere near a mere imagination. She has to be one of the patients, that explains her dress too.

But who would do that? Who would know about my sister?

THE DEVIL TAINTED US

CHAPTER SEVEN

AGATHA

I'm at the library, cleaning the shelves like I am usually tasked to do during the evening. The room is much darker compared to other rooms. Same condition as the others. But on the walls there is a series of repeated lines that covers every corner.

WE BELONG TO GOD ONLY. HEAVEN IS OUR HOME.

There are vast, tall shelves that nearly touch the ceiling. Most of them are filled with books or studies related to God and Bible, making me wish I had my favorite collections of Thomas Hardy and William Wordsworth. There is a long table at the center of the room with chairs on either side to read, but I rarely see anyone coming here to spend their privacy with books.

I'm done re-arranging the shelf, and walk behind it towards the store-room where the other cleaning supplies are kept. But as I reach for the door, my hand stops close to the knob when I hear a woman's muffled moaning coming through it.

I frown, taking a step back and looking left and right.

The moan comes again followed by a grunt this time. But in seconds, I realize it is Agnes inside with a man.

"Suck it harder, Agnes. You have been taught way more than that." It's Father Geryon.

"Yes, sir."

My mind keeps telling me to ignore it and walk away, pretending as if I didn't hear anything but when I hear her crying and struggling, I can't help but lean down to peek through the small crack on the door.

And the sight I see makes me gasp.

Father Geryon's hand cups Agnes' head, guiding her back and forth to suck his cock. She keeps her gaze up at his face with tears streaming down her face, while it looks like she is struggling to take him deeper. But he doesn't let her have the easy way, and pushes deeper into her mouth, throwing her head back and letting out a low groan.

"Yes, just like that. Please me and you shall be rewarded in the best way as always, Agnes."

She nods and keeps sucking him, resting her hands on his thigh. He thrusts his hips a tad faster and harder, making her choke while signaling with his finger pressing against lips to gesture to her to be quiet.

I can hear my heart drumming in my ears. My blood is racing with my nerves quaking from the sight. It is a forbidden sight and yet it turns my breathing shallow and deep.

"It is bad to pry into others' business, little girl," the familiar masculine, gruff voice whispers close to my ear, making me jolt up. But before I can yelp in surprise he presses a hand against my mouth, pushing me against the wall beside the door.

"I'm pretty sure you don't want Father Geryon to know you were looking at his cock getting sucked by Agnes," he whispers, pressing against my body. But when he gazes at my face a sinister smile crosses his face.

"Why is your face flushed, little girl?" he asks, taking away his hand and caressing my jaw with his thumb. "Did that sight affect you?"

I turn speechless all of a sudden, looking around nervously. He cups my jaw to make me meet his gaze to answer him bravely.

"Answer, little girl."

I shake my head. "I-I…It was nothing. I came to take the cleaning supplies…I didn't know-"

"That doesn't answer my question though. Making riddles will end up in creating lies. Answer directly. Did watching them turn you on?"

I answered him with silence. But that is enough proof for him to get the answer to his question. His nose takes a deep breath into my hair, making me close my eyes and goosebumps run along my skin.

"A sinner and a vixen. Dangerous yet tempting combination," he whispers.

Another moan echoes from the door, turning my body warmer. His thumb runs along my lip like he was outlining it. His touch skating down with his fingers touching the pulse point on my neck, moving lower…lightly caressing my breasts before continuing its journey downward.

"Please," I rasp.

"Please what? Stop?" he asks. "If you want me to stop then all you have to do is say the words, little girl. Say it and I will move back and leave."

Tell him no. Say no and walk away.

But the words I need to tell him don't come out, giving him the green flag to resume. Deep down a part of me wants this. Why? I don't have any answer for that.

A low grunt and a choking sound comes again, but his touch keeps my attention captivated.

"You are always breaking the rules. Every time I find you, you are doing something you aren't supposed to. And here you are again. Something tells me you crave it. Tell me," his hand hitches up my dress, tracing the panty lines with his middle and index fingers, "are you wet from seeing what Agnes and Geryon were doing?"

I lick my dry lips, swallowing deeply. My eyes closing on

its own feeling his fingers explore my skin. His face close to mine with his lips against my cheek as he mutters his words.

"Do you want what she is experiencing?" he asks.

I grind my teeth together, feeling anger starting to boil up from his words. If he thinks I'm going to be a slut, who would fall on her knees for him anytime he says, then he is dead wrong about it.

"I won't be a slut. Don't dwell in the illusion that I will let you use me just because of your bullshit obedience logic."

He snickers under his breath with a dark smirk. "Not what I meant, but let me clarify here. Do you wish to experience the pleasure and desire she is feeling? Relishing your body writhing and trembling that you are unable to think about anything. Feel your every nerve being controlled by desire, driving you insane until you beg for release. Is that what you want?"

Dear God. How can anyone deny such an offer?

His fingers go lower to the apex of my thighs, lightly grazing my pussy, making me gasp. I clutch onto his muscular arms, arching my back.

The moaning suddenly stops from the other side of the door, and is exchanged with a yelp and a cry, which soon gets muffled, followed by the slapping sounds of their skin.

"She is getting rewarded by his cock. What about you, little girl?" He touches me again and I can't help but bite down on my lip to keep myself quiet.

"Please."

"Say the words and you shall have it."

I have been craving for it since the first night he came to my room. After he left me yearning for more, I keep telling myself to stay away from this. But now he is reviving those sensations again, but this time it feels irresistible. Every inch of my skin is trembling with need…with desire.

"I want this. Please."

That is the only response he needs before he moves my panties aside, finding my already wet pussy. He lets out a raspy groan while I feel his chest vibrating against mine.

"You are soaking wet. I can easily slide myself inside you," he whispers, moving his fingers back and forth along my wet pussy lips. My legs start to shake, but I hold onto him for support. His other hand wraps around my waist, pulling me closer and I feel his erection digging against my hip.

I hear the moans turning ragged, the slapping sounds getting louder and rougher. He even increases his pace and circles my aching clit. I bite onto my lip harder, not caring if blood draws out. My insides are twitching for release as his fingers work their magic.

"Fuck, you already feel so warm. Let's see how tight you are," he murmurs against my cheek, before pushing his fingers inside me and starts to really fuck me.

His motion is fast and hard, hitting that sweet spot that is calling for attention.

"My God, you feel so tight. Your walls are clenching my fingers so tightly." He pushes deeper up-to his knuckles, pressing his fingers against my wall and moving back and forth rapidly that I can even hear the wetness pooling between my thighs and dripping down.

"You will come before she does. A second later and I won't touch you again. Understood?" he asks.

I simply nod, throwing my head back as I release a silent cry. My fingers digging into his shirt.

At this point I don't care who sees us, the only thing that matters to me is coming in his arms.

"That's it. You're getting close. So, fucking close. I can feel your walls twitching."

He keeps fucking me with his fingers. My mind goes insane with a sensation I've never felt before. I'm almost on the verge…I can feel it coming.

"Say, my name when you come, little girl. I want you to hear and remember who made you writhe and moan."

"Tell me your name," I barely get out my words.

"Eryx. Say it."

He increases his pace, hitting my spot vigorously that before I know it, I'm coming undone whispering his name.

"Eryx…Ah! God! Eryx."

For a fleeting moment my vision turns blurry as my head rests against the wall and Eryx leans his head at the crook of my neck. He slows down his motions, eventually coming to a stop before he pulls out his now drenched fingers.

He moves his head back and looks at me with those lustful eyes before he brings his fingers close to his mouth and sucks it clean. My jaw drops open in shock as I've never witnessed such a sight, and the amusing look on his face says he is truly enjoying my astonishment.

He hums in appreciation at my taste. "Sweeter than any delicacy I ever had. A flavor to cherish for sure."

With a smirk he smoothens down my dress and takes a step back. "When it's said that sometimes sin can bring the ultimate pleasure, it's not wrong."

He turns around and walks away, pretending like he didn't just make me come into the library room. I try to catch my breath, feeling my mind still in haze of the intense pleasure I experienced.

Realization soon hits me that I'm still at the doorway and that Agnes and Father Geryon can come out anytime now. Fixing my hair and dress, I rush back to the place I was before, pretending to stock the shelves.

Others around me are still focused on their tasks. I'm not sure if they heard what Eryx and I did, or if they are hiding it very well. My hands are still trembling with my mind playing the images of Eryx and his touch…his closure…his sensation.

I don't know what consumed me that I threw my senses out of the window and let him touch me that way. And yet, a part of me can't deny it was the best feeling ever. The kiss that night was just a little peek, a forbidden taste, he showed me. But today's moment was way beyond it that left me yearning for more.

Why is he affecting me so much?
Why him?

I'm standing in the line, with an empty tray in my hand, waiting for the girl in front of me to be done filling hers with food. We are at the dining room to have our lunch. I don't know if they lack the items for breakfast or if this is some religious bullshit they created but it is never served or even cooked here. And nobody here seems to have a problem with it.

The room is equally vast like the prayer room on the ground floor. There is a long table set against the left wall with all the food already served in a row. On the opposite side are the tables and chairs where a maximum of four people are allowed to sit together to eat.

My turn comes and I fill my tray with bread, a small bowl of soup, sliced vegetables and fruits, and beans. Most of the seats are taken, but luckily a seat is empty beside Beth. I don't think any further and make my way towards her at the very corner of the room. She is usually like this from what I have noticed, hiding in the corner like a lurking shadow, as if she doesn't want to be seen. I sit in front of her, greeting her with a gentle smile, but she avoids my gaze and continues to eat her meal.

I look over my shoulder to find Agnes standing at the doorway with her arms crossed, looking around like the warden she is.

I dig into my food, slurping on the soup and keeping my gaze down. But I have to talk with Beth. I need her to help me find a way out.

"Please, think about it, Beth," I start, noticing her shoulders becoming tense. "We can both escape."

She barely shakes her head. "If you want to escape, feel free. But I prefer to live."

I frown. "Live where? Here? In this rotten hell where you are treated worse than a slave. I can clearly see your bruises around your eyes and your hands."

She tries to hide her hand with her sleeves, still not meeting my eyes.

"You prefer this life over the one where you could be free of this pain and humiliation."

Her head snaps up and for the first time I see emotions reflecting in her eyes.

Anger. Sadness. Recollection.

"I know what pain and humiliation feels like, Agatha. And I would rather live here than return back to the life where

I was seen as nothing but a burden and an embarrassment."

She lifts her palms up, a dark emotion shadowing upon her flushed face. "Do you have any idea what these hands have done? The sin it committed that I will always remember for the rest of my life"

She leans her hands closer to my face, making a sudden nervousness shroud my heart. My nerves are starting to race with anxiety.

"These very hands didn't hesitate to take the life of the person I loved."

I gasp in shock as realization settles in me.

She nods with a humorless smile. "That's right, Agatha. I killed someone and I had to do it. She deserved to be dead. The day she fell in love with me, she was doomed. And my hands sealed her fate."

I remain silent, breathing heavily. My appetite vanishes in thin air after hearing the confession that Beth made.

"I killed her," she rasps. Her eyes are wide with a horrific look. Tears stream down her cheeks and I notice she isn't blinking for once. Her body is trembling like she is realizing the truth just like me for the first time.

"I killed her...I...killed...her," she repeats her words like a mantra.

"I killed her." She looks down at the sharp fork and before I know it, she stabs her own hand with it in one sharp move while she keeps screaming her words.

"I killed her! I killed her! I'm a murderer!" she yells. I move back in terror, watching the blood spurt out of her palm, but she keeps stabbing herself again and again like the pain isn't enough for her.

Her eyes wide and red, filled with fright and remorse.

I look around and strangely everyone is calm and quiet, enjoying their meal like nothing is happening around them. But Agnes comes towards us, holding down Beth and snatches the fork away from her grasp.

"Stop it, Bethany!" Agnes orders in a strict tone. "I said stop!"

And all of a sudden, she does, turning still as a stone.

"Come with me," she mutters before holding Beth's hand and guiding her out of the room. I remain planted in my spot, feeling my heartbeat drumming in my ears. Letting out a shaky breath, running a hand through my hair as my eyes land upon the pool of blood on the table. Few drops splattered on my food and Beth's too.

I'm no longer hungry, as I feel bile clogging my throat. My body starts to sweat suddenly, with my forehead thumping with a headache. I look around and notice nobody is still reacting. They won't even acknowledge me if I leave the room, but something tells me if I do then Agnes will come after me.

"Agatha," Father Geryon calls my name, making me look over my shoulder. I walk towards him, watching his stoic expression soon turning into a glare.

"Come to my chamber. Follow me."

Without waiting for me to respond he stalks away while I follow behind him. His chamber is on the ground floor towards the right side of the prayer room. There is a large wooden table with a few books and files resting on top. A bookshelf is set against the walls, filled with more books. The floor is covered with a dark brown carpet. A small couch is beside the window with a folded blanket resting on it. The room is somewhat clean compared to the other places of the building, making it the only normal room in the whole castle. A tall and wide window on the right side seems to be the only source where light passed through. It has curtains pulled together but I notice there is a small lock on the window handle that has the possibility to be opened.

He takes a seat, resting his foot on his opposite knee. I stand at the center like I have been called at the principal's office.

"As you've seen, Bethany had a little relapse back at the cafeteria," he starts, "Her hand would require a few weeks to be fully recovered but other than that she would be fine."

How can he be so calm about it?

"But why do I feel like you triggered her somehow?" he asks, arching an eyebrow.

I try to remain relaxed but it's hard to follow when he is so cold and distant. "I was just asking her about the food,"

I lie.

He remains silent for a second as if analyzing my words carefully.

"You better not be lying, Agatha. Because if you are then you will be severely punished, bear that in mind. And lies here aren't taken lightly," he warns.

"I'm not lying."

"Then why aren't you speaking your words with confidence, why are you avoiding my gaze?"

I shrug. "Perhaps I don't like looking at you. Also, I don't have any excuse to lie."

Just then the door opens and Eryx enters, instantly scowling at my presence like he wasn't expecting me to be here.

"Ah, Father Eryx," Father Geryon greets him as he makes his way towards the desk, dressed in a priest attire like Geryon.

"I heard from Agnes about Bethany," he murmurs, leaning against the table with his arms crossed, while he faces me.

"Agatha here seems to know what must have happened to Bethany to cause such a scene," Geryon mutters.

Eryx has a sinister grin crossing his lips before he stands right in front of me. God, he is so close I can feel his heat. But I didn't let myself crumble under his intense gaze, standing tall and strong.

"Is that true, Agatha?" This is the first time he called me by my name in front of another person.

I shake my head. "We were just eating and I asked about her food-"

"What did you ask?'

I gulp. "If she likes the soup..." my voice trails off.

Eryx remains silent for a while before he nods, looking over his shoulder. "She is telling the truth. Bethany must have been triggered by something else. I'll check on her in a few minutes to see what happened."

Geryon simply nods but he doesn't look convinced. However, he doesn't argue furthermore and gets up. "I will see if she has been treated."

With that he leaves the chamber and closes the door behind him. I turn as well, about to leave. But when I open the door, it is slammed shut by Eryx. He is right behind me while I face the door, both our palms resting against the wood.

"I thought you two are done with your investigation. I want to go back to my room."

He tsks softly, moving closer, pressing his chest against my back. "Father Geryon is done questioning you, but not me."

I swallow the lump in my throat, trying to calm down my nerves, but they seem to speed up every time Eryx is around me.

"You were lying."

I frown, looking at him over my shoulder, with his face so close to mine. "I...I wasn't. You said so yourself."

"I lied to cover up yours. I could see it clearly in your eyes that you were hiding the truth. Just to save you I had to commit a sin."

I glare at him, my teeth gritting together. "I didn't ask to be saved. And whatever punishment he has I would have handled it myself."

He chuckles softly. "Trust me when I say, no person has ever *handled* Father Geryon's punishment. It would have haunted you for many nights."

For some unknown reason I do believe him. A small part of me feels thankful that Eryx saved me. Again.

"But that doesn't mean I will accept your lies. Now tell me what triggered Bethany's scenario?"

I shake my head. "I'm telling the-"

My words are left unfinished as he grasps my jaw, glaring at me in annoyance. That dark and twisted emotion pooling in his eyes sends shivers down my body. Sudden fear is starting to hold me captive.

"I hate to repeat myself again and again, Agatha. Tell me right now what happened or else I'll punish you and believe me it will be painful," he threatens.

His words are filled with confidence and promise, as I feel sure he is serious about punishing me. But if I tell him

I was trying to convince Beth to help me, then I will be in bigger trouble.

"Answer me, Agatha. If it's your lie again then you will choose the option to be punished."

I gulp, feeling my throat suddenly dry. "I-I," I cleared my throat. "I didn't do anything. She suddenly started to scream and hurt herself."

Eryx is quiet and unmoving for a fleeting moment, as if giving me a final chance to tell the truth. But when he realizes I'm staying rooted to my false words, he grips my hair, guiding me towards the desk.

"Bend over," he orders in an emotionless tone.

I look over my shoulder, feeling uncertain and nervous, opening my mouth to protest before he stops me.

"The more time you take the longer the punishment will be, Agatha. So, do as you are told and bend over the desk, hold onto the edges. Do not let go unless you are told," he demands. He walks back while I bend over and feel the hard wood pressed against my breasts.

He soon comes back and I look over to find a handle-like object with long, wide leathers hanging like tails in his hand, with his sleeves folded up. My eyes widen in horror and I immediately stand up before he pushes me down again.

"Let me go! I won't let you hit me with that!" I protest, writhing against his hold.

"Then tell me what happened and this flogging will be

gone."

But I remain quiet.

"Then the flogger it is. Lift your dress up," he orders.

I swallow the lump in my throat, feeling my breathing turned ragged. My heartbeat paced up like a skyrocket.

I hear the sharp snap of the leather making me jolt in surprise. With trembling hands, I move my hands back and lift up the hem of my dress. He moves closer towards my side, leaning his hand forward to caress the back of my legs that is covered with stockings. His touch makes its way up until it reaches my panties, making me gasp.

Before I'm aware, I hear the ripping sound of my panties.

"What are you-"

"Quiet," he mutters in his deep voice. "Unless you want to tell the truth then speak or else don't."

I feel the cool wind caressing my skin, sending goosebumps everywhere.

"I will be hitting you until you speak the truth. I won't even stop when your skin turns red or your ass starts to bruise. Understood?"

I nod. But suddenly I feel the hit of the flogger against my skin making me yelp in shock.

"I asked you something so I expect an answer in words."

"Yes, I understand."

"Remember, everything stops when you are no longer lying," he mutters. Before hearing the flogger coming, I felt it landing on my ass with a sharp hit.

"Ah God!" I whimper at the strike.

It starts off slow, but with every smack he increases his pace and force. My whimpers soon turn into cries that I try to muffle against the desk.

Behind me Eryx grunts and starts breathing heavily just like me. But he neither pauses nor does he let me rest for a minute to get used to the pain. He wasn't kidding when he said his punishment will be painful. But I have to endure it or else the truth will bring a bigger chaos for me.

After God knows how many hits later, my skin starts to burn, my eyes are glimmering with tears that are threatening to be flowing down.

"The truth will save you, Agatha. Stop being childish and tell me," he says but my mewl is the only response for him.

"Tell." *SMACK.*

"Me." *SMACK.*

"The truth." *SMACK.*

"Ah!" I cry out loud at the top of my lungs, unable to hold back the tears. My legs start to tremble that I feel I will fall down anytime. But he doesn't stop.

Not for once.

Even though I can't see it, I can feel and guess my skin will be burning like a raging fire for days. I start to cry, hating him even more for causing me such immense pain and making me look like a weakling. And for that I'm never forgiving him.

But I'm also not going to fall for his pain so easily that I will tell him the truth. I have that much strength within me even till my last breath.

Eventually, my knees buckle and I fall on the ground. Crying and shivering from agony.

Thankfully, he finally stops, dropping the flogger. I'm still in the haze of pain, unaware of my surroundings as I keep shedding tears.

But eventually, I feel the warmth of a blanket engulfing me before he makes a move to pick me up, but today I hate his touch. I loathe it.

I slap away his hand and instantly sit up, masking my pain before I try to get up on my shaky legs.

"Don't you fucking touch me!" I scream in rage pointing a finger at him, tugging the blanket tighter against my body.

"Stay the fuck away from me," I warn, while his expression remains neutral like he even doesn't feel an ounce of remorse for hurting me like that.

And the bastard dares to take a step towards me.

"I said stay away!"

But he still comes close to me and before he can touch me again, I slap him right across his face. "I said no!" I yell at him.

"When someone says it, they mean it. I don't know how the fuck you have been raised but no means a *no*."

He faces sideways with his jawline clenching. I notice his hands tightening in a tight fist. It is clear he is boiling with rage but he is controlling it.

But not me. I can't control my emotions any longer after the pain I've been through.

"Stay the fuck away from me. I'm not telling you anything," I seethe through my clenched teeth and march towards the door, rushing back to my room.

I shut the door behind me and kneel down, bringing my chin against my knees as I continue to cry.

Anguish, misery and shame shrouds me.

My skin is aching badly so it needs to be treated but I don't know where to go. Fuck, it's been weeks now and I'm still anywhere close to finding my way to freedom.

Everything is going south. The more I try to discover the more hopeless I'm turning. Slowly, bit by bit, my chances are fading away.

And with Eryx, things are turning confusing. His presence feels forbidden and yet my soul and body yearns for him. His words hypnotize me like dark magic. But even his darkness comes with a prize that can only be paid with pain and distress. And today I paid for it.

It changed my perspective about him even more, making me wish I never allowed him anywhere near me.

Don't give him an ounce of attention, Agatha.

He was never worth it in the first place.

CHAPTER EIGHT

ERYX

My cheek is aching from her hit and takes everything within me to stop myself from punishing her again. Her tears…those fucking tears hold me back.

I breathe in and out to calm down my nerves. My blood is racing faster with every passing second.

It's been a few minutes since she left but I don't leave the chamber. But when the door opens again, I know it isn't Agatha.

Geryon comes in my view with a frown on his face. "What happened to your cheek?"

"Doesn't matter. I punished her," I state it like a fact.

He simply nods. "And did she tell the truth?" he asks.

She didn't. She is the most stubborn woman I've ever met. Way too adamant beyond her own limit. I saw how badly her skin was bruising and turning red from my hits. With every strike I landed, I kept telling myself she will tell the truth, she will cave in. But she didn't surrender for a second.

But I can't tell Geryon about it, when I'm well aware he will punish her way worse than me. He hates it when something doesn't happen the way he wants. It's probably best to never test his anger.

"She wasn't lying." He frowns like he isn't expecting that response.

But I keep a stoic face to not let him see through my lie. "What happened to Bethany was caused by a reaction from a pill she missed yesterday."

"What do you mean she missed a pill?" he asks, his tone growing serious.

"The delivery for her medicines got delayed yesterday so she missed one and it affected her today."

He glares at me, closing his eyes and pressing his middle finger and thumb between his forehead. I remain silent, waiting for him to burst out in rage. But he breathes in and out, trying to calm himself, which he rarely does in such situations.

"How many times do I have to tell you to make sure we get the deliveries on time, otherwise we don't pay them a cent?"

I shrug. "They had some issues-"

"I don't care what issues they had. It was your job and you failed. As always," he taunts me. "Now she is your responsibility until her hand is fully cured. Make sure to check on her rather than sticking your cock inside that new girl."

"Keep her out of this," I say in a warning tone.

He snickers darkly, placing his hands on his hips. "What? Her disobedience and adamant demeanor turn you on? Your cock gets hard in her presence because she is a challenge to you?"

He spews out offensive words knowing well it's triggering me bit by bit. But I remain quiet, trying to be as calm as possible. Acting upon his words with a fight will worsen the situation.

He points a finger at me with a threatening look. "I don't care if you fuck her or punish her, as long as you don't fuck up her treatment. Don't forget her brother-in-law gave us shit ton of money for her."

"I remember because you remind me every fucking day."

He grabs my jaw in a tight grip, urging me to meet his eyes. "Don't you fucking dare act like a smartass. A woman like her only uses men like us to find her goal which is freedom. She won't hesitate to dispose of you the minute she is out of here."

I breathe heavily, gritting my teeth.

"You know how I know that, Eryx?" he asks. "Because you don't have a heart. God didn't give you one unfortunately to make you feel loved. You have nothing but a dark and rotten soul like the devil. A woman like Agatha ends up with men who are wrapped around the fingers of their wives, while she takes away his wealth."

He lets go of his grip and moves back. "Treat her like your patient, help her get cured so she can get the fuck out of here."

He heads towards his desk, taking a seat to work on some paperwork.

"You know about her state, right?" I ask, straining my gaze on his face that he is trying to hide.

"You also know why she is here-"

"Get back to work *Father Eryx*. Leave." He only calls me by that name either to dismiss or to remind me of my place here.

I simply nod, knowing well it's pointless to talk with him about it. I head out of the chamber and take the stairs to check on Bethany, but instead my feet guide me towards Agatha's room. I stand at her door, raising my hand to unlock the knob, when I hear her muffled crying echoing through the door making me halt. I have heard several women crying at the Magdalene.

Some cried in pain, some cried in humiliation, while others cried in hopelessness. But none of them ever affected me like Agatha does. Since the day I brought her here, I saw a spark within her.

A determination and strength that I rarely see in women.

But she carried those attributes like a crown and it made her look so...beautiful.

But hearing her cry feels like a dagger stabbing against my soulless, dark heart again and again. An agony that I never allowed myself to feel. But she is starting to make me feel emotions that have vanished from my soul ages ago.

I know she must be in pain and I'm the only one responsible for it. But I have no other choice. At the chamber when I saw Geryon leaving me with her, without further questions, I knew he would be standing at the doorway to listen to her confess to me while I punished her. But she is too stubborn.

I can only guess that she was talking something personal to Bethany which triggered her today. Since day one, Agatha has been looking for a path to freedom, but despite her failure she isn't willing to quit.

Not so soon.

But little does she know, once one comes to the Magdalene then even God can't help that person to escape from this living hell.

She isn't realizing it now, but when she will acknowledge it, I know hopelessness and loss will engulf her in a dark path, just like the rest of the patients.

The only thing I can do at this point is warn her. But a part of me keeps telling me to help her way beyond my ability, to save her...even though it's impossible.

I shake my head to bury those thoughts deep in the graveyards of misery. Geryon is right, I should treat her like a patient and nothing more. I can't let her tears and sorrow affect me like this when I don't even have the heart to feel something for her. It's futile.

With my gaze fixated on the door while my ears ring with the sound of her sobbing, I take a few steps before turning away and heading to do my job.

It is nearly midnight. Rubbing my eyelids with my index finger and thumb, I try to ease down the tiredness a little. Opening my eyes, I focus back on the sheet that has the list of the deliveries that will be coming this week.

My chamber is illuminated by the candles, the only source of light used during the night times here.

I take a sip of the bourbon from the silver glass, before setting it down. I write down the medicine and painkillers that will soon be out of stock.

Suddenly, I hear the creaking sounds of the stairs, making me frown in confusion. Geryon usually retires for the night before midnight, and the other nuns have a different chamber at the back of the building.

Putting away the papers, I get up from the chair and head out, walking upstairs. The halls are vacant and dimly illuminated by the moonlight coming through the windows. I hear the screeching sound again and this time it is coming from the top floor.

I quickly go upstairs when a figure catches my sight. Frowning I stalk towards her and see her standing at the balcony. Her hair is waving with the wind, along with the ends of her dress. She is muttering something as if someone is in front of her, even though she is the only person. As I get closer, I identify the voice.

Agatha.

I stand at the doorway, feeling the cold air against my skin, passing through my t-shirt as well. I'm about to call her when she suddenly turns around with her eyes wide open. Her skin looks suddenly pale like she has seen a ghost.

"Agatha, what happened?" I ask, approaching her but all of a sudden, she lets out a screech and aims to hit me with the candelabra against my forehead. I instantly move back, blocking her another attack by catching her wrist.

"Agatha! Stop!" I order her but she keeps writhing against my grasp. But when I put pressure on her delicate hand, she lets the candelabra fall on the ground with a loud thud.

Her eyes are wild like a lunatic, as she looks everywhere, as if she isn't aware where my face is. There is a terror lurking in her gaze that makes me more worried for her.

"Who are you? What do you want?" she keeps asking.

What is happening to her?

Gripping both her hands in one grasp, I bring her closer to me, holding her jaw with my other hand to urge her to look at me.

Is she sleep walking?

"Agatha, look at me. Hey, follow my voice," I mutter. But she keeps looking everywhere except at me.

"Follow my voice. Listen to me. I'm here. I'm here for you," I whisper calmly, noticing her body is starting to relax a bit.

"Eryx?" she whispers.

"Yes. It's me. Follow my voice, Agatha. I'm here for you. Do not fear anything."

I'm here. I'll always be here.

Finally, her gaze meets mine like she found me and lets out a deep breath of relief, leaning her forehead against my chest. "Oh my god," she rasps.

"Shh. Breathe. Take deep breaths," I guide her, caressing her hair. She does as told, but her body still keeps shivering as if ice cold water has been poured over her. Her arms wrap around me tightly like she doesn't want to let me go even for a second. Putting my arms around her and I pick her up.

Her door is already open as I step in and set her down gently on her bed. She is still shivering.

I touch her forehead with the back of my hand to check for temperature but it's normal.

"Stay here, don't move," I mutter before rushing out of the room and towards the checkup room. I have had patients before who would face such scenarios, so I always have drugs ready for such emergencies. I quickly take the injection and the small bottle with cotton swabs and dashing back to her room.

I kneel beside her, taking her arm to find her pulse point. I fill the injection and disinfect her skin before inserting the needle and pressing on the syringe. Few minutes pass by when Agatha's body finally relaxes with her muscles loosening from the drugs affecting her nerves.

Her eyes are closed as she sleeps peacefully. But the dark circles underneath her eyes don't go unnoticed from my sight. Lack of sleep.

I know I can leave her room now as she has calmed down, but deep down I want to stay with her. I will wait for a few more minutes in case something happens.

Yeah, keep telling yourself that.

I notice her face constricting like she is wincing in pain. Then I remember how her bruises haven't been treated. I return back and retrieve some ointment.

I sit beside her and turn her to her side slowly. I pick up the hem of her dress, pulling down her panties and the sight that I witness sends dread coursing through my entire body. Her skin isn't flawless and smooth, dark and deep cuts are painted all over like a horrific vision.

You caused it. You hurt her.

But I had no choice. It was either me or Geryon. And I won't let him place even a finger at her. Putting the ointment between my thumb and forefinger, I gently rub it to warm it up. I carefully apply around her scars, noticing she lightly winces in her sleep. Thankfully, the drug will let her sleep peacefully for hours.

She looks really tired.

Few minutes later, I'm done applying the ointment before I pull down her dress and put a blanket over her. I'm done here, I should leave now and pretend this night never happened but the minute I get closer to the door, my heart starts to pound.

What if the drug has an effect on her? What if she needs something?

Question after question makes my steps indecisive. Although, I can't stay here. If I do either Agnes or Geryon will know and I can't risk that. With a heavy heart, I let out a deep sigh. I glance over my shoulder, watching her asleep in her bed with her body relaxing, her chest rising up and down with steady breathing.

She is safe now. She is alright.

You helped her when she needed it.

That's the only consolation I can give to myself before I open the door and walk away before I end up doing something that would put both of us at risk.

THE DEVIL TAINTED US

CHAPTER NINE

AGATHA

My mind is still hazy from last night. I remember nothing. It feels as if last night never existed. It has been wiped away from my memory.

But I have this nagging feeling that something bad happened last night. Surprisingly, the bruises on my ass no longer hurt. They are beyond terrible and as if a miracle happened, the pain is somewhat less.

The prayers are done and Agnes barks out the instructions to everyone for today's chores. It's the same as usual. I don't know why she even bothers to announce it every day. I follow everyone to the laundry room, and in a few minutes the place starts to bustle with us working.

I use the detergent, rinsing away the dirt on the blanket, while my mind runs wild with thoughts regarding last night.

Did someone come to my room? What exactly happened?

Shaking my head, I twist the blanket, rinsing off the excess water. I'm putting it away when I notice something dropping on the water. Frowning, I lean slightly closer and another drop falls. It's something red like... blood.

I instantly touch my face and nose, assuming I must be bleeding from somewhere, but there is nothing.

I look up at the ceiling but there is nothing dropping from there. My gaze returns to the tub which has now suddenly turned bloody red. I gasp back and look around with nobody reacting to this. I realize their bathtubs are filled with soap water unlike mine.

What in the world...

What the fuck is happening?

This can't be real. I shake my head, rubbing my eyes. But nothing changes. My heart hammers against my chest; my pulse starts to speed up. With my hands trembling, I rest them on the tub handle and lean closer.

Suddenly, blood covered hands rise up and grab my head before sinking me into the tub.

"Ah!" I let out a muffled scream with the bubbles roaming around me.

My throat starts to clog with fear and blood in mere seconds as my lungs begin to burn for air. But I can't do anything.

The hands keep me beneath as I struggle, unable to feel the rest of my body. I can feel some of the blood running down my throat, making me want to throw up at the same time.

Everything is dark and red around me; I can't even see properly who is drowning me…torturing me to death. Even though I give it all to calm down and think through this, my mind is still in the haze from fear of dying by unknown hands. My windpipe starts to constrict, making it even more difficult to breathe.

God. Please, please. No.

I feel nearly on the peak of losing my consciousness and my life. My pulse starts to slow down with every inch of my body turning slack…preparing to embrace death.

But another hand comes up, but this time from behind holding my neck and pulling me back. Light and air comes alive as I cough heavily.

My hair and half of my dress is wet. I can hear my heartbeat drumming in my ears as I give every ounce of my energy to try to return to normalcy. I feel a hand around my shoulders, and another cupping my cheek.

I blink rapidly to focus on the vision in front of me.

It's Eryx.

"Agatha, can you hear me?" he asks. His eyes wide with concern and seriousness.

I simply nod, unable to speak at the moment. Remembering the blood entering my body, nauseousness hits me like a train wreck as I push away from his hold and rush towards the nearest corner to throw up.

Eryx comes by my side, gently moving his hand up and down my back, holding my hair for me. Few moments later, when I feel half of my stomach is empty, I lean back with my tears blurry from tears as I wipe my mouth with the back of my hand.

"It's okay," he whispers, helping me stand up and taking me back to my room. My body is still trembling from shock and weakness. Opening the door, he wraps his arms around me and gently lies me down on bed.

"I need to shower…I'm covered in blood…" I rasp, feeling fearful of seeing my hands and face coated in blood.

He frowns like he can't process what I mean. "You would need a shower for sure but what are you talking about?"

"I'm covered in blood." My tone is shaky from fear. "Blood…everywhere."

He caresses my wet hair and I flinch away. "No, please. Don't touch me."

"Hey…it's okay. It's okay." His thumb lightly brushes my cheek. "And there is no blood. It's just tub water."

"No, no, no. You are lying."

He cups both my cheeks and leans his hands back for proof, revealing there was nothing but water droplets and soap foam. "See? There is no blood, Agatha."

My brows furrow together and I instantly sit up, touching my face and looking down at my dress and hands. Eryx is not lying.

There isn't even a drop of blood. My breathing turns ragged, my lungs begging for air. "But…I swear I was drowned in blood." I hold onto his arms.

"Hush, take deep breaths." His tone is gentle and light as a feather for the first time. One hand holds my cheek and the other covers my hands. I follow as he says, inhaling and exhaling deeply and he copies me like he understands that I need guidance. He even leans closer, pressing his forehead against mine, leaving a comforting feeling that I didn't know I'm yearning for.

His hand snakes up, digging into my hair. "You are safe now. You are safe."

I exhale a shaky breath before I open my eyes and look at him, begging him to believe my words. "Please…"

He swallows, licking his lips that I can't help but stare at his lips that has made me feel the most pleasurable sensations.

"Tell me from the beginning. What happened?"

And I reveal it all. "I first saw that woman in the hallway. I don't know what happened but I woke up and I heard sounds coming from somewhere. I followed it and she was there. When I got closer to her she tried to kill me by choking me and pressing me harshly against the wall. And last night I had these fragments from a dream…I was on the balcony maybe and I heard a group of people whispering to me that I'm a murderer. Then someone came to attack me from behind and after that I don't remember anything."

I lick my lips before continuing. "And today...I was just washing the clothes and saw the tub being full of blood. And I leaned closer to see what it was when a pair of bloody hands came out and pulled me inside the tub. It was dark... and blood was everywhere."

The whole time he keeps his gaze fixated on my eyes as if looking for a sign of confirmation for my truth. His face is emotionless but I can feel his mind running a mile with question after question to the events I'm spilling.

I don't hesitate to share how those moments made me feel, how lost and scared I felt in those times of horror. I've never been this vulnerable to anyone and yet with him a part of me feels safe...a part of me that trusts him, hoping deep down that he might help me.

When I'm done, complete silence fills the room with the crashing waves echoing from outside.I wait for his response but the longer he delays it the more I feel that hope crashing into those waves and disappearing forever.

He opens his mouth, kindling my expectations but no words leave those lips. He is speechless and is unaware of how to answer my worries.

He doesn't believe my words.

"Agatha...I-"

"Stop. Don't do it." I shake my head. "Don't you dare pretend and feed me with lies."

He frowns. "I wasn't-"

"You don't believe me. I can see it in your eyes." I back away. "Get out and leave me alone."

He approaches me but I slap away his hands. "I said get out."

Instant fury inks my heart and soul. "It's clear as daylight that you don't trust my words. So, save your lies and fake consolations and leave," I warn him.

He still remains quiet with an emotionless look. The longer he stays the more rage infuriates me. He comes closer again and I don't hesitate to slap him with a viper speed, his face turning sideways.

"Fucking leave-" My words are left incomplete when his hand instantly wraps around my neck with his fingers digging into my skin. He pushes me down onto the bed as he hovers over me with a cold, heartless look that makes my blood turn ice cold.

"I let that act slide yesterday, but don't make this a habit," he seethes through his clenched teeth, leaning my head back with his other hand fisting my hair tightly.

"Ah!" I groan in pain but that doesn't affect him.

"I don't know what is going on with you or if it's just hallucination from your mental breakdown caused by guilt."

He reads the confusion in my face and grins darkly. "What? You thought your brother-in-law wouldn't tell us everything? Guess what? I know how you tried to hurt yourself when you saw your sister's dead body. Your guilt is controlling you to your very core."

My heart is thundering against my chest at his words as I feel my throat clogging with emotions.

"You kept blaming yourself for her death. I don't know what happened to her but now that I see it, I too agree with you. Maybe your sister did die because of *you*."

His words poison my soul as I feel guilt and heartache swallowing me into a black hole. There is no regret glimmering in his eyes as he continues to lash at me with his words. "You could have saved her; she was your sister after all but I guess you were too busy being fucked by college boys. Am I right or am I right?"

Tears prick my eyes making my vision blurry, but I give it all to not let myself break down in front of him. I won't.

"You are brought here to be punished for that." He shakes my head by my throat, tightening his grip.

"I thought maybe you, just maybe, you deserve some kindness, but I was a fool to let myself even ponder about it. You are just like every patient here. Lost. Broken. And most of all, weak."

The tears I have been holding back course down despite my attempts as his harsh words stab me right through my heart with no scope for it to be healed. If he planned to cut right through my soul with his harshness then he has succeeded with flying colors.

With his jaw clenched, he pushes back and lets go of his grasp. But I stay immobile, gathering my broken pieces.

"I had enough of your acts and bitchiness. If it's some sort of plan you are pulling off to escape from here then stop wasting your time. You are not leaving until *I* state it legally that you are sane and cured. Get that through your mind or keep suffering."

I remain silent.

"Understood?" he asks but my lips don't move.

"Speak!" his voice roars through the silence making me jolt.

"Yes. I understand," I barely whisper.

"I will send Agnes to get you fresh clothes and then you are coming for the checkup."

My head snaps up to meet his cold gaze. "I-"

"It wasn't a question, little girl. You will be there even if I have to drag you there by your hair."

Before I can protest any further, he leaves.

I bring my knees to my chest and start sobbing as memories of losing my sisters hits me like a wrecking ball. It feels like a thunderstorm destroying every bit of my soul.

Eryx isn't lying and that is a fact I've been trying to avoid for so long, just to allow myself to keep moving in life. But such guilt will always follow me like a shadow till I take my last breath, because losing my sister was a grief, but being responsible for her death is a never-ending sin I've committed.

She died because of me.

A few days have passed by since that tub incident...since the day Eryx whipped me with his harshness.

Today I'm at the front yard, picking up a few dead plants. The clouds are gloomy and dark as always with the ground slightly muddy from the rain last night.

I reach towards the iron gate where several dead roses lay on the ground. Bringing the basket closer which is already pretty full from the dead plants, I stuff it more with the roses.

The thorn vines wrap around the gate rods, as I carefully pick out the deceased roses. I hear scrunching footsteps coming from behind, looking over my shoulder I see Eryx arriving and standing beside Agnes to talk with her about something in a hushed tone.

She nods and walks inside, leaving Eryx to watch over me and four other women who are doing the same task as me. His eyes meet mine which carries the same emptiness as it did the day he left my room. Looking away I return to my so-called work, accidentally prickling myself with the thorn as I hiss in pain.

I suck on my cut, trying to soothe down the pain. I look back, expecting for Eryx to come to help me like he usually does but instead he remains fixated in his spot, surveying others. I get up and walk to pour some water on my cut, but as I pass by Eryx, he grabs me by my elbow and pulls me back.

"Where do you think you are going?" he asks in a neutral tone.

"My finger got slightly cut by the thorns-"

"That's not enough of an excuse to leave your work." He pushes me back nodding towards the gate where I was working. "Get back to work."

"But it will get infected-"

"In case you have forgotten, let me remind you." He stands close to me and holds my jaw, pressing his fingers against my cheeks and demanding with his motion to look at him. "I'm the doctor here, and that little cut won't infect your baby soft skin. So, stop acting like a brat and get back to work, otherwise you know well what the consequences will be."

He pushes me away again without any reflection of remorse in his face. Swallowing the lump in my throat, I walk back and return to my task. For some unknown reason, his cold and heartless demeanor feels like a slap across my face.

I think of the time he was gentle with me at the checkup room. How it didn't matter to him that he broke a rule just to comfort me. How he touched me that day...making me feel alive like I've never felt before. But now?

All of those are gone in thin air. Like it never existed in the first place. But I'm not going to let him control my emotions like that. I have to keep reminding myself that he is one of the villains in my story.

Geryon joins him and gives one quick look at us before he starts talking with Eryx. "The supplies will arrive soon. The ship should arrive here in a week or two."

A ship?

I pretend to be focused on my work while I listen to their conversation.

"I will go and get them. And I have to go Vailburg for a few days," Eryx says.

"But the day hasn't arrived yet."

"I know but I have some important work to finish."

There is silence for a few seconds. "Alright. But be back in a week. No more than that."

"Alright," he agrees and with that Geryon leaves.

I can't help but feel a ray of hope blooming in my heart, finding out there is a way of escape. A ship is coming here and I can get there, sneak in there and be free. But I know I just can't run there as I have no clue which direction leads toward the exact shore area where the ship will stop by.

Only person to know it seems to be Eryx.

I have to figure out a way to get to know the location through him. I know he isn't going to tell me the direction, that is an impossible thought but I have to try another way.

By the time I'm done with my work, my hands are sore and prickling with more cuts from the rose. The clouds start to growl with thunder, signing for an approaching storm.

"Everyone, inside right now," Eryx orders with a gruff, loud tone and we all do as told.

I pick up my basket and head in, peeking a glance at Eryx over my shoulder, surprisingly finding him already staring at me before he looks away. He is my key to freedom and I will do anything to search for a way to get to him.

Chapter Ten

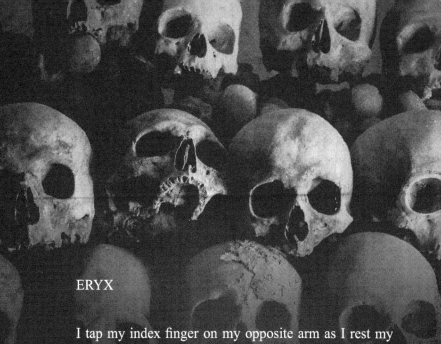

ERYX

I tap my index finger on my opposite arm as I rest my back against the check-up bed. My eyes glance at the door as I keep waiting for Agatha to arrive. My nerves rush with impatience.

I know she isn't going to come here that easily but I still want to give her a chance. Seems like it isn't worth it. Feeling my last thread of patience slipping away, I walk out of the check-up room in search of my little temptress.

When I reach her floor, I notice she is just entering her room, but the way her shoulders are hunching down tells me something is suspicious.

Frowning, I halt and wait for her to close the door.

I lean my ear against the wood but there is no sound coming, but when I heard a light scraping sound everything within me tightened in alert as I burst inside the room.

"Dear God!" she yelps from my sudden presence, leaning against the window side. The subtle movement of her hiding something behind her doesn't go unnoticed from my gaze. I stride forward until I'm standing like a tower in front of her.

"What are you hiding?" I ask in an authorizing tone.

She simply shakes her head, not uttering her response as if she knows she will get caught by me through her words.

"I asked you something, Agatha, so you better answer me before I make you."

Instead of having fear paint on her face, there is bravery and strength shrouding her, and those make her look so beautiful that it hurts. But I suppress those weakening emotions and give her a warning look.

She swallows, licking her lip which makes me want to lean down and lick it for her, tasting that sweet flavor I haven't forgotten since that night.

"It's nothing. Why the hell are you here?" She accuses me in return. "My chores are done for the day."

"Don't play games with me, little girl. You wouldn't like the consequences at all. So, don't make me repeat myself."

She still remains quiet, testing my patience even more.

In the next second, I grab her arm and pull her up in order to see what she is hiding. She yelps and thrashes against my hold. "Stop it! What are you doing?"

I expect to find something that she might use against me but what I see makes me pause my motions. It is a rose with its stem somehow balancing in one of the cups used in the cafeteria for drinking. The rose seems to be withering and probably will die soon in a few weeks, perhaps days.

"Why is this here? And how did you get the cup to your room?" I ask, facing her.

She casts a nervous glance at me before answering. "I found it yesterday when cleaning the area around the gate. I thought it deserves a chance to live a bit more, perhaps it could blossom soon if given the right care. And after lunch I hid the cup inside my pocket."

This time I turn silent, unable to think of the right words to respond.

"What are you waiting for? Go ahead," she mutters with a shrug, crossing her arms.

"What do you mean?"

"It's clear from your silence you don't want me to keep this rose in my room, just because I want at least a small source of life in my room. So, go ahead and throw it away." Placing the rose on my hand, she walks towards the bed and sits down, fidgeting with the fabric of her dress.

I look back at the rose feeling this sudden ache in my heart that I haven't felt for a long time. Leaning my hand forward, I lightly touch it, caressing the rough and oval ends of the petal between my thumb and forefinger.

"It needs more than water. You will need some soil," I state, not turning to gaze at her.

"I don't have a pot and I couldn't find it around."

"I have a jar in my room. You can use that and fill it with the essentials this rose needs."

"Why are you doing this?"

I meet her questioning gaze like she is going through a rough time to figure me out. It's futile but she is still trying.

"I don't need to justify anything to you."

She scowls. "I just wanted to know why you are showing interest in a flower."

You don't want to know, little girl. I almost say it.

"You are getting what you want, so, stop questioning about it and be thankful, little girl."

She presses her lips together and nods. "Thank you. I actually appreciate it."

"Why aren't you in the check-up room?"

She starts to fidget again with her dress, looking worried and nervous to mutter her words. I walk towards her direction and stand in front of her before sitting on the bed, tucking her hair back that she is using as a curtain to hide behind.

"You hate check-up rooms, that is no surprise there. But why?"

She gulps with her breathing turning slightly shallow and raw. Copper her cheeks, I can feel her nerves pulsing faster underneath my touch. This truly bothers her deep down.

"How will I fix it if you don't tell me, Agatha?"

"I don't need you to fix anything."

"I'm your doctor, so it is my job to fix your problems. You can tell me."

She lets out a humorless chuckle and shakes her head. "You won't believe me. Nobody ever does."

I skate my hand lower and cup her cheek, urging her to look at me. "I will believe you."

"And why is that?"

"Because you have nothing to lie about to a stranger. And your eyes will reveal it all to me, they are a mirror to your soul, telling me the truth I need to know."

Agatha remains quiet, trying to steady her breathing with astonishment painting her face. But it's also clear that she is struggling to find her words…to reveal the truth about her fear. Without a second thought, I dip down my head, pressing my forehead against hers and take steady breaths along with her.

"Close your eyes. Pretend you are disclosing your secret in a dark room. Nobody but you." She closes her eyes.

"Deep breaths, Agatha. Deep breaths." She does as told while I continue trying to sooth her with my touch.

"Tell me your fear, Agatha. Share it with me," I rasp.

"Tristen took me to the hospital where I was before. The doctors there were normally doing the check-ups but then…" her words fade away as she pauses for a moment.

"One of the doctors injected me with something during a check-up. I don't know what happened but I just froze.

I couldn't feel my body…every nerve within me felt motionless. He then slid my gown up…h-he," her voice starts to shake but she still gathers her courage to finish her words.

"He started to touch me between my…he then started to stroke himself right beside me."

I open my eyes and see hers closed with tears streaming down her. Every drop that falls, feels like a poison being poured on my heart, burning every nerve as if it's on fire and turning into ash.

"He had this devilish look in his face and it truly felt like a monster was in front of me, ripping me away from my own self with his sins…making me feel tainted inside out."

She lets out a shaky breath. "It felt like forever. I kept praying that the nightmare would end and I would get the hell out of there. But I was wrong…Tristen didn't listen to me and kept me there while I went through that horrific time several times. But when I attacked the doctor when I had control over my senses, only then he stopped. But I kept fighting him at every turn because I didn't trust him and what he might do. So, I would get whatever I could find nearby me and hit him until he bled."

She licks her lips, not caring it's now coats with her tears. "Every time I even hear about going to the check-up room, I would remember that gut wrenching moment, feeling helpless all over again," she shrugs with a sad smile, "-and there is my truth. My secret…a secret that no one believes because everyone thinks I'm insane. I can't be trusted."

"Look at me, Agatha," I whisper. The minute she does and I see the deep, dark pain she has been hiding in her eyes, I just know she isn't lying. It's all real.

The mere sight makes me want to take her pain. Not just this but every bit…every ounce of suffering she has been through because no matter what she has done, she didn't deserve that.

Nobody deserves that.

"What you have been through is the worse torture than death itself. You certainly didn't deserve it. But you know what I saw when you told me your truth?"

She shakes her head. "What?"

"A strong and brave soul. A woman who will rise up more powerful no matter how many nightmares she goes through. I have seen women who have been through horrific scenarios. Many remain silent and hide in the shadows, some even give up on their lives and quit. But not you. Your strength is your weapon and shield."

Her eyes glimmer with fresh tears.

"I believe your words because I see that agony in your eyes living deep down in your soul. It may have tainted you but it didn't kill your spirit. Nothing can."

"Nobody has ever said those to me."

"Because they are too blinded by lies that they don't see the reality in front of their eyes. That's the world we live in.

And as for your check-up, I give you my word, I won't do anything that will make you feel helpless and bound."

She keeps staring at me, searching for the promise my words hold, and when she sees it, she eventually relaxes and nods.

"I have your word?"

"You have my word."

She is nervous for sure, but she gives it all to hide her emotions. But I keep the door open, letting her know she can leave anytime she wants and I won't stop her. The memories triggered her panic attack where she knew she couldn't escape. But this time she has that option.

I check her blood pressure and temperature, making sure she has no side effects from the medications she is taking. She keeps toying with the loose thread from her dress, something she does whenever she is worried about something.

I lightly pull down the skin beneath her eyes to see the blood circulation, which is at normal level, but the dark circles tell me she isn't getting enough sleep.

I jot down at the necessary information in my black, leather notebook.

"Everything so far seems normal but you aren't sleeping properly. Why is that?"

She shrugs, casting her eyes down. "I have been having these weird dreams and it's so quiet here that it sometimes scares me."

I cross my arms and nod. "By any chance you feel nauseous or have a headache whenever you go to sleep?"

She shakes her head in response.

Strange but I also remind myself of the times I caught her at night outside of her bedroom, screaming and crying for help. "What about the times I found you in the corridor or balcony? How do you explain that?"

"I can only think of sleepwalking but I never had that."

"It doesn't seem to be that case, sleepwalking has different symptoms." Letting out a sigh and grab my notebook again to write down. "I will get you some sleeping pills, might help you to sleep better."

She remains quiet as I feel her gaze on me.

"What?" I ask, continuing to write.

"Just curious about you…"

"What about me?"

"Did you always wanted to be a doctor?" she asks, curiosity oozing in her tone.

"No. My parents wanted me to be a well-known doctor and so I studied in medical science in Vailburg."

"How old are you?"

"Thirty-seven."

Her eyebrows arch up in surprise. *Yes, I'm eighteen years*

older than you, little girl.

"Where are your parents?"

"That is none of your business. And never ask that question again." Instant annoyance claws me making me snap the notebook shut and nodding towards the door for her to leave. "Your check-up is done. You may leave."

Confusion dawns on her face but she gets the hint from my tone as she gets off the bed, stalking towards the door but pausing at the doorway. "Just like you trusted my truth, you can trust me with yours."

I pretend I didn't hear her, turning my back at her and going through some papers on the table. She waits for a moment but when she realizes I'm not going to budge, she finally leaves me alone. I let out a deep breath, relaxing my nerves and closing my eyes.

After what Agatha confessed to me earlier, I begin to see her in a different light. I see her in a way I've never seen a woman before. I know she is strong and determined, but I had no clue she is a warrior, protecting and fighting for herself through these nightmares. It makes me want to know who the doctor is so that I could fucking cut him into pieces and throw him in the sewer, where he belongs.

Maybe I will do that.

But at the moment, I try to focus on my task, though it's turning out to be difficult with Agatha filling my thoughts. Something about her reports start to nag me…like something is wrong. It's clear by the doctors' statements that she is mentally ill and usually harms herself and others. But so far, she has acted upon harming people in order to protect herself. She has her reasons and that's not an illness.

The brother-in-law is hiding something for sure, and there is only one way to find out the answers to my questions.

CHAPTER ELEVEN

AGATHA

I dash out of the bathroom as quickly as possible, looking around to make sure nobody is following me, but I suddenly bump into a strong, wall-like body. I nearly think it's Father Geryon and I'm in big trouble, but when I see those familiar black eyes, I let out a sigh of relief.

"What are you doing?" he asks.

"I was getting some water for the rose."

He nods and looks over my shoulder and nods towards the door of my room. We both get inside and I don't waste time putting the rose inside the cup. It still doesn't look much different from the last six days, but I don't give up hope.

"Here," Eryx says, making me look over my shoulder. "I brought you the jar I mentioned. It will hold more water and the soil it needs."

He hands me a large glass jar with a crisscross design on

the head area. With a timid smile I take the jar and replace it with the cup.

"You didn't use the soil from the front yard?" he asks.

"I tried but it didn't help much. Maybe it wasn't fertile enough."

"There is some good quality soil in the shore area. I will get them for you, don't worry." He turns to leave but I hold his wrist, urging him to turn.

"Can I come with you? I can bring the-"

"Nice try but you are not setting a single foot out of here." He smirks.

"You know I can't escape from here unless I get help. So, why won't you let me out?"

"Because you aren't allowed. End of discussion." He moves to walk out again but I rush and stand in front of the door, blocking his path.

"No, it's not. I want to go out and I can't think of any possible way to go out with you except now. This place is huge and it will take me forever on my own."

"You still aren't allowed."

"But you can allow me. I just want to go out with you for a walk, I need some air. Even if it's for a fleeting moment I want to pretend I'm not in a prison."

He stays quiet, assessing my face like he is looking for me faltering with my words. But I hold my head high, reflecting confidence and certainty.

He leans closer, resting his hands on either side of my head against the door, caging me.

"And what do I get in exchange?" he rasps, his face so close to mine that our lips are a few inches away.

"I didn't know this was a deal." My throat starts to feel dry with my heart pounding against my chest.

He smirks, running his nose along my cheek, sending shivers down my spine. "I'm breaking a rule for you, so I deserve to have something in return."

I swallow. "What do you want?"

"You."

One word. That one word is all it took for him to take me aback with surprise. "What do you mean?"

"I told you what I want. It's as simple as that, I want you."

"I'm still not getting it."

"I see how you love to be in control. How you defy everything and try to take control even though you know the consequences would be terrible. But with me, I want you to give up that control. Surrender yourself to me."

"It's an unfair agreement compared to what I want."

He shakes his head, lightly skimming his lips against mine but not leaning for a kiss, which makes me wish he did.

"It's fairly equal. You just don't want to go out for a walk on shore, you want to feel the freedom in your cage. Something I'm sure everyone wants here but you are the one getting it granted. So, for something like that I asked for an equal price. You accept it and I will take you outside."

My pulse is racing, not just from his words but also from his irresistible touch. His lips run lower until it reaches my neck and he lands an open mouth kiss right on my pulse point. I close my eyes, feeling desire coursing through my nerves.

It's turning out to be difficult to think through his bargain when his lips are so distracting. His tongue circles on my skin as he sucks on it at the same time. I can't help but let out a raspy moan, holding onto his muscular shoulders.

"Ah!" I whisper, feeling his lips move up. Opening his mouth, he licks his way up to my jaw before moving to my lips and kissing me deeply with his fingers digging into my hair. His abdomen pressing against my stomach and when I feel his erection, my body igniting like an inferno.

Dear God. He is big.

He lets out a deep groan against my lips, making me lost in his sensation. I move my hands to hold his face but he suddenly grabs my hands with one of his and presses them over my head, and his other hand moves back, grasping the nape of my neck.

He is controlling my body and for some unknown reason I don't mind it. I feel my body surrendering on its own to him.

"Say, yes, Agatha. I know you want this." He nibbles my

bottom lip roughly so that I nearly think it will bleed. But I don't care. "Say it."

"Please," I whisper. He moves his hips against mine, making my cunt clench, aching for his touch. He lets go off my neck and reaches lower underneath my dress, tracing my now wet pussy, groaning in appreciation.

"Fuck, you are so soaking wet that I can easily slide my cock inside you." His fingers circle on my wet spot while I wish he would just remove my panties and actually touch me.

"You want that don't you, little girl?" he whispers. His hot breath fanning my lips before he dives in for another passionate kiss that shakes me to my core.

He finally moves my panties aside and traces my pussy back and forth, lightly touching my clit. *God, this is torture.*

My walls are twitching already and as if the bastard can feel it, he grins and continues his torment.

"It feels like torture, doesn't it?" He coats his fingers with my juices before sliding two inside me. I cry out loud but he muffles that by placing a harsh kiss. "Every inch of you is yearning for release."

His fingers move in and out as he fucks me with his fingers in a torturous, slow pace. I groan against his lips, begging him silently for more. "You are soaking my fingers, little girl. But, I'm curious…"

He pushes his fingers deeper with his palms against my

clit. My legs are trembling, on the verge of losing balance.

"I want to see how much more wet you can be that you end up soaking the floor. What do you think, should we test it out and see?" he asks, licking my lips.

My heart skips a breath, and I hold no control over my body anymore as I move my hips to get some friction on my aching clit. I want the release so badly that I might cry.

He starts to move his hand back a little, making me whimper in protest. "No, please."

"If you want it then you have to say it, little girl."

"Please," I beg, leaning my hips forward but being the fucking sadist he is, he moves his fingers away that I no longer feel my insides full.

"I'm not giving you what you want until you give me what I want. Give up your control and I will show you the pleasures you've never even imagined."

Oh God.

"I promise you this, the pleasure will be dark and forbidden, but it will be an experience you won't be able to resist. Say you want it."

"I...I..." My voice fades away as my mind battles to resist him.

"Speak up, little girl," he commands.

"I want it, please I want it so badly. I will lose my mind if you don't give it to me," I finally utter the words he demands to hear.

"Good girl," he whispers with a smirk and the next second his fingers pushed deep inside me in one swift move. I yelp in surprise, throwing my head back.

"Ah, God-" my cries get muffled by his kiss as his fingers start to work their magic, moving in and out with the tips hitting my walls in that sweet spot. His hold on my hand tightens like he knows I ache to touch him.

But he is in control now. Not me. And I want that.

He pushes deeper like last time with his palm against my clit, hitting a spot that I've never felt before.

"Ah, there it is. You've never had something so deep inside you, did you?"

My moans are my only response. "I can hear you for hours and still won't be tired of your cries and moans."

His fingers move faster. I can hear the wet squelching sound which only makes me yearn for me. With him I feel greedy with everything.

"Your walls are clenching so tight. But remember what I said, I want to see you so wet that it's soaking the floor, so let's try that."

His motions suddenly turn so fast that my whole body is moving along with it. Every bit of my soul feels like it is on the verge of breaking in his arms as I feel this experience I've never felt before. I cry out loud that I'm sure someone will surely hear, but I don't care at all.

My walls are twitching and I feel my wetness streaking

down my thighs with his increased speed. Suddenly, I hear light footsteps coming from the corridor and I know who it might be at this hour.

Sister Agnes.

Eryx smirks like he can read my mind but he doesn't stop. "That day you were watching her and Father Geryon. How about today she hears you come, what do you think?"

I can't respond as I'm too lost in the haze of desire.

The footsteps begin to come closer to my room and I nearly pray she will leave us alone without knowing what is happening behind the doors. But a part of me wants her to watch…wants her to see how Eryx is pleasing me…how he only wants me.

I feel myself reaching the peak point of release as my legs shake so hard that I feel I will be losing my footing, but his hold on my hands are the only thing that helps me stay upright. The footsteps got closer and we know she is right outside.

The thrill is so high that I feel my whole nerves being controlled solely by it. But Eryx doesn't pause for a second, instead he paces up, whispering his commands against my ear.

"You will come right now for me. Come so hard that you will lose your mind," he grunts while I'm mere seconds away from coming.

"Come for me, little girl. And you better drench the

floors. Come."

And I do.

I come so violently that my whole body shivers as I let out a silent cry, throwing my head back and shutting my eyes tightly, when I feel something wet dripping between my thighs. I'm squirting. Eryx and I both look down, watching my wetness pooling on the floor while his fingers continue to move, eventually slowing down.

When it finally stops, he pulls out his fingers and circles my clit making my body spasm even more.

"Good girl. Such a good little girl." He kisses my cheek before moving to my lips. I feel like I'm in a different world where only him and I exist. But when I hear the retreating footsteps of Sister Agnes, reality returns to me. Eryx made me come and squirt while she was right outside the door. The thought would have repulsed me if someone told me a few weeks ago, but at this moment it feels beyond thrilling and exciting.

Eryx lets go of my hands and wraps his hand around my waist as if he knows I will lose balance with my body still coming down from that mind blowing orgasm.

I watch him lick his fingers clean and it is such an erotic sight to behold.

God. What is he doing to me?

He pulls down my dress, smoothening my hair back as I look at him with drowsy eyes, watching him grin like the sinister he is. Picking me up he guides me to my bed and lays me down.

"I will get someone to clean the floor. Be ready after dinner," he whispers before kissing me one last time and standing up. My body feels already tired from that orgasm, so I close my eyes to rest for a while, before I hear the soft thudding sound of the door shutting as darkness engulfs me.

There is a light knock on my door at night and I know who it is. Smoothening my dress and hair I stalk towards the door and gently open it, finding Eryx standing there.

Even in this dark night, he looks so attractive and enormous. He is so tall that every time he is close to me, I have to crane my neck to meet his gaze. His dark brown hair was pushed back with his black eyes glimmering from the moonlight coming from my window, but the glass lantern he holds onto illuminates his features even more. I nearly expected him to not show up but he kept his promise.

He has a black hooded cape draped on his arm before he passes it to me. "Wear this."

Without questioning I put it on and pulled the hood over my head. He nods, gesturing me to follow him as he softly closes the door. With steady and noiseless steps, we head downstairs and out of the door, but when we pass through the gate, I feel this surge of peace coursing through me. A breeze of freedom engulfing me as I try to avoid the reality where I'm still in my cage.

"Stay close," he mutters and leans his hand forward with the lantern guiding our path.

It's mostly muddy from the rain that happens here every once in a while. The leaves and few fallen branches crunch beneath our feet as we head forward. It's pitch black that it's impossible to see through anything without the lantern or the moonlight.

We keep walking for several minutes and at one point I feel worried if we have gotten lost. But I notice Eryx touching the trees every now and then which makes me wonder if that was his way of remembering the path. I carefully remember every spot we pass, even though because of the darkness it's tough to memorize clearly.

Finally, the crashing waves' sound gets louder and soon we reach the shore side. The water glistens under the moonlight with the wind gusting strongly, making the end of my cape sway vigorously.

It's so…peaceful.

The scenario is breathtakingly beautiful. I inhale and exhale deeply, the earthy fragrance of the sea wafting around my nostrils. It nearly makes me wish to stay here and never return to Magdalene.

"Follow me," Eryx mutters, making me slightly jolt

because for a moment I forgot he was even there. I follow behind him as he walks towards the right side, searching for something.

He stops nearby a tall tree and leans the lantern forward to see the ground as he kneels down. "This is fertile soil. There is a small pouch in the pocket of your cape. Pass it to me."

I pull out the bag and watch him fill it with soil until it's hefty and he ties it close, passing it back to me.

"There, it's done. Let's return."

"We aren't going to stay?" I ask, feeling my heart drop dead.

"You wanted to come with me to get soil for your rose. We got it so there is no point in staying behind."

"But I want to stay a bit longer. We just got here," I argue.

"We are leaving now."

I take a few steps back, shaking my head. "I want to stay."

Even in this dark night, I can clearly see his sinister grin, feeling my body shiver from a sudden thrilling feeling.

"You either walk or be carried over my shoulder. One way or another we are going back, so you choose which option you want."

He notices me taking further steps back as he seems to be thinking of something.

He snickers. "I can see your mind racing and it's clear

you want to run away from me. But no matter where you go, where you run," he leans closer to me, setting my skin on fire, "I will find you, little girl."

I gulp feeling my breathing speeding up.

"But on second thought..."

I frown. "What?"

He moves back as confusion fills me. "Run."

"What do you mean?'

"Exactly what I said. Run. Find your freedom in this cage as I chase you. If you escape me, I will bring you here whenever you want, if I catch you then you will face consequences."

Consequences?

What is he going to do?

Hurt me until my skin was raw with blood? Abandon me here?

I stay rooted to my spot, unable to understand his proposal. There is nowhere to escape as I'm stuck here, except to get back in Magdalene before he catches me.

"Run, little girl. Run as fast as you can."

Before I know it, my feet are moving back as I turn and start to run. Where? That I don't know.

I only hear my thudding footsteps, my raspy breath and my heart pumping faster. I look over my shoulder for once and see him standing in his spot. He isn't even following me.

But I avoid it and run faster until he is no longer in sight.

I reach the hill side and the only way forward seems to be the forest. Without thinking, I dash forward feeling my lungs burning for air. My nerves are slightly aching but I don't stop for once.

It's getting darker and darker the deeper I go. But when I hear heavy footsteps coming from behind, I give it all to pace up my speed. He's coming.

I feel this unknown thrill coursing through my body, highlighting the adrenaline.

I can hear him…feel him getting closer, like a predator about to have his prey. I see a wooden bridge ahead but even from afar it's clear it isn't stable. But I still take the risk and walk ahead, holding onto the ropey handles as I cross it. Eryx crosses the bridge too with ease not caring how shaky it is with his weight.

My blood roars in my ears as I continue to run, but when I see the distant sight of the Magdalene gate, I feel a ray of victory coursing through me.

I'm so close. I can do this. I can beat him.

Suddenly, a strong hand catches my elbow and I yelp as I'm dragged back and pushed against a tree.

He caught me.

But I still continue to fight, thrashing against his hold. I even land a few hits against his face hearing him grunt, but in one swift move he catches both my wrists and pins them over my head.

"You lost, little girl."

I wince from his grip, but my body freezes when he presses his body against mine, with his figure looming like a shadow upon me. Both of us are breathing heavily, craving for air.

I raise my leg to knee him but as if he sees it coming, he halts my attack and grips my neck in a tight grasp. I wiggle my back and hand trying everything possible to get away from him.

His twisted grin makes my nerves tremble with a dark excitement I didn't know existed.

His mere presence holds a dark promise. His touch is an ecstasy that is forbidden for me and yet it feels so good. Eryx is a poisonous paradise.

"Time to face your consequences."

Oh God.

Chapter Twelve

AGATHA

Holding me by my neck, he pushes me down as I kneel in front of him. He reaches for my cape and takes it off, using it to bind my wrist together.

"What are you doing?" I whisper, a hint of fear starting to ink my tone.

"Be quiet," he orders. He tugs on the cape making sure my hands have no room for space, before holding the end that is hanging between and pins it over against the tree. My hands are stretched up as far as possible and he has control.

Eryx looks down at me with a victorious smile before his other hand reaches down and caresses my lips with his thumb.

"That same mouth left a mark on my hand and since that day I couldn't stop thinking how this mouth would feel around my cock."

I gasp in shock, breathing heavily.

He snickers darkly as he unbuttons his pants and pulls down the zipper, taking out his cock which is already hard and raging with pre-come coating the top.

Dear God.

"What if I say no?" I ask.

"You won't."

"How can you be so sure?" I rasped.

He strokes his length, smearing the pre-come while I have this deep aching blooming within me.

"Because it is clearly written on your face how much you want this. There is no sign of fear or shame. It is filled with wanton and need."

He lightly traces his cock along my lips, hissing under his breath. I get the lightest taste on my lips of his salty yet addictive flavor. Never in a million times have I thought something like this would excite me so much.

"You can lie to yourself but you can't lie to me."

This is wrong...everything about it is wrong and shouldn't be happening. And yet, my heart yearns for it.

I want it...I need it.

Eryx provokes this unknown side of me that he himself carries too. Only difference is he acknowledges his side without shame, while I never thought it existed within me.

"Let's see more of that beautiful skin, shall we?" he whispers, moving his hand lower to the buttons of my dress and popping them open. I try to yank against my hold, trying to pry off his touch but he doesn't stop.

"This is absolutely unfair."

"A deal is a deal. But I can promise you, once this starts you won't think it's unfair."

He parts the lapels of my dress, bringing my breasts in view and letting the cool breeze send a chilling shiver through my skin.

"Fuck, so beautiful," he whispers, grabbing one breast and giving it a rough squeeze while I whimper. He even rolls my nipple between his fingers before giving it a tug that I can't help arching my back and moan. His cock twitches in response. He lands a harsh slap against my breast making me shriek in sudden surprise.

"Ah! Please."

"Already getting greedy, I see." He takes his cock and taps against my lips. "Now open that mouth so that I can fuck your throat until its raw and aching."

I open my mouth feeling his cock sliding in as he throws his head back and grunts in pleasure. "Shit…so good."

He slowly pulls out before pushing in as if letting me adjust to his size. But soon he turns rough and thrusts a bit harder, nearly hitting the back of my throat. I gag, finding it tough to breathe but Eryx guides me.

"Breath through your nose and relax your muscles." When I do, I don't feel discomfort anymore.

"Use your tongue, little girl." I do, swirling it around his head, tasting more of the pre-come. He thrusts in and out a few more times before pulling back slightly with the tip against my tongue.

"Open your mouth as wide as possible because I'll be fucking your mouth like you are my fuck toy."

When I do, he doesn't waste time pushing his cock in that he hits the back of my throat making me gag hard with tears pooling in my eyes while my whole-body shudders. He grabs my hair as leverage and fucks my mouth harder than before that it's aching.

"That's it. Take my cock like my greedy little girl. Let those tears fall."

I give my best to keep my mouth open as he fucks me like a fuck toy…just like he promised. Every inch of my soul is burning like hell fire with desire. I can feel my inside clenching, begging for release with wetness forming between my legs.

He is ruthless for sure, but deep down I loved this. His groans and my moans mingle together along with the squelching sound of my mouth. Spit started to drool down my chin falling on to my breasts while it even coats his cock. Tears stream down my cheeks as I feel my muscles aching.

"This is beyond words," he grunts. "I will be coming right down your throat and you will swallow my come when I tell you. Understood?"

My muffled moan is my only response as he increases his pace. His muscles are tightening as I can feel him getting closer to his release. Something possesses me as I bare my teeth, lightly scraping his skin and running my tongue faster. The motions click like a switch for him as he curses under his breath and turns still as he starts to come in my mouth.

"Fuck…" he barely whispers, keeping his cock deep inside with his body shuddering slightly. Few seconds later he pulls out with his length glistening with my spit.

Eryx let's go off my hand as they slump on my lap before he kneels down and grabs my jaw.

"Open your mouth and show me."

I do as told, letting him see his come resting on my tongue.

"Swallow and show me when it's done."

I gulp and open again, showing him there is no drop left.

"Good girl," he whispers, lightly brushing back my hair, kissing my cheek light as he unveils his gentle side. "You did so good. And even now you look more beautiful. Your eyes are hazy like you are still high on desire, and your spit drooling down on your body is the most alluring sight I've ever seen."

Cupping my face he kisses my lips lightly, feathering light touches with his thumb. "I promised to show you pleasures you've never imagined and I always fulfill my promises, little girl. This is just the beginning."

I wash the dishes at the cafeteria along with five other women against a long, stone table with sinks for each of us to use. Agnes is acting like the guard like always, walking back and forth behind us.

The window in front of us gives the side view of the forest with nothing but trees and dead plants everywhere. It looks dark and lifeless, but I have been getting used to it.

I set the clean plate on the right side of the sink where a stack of other plates rested. I look up and freeze when I see a figure standing nearby one of the trees.

It isn't anyone from the Magdalene but it's a person I know.

My sister.

The plate slips through my grasp, clanking with the others. My eyes stay fixated on her as I forget to breathe for several seconds. My heart is pounding so fast like I might have a heart attack.

I don't even blink feeling fearful she might disappear if I do. She is wearing a night dress almost similar to mine. Her raven hair was wet with sand bits dusting her strands. Her porcelain skin looks white as snow like she has no blood warming her skin. Her eyes even from far away look empty…lifeless.

She nearly looks like a living corpse but yet she is alive. She is here.

Without thinking, I dash out of the room and open the door that leads outside.

"Agatha! Where on earth are you going? Get back right now!" I hear Sister Agnes spewing orders but I don't care. Not even once as I rushed out to get to my sister whom I thought I'd lost.

To hold her…to say how much I love her.

She is still beside the trees but when I get closer, she starts to run too but away from me, into the deep woods.

"No! Helena! Come back!" I scream, rushing after her, watching her dress swaying with the wind.

"Please, Helena. Don't leave me," I beg through my ragged breathing. But she doesn't stop no matter how many times I call for her.

My throat is getting dry with my lungs burning.

She is getting closer to the bridge that I crossed last night but she is heading towards the gap.

"No, stop! Helena! Don't go there!" I warn her, watching her getting closer to the hole of death. Again.

No. No. No. No.

I can't lose her again. Never.

"Helena!?" I yell at the top of my lungs and she finally halts at the very edge.

I'm a few steps away from her and try to get closer.

"Please...Helena."

She gradually turns, looking over her shoulder with her hair curtaining her side. Her eyes filled with tears of blood and emptiness.

"Don't do this. I will help you," I beg her, slowly approaching her. But she shakes her head with the tears streaming down.

"You can't...you never did," her voice was broken with no sign of emotions in her tone.

"Agatha!" I hear the familiar voice of Eryx, calling me out. I look over my shoulder watching him and Father Geryon finding me. Distress paints his face with his eyes widening in shock, while Geryon offers me a death glare mixed with a hint of tension.

"What are you doing? You will fall, get back right away!" Eryx orders me.

I vigorously shake my head, begging him silently to listen to me. "No. I have to save her. I can't lose her again."

"Who?"

"Helena. I have to save her," my voice turning shrill as I'm falling on the verge of crying. "Please, I have to do this. She needs me."

"You don't have to, Agatha. Listen to me, please."

"I-I...I can't. She will fall if I don't save her."

"She is already dead, Agatha. Don't be a fool," Geryon retorts.

"No! She is alive! She is alive!" I turn to face my sister, to prove them wrong but I see her taking a step further as I feel my own soul leaving my body.

"Helena! No!" I instantly go after her to catch her.

"Agatha! Stop, no!" Eryx screams but I ignore him and go after my sister, watching her fall off. If she dies, I die too, and at this moment I will embrace my death with open arms.

I witness her fall down and I jump along with her. But the only difference she and I have is that she died again while I got saved by Eryx pulling me back. Grasping my hand as I live another day to drown in guilt.

I thrash against his hold, continuously hitting his chest as I sob in misery. "No! No! Let me go!"

"That's enough, Agatha!" Eryx snaps.

But I resume hitting him, channeling my pain on him.

"She just died again…I killed her," I cry out loud, feeling my body slacking against his hold in defeat as I kneel down.

"S-she…she…s-she is dead," I choke out my words, my body shivering from so much emotions coursing through me.

I sense him picking me up and carrying me away. I don't hear Geryon anymore, assuming he must have left earlier when he saw I was saved.

But I shouldn't have been saved. *I should have died.*

"I couldn't save her…I couldn't save her." I keep repeating the words like a mantra, resting my head against his firm chest, closing my eyes.

It hurts so much that I feel my soul shattering into tiny pieces. And there is nobody else but to blame myself. It's all because of me.

I don't know for how long Eryx carries me back, but when I feel the softness of the bed, I know we are at the Magdalene…my cage.

I'm still shivering when I feel the warmth of a blanket engulfing me. I frown and slowly open my eyes, finding Eryx coming in my view.

His expression is empty but his eyes hold the anxiousness. He caresses my hair, moving his fingers through my strands.

"Shh, it's okay. Close your eyes," he whispers gently.

I shake my head knowing he is lying. "Nothing is okay… it will never be."

"It will be. You have been through a lot, Agatha. Do not let your mind and emotions punish you furthermore before you lose your own self."

"I have been lost for years…years," I whisper.

He frowns, not understanding the meaning that I only know of.

"Close your eyes and I promise when you wake up, everything will be okay."

I don't believe his words knowing well he would fail or give up on me just like my loved ones did. But deep down, a part of me trusts him for once.

I believe you, Eryx.

I believe you.

I hear muffled voices that break my slumber. My eyes slowly open, adjusting to the dimly lit room, hearing the pitter-patter sound of the rain. It's nearly night time probably as there is a candelabra resting on my table. Except, it doesn't look like the table in my room.

Frowning I sit back and look around, finding myself in a different room which is the complete opposite.

I'm lying on a king size bed with velvet sheets, pillows and a blanket. There is a detailed, spiral carving design on the headboard. The walls are way cleaner than the ones in my room with a gray color coating them. A vast, dark brown wardrobe is positioned on the right side with a door beside it which I'm assuming led to another room. On my left there is a giant window with crimson curtains that overlooks the forest which is drenched from the rain. An ottoman is situated beside it along with a bookshelf close to the window side.

It's a much better room in the whole building…but whose room was it?

I get my answer when Eryx enters the room, shutting the door behind him as he stalks towards me.

"You are awake. How are you feeling?" He sits beside me and brings the candelabra closer, pulling my skin below my eyes like he did during the check-up.

"Slightly weak. My head still hurts a bit," I respond.

He nods, leaning back. "That's normal. You haven't been eating properly too for a couple of days. Care to explain why?"

He passes me a glass of water from the table. I take it and take a few little sips realizing how thirsty I am and gulp down the whole thing.

"I'm still waiting for you to tell me. What happened that time?" he asks. "Sister Agnes called for both of us saying you were screaming and running off. What was so important that you saw, that you were willing to risk your life?"

I shake my hand, looking down at the glass resting on my lap. "It was nothing."

"It wasn't nothing and you know it. You have to tell me Agatha, otherwise I won't be able to help you."

"Why would you want to help me in the first place?" I retort back.

"I know I shouldn't and just pretend it was caused by your physical weakness and lack of sleep. But I won't do that."

I gulp, licking my lips. "You won't understand."

"Then make me understand. I will believe you."

I let out a heartless chuckle feeling my eyes watering with overwhelming emotions returning back as I start thinking of what happened. "You won't. You will just think I'm acting like a crazy person and give me more medicine. Maybe who knows you will put me in some sort of room and lock me up in isolation for days or months." My voice starts to raise up bit by bit.

He remains silent, watching me lose my temper. The tears I have been holding back start to stream down as I speak with a broken tone. "I have stopped hoping for people to believe me. People never want to see the truth because they are scared of it."

His gaze never leaves my face.

"They just want to live in a mirrored world, where everyone is so used to the lies and deception that they don't want to see the reflection of truth. And when it appears, they break it without any hesitation."

I sense him getting closer and cupping my face. "You have to tell me who broke you, Agatha, otherwise you will fall into that false mirror and get shattered."

"I'm already broken."

He shakes his head, pressing his forehead against mine. "No, Agatha. Not yet. You are still strong and filled with hope. There is a chance but even that will fade away if you don't allow me in your darkness."

His thumb skims along my cheeks as always, like he knew his touch helps me soothe down. Every time he holds my face, my heart somersaults, wanting to be engulfed in his warmth forever.

Bending his face lower, he kisses away my tears, caressing my lips with his thumb. The rain falling harder with the thunder roaring loudly.

"You can trust me with your truth, Agatha."

Just like you trusted my truth, you can trust me with yours. I remember telling him those words and today he was reminding me of my own saying.

"I saw my sister...Helena." I wait for him to call me insane for thinking it but he doesn't utter a single word.

"I saw her through the window and she was there looking at me. Her eyes were just empty..." I shake my head, "I hate to say it but she nearly looked like a corpse. She didn't look like my happy and beautiful sister who would always welcome me with a bright smile and open her arms for her snuggling."

I let out a sad chuckle, remembering the times she would even swing me around by my arms when I was a kid. How she would even have tea parties with me and my dolls whenever I asked her. How she would even save me from mommy's scolding if I accidentally broke one of her expensive vases.

Those were the perfect times of my life before it was shattered right in front of my eyes.

"She felt so real. I didn't think for a second and went after her. But when she was near that bridge...my heart just stopped thinking she was going to jump...and she did," I barely whisper out my words before a sob breaks through my chest.

"I couldn't save her, Eryx. She died again because of me."

"Hey, look at me," Eryx urges as I meet his intense gaze which is filled with a hint of empathy. As if he knows my pain.

"You did not kill her. She was never there in the first place, Agatha-"

"I saw her, I promise you I'm not lying."

"It's not about you lying or being truthful. It's about this guilt you carry that is eating you alive and making you see things that your mind wants you to see."

"I'm not being delusional if that's what you are pointing at." The rage that I buried while revealing what happened today is starting to emerge back. "She is alive…was alive."

God, it hurts so much…it hurts so bad.

"Your sister was declared dead last year by the doctors. Her body is still in the graveyard, so it is impossible for her to be alive."

I pull away, feeling my nerves ravaging with anger as his words gut me deeper than anything. "Then how do you explain what I saw today? Are you really saying I'm a lunatic?"

He holds my hands for reassurance but I don't want any of it and I pull back.

"You are not a lunatic. Stop saying that. There is a

difference between being a crazy person and ill. What you have is signs of bereavement hallucinations. And there is absolutely nothing wrong about it. This is a normal stage people go through when they suffer the loss of their loved one's death."

"What are you talking about? My sister was still alive today! I saw her."

He runs a hand through his hair, letting out a deep breath before meeting my gaze. "I am your doctor, Agatha, so, I know what you are experiencing. I have been checking your progress and the unusual things you are experiencing. And it's all a sign of the hallucination. Your guilt is the trigger."

"Of course, I have guilt. I feel remorseful for Helena's death because I caused it."

He opens his mouth to explain more of his bullshit words but I'm not going to have any of it. So, I push my hands against his chest, even though he doesn't budge.

"Leave me alone! Get out!" I scream, continuing to push him away. "I said fucking leave!"

He finally stands up but I keep pushing and hitting him. "Leave! And don't you ever dare look at me like you understand my pain. A monster like you can never understand what it is like losing someone you love because you don't have a heart that is even capable of feeling emotions. No wonder you are alone because you know that you act like one of the rulers here, but you are also a prisoner, just like me."

I raise my hand to land another hit but he catches my wrist. When I see the cold, vengeful gaze burning in his eyes, my heart stops. Realization soon hits me, making me wish I could take back my words. But it's too late.

Eryx is infuriated and it's clear my words stroke him right to his soul. He nearly looks as dangerous as he did the first day he kidnapped me and threatened me with a knife against my neck.

It feels like he has been hiding that side for these past few weeks but now I triggered it back.

"I-I'm sorry…I-"

He raises his other hand, signing me to be quiet. "Not a single sound. One little word out of your mouth and I won't hesitate to break your hand."

Fear soon took over and I believe the promise his voice carries. "Get back to your room. I will send Agnes with your medicines. Now leave."

"Eryx, I didn't-"

His grip tightens around my wrist almost in a painful grasp making me wince. "I said, *leave.*"

I try to twist away from his hold but he lets go and I dash right out of the room, heading upstairs. I shut the door behind me and instead of crawling on the bed, my legs give out as I kneel on the floor, letting myself drown in my guilt and sins while I sob.

No matter how much I try, I end up doing the worst things

possible. Even though Eryx is my captor, he is also the only person here who treats me differently every now and then.

And what did I do?

I trigger something within him that should have been locked inside the walls he builds around himself. There is nothing but rage in his eyes that he nearly wants to hurt me, but he controls that urge…for me.

But is he really telling the truth about my hallucinations? Is my guilt making me imagine my dead sister?

I know she was real; she was right there in front of my eyes, and I saw her fall to her own death. But was it real though? Or was it my mind playing tricks on me, engulfing me in darkness that I couldn't realize what was real and what was imagination?

Oh, Helena.

I'm so lost, sister…so lost.

THE DEVIL TAINTED US

Chapter Thirteen

ERYX

I rest my feet on the small black table as I sit beside the window with my hands on either side of the chair. In one hand I have a cigarette letting me feel the soothing burn on my lungs, while an open book of Macbeth's story rests in my other hand.

The rain is pouring as usual as I read the tragic dramatic play by Shakespeare with the candelabra resting on the small table beside the chair. But the only issue is I have been staring at the same page for the past few hours with Agatha occupying my thoughts. And it infuriates me that I can't get rid of her even in my mind.

It has been a couple of days since she nearly tried to jump to her death. And after saving her she repays me by reminding me of my past that I never want to recall. She made me think of the reason I was here and how it changed me in a way I never thought to be.

I nearly had the urge to punish her but her tears from last time held me back. There is a light tap on my door bringing me back to reality.

"Come in," I call out, snapping the book shut and resting it on my lap as the door opens.

It's Agnes.

"How can I help you, Sister Agnes?" I ask, looking at her dressed in her usual attire of a nun. Even though she is far from that role.

She shuts the door behind her and timidly walks towards me, looking slightly nervous with her cheeks lightly blushing.

"I just came by to see if you are alright," she whispers, standing beside the table where my feet are.

I frown. "Why is that?"

She lightly bites her lip, looking at the floor. "You haven't come to attend the mass for the past two days and you weren't there during the round ups in the afternoons. I was worried about you-"

"It is not your responsibility to worry about me," I interrupt her saying, "-your focus should be on the patients rather than on me."

She moves closer, lightly tracing her fingers on my knees before skating them up. "I don't mind worrying about you… or thinking about you," she whispers, almost in a seductive tone. Her slender fingers continue its journey as she starts to kneel beside me, leaning both her hands towards the belt of my pants.

"I can help you with *anything* you want." She unbuckled my belt before pulling down the zipper.

Before she can make her next move to pull down my pants, I grab her wrist tightly, watching her face flinch in pain.

"I may have fucked you a few times but doesn't mean I will do it again. And last time I remember, I didn't tell you to come and suck my cock, so leave before I break your hand."

I push her away as she lightly whimpers from my force with hurt glazing in her eyes.

"Go to Geryon for all I care but never again dare to approach me to fuck you again," I warn her when there is a knock on my door.

Dismissing her I head to the door expecting Geryon to be on the other side but the person who greets me takes me aback with surprise that I try to mask.

It's Agatha.

She is in her night dress like every other night but her hair is braided, making me wish I could wrap it around my hands while I fuck her from behind against a wall. She looks a bit anxious with her hand wriggling before her gaze lowers on my unzipped pants.

She frowns with a questioning look. "I came here to talk but if it's a bad time then I can leave…"

Before I can mutter my answer, Agnes comes to the door, giving a death glare at Agatha whose eyes widen in shock.

"You shouldn't be here in the first place," she snaps, making it clear she is channeling her rage and hurt on Agatha.

But Agatha looks back and forth from me to Agnes as if she is connecting the dots to her presence in my room, coming to the conclusion that I must be fucking her. But I didn't make a move to correct her, she can assume whatever she wants. But the pain and hint of betrayal in her eyes makes it clear this whole scenario is affecting her.

"Go back to your room right away," Agnes comes to her side and grips her arm in a painful way.

But Agatha's eyes are fixated on me only while Agnes starts to get infuriated with her lack of attention on her orders. Before I know it she turns her around and slaps her right across her face, making Agatha fall on her floor with her cheek turning red instantly.

My hands clench into a tight fist but I don't lend her any help. She knows the rules and she broke them, so she had the consequences coming. And yet my heart pangs with an unknown agony seeing her suffering.

Agnes holds her by her hair, dragging her up. "You truly are a brat. Always breaking the rules. No wonder your family abandoned you," she seethes through her clenched teeth.

"You must have always embarrassed them and they were tired of you before they threw you out." She tightens her hold on her hair and slaps her again.

My control is on the verge of losing the more I see Agatha getting hurt, and especially her not doing anything to protect herself like she always does.

She isn't your responsibility.

"You certainly deserved it," she sneers, holding Agatha by her jaw tightly that I'm sure it must be digging into her bones. But that is the last straw to my control and before I know it, I grab Agatha's arm, pulling her towards me.

"That's enough!" I growl at Agnes watching her stunned look from my sudden outburst.

"But she-"

"I told her to come to me," I lie, not giving a fuck about it. "Leave. Right now."

"She isn't-"

"Not another word, Agnes. Fucking leave before I do something you will have nightmares about," I threaten her with a glare filled face. I witness the fear in her eyes as she looks from me to Agatha before shaking her head and finally leaving.

I guide Agatha inside my room before shutting the door and letting her sit on my bed. A little bit of blood, smudge the corner of her lips. I retrieve some cotton balls and a bottle of antiseptic, stalking back to her and sitting in front of her. I grasp her jaw but she hits away my hand, not meeting my gaze.

"I don't need your help," she whispers with a determinant tone.

"I would disagree with how you were getting beaten," I retort back. "Now let me get a look at your cut before it gets infected."

This time she lets me treat her cut but still doesn't look at me. I dab the wet cotton ball as lightly as possible. She hisses underneath her breath.

"What was your reason to come to me tonight?" I ask. But she responds with silence.

"You can either tell me or I can make you, and we both know I won't let you leave the room until you answer me."

She doesn't say anything for a few more seconds before she caves in. "I wanted to apologize for the other night…I shouldn't have said those-"

"You don't owe me anything. So, don't apologize," I dismiss her answer, not wanting to think about that night. I get up and put things back in its place, turning my back to her.

"You may leave."

"I didn't mean to interrupt your *time* with Sister Agnes."

"You didn't. And it's none of your business about whom I have my *time* with or not."

When I don't say anything furthermore, she gets my message and I hear her getting up. But she doesn't instantly walk towards the door, rather the book I've been reading catches her sight as she runs her fingertips along the title.

"I didn't know you are into literature."

I can't help but smirk as I stalk towards her, standing right beside her. "There are many things you don't know about me. But yes, I do read literature pieces too."

"I used to have many books too back at home. My father would get me my favorites during my birthdays." There was a small smile of nostalgia painting on her lips. As if she is remembering those pleasant memories. I rarely see her smile but when she does…it takes my breath away every time.

"Who is your favorite writer?" I ask, having the urge to know her other than the basic information I have on her as a patient. I wanted to know the real Agatha.

But why?

I have no answer to that.

"I have read mostly poetries over plays and novels. But I would say William Blake is my favorite."

"Why him?"

She shrugs. "I don't know…but whenever I read his poetries, I felt close to reality. He spoke about the truth…the harsh reality we live in through his beautiful words."

"That is true."

She nods, her eyes still on the book. "He expressed the sorrow and burdened life we all have but we deny it, living in a world where we think these dark times don't exist. He spoke about those bravely. I knew from a young age that literature pieces where they talk about love, innocence and nature…those are just imaginations. An escape."

"An escape?" I ask.

She looks at me with a sorrow filled gaze. "Exactly. When I got to see the true reality where those things don't exist, I confided in Blake's poetry where I knew my heart won't be disappointed as it painted a picture in my mind about the harsh world I was born in."

But something tells me she was greeted into the darkness with a harshness she didn't see coming. Was it her parents? Her father?

In the next second, I tuck her hair behind her ears, cupping her face as I run my thumb along her red cheek where she was hit. I should have stopped it earlier, but my ignorance and rage blinded me.

"What happened to you, Agatha? Who took away that innocence from you?" I ask, urging her to open up to me.

She shakes her head. "Sometimes it's better to keep some doors of secrets locked. It's where they deserve to be… hidden in the dark."

"But it would still be there, lurking your mind and filling your nights with terror of those secrets breaking the door and ruining your life. It's better to release them than keeping them caged."

She smiles sadly. "And yet, you keep me caged here."

Her words were like cold ice, stinging my heart. "Because

I don't have any other choice."

"Yes, you do. You just won't take it."

I remain silent and pull away but she holds my hand, begging me with her eyes to cave into the hope she has been looking within me for the past few weeks.

"Don't look at me like that, Agatha."

"Like what?"

"Like I'm your savior and that I will help you escape because we both know I can't do that."

"You can but you aren't even willing to try-"

"Because it will be a futile attempt. Not only will we break the rules but our lives won't be the same and you don't want that to happen to you."

"Why do you think that?"

I sigh, leaning my forehead against hers. "Because once you enter the Magdalene, it scars you to your soul for life. So, it's better to accept your fate than hold onto the hope that will lead to disappointment."

Her eyes glimmer with sadness as she pulls away before I do and walks by me, without a single glance over her shoulder. I look at her over my shoulder, witnessing the defeat she is feeling and I won't lie to myself when I say, it hurts more than anything else to see her like that. She leaves my room, closing the door lightly but my eyes are still strained even though she isn't there anymore.

I truly wish I could help her. I have never felt something

like this for my patients but also, I've never met a woman like Agatha. I don't want to lead her in a dark room with no sign of light, knowing well it will break her even more.

And that is what I have wanted when I first saw her, but that motive now seemed meaningless.

AGATHA

I wait.

Even though it's for a few minutes, it still feels like eternity. I knew I would be given the task today to work on the front yard. Everyone else is focused on their task, while I wait patiently for my freedom to arrive.

The ship is going to arrive today. I knew about it from last night when I saw the letter on Eryx's table beside his bed. While he was putting back the cotton and antiseptic, my eyes fell on the letter that said about the day and arrival time of the ship. Today is my only chance to escape and I couldn't fuck it up no matter what.

I look over my shoulder, finding Eryx dressed in a long black coat that I haven't seen him wear before, with matching boots, as he gets ready to go to the shore. I avoid his gaze and pretend to work as he walks out of the front gate.

When he is out of sight, I look around and find no sign of Agnes or any other person to watch on us. I drop my basket and slowly get up, my heart pacing up that I can hear it drumming in my ears. Keeping my eyes over my shoulder, I let my instincts guide me forward as I head towards the direction where Eryx went.

Nobody even bothers to look at me or go and complain to Agnes or Geryon. Letting out a deep breath, I don't think anymore and dash ahead, not looking back anymore.

I don't know how far Eryx must have gone and where I will hide in the ship, but I have to take this chance. *My only chance.*

Adrenaline rushes through my spine with full speed, with fear and anxiousness crawling through my nerves. I try to remember the directions from the night Eryx took me to the shore. I'm barefoot but ignore the little stings left by the stones and fallen branches underneath my feet.

My freedom is the only thing that matters to me.

The journey nearly feels like it lasts for hours but when I hear the sound of the waves closing in, I feel the surge of victory blooming in my heart. I'm so close…so close.

Few minutes later I'm at the shore but hide behind the trees to make sure Eryx isn't around. I look at my right side and surely the vast ship is positioned at the shore end.

Thank God.

It's a medium sized ship, painted in white and red. There is a seagull drawing but the surface looks partially scratched. Eryx isn't in sight but when I take a step forward, I see a few men carrying boxes on their backs. I immediately step back feeling this terror of being caught anytime. And then I see Eryx right behind them, ordering them to be careful with the packages.

I wait for them to be gone as he guides them towards the direction of Magdalene.

Patience, Agatha. Be patient.

When they finally leave and I watch for a few more seconds for anybody else to be around, I finally feel safe and walk towards the ship. There is a ladder and I don't waste my time climbing up. It seems to be empty. Perhaps all the members went out to help Eryx.

Every step I take ahead are steps of risk with unknown consequences. But I have no other choice. I leave everything to fate, letting it decide my freedom. I walk along the small corridor, hearing the low creaking sound of the floorboard, while silently praying I don't get caught. Just then I see an ajar door. Feeling my heart pounding, I carefully take a peek inside, finding a dark room which looks like a small resting room with a long table and chairs, along with a shelf filled with plates and cups. But when I plan to hide here, I feel a hand grasping my hand, pulling me back tightly as I let out a screeching scream. But it soon gets muffled by another hand.

"You never quit, do you?" It's a deep, gruff voice and it's familiar to me. But it's the one that I know will bring me nightmares. It's Geryon.

He holds me as tightly as possible, dragging me out of

the ship by putting me over his shoulder. I kick his abdomen and rain hit after hit on his back. But nothing fazes him when we reach the forest area but he is taking a different route.

"Let me go! Help!" I scream.

He only chuckles darkly that only highlights my fear even more. "You think Eryx will come to save you, huh? Sadly, he won't be here when you will be punished."

"No! No! Let me go! I want to leave! Please!"

"I have had enough of your acts. Today you crossed your limits and you will be severely punished. Neither Eryx nor God will save you."

I believe the promise behind his words, feeling the last bit of my hope for freedom fading away. We soon reach the Magdalene and I know it when we enter the gate…the gateway of hell. I continue screaming and thrashing, still hoping Eryx will hear me and come to save me. But by the time Geryon takes me inside I feel dread controlling my mind and heart. Instead of taking me to my room or to his chamber, he takes me to the back of the altar, where a wooden door is located.

"Where are you taking me?" I ask with anxiety and fear in my voice.

"Where you belong and should have been since the first day."

He opens the door before shutting it behind him, making the entire room pitch black.

"You thought I wouldn't notice you the day Eryx told me about the ship arriving. I saw how you were eavesdropping and felt your mind racing with plans to escape. I knew you would come to the ship, you fucking brat. But nobody has ever escaped the Magdalene unless they are allowed to, so, you are no different."

I feel the air being sucked out of my lungs as I sense something bad is about to happen. He flips on a light and continues down a stone paved stairway.

But luckily, I kick him on his groin as he drops me, letting out a grunt of pain, as I fall down the stairs. My body aching more and more until I land on the ground, clutching onto my head and arm. But before I can make my next move to escape, Geryon grips me tightly by my hair and makes me stand up. The agony is too much to bear that I feel he would tear off my hair from my scalp.

"Time for your punishment," he seethes through his clenched teeth, only making me realize my risk led to my downfall.

Chapter Fourteen

ERYX

I lean against the railing with my arms crossed over it as I look at the endless, vast sea. After putting the packages of medicines, I join the workers in their ship to travel back to Vailburg. I usually visit there for some personal stuff but this time I have different motives.

This time it isn't for me…it's for Agatha.

I hoped to see her again when I came back to deliver the packages but she was no longer at the front yard. But I didn't bother searching for her as I didn't want her to think something significant about my search for her.

Bit by bit, she was becoming someone who makes me… care. Every time I'm taking a step closer to see her truth, her walls of fear and ignorance would banish me. I was so close the other night to see what nightmares were haunting her mind before her walls stopped me.

But I'm going to find out the truth about her no matter what and I know I will get the answers in one place.

"Beautiful, isn't it?" My old friend, Julius, mutters from behind before leaning against the railing beside me.

With a tight smile I look at the sea again with a nod. "It truly is but nobody can ignore how deadly it is."

"You always have to find something negative in everything, don't you?" He snorts.

I shrug. "Nothing is perfect in this world. Not even nature."

"I thought you would be coming to Vailburg in a few days. Sudden change of plans I'm assuming." He lights a cigarette before taking a deep drag and blowing out the smoke in thin air.

Julius and I have known each other for many years. But the business connects us more, where he supplies me with the necessary medicines and drugs that's needed back at the Magdalene. His business is illegal for sure but he is the only supplier who agrees to work with us. Everybody else starts to get scared like a pussy just hearing about the Magdalene.

"Something like that."

"How long are you planning to stay?" he asks, taking another drag before offering it to me. I take it and let the smoke leave a soothing burn in my lungs and throat.

"A week."

"I bet Joana will be ecstatic," he mutters with a smirk,

shouldering me.

"Not in the mood to visit her this time."

"No problem. I will then."

"Your choice, don't even care. I'm here for work this time."

"Sounds serious already."

I nod. "It is and I need your help with finding something."

He frowns. "What do you need help with?"

"I want to know some background information on a girl. I need you to find everything possible and give it to me by tomorrow. I will pay you whatever price you want, but I need every detail on her as soon as possible."

Julius is quiet for a few seconds as if processing my sudden demanding demeanor, before he nods his response.

"I will get my brother on it and you will have everything by tomorrow."

Julius and I part ways at the Vailburg port. Resting my bag over my shoulder, I start to walk towards the town side and as always, the locals notice me and start with their gossiping.

He is back again.

What is he doing here?

Stay away from him, I heard he is a murderer.

Hush...he will hear you.

I wonder if he has murdering weapons in his bags. Don't let him stay at our motel.

I ignore them all and keep walking to a nearby motel. I'm used to their whispered gossips and judgmental looks like I don't belong there. It is true. I never belonged in Vailburg, but these people are no saints either who are living in this very wretched place.

I soon find a small, rustic looking motel with the name *Albatross* written in bold red letters on top of the roof. I head to the reception room, where an old, hefty man, probably in his sixties, is smoking with his gaze focused on the newspaper in his hand. The room looks really dusty with spider webs hanging from the ceiling. There are few landscape pictures but they are tilted, with the wallpapers scraping off. It's crystal clear the owner of this motel has no interest in running his business anymore.

I drop my bag on the ground with a thud, catching his attention. He looks once casually before returning his focus on the paper but as if he realizes who I am he quickly looks back again with his skin starting to pale before abruptly standing up. He's in a loose fitting, crumpled blue shirt with sweatpants which seems to be on the verge of falling down.

"We don't have any rooms-"

I give him a death glare that makes his words pause with fear glooming in his eyes.

"I have had a long journey. By the looks of your motel, it's clear you have barely any visitors coming. Just get me any fucking room or else I won't hesitate to break that fucking face of yours," I warn him.

He instantly goes through the drawer on his desk and retrieves a key with the number ten engraved in it, before he passes it to me. "T-the room is on the right side of the hallway. Third d-door."

I grab the keys and head out, entering my room. It's no different from the reception room, except there is a single bed with a wardrobe. A smudgy, small mirror is attached to the wall beside the wardrobe, along with a door that leads to the bathroom. I decide to relax for a few hours as I get freshened up and change into new clothes before lying on the bed and watching the fan rotating on the ceiling followed by a creaking sound.

But my mind is only consumed with Agatha's thoughts. The more I think about her the more a heart-clenching and uneasy feeling crawls to my heart. Like something bad is happening.

The only thing I know is that with every passing day, her sorrows and nightmares are pulling her away from her true self. I might be her only hope to bring the real Agatha back to her, but for that I have to know her past.

I have to.

For her

True to his words, Julius hands me a few papers that have the necessary information regarding Agatha. We are at the bar, having drinks, while the people around there are already getting uncomfortable with my presence.

Some are even leaving, giving me nervous glances from the corner of their eyes.

"How long have you known this Agatha girl?" Julius asks, passing me the papers, before taking a sip of his beer.

"It has been a few weeks, perhaps more than that."

"Is she your patient?"

I simply nod, starting to go through the papers already. It mostly talks about her family, education and recent medical information. Agatha is the youngest daughter of the late Mr. and Mrs. Adamos, who were the sole owners of Adamos Interiors company but it got discontinued after their death from a car crash. Her sister, Helena, got married to Tristen, and they took in Agatha in their house after their family passed away. Agatha finished her high school studies, learning about art and literature. Not many relationships and no criminal records too. But it says after her sister's death she started to lose her mind and attempted to murder Tristen one night. But she failed and the next day was taken by the police before she was transferred to the mental ward of Vailburg Hospital.

That was the story. But it leads me nowhere near the truth I'm searching for.

"Anything else your brother found?" I ask, feeling a tad irritated and impatient.

He shakes his head. "Nothing else. Everything he could find is on the papers. But I can tell, this is very serious for you. So, I think I know someone who can tell you more about her. I heard she used to work as one of the maids in Tristen's house, so she might know something we couldn't find."

"Where can I find her?"

"She lives in my neighboring area. I will take you there."

I simply nod and drink my scotch, but I can feel Julius still looking at me with a questioning look. "What?"

He shakes his head with a shrug. "You have several patients but I don't think I've ever seen you so invested in one."

I look away, knowing well he will read my mind. "There wasn't much about her in the files."

"Lie to me all you want but we both know that's not the case."

I scowl. "What do you mean?"

"What did her brother-in-law tell you about her?"

I can't tell him. It's a secret that I can't unveil, because then I will feel guilt consuming me. And I don't want to be in guilt because of her.

"Nothing much." I try to brush off the conversation, but

like the asshole he is, Julius continues to poke his nose into a subject that is none of his business.

"Lies, again. That would only leave the assumption that he paid you for-"

"Don't fucking go there."

He smirks, bringing the bottle to his mouth for a sip. "It's the truth, Eryx. It's one of the things you and Geryon are known for but it's kept as a secret. Only to be revealed during the dark times."

He is telling something I already know about. It's what I signed up for since day one, without knowing. But that's a part of me now and I should be ashamed of it. But that feeling never struck me before…before Agatha came in.

"If you feel she doesn't deserve to be a part of that fucked up world, then get her out of there before things slip through your hands."

"You know I can't. I have my reasons, too."

He nods. "I know that but I just feel maybe deep down you want to go against your reasons for the first time, just for this girl."

"She isn't worth it."

"That's for you to find out with time, my friend."

I remain quiet, not knowing how to respond to that because a part of me starts to have the urge to set her free. But the other part of me is holding tightly onto the rope of my reasons even though my hands are bleeding.

Maybe time will tell…or maybe not.

After our drink, Julius takes me to his house, which is on the poor side of Vailburg. It is overpopulated with homeless and jobless people, living in buildings which look like they are on the verge of collapsing. But they are willing to risk their meaningless lives to have a roof over their head. Cries and shrieking of children and women who probably work in brothels are screaming and cussing, filling the atmosphere with ear piercing noises. Young boys and men are in old, ragged clothes with their bare feet covered in mud and dirt. While women and girls are mostly dressed in frocks that must have not been cleaned or pressed for years, like their messy hair.

The whole scenario is the opposite portrait of a rich and luxurious life.

Julius guides me along a dark and congested alleyway, where we pass by a lane of brothels, with women touching our shoulders and winking at us with seductive looks, appearing somewhat decent than the others. But none of those ever appeal to me. One even holds Julius's hand, pulling him to her as they both laugh huskily.

"I missed you. Where have you been?" she asks in a sultry tone.

"Work, as always, Scarlet."

Scarlet looks a year or two older than Agatha, wearing a revealing red dress that showed off her porcelain toned legs and cleavage. She has put on a matching lipstick with her blond hair tied in a ponytail.

"Why don't you come in and I'll show how much I missed you." She kisses his lips in a teasing manner before pulling away with a smirk. Her gaze finds mine as she frowns with a look of curiosity.

"Who is your friend?"

"Just a friend."

"Does he want to join us?" she winks at me.

I can't help but roll my eyes, getting irritated with every passing second.

"Actually, I brought him to meet your aunt."

She frowns again but this time she looked a bit tense before taking a step back. "What do you want with her?"

"He wants to know something about one of his patients and your aunt used to work for her. Is she home?"

"She is but she is in bed rest. Her condition isn't improving."

Julius nods, tucking a loose strand of hair behind her ear, nearly reminding me of the same gesture I did whenever I was with Agatha to comfort her.

"We need to see her now. It's very important."

Scarlet nods before walking ahead and taking us to the side of the alleyway end, where a small, uneven, stairway leads to the second floor of the building. Retrieving a key from her bra, she opens the door and lets us inside a small, untidy room. There is a bed at the corner where her aunt is lying, breathing so heavily that we can hear it clearly from afar.

"Hey aunt, someone is here to meet you," she calls out to her and she gradually stirs awake. Scarlet stalks towards her and helps her sit back. The woman looks pale and weak, like she is one step away to the door of death.

"Who is it?" she asks in a low, stuttering tone like she is having difficulty to even talk properly.

"I don't know, see for yourself. I'm off to work," she mutters before lowering her face to kiss her forehead. "Julius, you want to join?"

He doesn't wait to think and leaves the room with Scarlet, closing the door lightly, while I take a seat beside the old woman giving an emotionless expression.

"Do I know you, son?" she asks, squinting her eyes.

I shake my head. "We have never met. But I want to know about someone you used to work for."

She lightly hisses in pain when she tries to get comfortable against the headboard. The only light coming into the room is through the small window beside the entrance. Her gray hair is tied in a loose bun with wrinkles and spots covering her face. When I make a move to help her, she shakes her head, before leaning back properly.

"I have worked for many people and some I don't remember anymore."

"Have you worked for Mr. Tristen Arthur?" I ask.

Right away, she tenses and her eyes widen with a sudden shock. "Yes, I did and that was the last place I worked before I was fired. But what do you want to know about him?"

"Not him, I want to know about his sister-in-law, Agatha. She moved into his house after her parents died. So, you must know something about her."

She remains silent as if letting me elaborate more.

"She is one of my patients and I feel her illness is connected with her past times. In order to find a cure for her, I have to know what happened to her and what changed her."

Silence fills the room with my patience slipping away. But she finally speaks, starting to reveal Agatha's truth.

"I know I shouldn't tell this to a stranger like you because it might lead me to consequences but I do not care anymore. My life no longer holds any value so it doesn't matter what happens to me."

She lets out a shaky breath before meeting my gaze.

"I worked at the Arthur residence for nearly fifteen years. I knew every piece of secret the family tried to bury in their grounds. And what happened to Agatha and her sister was one of those many secrets," she swallows, "when Agatha came to live with Helena and Tristen, she was closed off most of the time. Everyone thought it must be because of her parents' death that traumatized her. She only talked with her sister as she was her only family left. She spent most of her time in her room doing artwork or studying for her college. But I noticed how she would keep her distance from Tristen as much as possible, it felt like she didn't want to be close to his shadow. And I should have understood at that time and informed Helena about this, but I was worried about my job at that time. And I did not want to get into any sort of trouble. But one night something happened…"

I lean closer with a frown, feeling my heart pounding faster and faster, with realization hitting me about where Agatha's story must be leading. "What happened?"

Her lips start to tremble along with her eyes starting to glimmer with remorse and sadness.

"Helena went out of town to attend a small family get-together with Mrs. Arthur. I stayed with Agatha that time but when Tristen returned home with his father, he dismissed me for the rest of the night and told me to return home."

My throat starts to constrict as I'm struggling to breathe and think properly. I can feel it to my bones that whatever she is going to tell me will change my entire perspective about Agatha.

"I was halfway to my home but I remembered I forgot to bring some of the leftover food. So, I returned back and when I was close to the stairway, I heard a sudden screaming sound. It was Agatha's."

Tears start to fall down her cheek as she looks away towards the wall, as if getting lost in that very memory.

"I immediately went to her room, thinking maybe some burglars came in. But then…I-I see…" her voice starts to shake, "I see Agatha in her room…her hands tied behind her back while she was being raped by both Mr. Arthur and Tristen."

She starts to sob, putting her hand over her mouth.

My muscles are trembling at rapid speed with anger and ferocity firing my mind and soul. The vision of Agatha being helpless and abused by people who should have been her family burns in my memory, and it's a sight I will never be able to forget.

"Tristen was behind her and Mr. Arthur in front…s-she couldn't move or scream for help. I could tell she was crying…begging to be away from that nightmare. I couldn't look at that horrible sight anymore and decided to call Helena about it. But I accidentally knocked down a vase and they heard me. Before I could run downstairs, Mr. Arthur caught me."

She sniffles before continuing. "He threatened to not only fire me but also kill my family if I told anyone about it. And he even reached underneath my skirt to prove his point about what else he would do. I was beyond terrified and returned home. But I couldn't stop thinking about Agatha for one second, knowing she was suffering and there was nothing I could do…"

"Did her sister ever get to know?" I ask, trying to control

my rage but it was beyond my control.

She shakes her head. "That I do not know of. Her sister was already suffering emotionally after having a miscarriage and then on her second time being pregnant, she lost her baby again before three months of giving birth. She even went to several therapist to help her but none of them did anything for her, and she later committed suicide by shooting herself."

Fucking God.

"Mr. Arthur also had a sudden heart attack a few days later and died at the time before passing his inheritance to Tristen."

The fucking bastard had an easy way out by dying from a heart attack, He deserved to be tortured to death.

"I was fired a few weeks later after Helena passed away. And since then, I lost every connection with that family."

Letting out a deep breath, I stand up, running a hand through my hair as I try to process the truth, but the only thing I have the urge for is to hunt down Tristen and bury him alive into the deepest grounds.

But even that won't be enough for what he did to Agatha. He deserves way worse than that mere punishment. She was introduced to the actual living hell from a young age. She lost her innocence…her hope…her everything to such monsters who don't deserve to breathe in this world. He didn't even deserve to be anywhere near Agatha, but that monster didn't hesitate to corrupt and crush her soul.

"I still feel remorseful about that night and uncountable ones," she whispers, still crying.

"Uncountable nights?"

"They both kept raping her whenever Helena was out of town."

I close my eyes, feeling the inferno of vengeance burning my heart. I swallow feeling my throat turning dry. She is nineteen now but according to the information I got, Helena got married to Tristen when Agatha was fourteen. God knows if he has been advancing on her since the first day, but it's clear she has been suffering for years with nobody to look upon to save her.

She was all alone.

She is still alone.

"I will never be able to forgive myself," she murmurs.

I look at her over my shoulder with a cold smile. "You shouldn't forgive yourself. And no matter what you do, I'm sure your soul will rot in your grave when you die."

She starts to sob louder, casting down her eyes in shame that was hit by my words.

"You could have saved her...you could have done a good deed that would have helped you repent for your sin but you failed. So, there is no point in feeling guilty because when you die it won't be God greeting you, it would be the devil."

"Please...don't say that," she whispers through her cries.

"You and I both know it's the truth. And you deserve it.

You are no less sinner than those two monsters who ruined Agatha and her youth which was supposed to be filled with love and innocence."

Her body shakes from her crying with tears coursing down continuously. I don't try to console her and leave the room, heading out of the area without telling Julius about it. I need to clear my mind, but the more steps I take the more I get blinded by rage.

I reach the shipping dock, standing at the very edge of the deck, watching ahead where Agatha is miles away. I have to return to her as soon as possible before she is drowned in guilt of her sister's death and the horrors she suffered.

Images of her being raped again and again fill my vision that I nearly want to throw up, which I've never done. I have had patients before who had been preys of rape, but Agatha was trapped in the net of both betrayal and pain that she never expected to happen.

I breathe heavily, closing my eyes to calm down my nerves, but the minute I do a vivid picture of Tristen being on top of Agatha flashes in front of me. She is writhing and crying in pain and helplessness, looking at me with desperation and begging me to help her. Tears streaming down her cheeks as she screams for me to save her from this darkness. Her clothes are torn off while Tristen grins like a sadistic monster before lowering his head to take advantage of her.

I open my eyes instantly to be away from that vision only

to be greeted by the enormous sea...the same route which Agatha took with me to another hellish place.

She went away from one agony, just to be handed off to another where she is searching for her freedom, day and night. And I don't blame her for it, because it is something she deserves and should have got from the start until Tristen came into her life.

But I'm no different than Tristen and his father.

I'm ruining her even more than she already is. And at an unknown price that I'm not sure if it existed or not.

But I also have no other choice because of my cruel fate binding me to my motive. Only if I could go back in time and change the past then I would, but a part of me has no remorse for the sins I committed.

I have had several patients and I cured many, feeling it like a duty I have to fulfill. But with Agatha, it feels different...everything is different now. I'm her last hope and if I fail her, then there is no turning back for her. She will be lost forever...just like her sister.

It is now my purpose to guide her out of this cave of remorse so that she can be in the light of hope and happiness... where she belongs.

But I have to think through everything carefully because I can't risk any chances for her.

I have to leave soon but before that there is something I need to finish. And it's more for me than for Agatha. I have never hesitated to commit sins, so what was one more?

"I'll save you, Agatha. I promise on my life," I vow to her and to myself.

CHAPTER FIFTEEN

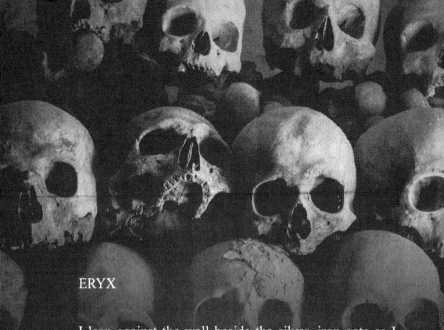

ERYX

I lean against the wall beside the silver, iron gate as I watch the black, expensive looking car taking a turn and getting inside the mansion.

The Arthur's Residence.

The guards close the door, as I take out a cigarette and light it up, watching the man I want to torture till his last breath get out wearing a gray suit. A woman follows him out as they exchange a smile before heading inside. I puff out the smoke while my eyes are strained on the enormous mansion he lives in, whereas Agatha lives in an opposite world…all because of him.

One of the guards, from the other side of the gate sees me and instantly recognizes me. He stiffens but he somehow gathers up his leftover courage to speak with me in a stuttering tone.

"Umm...sir, I'm sorry but you can't be here."

I step closer, narrowing my eyes. "I don't see how it's any of your fucking business to tell me where I can or can't be."

He gulps, looking away.

"Tell your master that Eryx is here to see him."

"He isn't-"

"Tell him now, before I'm tempted to break your back and smash your head right against the gate where you fucking work like a worthless slave."

He right away staggers back and picks up the DynaTAC phone which is attached to the wall beside the gate, making a quick call to Tristen. "Sir, a man named Eryx is here to see you." There is a pause. "Yes, sir. I will let him in."

He hangs up and doesn't waste time to open the gate, letting me pass in with a maid coming from inside to guide me towards an office room. I sit in one of the armchairs with my hands resting on the handles with my feet perched up on the opposite knee. The office is a vast room with every piece of furniture looking expensive and perfectly polished, including the table, chairs and bookshelf. There is a gigantic painting of Vailburg farmland area hanging on the opposite wall facing his table.

Few moments later I hear the thudding steps of Tristen's feet as he enters the office wearing a gray T-shirt and pants. A questioning look passes his face as he sits in front of me.

"Dr. Eryx, did not expect your visit." He copies my posture. "How may I help you?"

I remain quiet, looking for that guilt…that remorse in his eyes. But he is sitting with a prideful expression, hiding his sins like he never committed one. Though, with the silence he starts to get uncomfortable. There is a small table with drinks set on it, and he pours two glasses with bourbon, passing me one. But I remain unmoving.

"Is there something you need, Dr. Eryx? Is it about Agatha?" he asks, sounding concerning but I know it's a façade. Even hearing her name coming from his mouth makes me feel like cutting out his tongue and feeding it to him. Maybe it is one of the things I will do.

"Is she-"

"How do you do it?"

He frowns. "I beg your pardon?"

I tilt my head sideways with a shrug. "How does your tainted soul not feel an ounce of guilt for what you did?"

I can see the hint of fear coming out, but he immediately hides it. "I don't understand what you mean."

I snicker with a dark smirk. "We both know what you did, Tristen and we also know what you are doing now."

His face starts to turn serious with a sudden rage as he gets up and starts to leave. "If you have no work with me then I suggest you to leave, don't waste-"

"How did you look at your mother and wife after daring

to put your hands on Agatha and ripping off her innocence?" I ask, making him halt at the doorway, watching his body tensing.

"Did the devil taint you so much that you didn't think for once that what if the same happened with your mother? What if she was fucked and touched by men every night while you were sleeping peacefully in your room?"

He turns, glaring at me like he might kill me. But he can't.

"What if you saw her every day and didn't know how men took advantage of her in your own house and you couldn't do shit about it?"

"One more word about my mother and I will-"

I get up, stalking towards him like the devil himself who is going to punish him for his sins. "You will what? Fight me? Kill me?"

Standing in front of him, I grab his jaw tightly, enjoying his face flinching in pain while he tries to pull away from my hold.

"Coward men like you only use words to fight, but never know how to do it physically." I pull out my knife, witnessing his eyes widening in horror.

"W-what are you doing?" he asks.

I shake my head with a humorless chuckle. "Just seeing a knife is scaring you already? Fucking wimp. Like father, like son."

Shock paints his features when he realizes I know every bit of his truth. "H-how...what do you want?"

I push against the door, shutting it close, slamming his head against it. Leaning the knife close to his face, I use the sharp tip to trace the side of his face slowly while he remains still like a statue, being fearful one wrong motion will hurt him.

"I want you to tell me why you did that to Agatha?" I ask.

He gulps, watching the knife moving close to his eyes. "It was a mistake. I'm sorry-"

"Not the answer to my question. Why did you do it?"

"You want me to apologize to her-"

I move back and look at him with a death glare. "Sit on the chair."

He is hesitant at first but he complies and sits back on the armchair with his eyes fixated on the knife. I go towards the window side and cut off the white curtains, using it to bind his hands on the handle tightly, leaving no room for escape.

"If you want more money, I will pay you. I will even pay Geryon." He keeps blabbering his nonsense when I finish tying him and dragging the other chair in front of him before I take a seat. Perspiration starts to form on his forehead and neck from terror and anxiety.

"I'm going to ask one last time. If you don't answer correctly," I lean closer to his right hand and place the knife right above his thumb as I hold it, "the next second I will cut your fingers."

His face turns gray like he is going to be sick.

"Why did you rape Agatha?" I ask.

He swallows, breathing heavily as he begs me with his eyes to free him. "I...I don't know why I did it. I wasn't thinking."

His voice trembles with fear.

"It was the thrill...or maybe the fact that I couldn't have her...I don't know the exact answer."

Thrill?

He raped a fourteen-year-old innocent girl for thrill.

Before he can blink, I cut off his thumb, instantly covering his mouth, muffling his screams with my hand which is now covered with his blood. His eyes start to water as his body writhes in agony.

He breathes heavily with his lips trembling, whining like a pussy when I move back my hand. I pick up his bloody thumb from the floor while he follows my gesture as his body writhed from the pain.

"And how did you manage to look into your wife's eye after having your *thrill*?" I ask.

His face bends down with his eyes shut close as he shakes his head slowly. "I...I..."

I place his thumb on the table before I take his index finger.

"I'm not going to ask you again, so answer before I cut the rest of your fingers too."

"I don't know! I swear! I have no answers to your questions!" he whines.

I cut off his index finger too but when he opens his mouth to scream, I stuff it with his blood covered fingers. His eyes widen in horror and disgust but I know he will spit it out and I intensify his punishment more by grabbing his thumb and putting that inside his mouth too before putting my hand over his lips.

"Hmph hmph," he groans against my hand, his body trembling spontaneously.

"This is how disgusted she felt when you dared to touch her with your hands. This is how horrified she was when you raped her."

I move back, relishing in the sight of him coughing out his fingers and throwing up with his vomit drooling down his chin, ruining his shirt.

"Please let me go. I promise I won't tell anyone," he mutters in a raspy tone before he coughs.

I let out a dark chuckle, watching his eyes shut in disgust and terror as he continues to puke.

"She begged you to stop, didn't she? And did you stop?" I ask even though I know the answer.

Spit drools down from his mouth as he keeps his eyes cast down like he is finally ashamed of what he did. But I know it's all an act to escape this torture.

Standing up, I move closer to him and push his back by his hair, leaning the knife closer to his lips, enjoying the way every inch of his body is trembling like he is going to have a seizure.

"These were the same lips that dared to taste her skin and poison her so much that she never wanted to look at herself the same way again because all she could feel was shame and disgust." I slide the blade along his lips, making an X mark while he roars in agony with tears streaming down from his eyes. Blood oozing out of his cut with his face turning red and veins popping at his forehead.

A knock on the door catches our attention.

"Darling, is everything okay? I heard something…" the woman who came with him asks from the other side with a worried tone.

Tristen's horror fills eyes meet mine.

"Tell her, Tristen. Let her know if you are okay or not. But remember who has got your life being held on it's last end."

"I-" he winces when opening his mouth to speak but tries again, "I'm okay…I-I'm busy." His eyes clenched shut tightly. "Y-you leave."

"What? But you said we-"

"I said go!" he warns, suppressing his pain. "I'm busy so fucking leave now!"

There is silence from the other side before there is a soft crying sound coming followed by footsteps fading away, signaling she left.

"Let's resume, shall we?"

"Please I beg you...P-please..."

"I've just begun, so, it's a long journey of torture for you. And you deserve it for daring to touch her."

"I will apologize to her...I will... I swear."

I slice through his cut again, deepening and intensifying the pain as he screams at the top of his lungs.

"Your meaningless apology won't bring back her innocence back, it won't return her beautiful times which you tainted without a second thought. Every sin has its punishment. You would have received it by God when you rot in hell. But that is a long wait for the sin you committed. So, I'm taking that responsibility."

"What do you want me to do?" he pleads with a shaky voice. "I will do anything to repent...I will apologize to her...I will pay more money."

I narrow my eyes. "I really wonder how a fucking moron like you runs a family business so successful. If you still think, I'm here for money then you are dead wrong."

"Then why are you doing this? D-did that bitch let you fuck her and now is controlling you with her pussy-"

I grab his throat in a vise grip, nearly cutting off his ability to breath. "Call her a bitch again and I will cut your tongue out."

I press his windpipe tightly watching his eyes nearly bulge out. "You deserve to be punished for what you did. And you will take it without any questions asked like the little, whiny and worthless *bitch* you are."

Letting him go he takes a deep breath while coughing.

"I only have today left before I leave Vailburg, but I will make sure the second I step out, every time you move, you will think of me. Every time you look at yourself in the mirror you will shiver in terror remembering this moment. And if you even dare to think of Agatha or hurting her, I will bury you alive, letting you guide you to death while you are helpless."

"Y-your superior won't let this pass when I tell him." He tries to threaten me and I laugh darkly in response.

"If you have the balls to do it, go ahead. But just a reminder, if you do it, I will be at your doorstep the very next day and let you see actual hell."

I step back and pull down his pants while he gives me a mixture of an alarming and fearful look. "W-what are you doing? No stop!"

Despite his protest, I drop his pants on the floor as he sits there, naked underneath with a flaccid dick.

"You didn't stop when she begged. So, what makes you think I will stop?"

He has to suffer and today he will.

It will be a day that will haunt him day and night, and I will make sure of it.

Chapter Sixteen

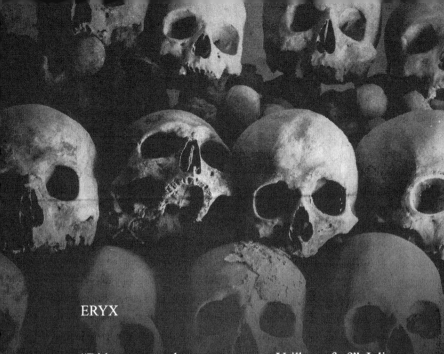

ERYX

"Did you get what you came to Vailburg for?" Julius asks, sitting beside me at the deck area. I was returning back to the Magdalene, to the place where a man like me belongs. Only a few minutes left until I reach my destination.

I nod my answer, looking at the wooden flooring.

"It seems like it wasn't a success."

I shrug. "I don't care."

He snickers under his breath. "If you didn't care then you wouldn't have gone so far for a girl you barely know to hurt her brother-in-law so severely."

I have no regrets about that. He deserved to be punished.

I left scars and cuts almost everywhere on his body as a reminder to never be near Agatha or me. I bet he is still in deep agony after I cut off his balls. He will survive but he will be living a painful and miserable life, regretting his actions every second of his passing days.

After I left his residence, I went to the hospital where Agatha was previously admitted. I soon found the doctor who was handling her case and didn't hesitate to punish him the same way. Only difference was that Tristen is still alive and the doctor's dead body must be somewhere in the dumpster.

I returned back to the motel and stayed a few more hours to calm down my nerves. I knew the word about what I did to Tristen would spread soon and I'm sure either the guard or one of the maids gossiped about it after I left. Probably half of Vailburg knows by now but I don't give a shit.

I stopped caring about what that town thought of me years ago.

"I will send you a message through the radio about the new packages if needed." I stand up and head to the room to get my bag with Julius following behind me.

"You know you can't ignore this. I have never seen you behave so possessive and act like a maniac for a girl."

"I didn't do it for her…I," I hesitate to answer.

"You did do it for her otherwise what motive would you have for torturing one of the richest businessmen in Vailburg."

"Why do you want to know so badly about it? Since when have you turned into a pussy who gossips?" I retort back with anger rushing through my nerves.

"It's not about gossip. It's about the consequences, Eryx."

I clench my jaw as I pick up the bag and put it over my shoulder before leaving the room, wishing for the ship to reach the shore as soon as possible. I have no interest in talking about this topic.

But Julius doesn't let it go as he turns me around by my shoulder, enraging me furthermore.

"You know well, Geryon will soon know what you did and he won't forgive you for it after he puts the pieces together. You can't hide this from him forever."

"Neither me nor you are going to tell him. And I'm pretty sure Tristen wouldn't dare to open his mouth, especially after I cut it."

He shakes his head, running a hand through his hair, looking frustrated and worried about me. "But when he finds out, you know what he will do."

I know that well. Geryon wouldn't think twice before twisting that knife of guilt and control he holds over me. But I'm aware in that scenario, Agatha will be gutted like me.

"Is all of this risk worth taking for a girl who will leave you when the time comes?" he asks a question that has been at the deepest graves of my thoughts but I never let it come alive, knowing well I will be dreaded by the answer.

"You might have feelings for her-"

"I *don't* have anything for her-"

"Lie to yourself and others all you want, Eryx, but you

can't lie to me," he cuts off my words, "-I saw it through your actions these few days…I saw how desperate you were to know the answers."

I gulp, feeling my heart racing as I remember the moments when I was searching for every possible way to know about Agatha. I came here to help her heal but after the things I discovered, healing her didn't seem to be my only motive anymore.

"You are trying your best to ignore your feelings for her and I don't blame you for it because you have other priorities. She will be there for a limited time and will leave you. She has seen your true side; she witnessed the devil and I can tell she won't be ready to embrace that part of you."

I remain quiet, feeling the ship starting to slow down as we get closer to the shore.

"You are my only friend I care about. Don't walk into a deep forest where the beauty may lure you but darkness will summon you into destruction."

"She doesn't mean anything to me. She is my patient and maybe knowing the man who hurt her will help her get cured faster and leave as soon as possible," I spit out my words with irritation crawling in my heart.

The ship finally stops at the shore and Julius helps by drawing the ladder down. I step down and nod at him over my shoulder as a farewell before I start heading towards the Magdalene.

A strange gutted feeling grows within me with every step I take. Even now my mind races with thoughts about Agatha. Various scenarios of how she will react after she knows what I have done to Tristen, flashes in front of my eyes.

I can't stop thinking about what Julius said as well. I did all of these for Agatha, to help her be free from her nightmares, but why do I care?

Why does it matter to me if a man had the audacity to touch her?

Why?

I reach the gateway of the Magdalene where some of the women are already working, cleaning the porch side as usual with Agnes watching over them. I don't spare her a glance as I walk ahead, not in the mood to deal with anyone at the moment. As I enter, I find Geryon coming from behind the altar area, dressed in his priest attire as always, with the sleeves rolled up. Few of the women are sitting at the benches, chanting prayers softly. The mere atmosphere feels cold and dark.

"Welcome back, Eryx," he greets me, stalking towards me.

I simply nod as my eyes look around for the girl I went to Vailburg for.

"How was your trip?" he asks.

"Good. Everything was alright here?"

"Yes. And the medicines have been stocked until next

month."

I open my mouth to let him know more about the packages when I hear a faint screaming sound, making me frown with a sudden worry consuming me.

I look around. "What was that?' I ask.

He looks over his shoulder with a shrug as the screaming continues. "Just letting one of our patients know what happens here when rules are broken."

I don't know whom he is referring to but a part of me has a hunch about it that I feel my blood running cold like ice.

"Who?"

"Agatha." He shakes his head looking unaffected by his actions. "She tried to escape on the ship-"

"Where is she?" I interrupt him, dropping my bag.

"The cellar but-"

I don't listen to another word before I dash to the cellar which is behind the altar. I burst open the door, taking the nearest hanging candelabra with me as I take two steps at a time downstairs. My nerves are twitching and firing at a vigorous speed.

My body prepares me to fight the most dangerous battle with anyone who would try to come between me and Agatha. I follow the cries and whimpers.

What I see makes me halt instantly.

Agatha sitting on the ground with her white dress covered with dirt and the shoulder part torn. Her hair is a mess curtaining her face. Both her hands are hanging from the wall behind her with heavy cuffs around her wrist. There are a few cuts on her legs which are soon going to be eaten off by the giant, dark rat approaching her.

Without thinking twice, I kick away the rat hearing it squeal before running away to another corner. I kneel beside Agatha, placing the candelabra beside us as I tuck back her hair.

"Eryx," she whispers, letting her choked voice tug at my heart.

Her face is covered with bruises like she was punched and slapped several times. The dark circles also proves she didn't have a wink of sleep. Her lips are chapped as she gulps like she is in desperate need of water.

Rage is the only emotion I'm able to convey at the moment. I quickly look around, finding the keys hanging at the opposite wall. I retrieve it and instantly unlock the cuffs, witnessing the dark, red bruises on her wrists.

The moment she is free, she moves into my arms, hugging me tightly like she doesn't want to be parted away. I move my arms underneath her and pick her up, heading out of the cellar.

"I got you. It's okay," I whisper to her.

Geryon is already waiting where I left him with a fuming look. But I don't pay him an ounce of attention as I head to my chamber.

Her body trembles as she starts to sob against my shoulder, her hands tightly tangling around my neck, digging into my skin.

I shut the door behind me, placing her on my bed. But when I try to move back, she tightens her grasp. Trying to control my racing heart, I shift and let her rest on my lap with my back against the headboard. She lets her emotions be poured without any hesitation while I caress her hair.

"Y-you came back..." she rasps.

"I did." That makes her cry harder that even my body is starting to shake with hers.

"I was so scared...I-I...I thought you would never come back."

"Hush. It's okay now. I'm here," I mutter against her temple, lightly caressing her back.

"I tried to escape," she starts, keeping her face pressed against my neck like she can't look me in the eye to confess. But I remain quiet, listening to her truth.

"I knew about the ship and tried to hide in it, so that I would leave along with it back to Vailburg," she swallows, "but Geryon caught me and said I would face the consequences for my actions. H-he put me inside that cellar and cuffed me all this time. Visiting me every now and then to hit me or slap me, punishing me again and again..." her words fade away but I can clearly understand whatever he did to her, traumatized her furthermore.

"It's okay. Nothing will happen to you. I've got you," I whisper as she continues to shed tears. We stay like that for a long time, before her body starts to soften under my touch. I look down and notice she has fallen asleep from exhaustion of the past few days.

If I knew she was going through this nightmare, I would have never left her. I have seen other patients suffering like this by Geryon whenever they attempted to escape and, in those times, I have remained silent. I didn't protest once whenever I heard their cries echoing through the Magdalene all day and night long.

But not this time. Not for Agatha.

I slowly pull away from her and get the first aid box from my drawer, to tend to her cuts at first. She winces and hisses lightly in her sleep but doesn't wake up. I put bandages over her wounds and cover her body with a soft blanket before I stalk out of my room to face Geryon.

He is at the prayer hall, sitting at the front bench with his right elbow resting on the seat with his feet resting on the opposite knee. The room is empty, making me assume he must have ordered everyone to leave.

His eyes are poisoned with anger and frustration before he gets up when I stand in front of him.

"She didn't deserve that," I mutter with an irate filled tone.

He smirks in a humorless manner. "Just because you are

fucking her doesn't mean the rules don't apply to her."

Without thinking I land a punch across his cheek, making him stumble down the bench.

But he recovers quickly and hits me in the same manner making my jaws ache instantly. He aims to strike again but I dodge it with my arm before holding his hand and twisting it. Using my other hand, I punch right on his nose with all my strength.

"Fuck!" he grunts and I take the opportunity to hit his forehead with mine watching him fall on the ground.

But he makes a quick choice and kicks my leg, losing my balance and gets on top of me, raining hits after hits across my face until I feel the metallic taste of the blood on my tongue.

He is stronger than me in every aspect possible but I'm more determinant than he ever will be.

My nose is starting to bleed and I can feel the bruise on my lips too. He raises his arm for a hit but I hold his fist when it's close to touching my face. Pulling him down by his collar I strike him with my head twice in a row. He falls on his side and I take the opportunity fist his hair and smash his face against the wooden bench continuously until I see blood dripping on the floor.

But I don't stop when he grunts in agony.

I don't stop when he lets out a loud cry, letting me know he is reaching his limit.

My thoughts are blurred with images of how vulnerable and helpless I found Agatha at the cellar…how she sobbed in utter horror and weakness that she found shelter of protection in the arms of her captor.

I keep hitting his head against the bench again and again like a mad man, relishing in the sight of his wounds and pain.

"She." *Thud.*

"Didn't." *Thud.*

"Deserve." *Thud.*

"It." *Thud.*

I crane his head back, demanding him to meet my gaze and know the promise my words hold. "Touch her again or try to even think of hurting her and I will kill you."

Thud.

I let him go watching his body slump on the floor like a dead body, even though he isn't dead yet. I spit out the blood from my mouth onto the floor, suppressing my urges to hurt him until he took his last breath here. I start to walk to my chamber when I hear Geryon chuckling in a sinister way like the pain doesn't affect him at all.

He is still lying on the floor giving me a blood covered smile.

"Since when did you start to have feelings, Eryx?" he grunts out his words.

"I have known you for so many years and some things about you may be a mystery to me, but I do know you don't have a heart to feel anything...not even love."

I remain quiet, listening to him state things I already know.

"If you think she will change her mind and fall in love with you then you are delusional, *brother*."

He calls me by the title that I wish I never had, especially by him.

"Once she knows the truth and sees the devil within you, she won't hesitate to run away and leave you forever. You and I both know men like us don't deserve to be near the shadow of love and care."

We never earned it in the first place.

He tries to get up but fails so he leans up on his elbows, facing his body sideways to me with blood dripping down his chin.

"We both are bound to be together, even after our deaths. You and I built this place after the darkness we were raised in and swore to accept this life. So, don't let a fucking girl change you when there is no hope for it."

"She isn't changing me-"

"I don't believe anything anymore from you about her. She is controlling you with her pussy but that's what she will be. A pussy you will fuck and forget when the time comes for her to leave."

I clench my jaw with my hands fisting tightly, itching to hurt him again.

"And even if she does stay, when she knows what you did to her, she won't see you the same way ever again. She will loathe you till her last breath. Stop fantasizing about a life which will never belong to you."

I point my index finger at him with a threatening look. "Stay the fuck away from her. Touch her and you die."

I continue to walk while his words echo through the wall with a dark chuckle. "You are brave, Eryx, but not so brave to kill your brother."

AGATHA

My eyes flutter slowly and the first thing that greets me is pain. I wince as I try to move, hearing the distant sound of running water. I look around, finding myself in Eryx's chamber, lying on his soft, vast bed.

Tiredness still consumes me from not sleeping for four straight nights. I sit up slowly, finding bandages wrapped around my cuts that Geryon left.

I can feel my swollen face from the bruises but I still have this fear within me of Geryon coming back and resuming his torture.

Just then Eryx comes out of the bathroom, wearing gray pants and black T-shirt, showing off his muscular arms which are inked with tattoos that I have the urge to trace. There is a monotonous look on his face, but his eyes tell a different story that he is trying to hide. There are a few light bruises on his face like he has been hit but I refrain from asking him at the moment.

He heads towards me before sitting in front of me and starts to inspect my bruises.

"How are you feeling now?" he asks, lightly touching the marks around my cheeks and eyes.

"Painful. Tired."

He nods. "You need bed rest for a few days or perhaps weeks. Your wounds will start to heal soon and I will give you some extra dose to help you sleep better."

I simply nod as he moves to my arms, retrieving the bandages from the side table and wrapping it around the cuts more.

"This should help keep your wounds dry while taking a bath," he stands up, offering me his hand, "time for a bath."

I accept his hand and walk with him inside the bathroom, where a bathtub is already filled with foamy water that smells like lavender with a bar of soap and loofah resting on a small stool beside it.

I face him, feeling this deep ache in my heart…something that I felt when he was gone.

"Do you need help?" he asks, not meeting my eyes.

Do the bruises affect him?

I nod my response and he finally meets my gaze, holding the hem of my dress and lifting it up. I stand there naked with my underwear on while his eyes never leave my face. Even when he kneels down to take it off, he doesn't look anywhere but at me. He takes both my hands and guides me into the bathtub as I feel the warm water soothing my skin with the sweet fragrance wafting around my nose.

"Ah," I sigh with comfort, closing my eyes as I relish on the feeling. The water slushes up reaching up to my breasts as I stretch my legs forward with my back against the tub.

Eryx leans behind my head, gathering my hair and tying into a bun. He takes my hand carefully and dips the loofah into the water before running it along my arm, avoiding the bandages before skating it up my shoulders and neckline.

Every muscle within my body started to relax from his motions. This is the very first time I'm seeing him acting so...caring and gentle. He doesn't seem to be my captor who was cold and distant in our first meeting.

But I can still feel a hesitance in his demeanor as if he is trying to hide something. He works on my other arm before taking my leg and washing them from my feet to my knees.

"Sit up," he mutters before moving behind me and cleans my back with slow, circular motions.

"Do my bruises bother you?" I ask, feeling him suddenly stop before he looks at me.

"You are looking at me in a different way..."

"What way?" he asks.

"There is hesitance and ignorance in your look."

He shakes his head before resuming to wash my back. "It's not you. Don't bother about it."

"But I want to know. Why won't you look at me like you did before…before this?"

He remains quiet and grabs the nearest hand shower, guiding me to stand up and washes off the soap from my skin, making sure the bandages are dry.

After I'm cleaned off, he grabs a towel and helps me out of the bathtub and pats me dry gently.

"You didn't answer my question," I mutter when he moves to my neck.

"I don't owe you any explanation. So, stop asking questions that you won't get answers to. It's useless," he dismisses the subject and wraps the towel around me, taking me back to the bedroom.

He pulls out a dark brown T-shirt and sweatpants, passing it to me. "I don't have extra clothes and I couldn't find your clothes in the suitcase. So, you can use mine. I will get something for you to eat."

He heads to the door when I call out his name, halting his steps.

"Eryx…" He looks over his shoulder at me with a frown.

"Are you going to leave again?"

He pauses, as if understanding the meaning behind my question. He knows my fear of being tortured by Geryon again is still lurking in the back of my head.

"He won't come anywhere near you."

"Do you promise?" I whisper.

"You can trust me with my truth like I trust yours."

My heart races faster from his words only but before I can talk further about it, he leaves the room, closing the door behind him.

My truth.

What does he know about my truth? How...?

I look at the clothes he left me and pick them up as I drop the towel, changing into the clothes. I can smell his musky and woodsy fragrance in his clothes, feeling his presence close to me even though he isn't in the room.

A closure I was imagining about the whole time I was at that cellar. I didn't know when it was day or night time. But whenever Geryon came in to hurt me and verbally abuse me I knew it was time to go through a nightmare. I have been hurt before but those times at the cellar would be unforgettable. I tried to find every way possible to escape from there but with my hands being cuffed so high and the whole time, with no food or water functioning my body...I could barely think it through. Geryon tried to break me physically and mentally but Eryx came again for my rescue. And deep down I was wishing he would come soon to get me out of this nightmare.

Biting my lip, I look around his room, not knowing what to do at the moment. I sit on the bed, touching the soft blankets. My gaze shifts to the window side where it's raining with a crow landing at the other side being all wet. Its head moves continuously in all directions as it shakes its whole body to get rid of the excess water before lightly tapping on the glass.

Another crow joins in and follows the other's motion. But both are tapping their beaks against the glass which sounds more vigorous. I'm so invested in those two crows that when I look out the other window, I don't notice there are four more crows doing the same. I frown in confusion.

The tapping starts to get louder and louder with more crows coming at the window. When there is no more room then, the others hit their beaks against it while flying.

My heart starts to pump against my chest at full speed with a sudden fear and anxiety tightening around my throat. My eyes turn wide in horror when the entire window is covered with crows, the tapping cawing sound got louder and louder that I feel it piercing through my ear drums.

The room turns dark with the crows blocking the light from outside. I limp run to the door but before I can even get to the handle, I hear the loud shattering sound of the window with all the crows bursting inside the room and attacking me with their beaks and claws.

"Ah! No!" I scream, trying to save myself from the strikes but I can't see anywhere because of their wings.

"No! Ah! Stop it!" I yell at the top of my lungs.

I feel the claws digging into my skin and on my bandaged

wounds too with blood oozing out. It is agony all over again as I writhe and try to defend myself. My eyes start to blur with tears. But panic set my nerves on fire, making it hard for me to breathe and think.

With agony spiraling through my body, my legs give away as I kneel and fall on my side and cover my ears with my hands, praying to be saved. But none of it helps.

Terror is shadowing upon me just like the crows and I scream in pain and fright, shutting my eyes closed, feeling tears streaming down my cheeks along with my body shaking like I'm hyperventilating.

"Agatha," I hear someone calling me but it feels like a faint voice as if it's muffled.

"Agatha, what happened? Agatha, are you okay?" It's still muffled but it's a feminine voice. My body trembles more with the faint voice starting to become clear.

"Agatha, wake up." Concern and tension painting her voice.

The cawing starts to lower down but I still keep my palms pressed tightly against my ears.

"Agatha, please open your eyes. Please. Oh God," she rasps, as I feel soft hands tugging my hands away.

"Please Agatha."

I gather up every ounce of courage I have and slowly open my eyes, expecting the crows to attack me again, but it's the absolute opposite. There are no crows or broken shards of glass anywhere.

I start to sit up slowly and look down for blood and cuts but there are none except for the ones that Eryx bandaged.

"Agatha." I follow the voice and see Beth sitting beside me with utter shock and concern. "What just happened?"

I look around frantically, unable to understand what just happened. "I…I don't know what…"

"Come on." She helps me stand up and takes me to the bed before carrying a plate of food and placing it beside me. She sits down and puts her hand on mine.

"Father Eryx sent me to give you some food and then I heard you screaming from outside. You were shaking and screaming to stop being on the floor."

I pull my knees close to my face as I shake my head in confusion and stress. "I really don't know what happened. I was changing my clothes and then thought to rest. Then I see this crow," I point at the window, "it was tapping on the window and before I knew it there were hundreds of crows bursting inside the room."

She frowns. "But the window is shut and nothing seems to be broken. Are you sure you weren't dreaming?"

"None of it felt like a dream. The crows were clawing my skin and hurting…I felt the pain and it was too real. I'm not lying, I promise. I have been seeing these things and I don't know myself if those are dreams or reality.," I shake my head feeling more tears emerging, "I can't stop thinking about seeing my sister…and blood everywhere."

My voice starts to get choked up.

"I don't know what is happening anymore-"

"Hey, it's okay." Beth moves closer before engulfing me in a hug, letting my rest my chin on her with my arms around her for comfort that I'm desperately wishing for.

"Shh. It's going to be okay. Take a deep breath. Come on with me."

She and I inhale and exhale deeply, as I close my eyes to let my nerves relax a bit. I feel her hand lightly brushing my hair as we both continue breathing.

"All will be okay. You have been through a lot because of Geryon. It must be your mind still recovering…give yourself some time. Everything will be alright soon," she whispers, tightening her hold on me which I don't mind for once.

Several moments pass by as we remain in the same position but I eventually pull back, letting Beth cup my face and tucking back my hair.

"I'm here…I'm here for you."

I feel overwhelmed with many emotions that I feel everything being out of control. I feel trapped with every passing day that I sense myself being back in those dark times of my life that Tristen tainted.

Every time I try to escape this darkness, it crawls back to my life, hiding in the shadows only to emerge to ruin me. It feels like an inescapable fate that I'm stuck with for the rest of my life.

I look at Beth who is looking at me with a softening gaze, lightly caressing my cheeks. I notice her eyes staring at my lips with an expression I haven't seen before.

Care. Concern. Fondness.

She wipes away my tears before slowly leaning forward. I'm still in the haze of what happened moments ago, unable to think of what to do next. But before I can contemplate, I feel Beth's lips touching mine in a soft kiss. Both of us close our eyes, getting lost in the moment.

My lips remain still but her's continue their motion with tenderness and gentleness like she truly cares about me. She lightly nibbles my bottom lip before sucking it and using her tongue to trace my lips. I hear her moan under her breath, feeling her hands lower down to my chest.

But before things can go further ahead, I instantly move back, finally feeling the surprise dawning at me. My brows furrow together in puzzlement as I touch my lips while looking at Beth who kissed me like I matter to her.

"What…why did you do that?" I whisper.

She bites her lip, looking down at her lap. "I know I shouldn't have done it. It's wrong and I should be mortified because this is the illness I was blamed for."

I shake my head, holding her hand. "It is not an illness, Beth."

She lifts her head, meeting my eyes. "It just felt right in

the moment for me."

"Having feelings for someone can never be an illness, especially when those emotions are true and pure coming from the depths of your soul. Whether it's a girl or a boy, it doesn't matter. But…"

"But you didn't feel this right," she mutters.

"I don't know why you kissed me. But I do know I'm not worth having feelings for. I'm not the one for you Beth. There is a person out there, who will cherish and love you for who you are. You may think you have lost yourself. But deep down your true self is still alive, you just have to let it emerge back before it's too late."

She swallows. "It's just since the day I saw you…you have been different from others. I instantly felt something and gave it all to avoid it…to suppress it because I knew it's wrong. And it triggered my anxiety, making me remember how I was brought here. But after seeing what you were experiencing a few minutes ago, I sensed that you would understand what I have been through."

"One way or another we have all been through darkness and pain. We are just the unfortunate souls who are bearing with it even though we did nothing to deserve it."

I lean forward, cupping her face, offering her a small smile. "But I want you to know, this doesn't change my perspective about you. It never did in the first place."

She gives a sad smile with her eyes shimmering with

tears. "I'm sorry that I let fear control me so much that I let you drown in suffering more than before. But now I promise you, I will help you."

"What do you mean?"

"I will help you escape. I don't know how we will do that but I will be there for you."

I feel warmth and hope soothing my heart as I can't help myself but hug her tightly. "Thank you…thank you so much."

"We both will escape from here."

"Thank you."

We will escape. We will be free.

But deep down I can't also stop thinking about Eryx who is turning out to be something more than just my captor… someone who is becoming my savior.

THE DEVIL TAINTED US

Chapter Seventeen

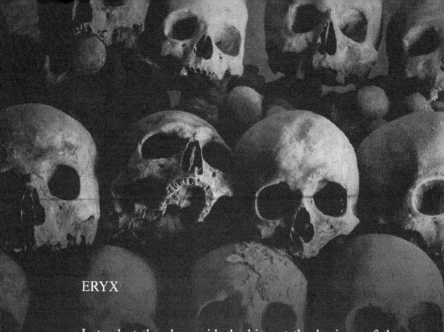

ERYX

I stand at the shore side looking at the horizon of the sea, letting myself feel the calmness before I have to face the storm back at the Magdalene again. It's turning dark and raining as usual but the weather doesn't bother me anymore as I'm used to it.

But every time I try to keep my mind blank, it's filled with the look of sheer terror and fright Agatha was in. I was in guilt before but now I'm drowning in shame too.

I keep blaming Tristen for making her life miserable but how am I any different.

I am no less than Tristen…perhaps more devious than him for what Agatha is going through.

While washing her at the bathtub, every time my eyes casted on her scars and bruises, I felt the hurricane of rage and remorse. It took everything within me to not go back and kill Geryon for what he did to her.

But I am to blame as well for not being there for her.

Although, the more I saw her scars, the more the urge to let her be free was consuming me. I swore I wouldn't let her leave until she was cured, but she is better off being on her own and being miles away from this world of darkness.

She doesn't deserve all this.

But a part of me doesn't want her to leave…a part of me wants to protect her till my last breath even though she will loathe me…hate me to the depths of her heart when she knows the truth.

Sighing, I inhale the earthy fragrance of the sea and sand, before I walk back and turn out to return to my dark world. It has been a couple of days since I rescued her from the cellar. She healed quite quickly with all the care and medication I could provide her with.

She has been settled into my room since that day, sleeping in my bed while I slept on the chair. It's uncomfortable but nothing I'm not used to. But even now whenever I look at her, I can't help but feel the pang of guilt poisoning my emotions. She is in that state because of going against the rules, but I still feel…broken, for not being there for her.

I enter the hallway and pass by Geryon, whose face is still fucked up from our fight. But I don't give him an ounce of my attention and head to my room.

Opening the door, I find Agatha sitting on the chair

beside the window, looking outside at the forest.

Seeing her in my own clothes while being lost in her own little world, makes me wish I could stop time and capture this moment forever. She looks so beautiful and angelic even from this distance. Her skin is glowing under the natural light streaming in, bringing an urge to go to her and kiss that soft skin, marking her as mine.

Her hand rests against her lips with her index finger and thumb lightly caressing her bottom lip. Fuck. What would I give to kiss those lips like they are meant to be kissed and tasted by me?

I feel the spark of desire igniting within me, but I control myself, not wishing to be a selfish bastard when she is in such a state.

I walk inside catching her attention with my footsteps.

"Where did you go?" she asks, sitting up as she looks at me. But I avoid her gaze knowing well I will be reminded of the moment I saw her at the cellar.

"Just for a walk."

I grab a towel, deciding to have a shower. I remove my wet clothes, unbothered by my nakedness in front of Agatha. But hearing her gasp makes the scenario a tad amusing to me. I can feel her heated gaze from back, imagining her looking at my body and tattoos that cover my back.

I head inside the bathroom and stand underneath the showerhead, tilting my face up. I stay there for a while to feel relaxed but none of it is helping when Agatha is in my head all the time. I soon finish and head out with the towel wrapped around my waist with a few of the water droplets glistening on my chest and abdomen.

I notice Agatha peeking at me from the corner of her eyes, pretending to ignore me but unable to help herself from looking.

"You can look all you want. I don't mind it at all," I mutter with a grin before pulling out a T-shirt and pants.

She shakes her head, looking at her lap. "I wasn't looking-"

Her words halt when I drop down my towel to put on my clothes. Her eyes right away landed on my cock followed by a gulp with her breathing turning shallow.

It amuses me to see her so affected by me just from my sight, because I know that exact feeling from experiencing it whenever I see her. She has a charismatic spell casted on me just from her beauty and innocence.

She notices my gaze upon her and instantly blushes from what she did and looks away towards the window.

Snickering under my breath I put on my clothes when she asks a question out of the blue.

"Why does it rain here so much? I don't think I have seen the sun for once here."

I go to the drawer to get new bandages to replace with her old ones. Taking a seat on the table, I drag it closer to her and place her feet gently on my thigh before I start to unwarp the bandage and answer her question.

"It's a myth some people believe in about Merry Heights." Her wounds and bruises are all healed and few even faded away, but I still attend to them just in case.

"What myth?"

I get the ointment and put it on her wound carefully. "People believe this place has been cursed by God because it has always been filled with greed, lies, sins and darkness. Day and night our ancestors would come here to be part of this dark world and never looked upon God. They worshiped the devil, considering him as their God. They even started to force the innocent ones to come here and be tainted by him."

She hisses under her breath but recovers quickly.

I move to her other wounds on her hands, leaning closer to her. "What happened then?" she asks.

"The scenario saddened God and then He sent a warrior and angel to help those innocent ones and punish the sinners. But their sins shadowed upon this place like an imprint which seemed impossible to remove. And they say, since then the curse has been raining on Merry Heights and hasn't stopped for once."

"It is always so cold and dark here…everything here feels cursed."

"That it is."

"But why have the Magdalene here?" she queries with

her brows furrowed along with curiosity glimmering in her eyes.

"Because this is the same palace where every sin was committed."

"It's still continuing…"

I meet her gaze seeing her unafraid of the myth this place carried. "Sin is like an addiction that is hard to get rid of. Once you get into its cave, there is no turning back."

"If you have the will then even in the darkest caves of sin, a ray of hope is enough to turn a sinner into a saint."

My motion pauses as I feel something unknown from her words, looking at her gazing upon me like she is speaking to a part of me that I have forgotten, and is trying to revive it back.

"Don't look at me like that," I whisper, finishing replacing the last bandage.

"Like what?"

"You know well. Stop searching for something that doesn't exist within me. I'm not going to be the hero of your story, so don't attempt to make me one."

"Who said it always has to be the hero to save the day? The villains always break the rules but that doesn't mean he can't carry the intention of saving someone. It has become an old tale where the hero is the good person and the villain is defeated at the end. Maybe it's time to change that story."

The atmosphere between us suddenly feels heated and

raw. The urge I was controlling to claim her as mine is starting to bloom again but this time it feels too strong to suppress. Her natural, flowery and vanilla fragrance sends fire through my nerves as she starts to get closer to me that our faces were only inches apart.

All I wanted to do was rip off her clothes and make her body writhe until she can't think straight with my come dripping out of her cunt.

"Now you stop looking at me like that," she whispers with her warm breath caressing my lips.

"Like what?" I lick my lips.

"You know well. You want to control that rough and devious side of you that you introduced me to. I thought I would be scared of it but after seeing it, I'm craving more for it. And seeing you control it is feeling like a torture."

"I don't want to hurt you, little girl."

"I'm not made of glass. I'm strong enough to deal with a man like you. So, do your best."

And right there I let it go. I let the last thread of control be torn as I grip her hair, hearing her gasp in surprise and anticipation.

AGATHA

"Trust me, little girl, this is nowhere near the torture I would plan for you. And you know why? Because I can see it in your eyes how much you are enjoying this. You are trying to hide your dark side but deep down you want this darkness like the little slut you are."

My breath hitches as words vanish from my mouth while he reveals the secret I differ to ignore. Any other girl might have felt disturbed by his words but for me...his words are like a dark magic that is sinful and yet irresistible. But deep down a part of me is truly yearning for it.

"What do you want, little girl?" he rasps, tightening his grip on my hair before his other hand comes around my neck.

"Do you want to suck my cock like you did in the forest that night?"

I nod with a whimper, feeling my heart racing that I can hear it drumming in my ears.

"I will happily give you this pleasure only if you speak in words. Say, you want to be choked like a slut and be filled with my come while my hand is around your neck. *Say it.*"

Oh God.

A deep groan vibrates against his chest, sending shivers down my spine.

Some may see me as a freak for wanting such a dark desire...it is insane for sure. But dear God, I am starting to want it more and more. Never did I think this is what I will want with a man who captured me and brought me to this living hell.

But after so many fucked up events in my life, what is

one more?

"Say it, little girl," he rasps against my cheek.

"I...I," I whisper.

"You say it and you get it, little girl. You are bold enough to utter those words and the bravery within you that turns me the fuck on every time. Say it."

"I want to be choked like a slut and be filled with your come while your hand is around my neck. Take me, Eryx."

He groans as our lips crash into a rough kiss that sets my whole body on fire in mere seconds. I hear clanking sound of the ointment bottle as it falls on the ground but neither of us gave a fuck about it. He puts arms underneath me and picks me up, never breaking the kiss.

His tongue peeks out, mingling with mine in an erotic dance while I moan loudly. He places me on his bed at the very edge before moving back to take off my clothes like he is on the verge of tearing them if possible.

I sit there naked while his eyes access me from top to bottom, making me crave for his touch even more.

He reaches out to caress my cheek with his knuckles before leaning his thumb close to my lips and putting it in. Without thinking, I start sucking like I would suck his cock, watching his eyes darken with burning desire.

His other hand goes down and parts my legs, skating towards my pussy which is already wet from his kissing.

"Fuck," he rasps. "I could fill you up with my cock and

stretch that cunt. You are soaking wet."

He traces my wet pussy lips before lightly circling my aching clit, making my hips buck forward to have more of his touch. But he tortures me by pulling away with a devious grin and goes back to gripping my hair, tilting my head back.

"Look at you, already wet and aching for my cock like a slut. Open your mouth wider," he orders.

I do and he pushes his thumb deeper, letting me swirl my tongue around it. He pulls it out and holds me by my jaw before spitting into my mouth.

Holy fuck.

"Drool it down to your pussy. Make it more wet," he groans.

I do as told, letting the spit skate down to my pussy before he uses his fingers to coat it further with circular motions.

He bites his lips and takes off his T-shirt and pulls down his pants, letting his rock-hard cock be free. He gives it a few strokes, making me gulp and beating my heart faster as I feel my breathing turning ragged.

"Turn to my direction, head on the edge of the bed. Now," he demands and I take the position. My world tilts upside down as he comes closer, tracing his pre-come filled cock's tip against my lips.

"Open your mouth as wide as you can."

I part my lips wide and he pushes his cock inside, hitting the back of my throat. I gag instantly but try to breathe through my nose when he starts to move with harsh and deep motions, grunting at the back of his throat. I feel more wetness forming between my thighs, aching to be touched more than anything.

"Fuck," he rasps. I feel his hand caressing my neck before he wraps his fingers around my throat, highlighting the thrill and pleasure even more.

His other hand reaches for my breast giving it a tight squeeze. I moan in response, feeling my entire body quivering with pleasure overload. Eryx doesn't hold back as he fucks my mouth and it is something I'm truly relishing in.

"So, fucking good. I will come deep down your throat that you won't be able to spill a drop."

His free hand moves ahead going to my wet pussy like he knows I need the release more than anything.

"You are dripping wet. Fuck. You're already soaking the bed sheet with your juices."

He touches my clit, making my eyes close as I feel my nerves trembling with need. He puts two fingers inside me and then finger fucks me while continuing to thrust into my mouth.

Fuck. Fuck. Fuck.

This is the best feeling I've ever experienced; I feel this euphoric sensation that drives me insane. I am lost in his touch and never wanted to come back to reality.

"You're already going to come, huh? You have been

aching that badly," he teases, increasing his speed and movement. "You will come the second I spill in your mouth, little girl. Understood?"

My whimper is my only response as I start to feel his cock swelling slightly and my insides tightening and twitching, bringing us both on the peak of release. My spit coats his cock, some of it drooling down and landing on the floor.

But neither of us stopped for once, getting lost in this dark, intense and forbidden connection. He grunts and hisses under his breath with his body starting to tense up along with mine.

Few more strokes by his cock and fingers and before I can realize it, I'm coming hard with every inch of my body shaking and shivering. I whimper and moan loudly against his cock as I feel him releasing his come inside my mouth, tightening his grip on my neck furthermore.

It's intense. It's euphoric. It's insane.

It is everything.

I swallow every drop, feeling my pussy still twitching from the orgasm. He pulls out and I can see a bit of the last few drops his come remaining on his cock. He scoops it on his fingers and smears it on my pussy.

"Fuck yourself," he orders.

I frown in confusion. "But…I just came."

He grins with a mystic chuckle. "You didn't think I was going to make you come once this time, did you? You will come again and this time with my come on your cunt."

"I don't think I can." My body is already sagging from exhaustion.

He kneels before cupping my jaw.

"You can and you fucking will," he groans. "Otherwise, I will tie you up and fuck you with my tongue, fingers and cock until you pass out from coming again and again."

Dear God, save me.

His other hand grips my hair, craning my neck before he lightly slaps my cheek just to hold my jaw again. "Fuck yourself, right now."

The electricity returns back instantly in my body, rippling me with desire all over again, until I feel my heart slam.

I slip my hand down, feeling my pussy clench and all the hair on my body lifting up with adrenaline pumping through my nerves. I feel his thick, creamy come mixing with my juices as I start to touch myself.

"That's it. Good girls following orders get rewarded and you shall have yours, little girl."

The promise behind his words knocks the air from my lungs. I keep looking at his darkening gaze as he leans and lands an open mouth kiss, letting his tongue explore my mouth.

"But I bet you wouldn't have any objection with me tying you up, would you?"

I moan against his lips, imagining the intense scenario in

my head vividly.

He smirks. "Just what I thought. I'm happy to oblige but it won't be anything slow and gentle. You will be at my mercy, for my pleasure. Would you please me?"

"Yes," I whisper, circling my clit faster.

He gives my hair a tight pull as a warning. "I said to fuck yourself. Stop taking baby steps and get on with it. Fuck your cunt with my come until you are squirting on my fucking bed."

I whimper and put two fingers inside my pussy, pushing it in and out like he did a few minutes ago.

"Put another in."

I enter a third finger, feeling my walls aching and clenching from his words.

"That's my good little girl," he rasps before slamming his lips against mine. I groan, returning the same roughness with my lips.

He pulls back as I suck in a deep breath before his lips moves to my cheek, licking his way down to my neck and bites me. But he even tries to sooth down the ache by sucking on the spot while my fingers never stop their movements.

"Only if you could see yourself from my vision. You look absolutely alluring. Makes me want to take you up on the tying idea."

"W-what would you do?" I ask with a hoarse voice.

His grin tells me my question surely amuses him. "I love

seeing your bold side. But to answer your question, I would do *anything* I want."

My mind turns hazy with images of him doing every dirty and forbidden act upon me, driving me insane with pure pleasure.

"I would eat your pussy like it's the last meal of my life and won't stop even when you can't handle it anymore. Then I would stuff your cunt with my cock and stretch you so that I can fuck you raw for hours. You would like that wouldn't you, little girl?"

"God, yes!" My eyes shut tight as I felt myself reaching close again which I thought was impossible.

"Your cunt would be seeping with my come, even when you walk out of this room, it will be dripping on the floor, letting everyone know you belong to me and that I've claimed you as mine."

My eyes flutter open with a warmth settling in my racing heart from his words. "Am I yours?"

He licks the seam of my lips before whispering. "You are only *mine*."

Something about the possessiveness and roughness in his tone makes my walls clench.

"Yes, my little girl. Come for me." He nibbles my neck, making me shriek and sending my body skyrocketing with another wave of release.

"Oh God. Fuck!" I cry out loud, not caring if anyone

hears from outside. I swear I see white from that orgasm that for a moment I lose my mind. My body trembles as he continues to kiss my shoulder and moves up to my face, kissing every inch of it.

"That's it. That's my good girl," he praises with a hushed tone, caressing my cheeks with the back of his knuckles.

But what I do next even takes him aback with surprise when I bring my fingers coated with my juices and his come and suck it clean, humming while looking at him. He grins darkly and kisses my forehead. "My dirty little girl is turning greedy."

"Maybe."

"Just how I like it. Dirty. Greedy. Slutty."

He moves back and rests against the bed, sitting on the floor beside me. He closes his eyes and leans his head back, trying to relax from our moment.

But my eyes never leave his face, looking over his rough features. He is surely older than me. And not the man I was expecting to meet in this way and start getting addicted to.

I look at his five o' clock shadow that covers up-to his neck, making him look more intimidating. His arms are inked with thorns that go behind his muscular back where I see a broken clock with more thorns and roses wrapping around it. As his breathing turns even, I see the way his muscles contract, making me yearn to touch them…trace them.

His cock is now limp but still looks quite big, as I thought about the soreness I might experience for days maybe if he fucks me.

"I went to see Tristen."

Like a switch being flipped on, my nerves tense up just from hearing Tristen's name as I frowned in utter confusion.

"And I got to know everything he did to you," he whispers.

I swallow the lump in my throat. "What do you mean?"

He turns his head, meeting my gaze. "I know what he and his father did to you, Agatha. And he paid for his sins. I now know your truth."

He knows. He knows everything.

"I didn't ask you to do anything for me."

He shakes his head. "You didn't but I could see it in your eyes how much you wanted to break away from the nightmare he put you through. How much you wanted to spend even a second that won't be scared by his sins. So, I did what was right."

"Is…is he dead?" I ask.

"Not yet. I didn't want to take away that decision from you. He harmed you, not me. But if you want me to kill him, I will do it in the blink of an eye."

"Why did you do it?"

He is silent for a fleeting moment like my question catches him off guard and he doesn't know how to answer properly.

"Because I didn't want you to be afraid anymore."

I sit up, unashamed of my nakedness as he looks at me over his shoulder, but soon joins me on the bed sitting in front of me.

"I'm not afraid of him. I was before but not anymore."

He frowns. "He is the reason your innocence was ripped away from you. He was supposed to be your family, whom you trust with everything but he broke that bridge."

I shrug, feeling my throat tightening with emotions. I blink rapidly as my eyes burn with tears threatening to be shed.

"I did blame him for what I have been through but I blame myself the most for something I can never take back."

"Blame yourself for what?"

I shake my head, looking at my lap as the first tear dropped onto my skin. "I can't…I-I…You won't see me the same way the next time you look at me."

He leans closer, cupping my face and urging me to meet his eyes that are filled with a soft gaze I haven't seen before. Harshness and coldness are the only emotions I have witnessed within him, but this is a rare sight that he is offering me as a touch of comfort, telling me without words that nothing will change.

"You can tell me, Agatha. Nothing will change my thoughts about you," he mutters.

"You say that now but your words won't remain true."

"We all carry our own secrets, Agatha. Our lives are rooted with guilt and sins. Nobody is ever perfect because everyone has tainted souls. But yours was forced to be part of this sinful world. Confess your truth to me, Agatha…relieve your heart of the burden you have been carrying so long that is eating you alive every day."

He presses his forehead against mine. "Confess to me, Agatha."

Something within me just shifts, making me feel that ray of trust that was crushed years ago returning back bit by bit. And telling Eryx about my guilt…my truth is the first step I have to take on my own.

Though deep down I'm sure he will see me the way my family did before abandoning me. After the things Tristen did to me, I became detached from my own family that they couldn't recognize their daughter anymore. Sometimes Tristen even poisoned their minds with lies about myself, saying he has seen me being intimate with strangers. And my parents…they believed him. Despite my protests and honesty behind my words, they accepted his truth.

So, I know Eryx is not going to be any different from them. And yet, I want him to know this part of my life and believe it.

"What is killing you, Agatha? Tell me," he whispers. "I want to help you and it can only be possible when you let your heart guide towards the path of trust."

I feel the warmth of his palms as we both inhale and exhale deeply. Our eyes are closed as I finally gather my courage and reveal it to him.

"My sister died because of me. *I* killed her."

THE DEVIL TAINTED US

Chapter Eighteen

AGATHA

I'm losing my sister. Helena is lost despite having the people she loves around her.

She is sitting on her bed as usual, looking out at the balcony which overlooks the other houses and forest side of Vailburg. Her eyes are vacant just like her soul.

She is suffering day and night after the tragedies she has been facing, and there is nothing I can do to help my own sister.

If I could carry her pain and distress then I would accept them with open arms just to have my sister back.

Carrying the tray of some of her favorite food, I walk inside her bedroom. Placing the tray on the side table, I sit with her, placing my hand on hers and give it a gentle squeeze.

Her face looks pale with dark circles underneath her

bloodshot eyes.

"Helena, you haven't eaten anything since yesterday. Please, you have to eat something...you are fading away," *I mutter, begging her silently to look at me.*

"Why am I being punished?" *she asks with a choked voice, making my heart pang with hurt and sorrow for her sufferings.* "What did I even do to deserve such cruelty?"

I shake my head, cupping her face, urging her to meet my gaze. But when she does, my eyes water up from seeing how empty her eyes are.

No emotions. No hope. Nothingness.

"You didn't do anything wrong to deserve this, Helena. It is just fate being cruel to you. You just need to give yourself time to heal-"

"I did had time to get over my first tragedy," *she interrupts me, reminding about her first miscarriage.*

"This time we took every precaution and made sure nothing went wrong. And yet here I am...losing my second unborn child," *she murmurs with her tears streaming down her cheeks, dropping onto our hands.*

"Maybe I don't deserve to be a mother..."

"No, Helena. Never think that. You deserve every ounce of happiness in this world. You care and love every person who matters to you deeply. And I can say without a shadow of doubt that you will love your child unconditionally."

She suddenly starts to sob, getting wrecked with her

emotions and sadness. She digs her hands into her hair as if having the urge to rip them off with her body starting to shiver.

"Leave me alone!" she orders.

"Helena, please, listen to me-"

"I said leave! Leave! Fucking leave!" *she yells on top of her lungs, throwing the try across the room, hitting it on the wall.*

She screams while sobbing, looking completely destroyed by heart wrenching pain. "Leave!"

But I don't. I have left her alone several times but not today. She needs me despite saying she wants to be alone, but I know how much she is craving to have a shelter of support in these dark times.

When she notices I haven't moved it enrages her more and she grabs my shoulders, making me get up before pushing me towards the door.

"I said leave! I don't want anyone!"

"No!" *I yell back, pushing away her hands.* "I'm not going to leave you. I will never leave you."

She breathes heavily with her lips trembling along with her eyes wide open in shock.

"Push me away how much you want but I will stay with you till your last breath. You are my only family I have left and I won't lose you too. I won't lose my sister."

We both just stare at each other, feeling overwhelmed

with distress and misery. Both our minds are in a haze of loss with neither of us finding our way back to sanity.

She starts to cry and kneels down, and I don't hesitate to join her, wrapping my arms around her. We both sob, pouring out our emotions as we stay in each other's arms. Her head against my shoulder with her body shaking from crying. "I cannot endure this anymore, Agatha. I can't…"

I run my hand along her hair, rocking back and forth lightly.

"I know. I know."

"Please make this stop, all of this is unbearable…please stop this," *she begs.*

My heart shatters into uncountable pieces from seeing my sister so broken like this that I didn't know how to put herself back together.

They say time heals everything, but they never said time can even bring your downfall.

"Everything will be okay…Shh. I'm here for you, Helena. I will always be here for you."

"Fuck," *he grunts behind me, pressing my face harder against the wall as he continues to thrust inside me.*

I remain motionless like a statue with tears of shame trailing down my cheeks.

"Feels so fucking good," he rasps, leaning closer with his breath against my temple, making me feel more disgusted. I keep praying for this moment to be over as soon as possible but it feels like an eternity.

My eyes are strained on the window of the kitchen where it views the dark backyard, with the stars glimmering in the sky. It's the only way I can pretend I wasn't experiencing a living nightmare.

He thrusts a few more times before coming inside me with a groan, pressing his chest against my back, finally finishing. He moves back but tilts my head back to place a hard kiss on my lips, knowing well I hate it more than anything else. And yet he does it every time.

Turning me around he caresses my hair while I feel his come dripping out of me and sliding between my thighs.

"Why the sad face?" he asks with a smug smile that I wish I could just cut it out of him.

"If it's because of Helena, then don't bother. It's her usual act now and she will get over it soon."

He steps back, drinking a glass of water and buttons up his suit back. Going to the sink he washes his hand and smooths his hair back before going to the countertop where his briefcase is.

"Tell Helena I'm leaving and will be back in two days."

I remain quiet, avoiding his gaze. But he doesn't care and grips my jaw. "I said something, Agatha, so I expect an answer."

I simply nod my response and he smiles before kissing me again while my lips remain unmoving.

"When I come back, be ready in your room at night. Understood?"

I nod again.

He finally releases his grip and walks past me towards the main door and leaves. When the roaring of his engine fades away, I finally feel myself breathing in relief. I immediately rush to my bedroom and rip away my clothes, getting inside the shower. Turning the shower head at full speed with hot water raining upon me, I take the bar of soap and rub it all over my body.

But it doesn't feel enough.

I get the loofah and start scrubbing my skin, going to every inch, every part Tristen touched. My skin soon turns red from the vigorous rubbing but it does not help to cleanse my soul that is dirtied by my own brother-in-law.

I finally let the tears stream down as I continue scrubbing while the images of Tristen touching me...raping me, flashes in front of me. One of many wretched memories that I wish to erase from my mind forever.

I don't know how long I keep cleaning my body under the hot water but when I see a bit of blood draining along with the soap, I finally stop. Running a hand through my wet hair I try to relax my mind and nerves, finishing my shower after a while. I get out with a towel wrapped around me and change into fresh clothes to sleep for the night. When I finish drying my hair, I decide to tell Helena goodnight and return to my room.

It is just me and Helena at the residence. The night guards are at the main gate as usual and even the maids are dismissed for the night.

The door to her room is already open as I step in. But she isn't on her bed, making me frown.

"Helena?" I call out her name. I check the bathroom but she isn't there either. So, I head to the balcony where I do find her.

But something seems wrong.

The atmosphere feels so ominous and cold that I suddenly feel my heart pacing faster and faster. Helena is standing against the concrete railing with her back facing me. She is wearing her usual peach nightgown with her dark hair being free as it touches up to her hips.

She doesn't turn when she hears my approaching footsteps. A sudden worry and fear settles in my chest while my throat feels clogged.

"Helena...what's wrong?" I ask her with a whispered tone.

She remains quiet that the only sound is the crackling of thunder coming from a far distance, signaling the arrival of a storm.

"You lied to me," she mutters. Her voice holds no emotion that sends chills down my spine.

"What are you talking about?" I ask, standing beside her.

She turns to face me with her eyes bloodshot but there are no more tears like she has none left to shed.

"How dare you? How could you even think of doing this to me…to your sister?"

I shake my head, unable to understand clearly but I have an assumption at the back of my head.

"You know well and it makes me wish I never had a sister in the first place."

And that's when realization hits me like a wrecking ball.

"I saw what you and Tristen were doing downstairs before he left…I saw it all and heard it all."

She knows. She knows about me and Tristen.

I lose the ability to breathe for a second, wishing the ground would swallow me and lead me to death.

"Helena…I wanted to tell you but I couldn't. I-I didn't think you would believe me…" I stutter, reaching for her hand. But she pulls away, taking a few steps back.

"When have I not believed you? How could you even think that about me? Since you were a child, I was always there to protect you and you thought I wouldn't be able to protect you from Tristen?"

The disbelief in her voice made the guilt weigh heavier

within me.

I shake my head as my eyes blurred with tears.

"I do trust you and I know you would do anything to save me but-"

"But you didn't trust me enough and let yourself be a victim of Tristen's cruelty."

"No, no, no. Please, try to understand, Helena. It all started when he first came to see you at our house-"

"Since the first day...he has made you his prey for years and you didn't tell me. You rather decided to endure it than speak up to me about it."

She looks at the vacant and dark backyard with the thunder crackling harder and getting closer.

"I failed you, too," she whispers.

"No, you didn't, Helena. It is me who failed you and I'm so sorry for not being brave enough to reveal his truth. I just saw how deeply in love you were with him and I didn't want to come between your happiness. I swear I did everything for you because your happiness matters to me more than my own."

"Am I happy now?" she asks.

I remain silent.

"I was never happy in the first place. He stopped loving me just a few months later after our marriage while my heart still belonged to him. I did everything possible to be the perfect wife, but I didn't try enough."

My body stills as I finally see she was actually never happy. She has been suffering too but never spoke about it just like me. And she still isn't content...she is in misery.

"I promise, Helena. I swear I will fix everything for you."

She shakes her head and meets my gaze while I silently beg for her to see through me and have the courage to take a leap of faith this time.

But what happens next, gives me the answer I was hoping to never see.

She holds a gun and clicks open the safety button off. Looking down at the gun I can tell what is running in her mind which makes pure terror gripping me...controlling my body and mind.

"Helena...whatever you are thinking about, don't do it. Please," *I whisper, begging her to listen to me.*

But she shakes her head and with a trembling hand brings the gun closer to her head before pressing it against her temple.

"I failed you."

I start to cry and shake my head. "No. Please, please, please, Helena. Please listen to me. I'm sorry I didn't tell you before...I'm sorry for being a coward but please don't do this to yourself. You could never fail me...I trust you. I love you," *my throat starts to tighten with tension with fret spiking my nerves as I start to struggle with breathing.*

Her eyes are blank as she sheds a lone tear, looking lost

and vulnerable.

"I failed as a wife. I failed as a mother. And I failed as a sister. I couldn't protect any of those relationships."

"You can still survive this, Helena. I'm begging you, please listen to me."

"I cannot. I don't want to survive anymore." *She rests her index finger on the trigger while I feel the last bit of my heart being ripped off.*

"I want to be free. I'm sorry," *she whispers and closes her eyes. But I take the chance and rush towards her to grab her gun.*

"No! No! No!" *Her eyes snap open with a wild look painting in her eyes like she isn't going to give up on her motive to end her life.*

But I'm not going to give up on her.

Never.

"Helena, stop this madness!"

Her grip tightens on the gun as we both struggle. I give it all to pry her hands off it, but she twists away from my grasp. But I put force and lower the gun, trying to click the safety on.

BANG!

Both of our bodies jolt with our eyes wide open. My heart stops and my blood runs cold like ice.

I'm fearful to look down and witness the outcome that will never be reversed. But I know I have to face this harsh reality.

My eyes lower down where I see my hands on the gun with my finger on the trigger. Helena's night gown is now drenched with blood from being shot on her stomach.

I stand still, unable to breath or think.

She looks down too and sees the sight I'm witnessing which will be burned in my memory forever. Her body sways as she staggers back and after a few steps her legs give away before she falls on the floor with a thud.

My entire body trembles but I still can't move an inch as shock shrouds me, cutting off my sanity. I do nothing but stand there, with my hands covered in my sister's blood along with the gun in my grasp. She looks at me, her chest heaving up and down with choked breathing.

But before I can contemplate, her movements slow down until she turns still...like a lifeless body. Blood keeps oozing out from her wound, turning her skin pale and white with her eyes no longer holding any emotions. Her blood starts to spread on the ground until it reaches my feet, coating my sole. That is when the bitter and harsh truth hits me like a hurricane, with guilt killing me as well.

She is gone...Helena is...gone.

I killed my sister.

I killed her.

She died because of me.

Me.

THE DEVIL TAINTED US

CHAPTER NINETEEN

ERYX

I listen to each and every word she utters about her past. The same past that she has been carrying as a burden on her shoulders since her sister died.

A death she blames herself for even to this day.

"Later one of the guards heard the sound of a gunshot and came to see what happened. He informed Tristen about it and rushed back home. But I just stood there looking at Helena's dead body."

Fuck.

"I was even prepared to go to prison because I knew I committed a crime and deserved it. But Tristen made it look like Helena killed herself from the grief of her miscarriage."

Agatha is now sitting on my lap with her arms tangled around my neck and her head resting against my shoulder. My arms are engulfed around her, letting her feel the warmth of comfort while she confesses to me. At one point when she started to break down in tears from her story, I didn't hesitate to pull her in my arms, knowing well she needed it.

I feel her tears streaming down as they drop on my chest, but the only thing bothering me is seeing the utter sadness in her heart that she has been trying to treat on her own for so long.

From what she has told me, it's clear all of it was an accident. She only meant to save Helena but fate had other plans and took her sister away from her.

"I will never be able to forgive myself for what happened to Helena. All I wish is at least when I'm on the gateway of afterlife, God gives me the chance to apologize to her and to tell her that I love her with all my heart. It was *me* who failed her."

"I think that's where you are wrong," I whisper.

She frowns looking up at me. "I don't want you to pity me for what happened."

I shake my head, playing with the ends of her hair. "It's your guilt that was your downfall. What happened to you is something no girl ever wishes on her enemies even. Tristen used that as his weapon to play with your young mind and made you believe that nobody will trust your words."

She remains quiet, listening to me intently.

"He controlled you and your sister. He was the one to blame for the chaos he started in your family...in your life.

Everything you thought was for your sister."

I caress her cheek with the back of my hand, wiping away her tears. Her cheeks are flushed and her eyes filled with distress that I wanted to release her from.

"You tried to save her but sometimes some things aren't in our control."

"How can you think of me like that after knowing the truth? Don't you see the stupid, careless whore that people looked at when they started to think I might have had an affair with my brother-in-law?"

Rage courses through my nerves just thinking of the people who dared to see her in that light. I bet, Tristen spread that rumor just to escape from Helena's death and look like a victim.

"All I see is a girl who was caught up in the shadow of darkness that people like Tristen put the innocent ones in just for their advantage. But you are the bravest girl I've met who didn't lose hope to escape from here. And I can also tell once you heal fully, you will plan to escape again."

Her body tightens confirming my assumption. But I don't blame her for it. Not anymore.

"And I know you will succeed. Because your bravery and stubbornness is your true beauty. You are like a queen who was used to sacrificing only, but now she is able to fight her own battles by hook or by crook. Only time will tell if you will gain your freedom."

"I will escape and nothing will stop me from it," she mutters and rests her head back on my shoulder.

Now I understand why she wanted to be free from this prison so badly...why she is hopeful of escaping from here.

She wants to be away from this dark world and be in a place where her guilt and past won't taint her anymore. And the mere thought that just her freedom means so much to her that she is willing to risk her life, makes me wish I never kidnapped her here in the first place.

It makes me wish to go back in time and never accept the offer Tristen made with me and Geryon.

She found shelter in my arms but once she knows the harsh truth, she won't waste time being away from me. She won't even look at me the way she is doing now, and it hurts me even more, reminding me that I will indeed always be the monster.

The devil.

The villain of her story.

Her gaze holds a gentle and softening emotion, making her look even more beautiful. I look at the window to see it's starting to turn dark.

I move us towards the headboard with my back resting against it as I lean to get the lighter from the drawer to light up the candelabra.

We settle in the quietness, hearing the pitter-patter of the rain from outside as we relish in each other's warmth.

"Why are you always there for me even though I can see it in your eyes you want to suppress that urge?" she asks with a hushed tone, lightly touching my chest.

I lick my lips, letting out a sigh. "I wish I knew."

"If you have the will to save me from the dangers here, then why can't you help me escape from here?"

"It is complicated."

"What secret does this place hold against you that you are so devoted to it?"

Her question hits me to my core as I remember why I'm tied to this place…why my life is controlled by the Magdalene.

But I don't answer her. I don't confess my truth to her knowing she will see a part of me that I won't allow anybody else to see. I have been vulnerable once but not again.

Never again.

I gently lifted her off from my lap and put on my clothes.

"I will get you something to eat." Before she could ask anything else, I leave the room.

AGATHA

The next few days pass in the blink of an eye. My wounds finally healed along with my soul that Geryon tried to break. Every angel has her fall, but just because they fall doesn't mean their wings won't raise them up with power.

Eryx has warned me beforehand that once I healed things will have to return back to normal for me.

I don't protest, knowing well I need to leave his room and keep finding ways for my escape.

I change into my new dress for the morning prayers. Eryx left early in the morning before I woke up but he left me some buttered bread and omelet to eat.

After getting ready, I head to the prayers and sit beside Beth. Eryx and Geryon soon enter with a Bible in their hands before they start to recite the verses.

I pretend to be a part of it, but I look around and see the usual scenario where all the women are like lifeless puppets dancing in Geryon's tune.

But the question was…why?

Why are all these women like this but Beth is different?

What control does Geryon hold on everyone here?

I try to avoid Eryx's intense gaze upon me that I always feel to the core of my soul, setting my skin ablaze with an unknown, dark need. After he revealed his…thoughts about me for what I have suffered, I had this little hope that maybe I can change his mind to help me be free from this place.

It may be an unknown chance where I don't know the outcome, but it is still a risk I'm willing to take.

Instead of dismissing us as usual after prayers, Geryon calls out a few names. Six women stand up, looking ahead without portraying an ounce of emotion.

"The six of you will meet me after dinner for your departure. It is time for you to leave," Geryon mutters in a sharp tone and leaves the room along with Eryx.

I frown in confusion. *Departure?*

Those six women will be leaving the Magdalene today and will be free from this living hell. I notice the ones he chose are usually the ones who scream or yell every now and then, having a sudden breakdown. But today they are quiet and still like others.

But why did Geryon pick them?

And why only six?

Later, while cleaning the shelves in the library, I find Beth and gesture at her to meet me at the corner. She nervously looks around and takes a chance to join me.

"Do you know anything about this departure?" I ask her with a hushed voice. My eyes every now and then peeking glances through the gaps of the shelves to be aware of someone's arrival.

"Usually at the end of every month, Geryon picks six girls and they leave with him after dinner. Today seems to be that day."

"Do they leave by ship?"

She shrugs. "Nobody has seen it. But once they leave this building, they are never seen again."

"We can follow them tonight," I suggest. "We can see how they leave and if it's possible then we can follow them and get on board with them."

"But Geryon will be with them. He will easily find us."

I nod. "I know but at least we will know of a way and plan stronger for it the next time."

She swallows, a hint of uncertainty glimmering in her eyes, before she nods in response. "Alright. But what about sister Agnes? She sometimes makes rounds at night."

She is indeed an issue that is hard to tackle. "I will think of something. But be ready after dinner. I will knock three times on your door for a signal. Now go."

She turns and quickly returns to her previous spot.

My mind starts to race with every possible solution to get rid of Agnes from our path to freedom. But thankfully a plan comes up in my head.

After lunch time, I quickly go to Eryx's room and start to rummage through the drawer chest where he keeps small, thin sized capsule glass bottles, with medicines stored in it.

I'm searching for the sleeping pills and luckily found them. Looking at it, I know I have one shot at this and that I have to be careful. I put the bottle inside my dress pocket and quickly close the door, when the entrance door opens too.

Eryx enters and his eyes instantly fall on me with a questioning look. Suspicion is shadowing upon his face as he stalks towards me.

"What are you doing here?" he asks.

I shake my head. "Nothing," I whisper, feeling my nerves

tightening with tension.

He stands so close to me that I can feel the heat of his body even from a few inches away. His eyes darken as they assess me up and down like he is searching for something to confirm his suspicion.

"I should get going," I mutter and walk past him, trying to escape the scenario.

But he grabs my wrist, halting my steps and speeding up my heart.

"If you are thinking of escaping today with the women, then don't even attempt it," he mutters over his shoulder. My pulse races with a sudden nervousness.

"Don't do something reckless. You have tried it once and you've seen the consequences."

"I don't know what you are talking about," I murmur.

He lets out a dark chuckle under his breath as a gesture he isn't buying my excuses. "The minute Geryon mentioned about the six women being free, one glance at you gave me the answer that you were starting to plot your escape already."

He pulls me back, making us stand side by side. Him facing the side of my face while I kept my gaze forward.

"You will be disappointed at the end. So, do not even think of doing anything tonight. I may have saved you once but I won't be able to every time."

I smile humorlessly, meeting his gaze. "Because you are a prisoner like me."

"We are all prisoners in this world. Even if you escape this place, there will be another jail waiting for you to ruin your life and trap your freedom."

He leans closer with his warm breath caressing against my lips. My skin is heating up with the familiar sensation I always sense from his closeness.

"I'm warning you for your own good. I don't want you to suffer again, you've already been through a lot."

"If you cared so much about me, then you would at least have the courage to help me be free," I retort. "I have fallen many times. But no matter what happens, I will always come out stronger than you'll ever imagine."

"Don't say I didn't warn you," he murmurs before loosening his grip on my wrist. I frown in confusion and take the chance to leave his room.

Though I can't stop thinking if Eryx will go behind my back and alert Geryon about what I might do, or if he is actually not going to stop me.

It's nearly night time and everyone is busy with their chores. I keep an eye on Agnes who is standing at the corner of the prayer room, while we clean the benches and mop the floors.

It's turning dark and from afar we can hear the rumbling

of thunder.

Few moments later, we are done for the day and everyone starts to line up to leave the room, returning back to their rooms. But instead of following them, I sneak into the kitchen and quickly look for the jar where the tea leaves are kept.

I have often seen Agnes drinking tea. During keeping an eye on us or sometimes after we were dismissed at night, and it seems like she is the only one. I find it, trying to steady my trembling hands. I pull out the small sleeping pills, crushing four of them into powder and sprinkling it into the jar. I give it a quick shake, placing it back on the shelf.

Fortunately, nobody notices my short absence and I quickly join the line. Keeping my head down like others we go upstairs to our rooms.

I wait for an hour, which nearly feels like forever, before I open the door and tip-toed downstairs to the kitchen.

I slowly open the door and find Agnes, with her head resting on the table. I stalk towards her, trying to make the minimum sound. Her eyes are closed and her body is relaxed, gesturing she has fallen asleep from the pills.

The tea cup is sitting empty on the table, with few remains of the tea leaves.

I let out a breath of relief and left the kitchen. I quickly make my way to Beth's room, knocking three times.

She opens the door with a hint of uneasiness in her eyes.

"Are you ready?" I ask.

"What about sister Agnes?"

I hold her hand, guiding her to the corner of the stairway. "She is taken care of. Just be quiet and when Geryon comes out we will follow him."

She nods. We kneel beside the stairway handles, waiting for Geryon to be seen or heard. A few moments pass by when we hear heavy footsteps. I feel Beth's body turning tense beside me as she grabs my hand tightly for support.

I look at the gaps of the railing, finding Geryon coming to the prayer hall with the six women right behind him.

"Follow me," he orders. They head to the front door and that is when we get up and slowly descend downstairs.

Perspiration coats my forehead and neck, dripping down my back as well.

My heart starts to race with a high speed that I can hear it drumming in my ears.

Both of us keep a general distance from Geryon and the women as we start to follow them. The women are dressed in their usual nightgowns with a suitcase on each of their hands.

They walk through the gate of the Magdalene, crossing the territory but instead of heading forward, Geryon turns to the right side of the building and walks along the dark path of the forest side that leads to the backyard.

I frown in confusion being left clueless of what Geryon was doing.

Why didn't he go to the shore side?

CHAPTER TWENTY

AGATHA

For the next several minutes, Beth and I keep following them, into the depths of the forest. It's starting to get slightly difficult to see but the moonlight peeking through the tree leaves helps a bit.

But when I notice Geryon suddenly stopping, I instantly take Beth's hand and pull her behind a tree.

Shit.

We both start to breathe heavily from sudden fear of being caught. But there are no footsteps scrunching on the fallen leaves to signal us about Geryon approaching us. There is only pin drop silence.

Ever so slowly, I try to sneak a peek and see them standing still on their spot, absolutely unmoving.

"What is happening?" Beth whispers.

I shrug. "I don't know. They aren't doing anything."

Few more seconds pass by with them doing nothing. Geryon finally turns and says something to the women. They all drop their suitcase in unison and start to stand a few inches away from each other, forming a circle. Geryon walks forward as if searching for something, while Beth and I take this chance to get closer and hide behind another tree.

He soon returns with a thick branch in his hand and traces a circle around the women. He goes to one of the suitcases and retrieves a few candles and a lighter, placing them around the circle.

After finishing the task, he stands in the center and looks at them with a prideful and vicious smile...almost looking like a monster...a demon.

"Do you all want to be free from your sins?" he asks in a rough voice.

"Yes, father," six of them answer together, in a cold, emotionless tone.

"Are you willing to sacrifice anything?"

"Anything, father."

He nods in approval and kneels, placing his palms on his knees and leaning his head up in the dark, gloomy sky, with the women following his posture.

We have no idea what is happening and why, but deep down I can feel something ominous about to happen... something that will change everything. But I need to know...I have to.

"What on earth is he doing?" Beth whispers, sounding nervous and hesitant.

But I have no response to her question. I'm as confused as she is.

"Pray to be forgiven, my children. Pray to repent for your sins," he orders.

The women raise their hands for prayers and close their eyes with their hair curtaining around their faces. They all seem not bothered at all with what is happening. Nobody questions anything or does something to escape. As if Geryon has put strings on them and it's pulled and controlled by his words like a puppet.

He goes to a nearby tree, removing some branches and leaves like he hid something there. But he extracts out, makes my throat clog with fright. It's a giant bull skull that has little dirt on it and long curve-like horns. He returns back and puts it on like a mask as if he is showing his true devil side. Geryon goes to the same suitcase, but this time he pulls out a sharp, long dagger before standing in front of one of the women with blond hair. He touches her head gently while she leans forward for his touch more. Her breathing turns shallow when his hand skates down to his cheek before it glides down to her slender neck that was arched up.

"Oh my God…" I rasp. What I see next makes my eyes widen in horror as I feel terror coursing through my entire body.

Geryon places the dagger against her throat and dives it deeper into her skin until her throat is cut and blood spurts out of it, making her choke.

I hear a light gasp from Beth and instantly put my hand against her mouth to keep her quiet as we witness the horror in front of us. But not for once the woman screams in agony like she doesn't feel the pain at all. Before I know it, he digs the dagger deeper and cuts her head from her body as it limps back on the ground.

She is dead...he killed her by chopping her head off.

I feel my throat clogging as it becomes hard for me to breath or even move. I can't believe my eyes for what I'm witnessing.

"You will be forgiven, my child," he murmurs and throws her head at the center where he was previously. None of the other women open their eyes or react against it.

He moves to the next woman and does the same, while I watch in horror. And I just know that this image will forever be tainted in my memory.

It will haunt me for several nights until my last breath.

I only thought this place was wretched with monsters like Geryon who tortured and tormented victims like us. But now this place has a completely different story.

A deeper, darker and harsher truth that nobody is aware of except for the monster himself. Eryx told me how this place might have been cursed because of the burden of sins, and now I have got the proof of it too.

Geryon chops the heads of all six of the women, piling their heads at the center as their limp bodies circling around it. I feel like throwing up at this atrocious sight, but I give it all to calm down even though it's impossible in this scenario.

After killing them all, he goes back to the suitcase and takes out a small shovel. Stalking near the bloody heads he kneels and starts to dig out something.

It's a skull, covered in mud and few earthworms crawling over it. Geryon dusts it off and places it beside him, before he leans to the blond woman's head and gouges out her eyeballs with his dagger. I can't help but look away, shutting my eyes, only to return my gaze onto the sight a few seconds later.

He places the eyeballs on to the skull's eye socket, and positions it on top of the pile of heads. He stands up and uses the tip of the dagger to line out a star-like shape inside the circle. After finishing he spreads his arms and kneels outside the circle, looking at the sky that is rumbling louder and louder, signalling an upcoming storm.

"I serve you, master," he yells, looking like he is surrendering to someone from the depths of his dark soul. The madness reddening his eyes with an addiction of serving to his so-called master.

"I only ever serve you and always will till the time comes I give you my last breath. Accept my sacrifice and repent me from my sins. Repent them from their illness, and let their souls be part of your beautiful world. Accept it, master," he takes the dagger and cuts his palm, squeezing out the blood on top of the skull, "accept it."

CRACK. CRACK. CRACK.

The thunder crackles. And soon raindrops start to fall from the sky. My clothes and hair become wet and it turns a bit tough to see Geryon clearly with the candles extinguishing in thin air. He pulls out the bull skull and places it right behind the human skull before continuing his words.

"Free them, master. More will be served in time that I promise.. Let them be witnesses of my acts and let me be part of heaven. Wash away my sins, master." His voice is hoarse and raw like he means each and every word.

But I know if we stay longer the more chances Geryon will have of finding us.

I look at Beth, whose face is pale as snow from what she witnessed with her glistening eyes wide open. I'm aware of the shock she is going through as I feel the same. But I lightly shake her, bringing her attention to me.

"We have to go back. Right now," I whisper.

She gives a shaky nod, feeling loss of words. Keeping my gaze over my shoulder, we slowly turn, giving it all to walk away slowly.

With every step I take, I feel my heart beating rapidly against my ribcage as if it will come out of my body. I have never been frightened and terrified of something so much.

And I'm already praying that this sight vanishes from my memory someway possible, even though it's futile... because God doesn't exist in the Magdalene.

This is the kingdom of the devil, where God's shadow is used as a bait for victims like those women. And I'm one of them.

A bait to be served to the devil.

Thankfully we are several feet away from Geryon who remains in his position inside the circle. I take a chance and face ahead when suddenly I let out a yelp when I feel a pointy branch prickling my feet.

I instantly cover my mouth but it's too late.

"Who is there?" Geryon yells.

Without waiting or thinking, Beth and I start to run as fast as possible. I give every bit of strength and will I have to escape from Geryon.

Our breathing turns ragged as we dash through the dark forest, but I soon hear thudding footsteps following us which only paces up my pulse more than ever.

Oh God. Please, no.

When I see the side view of the castle, I feel a rush of relief running through my nerves. We quickly get inside and rush upstairs but I halt at the corridor, grabbing Beth's arm.

"You go to your room and don't come out. Dry yourself as much as you can and pretend to be asleep," I mutter quickly, feeling a surge of panic crawling to my soul.

She frowns with the water droplets skating down from her lashes and chin to the floor. "But what about you?"

I turn her around and push her shoulder slightly, urging her to move quickly. "Don't worry about that and go quickly."

She rushes to her room without a backward glance and I take this chance to run downstairs where I know who can save me from this.

Eryx.

By the time I reach the last step, I can see Geryon's shadow enlarging on the main entrance. I quickly hide behind the stairway, waiting for Geryon to head to my room. His thudding footsteps echo to the second floor and I don't waste time going to Eryx's room.

I expect to be unlocked but when I turn the handle and the door doesn't open, I feel my throat clogging with fear. My heart starts to beat rapidly as if it will jump out of the body anytime. I slap my palms against the door again and again while keeping my eyes on the stairway.

Please, please. No…this can't be happening.

"Eryx. It's me, please open the door. Please!" I mutter with panic painting my voice.

But the silence feels like daggers of betrayal stabbing into my soul. "Please, Eryx. I know you are in there."

The second I hear Geryon's heavy steps descending down, the little hope I have left is starting to vanish in thin air.

I'm well aware the moment he knows it was me and that I have discovered the actual reflection he carries behind the Magdalene, he isn't going to hesitate to hurt me...or most probably kill me.

I see his shadow on the pillar and nearly accept my fate, when the door suddenly opens and I'm pulled inside. I gasp from the sudden movement and hear the soft thud of the door closing. I look over my shoulder, facing Eryx's back who has his head casted down with his right hand tightly gripping the knob.

"Go to the bathroom and turn on the shower. Lock the door and don't come out until I tell you," he mutters in a cold and distant tone.

But emotions overwhelm me, freezing me on the spot.

"Right now!" he orders. His rough, deep voice brings me back to sanity and I rush inside the bathroom, doing as he instructed.

I lock the door and let out a deep sigh, giving it all to calm down my nerves. I swallow the lump in my throat and rest my forehead against the wood with my palms against it.

It's going to be okay...everything is alright...

My ears start to ring despite the muffled voices coming from the other side. Dread keeps climbing its way to the depths of my soul with every second passing by as the horrific scenario I witnessed tonight keeps flashing in front of me.

The sharp sound of the dagger slicing the women's

heads. The gushing sound of their blood spurting out. And the thud sound of their lifeless bodies falling behind.

It's a vivid picture that I will always remember.

The maze of secrets behind this place starts to make sense but some major parts are missing. But in conclusion, I have to leave this place quickly before I become one of those victims.

And I defy to accept my fate that way.

I don't know for how long I stay inside but when I hear Eryx's calm voice I finally bring myself back to reality.

"You can come out. He is gone."

But he won't be gone from my memories.

I slowly open the door, looking for any sign of Geryon's presence but I'm glad when he is nowhere in sight. However, when my eyes land on Eryx, who is facing the window with the heavy rain droplets clashing with the window, suspicion and distrust starts to bloom within me.

Eryx knows what Geryon does and yet he is unfazed by it, which can only mean he is part of his sins.

"You knew, didn't you?" I ask, stalking towards him as I feel my wet skin forming with goose bumps.

He remains quiet, keeping his gaze fixated on the pitch-black forest.

"You have to answer me after what I saw. I deserve to know the truth, Eryx." Even to me my voice sounded broken but it held the determination to know the darkest secrets.

"I warned you," he barely whispers, meeting my gaze over his shoulder.

"That is not enough. You know he kills the women of this asylum and yet you let it happen," I let out a sad chuckle, "-you tell me to trust you but after what I saw…it's impossible for me to even try it when I know if I'm chosen next you will stay behind and won't do shit about it."

He fully turns, walking towards me, but I take a step back and raise my hand as a gesture to halt his steps.

He stops wearing an emotionless expression that only riddles my mind with more questions.

"I want to know everything. This place…about Geryon and the things he did…and *you*. I deserve to know before you let me be one of his sacrifices."

He shakes his head. "I won't let him hurt you."

"I don't believe those words anymore."

Silence draws an invisible wall between us, filled with doubt and secrets.

"Tell me," I mutter. "I need to know."

ERYX

I don't know where to even start. I was well aware she would do something tonight but I didn't expect such a reckless act. Even when I found Agnes unconscious in the kitchen, I knew Agatha must have been behind it.

If Geryon discovered her presence he wouldn't have given a second thought before killing her. Even when he came to my door asking about her, his eyes were darkened with a wild craving for sin...for blood.

The second I heard the first knock at my door, I knew it was Agatha. But for several seconds I remained rooted to my spot, telling myself not to help her because of Geryon. I couldn't take the risk. Especially, after he reminded me of what he holds against me...I had to back away.

But the desperation...the fret...the fear of seeing her hurt, crumbled my walls and I didn't waste another moment to save her.

But now, after witnessing one of the darkest sins the Magdalene carried, she sees me under a different light, thinking I'm part of this darkness.

She isn't wrong.

And after all the things she has been through, she at least deserves to know the truth that no other woman here got to know.

I simply nod, inhaling a shaky breath, as I open my mouth to reveal the truth, while my mind goes back to the moment I stepped into this dark world.

THE DEVIL TAINTED US

Chapter Twenty One

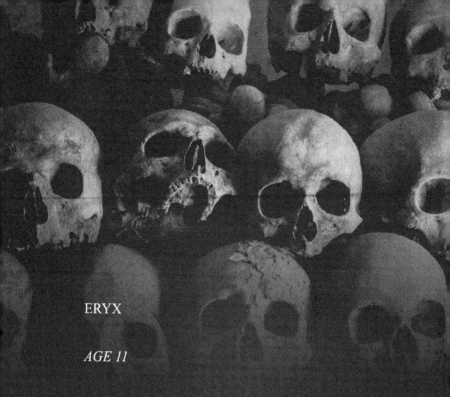

ERYX

AGE 11

Something wakes me up...a sound...a gasp.

My eyes flutter open as the night greets me. I rub my eyes with the back of my hand and look over to the opposite bed where my brother is fast asleep after his soccer practice today.

Looking at the clock I see the time being after midnight.

The gasp echoes again making me frown in confusion as I sit up. Sleep escapes from my eyes as I start to stalk out of my room. My feet lightly make the wooden floor screech.

But the more steps I take down the hallway the more the gasp turns louder.

But something about it makes an agitation course

through my nerves.

At the end of the hallway are our parents' room, where the door is slightly ajar with the light from the room streaming out. And the sounds are coming from there.

"Oh God," I heard the familiar voice of my father in a raspy tone.

I feel my heart racing against my chest as I hear the THUMP THUMP sound in my ears.

I stop beside the door frame and lean forward to see the light illuminating on my face with the rectangular gap size. But what I see makes my eyes widen with shock and my body is still turning like a statue.

"It feels so good, dear God," father whispers while he stands naked behind a woman, who isn't my mother. She has short blond hair unlike my mother's black hair. He holds onto her waist tightly and the woman seems to be in pain as her eyes are shut tightly.

Tears stream down her face as she cries out loud but father doesn't stop.

My whole body starts to shiver as I feel…disgust…dread looming over me.

"Ah God!" he grunts, increasing his motion and holding onto the woman's hair into a tight fist.

Gulping nervously and feeling my breathing turning shallow, I think about returning back to my room. I want to go back and pretend this night has never happened and it's possibly a nightmare.

But when I take a few steps back, I feel my back hitting another body. I quickly turn with a gasp and see mother standing with her brows furrowed.

Without thinking, I quickly warp my small arms around her waist, hugging her tightly. A wave of relief and comfort washes over me...just like it does every time mother is with me.

"What are you doing here?" she asks.

Should I tell her?

"I...I heard something," I whisper against her belly.

"What did you hear?" She kneels in front of me, pushing back my hair before her hands cup my face.

"I saw...I...father with..." I stutter, unable to think of my next words.

But as if mother understands my words, I see the realization crossing her face followed by a small smile.

"We thought to wait. But now that you have seen it, then you have stepped into the world."

I frown in confusion, waiting for her to explain further.

But rather than speaking, she takes my hand and guides me back to her room where father is still with the woman in bed. I try to pull away from my mother's hold with my eyes tight shut.

"No, mother. Please, no," I beg, wanting nothing more but to leave the room.

She doesn't listen and locks the door.

"Wilson," she calls out father's name and I hear the sounds stopping.

"What is he doing here?" he asks in a shocked tone.

"It is time for him."

"Are you sure?"

"Absolutely. The sooner the better."

There is silence for a moment and taking a risk I open my eyes, seeing my parents gazing upon me. But the look is serious and distant that sent shivers down my spine. I have never seen them this way and at this moment, I don't feel they are my parents...they are strangers.

"Please, mother...I want to go. I don't want to be here."

She shakes her head, gesturing me to be quiet with her index finger against her lips.

Tears start to blur my vision as she guides me to the bed where the woman is with father moving aside and putting on his pants.

I look away, feeling ill all of a sudden. Sweat starts to course down from my neck to my back.

"Eryx, look at the woman," father orders.

But for the first time, I deny him. I can't and I won't do it. Suddenly, I feel my father's hand gripping my jaw with a familiar grip as he forces me to turn and face the woman.

She is in a kneeling position, showing her naked body.

I shut my eyes and try to look away, but father intensifies his grip, urging me to look back.

"She isn't just a woman, Eryx. She is an angel," mother mutters.

What? An angel?

"What?" I whisper.

Mother sits beside the woman who looks like every ounce of emotion is wiped away from her face. It's like moments ago even the pain she felt was no longer there.

She is like a living statue.

Mother cups the woman's face, caressing her cheek like she does to me. "She will be sent back to God and we will be rewarded later for it."

"What? I...I don't understand."

"You will understand everything soon, my sweet little boy. But tonight is your beginning...your first step towards the Magdalene."

Nothing but discomfort, pain and revulsion shadows upon me. I can't help but start crying as I beg mother to let me out of here.

"Please, I want to go back to my room. Please, mother. I don't want to be here or near her...please."

"You have no other choice because you will need to please the angel before she is sent back to heaven."

I scowl. "Please her?"

She nods. Turning towards the woman she urges to face her and before I know it their lips touch each other.

I shut my eyes again feeling repulsed.

"You have to watch, son," father mutters, close to my ears. "Do it or else I will beat you until your skin starts to bleed."

I don't doubt my father's words because I have experienced that pain several times from him. Finding no other choice, I open my eyes and have to forcefully witness my mother kissing a stranger, whose skin is turning red like she is blushing.

But when their kiss broke, she became emotionless again. Mother looks at me with a soft smile and holds onto my shoulder.

"Now your turn," she whispers.

What?

"You will please her just like I did. If you do then the angel will help us be part of heaven."

I shake my head vigorously and try to get down from the bed. But father tightens his hold and pushes me towards the woman.

As if understanding my hesitation, she leans forward and in the next second I feel her lips on mine. My mouth is immobile and still while she moves her lips and uses her tongue to trace mine. I feel bile forming in my throat as I want to puke badly. My heart is thumping faster and faster while the tears won't stop streaming.

Let this be over soon, God. Please let this be over.

Thankfully it does and she moves back. Mother and father offer me a prideful smile even though I don't feel an ounce of honor.

"She is pleased by your act, son," father murmurs while caressing my hair and mother touching my cheek.

"There is nothing to cry about, sweetie. It's part of the Magdalene. And tonight, you took your first step. There is more to come. But now it's time for our angel to go. Let's bid her farewell," mother says and the three of them get up.

Mother takes my hand and guides me with them towards the basement- whereas I want nothing more but to escape from this horrific night.

Father locks the basement door when we reach the room. Unlike other times, the room is illuminated by candles that are placed around a circle. There is a star shaped mark inside it and there is something white and dusty, with huge horns and black hollowed eyes…it looks like a monster.

"Come with me," mother speaks to the woman who follows her to the center of the circle.

Father stays behind me, holding my shoulders, witnessing the sight like me.

What is happening?

Why is mother doing this? Why did father force me?

Who is this woman?

So many questions roam in my head but I don't achieve an answer for one.

The woman faces the white monster and kneels in front of it with her head casted down. Mother stands right behind her and retrieves something from the ground.

"She will be returning to God, Eryx. She is going to be free from here, happy and pleased."

The way my mother's eyes darkened with an overwhelming happiness that I have never seen before, makes me scared of my own mother for the first time.

I have been afraid of my father mostly because of the way he punished me and my brother for the smallest mistakes. But with our mother we seek comfort and protection.

Tonight, even that notion is proved to be wrong.

Because what happens next, paralyzes my mind and soul.

"Do you wish to be free?" she asks the woman who simply nods and arches her head back.

"We serve you, master. Let her be free and come to you. Let our sins be forgiven and allow this angel to be the witness and evidence to help us repent," mother mutters, her head leans back as she looks at the ceiling.

Her voice sounds as if she means each and every word from the depths of her heart.

Before I can contemplate, I see a knife in her hand with its sharpness being highlighted by the candles. Mother brings it towards the woman's neck and cuts her neck.

Instant fright shakes me to my core, making my body tremble as I see the woman's neck gushing out blood and soon being cut off from her body.

The rest of her body falls forward with mother holding her head.

I can't move...can't think...can't speak.

The woman is dead...mother killed her...she is dead... dead...

That is the last sight I envision before my world turns from blurry to dark and I collapse on the ground letting myself be engulfed by slumber that I want to stay in forever.

A week passes by after that night.

The next day when I woke up, it all felt like a dream. I immediately rushed to the basement but there was no sign of the circle, candles or the white monster.

Mother found me there but instead of lashing at me she greeted me with her chirpy voice and guided me back to the house. Even my father pretended like nothing happened the other night.

He was simply reading his newspaper while mother was making breakfast.

Everything felt...normal.

Was I dreaming?

I didn't see that woman again though my mind couldn't stop seeing the flashes of her head being cut off from her body.

For the next few nights, I couldn't blink a sleep. I tossed and turned, thinking about the woman again and again. But eventually, I made myself think it was just a nightmare and the woman didn't exist.

With that comforting thought I let my mind feel the calmness I lost a few days ago.

It was a dream...a bad dream.

None of it happened.

But it turns out to be a lie one night.

I'm in a deep sleep but it's broken by a hand shaking me by my shoulder vigorously. My eyes snap open to my younger brother. He is in his white pajamas like mine with his raven black hair tousled in a mess. But what catches my attention are the tears of distress streaming down his face.

"Eryx, wake up. Please wake up," he begs with a choked-up voice.

I instantly sit up and hold his hands for comfort. "What happened? What is wrong?"

"Mother...father...t-they."

I frown and the only scenario I can think of is that night. "They are what?"

He continues sobbing and hugs me tightly. "T-they... knife...I saw a woman...she is...mother she...-"

His words get halted when the door of our bedroom bursts open with our parents entering like the dark monsters we always thought hide under the bed. But we never thought those monsters lived with us.

This is reality and so was that night.

My eyes land on the blood-stained knife on mother's hand but this time father's hands are covered in blood too.

Protectiveness overpowers me as I cage my brother in my arms with a harsh grip as I lean us towards the corner of my bed. There is no other place to go but I will do everything in my power to protect him. Even if it required me to sacrifice myself...I will do it.

Our parents have forced me to step into their dark world but I won't let my brother be a part of a world where he doesn't belong.

"No! Stay away from him!" *I shout at them for the first time.* "Don't you dare touch him!"

"Eryx, sweetie," *mother starts while heading towards my bed,* "-we want you to be a part of this. Both of you. Because when we die and go to heaven, we want you both with us and this will secure that motive."

"Listen to your mother, boys. We just want the best for you."

"By killing strangers in front of your sons?" *I yell while my brother's sobbing makes my body shake. I try to soothe him by caressing his back even though I know it won't help much.*

"We aren't killing strangers, sweetie. We are sending the

angels back to heaven. It's part of the Magdalene."

"We don't want to be part of anything. This is sick! You two are insane and unworthy of even being called parents," I sneer.

Father strides towards me and doesn't hesitate to slap me across my face so hard that it darkens my vision for a moment. "How dare you insult your parents like that? God doesn't forgive those who disrespect their parents!" he yells, with a sudden vengeful anger boiling in his eyes.

"You will be part of the Magdalene like us. This is where we belong and so will you two…by hook or by crook."

His warning is enough for me to know that our parents are serious about this and nothing will change their minds. Whatever this darkness is…it has blinded them deeply that they didn't care how it would be affecting their sons.

"Tonight, is time for another angel to go. Both of you must join," mother whispers, lightly caressing my cheek where father slapped me.

"You have always made me proud, Eryx. Do this and I will be prouder knowing our son wants to be with us when we go to heaven."

I shake my head. "I won't be part of your sick world."

Her soft smile disappears in the blink of an eye and she leans back with the same emotionless look that woman carried.

I have never feared my mother so much as I do at this

moment.

She simply leans forward and brings the bloody knife close to my face. I try to mask my fright but my shivering body gives it away.

"You will do this. You have to otherwise," she brings the tip of the knife towards my brother's hair and skimming it lower to his neck, "I won't hesitate to send him with the angel tonight."

My heart skips a beat just from the thought of losing my brother by my lunatic parents. I tighten my hold around him while he does the same like he doesn't want to let go of me for a second. He is as scared as I am but I have to be there for him and be brave.

"You will be a part of the Magdalene and keep continuing this tradition until you take your last breath. With time you will know how to find an angel. And when you do, you will please them and help them be sent to God. They are trapped in this sinful world like we are, sweetie," her voice turns soft all of a sudden, with her eyes glimmering, "-if we could escape, we would. But poor and innocent souls like us are imprisoned in this devious world. We have all committed sins and will be punished despite leading this miserable life. This can't be the world God made for us…it is tainted by the devil. The devil tainted us."

She smiles again, cupping my cheek with one hand and while holding the knife she strokes her other son's hair- who is in no condition to feel the affection of a monstrous mother like her.

"*But by the help of the angels we can be together in the afterlife,*" *she whispers.* "*They will be our key to happily ever after. So, you need to do this for us...for yourself. Will you do it, Eryx?*"

Rather than answering her, my gaze shifts to the knife she holds close to my brother's head while faking she cares for him...and for me.

But it's all an act...a trap they want me to fall in. But I know at this moment it is impossible to escape this nightmare. I don't want to risk my brother's life and let his innocent soul get darkened.

So, I do what I have to do for my brother...only for him.

My gaze returns to my mother and then to my father, while I question God why he let us have such parents.

There is no solution but only one that I wish wasn't an option. I let out a shaky breath, trying to control my emotions before I give a simple nod.

"*Yes, mother. I will do this.*"

THE DEVIL TAINTED US

Chapter Twenty Two

ERYX

Agatha remains silent when I tell her about my past...a past I wish never existed in my life.

"For years they made me do this. I would find women who were beautiful and innocent-"

"Like an angel," she completes my sentence.

I nod and look away, returning my gaze to the raging storm outside.

"I would bring them to our house where my parents would talk with them and make them drink tea that had drugs in them. They would then feed them with their bullshit about the Magdalene and make them think they are actually angels."

Every time I brought a woman with me, I would feel the weight of guilt heavying upon my shoulders more and more. Each and every one of them were innocent who thought to be part of my life as a friend or something more.

And what did I do?

Trapped them like innocent birds into the cage I was in and let them soon become targets to my parents. I watched them get killed, their heads being cut off...their blood staining my hands when I buried them in the grounds.

"But why would anyone believe in such a horrific and gruesome act?" she questions.

"The world isn't full of innocent people who will follow the righteous path God tells us to accept. My parents were brain washed by some fucked up pastor and made them believe with his lies that God has sent angels on earth to witness our actions. They must see it and be sent back to God, and the only way to do it is please them and then fucking kill them as that's the only way any spirit leaves the world. I thought maybe my parents were the lunatic ones but when I got to learn more about this, I saw so many people actually falling for this trap."

"Why didn't you ever tell anyone else?" she asks.

I let out a dark chuckle. "You have been part of a rich family, and I'm sure you had other people to talk about what Tristen did to you. Why didn't you?"

She remains silent, validating my point: *Nobody would trust my words.*

"People at Vailburg always have this painted image of rich people being perfect and living their lives with honesty and power. Only if they would get their heads out of their asses, they would see the dark reality those rich bastards live behind those expensive residence."

"Are your parents still alive?"

I move my head sideways as I respond to her question.

"No. Me and my brother killed them."

She gasps with her lips parted as she is taken aback with surprise. "If they are dead then why are you continuing their sick ways?"

"Because of Geryon," I mutter, running a hand through my hair as I let out a shaky breath. Just remembering what that fucker did to me makes me wish I could cut him into pieces and bury him in the Magdalene. "He believes in this ritual with every living fiber in his body. He believes it so much that he calls God his master and for Him, he will do anything. That's why from Vailburg he would get innocent girls who are labelled as unwanted or lunatics there. If he sees they are worthy of being sent to God then he would use them as sacrifices and if not then he sends them back. In daylight he acts like a priest, repenting for his so-called sins to God, and at night he performs those sins thinking it's a pathway to heaven."

"Did Geryon drug all the women here? Is that why they look so…"

"Lifeless. Yes. He lets them settle in this dark place and when the time is right, he starts to drug them, making them believe whatever he says is right and they are angels."

"Did he drug me too?" she asks.

I shake my head. Not giving her the full answer because I'm not brave enough to see her fall into the depths of lies more than she already is.

"And what happens to the women who aren't affected by it or don't fall for his traps?"

I shrug. "I help them get cured as much as possible, mentally and physically like a doctor should."

Agatha stalks towards me and stands right in front of me. Her eyes filled with doubt and curiosity.

"So, you aren't an actual priest then?"

I shake my head. "I'm like a wolf disguised in sheep's skin. Geryon made me play this part to keep the façade of this place being holy for the world and thinking I would wholeheartedly be a part of the rituals too. But I have no intention to follow in his footsteps, that's why during the prayers, even though it's false, I pray to God for my sins. I pray for the souls of those innocent women who didn't deserve such inhumane deaths."

"Is Geryon your brother?" she asks in a low tone.

I nod, looking right into her deep black eyes. "He is my brother but not the one for whom I stepped into this fucked up world."

She scowls in confusion. "Then who is he?"

"He is my elder step-brother. My parents were part of the

Magdalene ritual before they got married. Father fucked one of the members of it and she got pregnant. He didn't want to take any responsibilities of it so the woman committed suicide and Geryon was left in an orphanage. But he somehow got to know about us and the Magdalene. He gave me something I needed and in exchange he told me to continue the ritual…to resume being part of the Magdalene. We may be priests from outside but from inside we are sinners."

"What did he give you? And where is your other brother?"

I snicker. "What will you gain knowing about those? You wanted to know the truth about Magdalene and me. So, I told you."

"You are still hiding something and I need to know-"

"I already told you that's important for you. Knowing about my brother or Geryon won't be helpful."

I snort. "What will you do? Help me? Go against him and save yourself and me?"

She swallows before I see determination and strength empowering her features. "If it's part of our escape, then yes. I will help you."

I shake my head. "Since when do you care about my escape? Neither do I need to leave this place nor do I need your help. Worry about yours first. Tonight, you could have died for your reckless act. Fate won't be on your side again and again. He will find out one way or another and won't spare you. That time I can't help you no matter what."

She leans closer.

"I know you will save me. You swore to be the villain of my story but this villain will be my savior."

She cups my face, bringing my face closer to her. "I want to help you because that would mean saving myself. You and I are different people but we both carry the same reflection of darkness that we forcefully faced."

I remain silent, feeling my heart racing by her words.

"We both were thrown into the darkness of the Magdalene by the people we thought we could trust. But despite being strangers, you still saved me. And this time I will save you."

My jaw clenches as a wave of anger starts to crash through my nerves.

"You can save me and I will save you."

Nobody has ever saved me. How can she be any different?

"Your truth has put you under a different light in my eyes and the person I see is begging to be set free from this place. I will do that for you."

I push away her hands, caging behind her back while my other hand holds her jaw.

"Don't make promises you can't keep, Agatha."

Our breathing turns ragged as the atmosphere turns intense.

"I have been disappointed and betrayed several times in life to teach myself that trust doesn't exist. So, don't make me trust you because when you fail me, even the last bit of my true self I have left, will be gone forever."

I bend my head lower to hers with my warm breath skimming over her lips. "Don't save me because there is no hope for that."

"I have been betrayed too, Eryx. I know what it feels like and how much pain it can bring. But you still sparked that trust back within me."

"Just because I helped you few times doesn't means-"

"It means more than you'll ever know. You could have ignored it just like you do for others here. But you promised to be there for me and tonight you proved it again. I won't back away from my promise-"

I shake my head as a warning. My heart starts to rise up with the ray of hope she was shining upon it, intensifying my fear.

"Don't do it, Agatha. You will regret it."

"I will regret it more knowing I didn't try hard enough to save you when you needed me the most."

Her words start to bloom my lost hope despite my attempts of suppressing it. But it's the honesty…the truth in her eyes that is trying to break down my walls.

"I don't want your help because of your pity," I mutter. Our lips are so close that only a few inches gap exists.

"It's not out of pity. It's because I care."

"And why should I trust you?" I ask against her lips.

"Because just like you trusted my truth, you can trust me

with yours."

And with that she breaks the walls I had built around myself for years.

I close my eyes, breathing heavily and pressing my forehead against hers. I breathe in her sweet scent, relishing in her sweetness that makes my heart race every time.

"We can save each other. All I need is your trust and help so that we can leave this living nightmare."

I caress her lips with my thumb and open my eyes to meet her beautiful ones.

"You will have your freedom. I promise in my life, Agatha, I will do everything in my power to protect you and get you out of here."

She looks at me with an overwhelming emotion like she wasn't expecting me to agree. Her eyes glimmer with tears of joy before they course down her cheeks.

Letting go off her hands, I bring both my palms to cup her cheeks and kiss away her tears.

"No more tears, little girl. You have suffered enough and soon you will be free from them," I vow to her.

If she gets to know the truth I'm hiding from her, she will loathe me for the rest of her life but I'm serious about setting her free. I won't let her be tainted by the devil.

Not anymore when she sees and believes in a part of me that I thought was dead years ago.

She sees him and trusts him.

She keeps her gaze fixated upon me as we both feel the undeniable attraction pulling us closer with an intense fire of need burning our bodies.

"I..." she whispers. "I want you tonight."

"What does my little girl want from me?" I rasp against her lips, watching her lean closer for more, but slightly move back to make her yearn for my touch.

"Everything. I want to be yours." She licks her lips that ignites my racing blood.

"And how would you want it to be?' I trace my tongue along her bottom lip, relishing in the alluring sound of her moaning.

"Raw. Deep. Harsh."

I smirk. "Seems like my little girl craves the dark pleasure like I do."

"You made me fall in love with this dark side and now I want more...I want it all."

I move my hand towards her throat and hold it, pulling her to me and crashing my lips against hers in a deep, passionate kiss. Her sweet, honey-like flavor makes me release a deep groan in my chest. My blood pumping faster through my body just from her plump lips.

Fuck.

My cock aching against my pants, begging for release and having Agatha's warm, wet mouth wrapped around it.

I lean back watching her eyes darken with desire with

her cheeks flushed.

"On your knees. Now," I order.

She kneels looking at me with those innocent eyes that makes me want to fuck her harder. But tonight, I will be claiming every part of her, even her pussy that I have envisioned many times while jerking off.

I touch her jaw and lightly caress it with my thumb before I slide my hand behind her head and fist her hair.

"Take out my cock and make it wet so that it's ready to fuck your cunt raw," I grunt.

She mewls and starts to work on my pants and pulls down the zipper. My cock springs free through the gap, lightly resting against her lips. I hold my cock, giving it a few strokes and tap it against her bottom lip.

"Open that mouth. I want to see my little girl choke on my cock."

She opens her mouth as wide as possible before I thrust in my cock, hitting the back of her throat. My head leans back with my eyes closed with pure pleasure coursing through every inch of my body.

Her warm, wet mouth and her throat clenching around my cock makes me want to spill my come already, but I want to relish this as much as possible.

Using my other hand I fist more of her hair, controlling her motions by her head.

"First I will make your throat ache with my cock, and

next will be your cunt, little girl," I mutter.

She simply nods eagerly, pleading silently for more.

Whatever my girl wants.

Before she can contemplate, I start to thrust faster and deeper into her mouth, moving both my hips and her head.

The sloping and squelching sounds of her gagging and spit fills in the room along with the heavy rain falling outside. It feels so fucking good…so heavenly.

But the best part is seeing her mouth adjusting to my size while her eyes water with tears. Spit starts to drool from her mouth and fall onto the floor. But despite my rough treatment she doesn't show an ounce of hesitation.

That's my girl.

"Such a good little girl, taking my cock like a hungry slut," I groaned. My words trigger her moaning further as I feel it on my cock as well.

She whimpers and mewls, savoring every second of this moment. Her hair is a wild mess now and skin turning into a shade of rosy red.

I pull out my cock and she inhales in a deep breath with her tongue out and mouth apart.

"Do you want my come in your mouth or cunt?" I grunt while she tries to come out from the euphoria. But I don't let her and pull on her hair.

"Answer me," I ordered.

"Both," she rasps heavily. "I want both."

I let out a dark chuckle, arching her neck more by her hair. "Greedy little girl," I hissed.

I shove my cock in her mouth again, fucking her harder like there is no tomorrow. She is loving the roughness…the pain.

Any other woman would feel used and hurt by my acts, but not Agatha. She embraces this side of me with open arms without any judgements.

"Mmmm mhmm," she hums with her eyes closed placing her hands against my thighs. She skates them up and cups my aching balls, massaging them and heightening my pleasure even more.

"So fucking good. Fuck!" I let out an animalistic growl feeling myself on the verge of spilling anytime as my muscles tightened.

"Fuck…I'm going to come deep in your throat and you better swallow every last drop like good girl."

She nods and tries to relax her mouth, letting me increase my pace. I soon find my release and come inside her mouth with a deep groan.

"Fuck, fuck, fuck," I grunt feeling my muscles turning relaxed with my nerves loosing up a bit. I breathe heavily and pull out, watching her open her mouth wide to show me she swallows it all.

I lean forward and kiss her deeply. "Good girl. Is my little girl's cunt wet and aching?"

I see her hips slightly gyrating like she was seeking for relief. I lower my hand and trace her pussy over her now wet panties.

"Just sucking my cock made you so wet. Dirty little slut," I groan and nibble her bottom lip, earning a whimper from her. Her eyes are dazed with need like never before.

"Lie on the bed, legs spread," I ordered her, watching her stand and quickly lying down in bed with her legs spread. Grabbing her dress by the neckline in a tight fist, I rip it open hearing her gasp in surprise and pull off her dress. I do the same with her panties until she is fully naked in my bed. Every inch of her skin is flushed with her chest heaving up and down as she breathes heavily.

Fucking gorgeous.

I want to claim her so badly but I need her to relax at first in order to take me. I lie beside her and wrap one hand around the back of her neck, kissing her harshly. Our tongues mingle together like we can't get enough no matter what.

My hand moves down and circles her wet cunt while I swallow her moans.

"I bet you want to come so badly that in seconds you will be screaming and writhing, right?" I rasp.

"Yes...please. Please, touch me," she begs.

I lick my fingers groaning at the sweet flavor of her pussy. I spit a bit on my fingers and lubricate her aching cunt more. I push in four fingers together and start fucking her vigorously, not allowing her any gentleness.

She wants it rough. She will have it.

Her whole body starts to shiver as she cries out loud with her thrown back, being hypnotized by pleasure.

The squelching sound of her cunt and her lips letting out those moans are like music to my ears.

Her eyes are shut and she grabs my shirt for support as my fingers pace up their motions. Her cunt squeezes so tightly around my fingers that I feel it on my cock which is turning hard again.

"Kiss me," she whispers.

I bring her closer by her neck and kiss her. She returns the same roughness by biting my lip, making it painful that my mind goes wild.

Fucking little minx.

My fingers hit that sweet spot inside her pussy and feel her coming around my fingers with her wetness squirting out and pooling on the floor. Her hips buck up and down but I don't stop for a second.

She nearly falls back from the intensity of her release but I hold her against me and continue kissing her until she returns to reality. Leaning back, I watch her face lost in the ecstasy brought by my touch.

I stand up and start working on my shirt and pants, until I stand naked in front of her. She lay there and parted her legs more, watching me with those lust filled eyes.

I notice her gaze dropping on my cross chain around my neck and that is when a wicked idea hits me. I take off my chain and place it against her belly.

Kneeling in front of her I put my mouth on her wet cunt letting her legs straddle around my head. I devour her like she is my meal, flicking her clit with my fingers and fucking her cunt with my tongue.

Her back arches as she holds onto my hair for leverage and cries out loud.

"Oh God! Ah! Eryx!" she screams, writhing against my hold. I move my mouth a bit lower and let my spit drool down to her asshole. I even smear her pussy juices on her asshole to lube it up more before I take the cross chain in my hand.

She frowns in confusion and leans on her elbows.

"What are you doing?" she asks with a groggy voice after screaming so much.

"Giving you the most intensified pleasure, you will ever experience, little girl. Trust me on this," I murmur, licking my lips and tasting her juices.

She nods. "I trust you."

My heart thumps against my chest faster while she breathes heavily.

"Hold your ass cheeks apart for me and relax your body." She does as told and I move the pendant on her cunt first, coating it with her juices before skating it lower...lower.

The cross is almost the size of my finger and it will require her to stay calm and relax to feel the pleasure I'm giving her. I circle it around her and then ever so slowly push the cross inside her asshole.

"Urgh! Ah!" she whimpers with her legs trembling and her asshole squeezing around the cross.

Fucking beautiful.

"That's it, take deep breaths," I whisper, letting her adjust to it. She takes it in until the chain is dangling out. I look back at her and smirk seeing her lost in the haze of desire.

"Now time to make you mine," I groan, taking my cock and stroking it. Placing it against her wet pussy lips I slide it up and down, loving the way she whimpers for my cock.

"Please…" she whispers.

"Please what, little girl? Say what you need."

She gulps licking her lips. "I want you to claim me. Please put your cock inside me. I need it."

"Whatever my little girl wants."

With that I sink my cock inside her tight cunt and can't control the deep moan vibrating from my chest.

Fucking Lord. She feels too perfect.

"Fuck…" I grunt and land my gaze on her face which is constricted like she is in pain.

I'm on the verge of pulling away and as if she can read my mind, she cups my face and shakes her head.

"No. Don't. I want all of it, including the pain," she

whispers.

"But I don't want to hurt you too much."

"I don't want you to hold back and treat me like a fragile flower. You and I connected with darkness, and now I want to be with you in this same darkness where we are each other's light. I want every part of you." She kisses me harshly and clenches her pussy on purpose.

Dear God, give me strength.

"Claim me and fuck me like I was born to be yours. I want it to hurt, I want to feel it through my bones…right through my soul. Fuck me, Eryx."

Her words work like a trigger and I let myself lose control. I lean over and cage her hands above her head with one hand, while the other grabs her throat. I give one deep thrust and pause to listen to her cries. Another thrust brings out another cry before I thrust again and this time I don't pause.

I start fucking her.

Raw. Deep. Harsh.

"God yes! Yes! Please more," she moans out loud that it rings louder than the rain outside.

"You feel so fucking good. Absolutely perfect," I mutter against her lips before leaning low and kissing the nape of her neck.

Every time my cock hits deep inside her cunt, my blood roared with possession. The primal need to have her all to myself felt too strong.

Our moans and grunts echoes through the room, mingling with our ragged breathing.

But when I look at her eyes that are filled with more than just lust, my heart hammers faster, making me feel something…a wave of comfort that I haven't felt for a long time.

The sense of trust she carries in those beautiful eyes makes me wish I can take her away from this rotten place right now. But we have to wait for the right time.

I'm willing to risk my life but not hers.

"I want to touch you," she murmurs and I let go of her hands as they make their way to my shoulder before leaning towards my back.

Resting my forehead against her temple I kiss her jaw and keep thrusting in and out of her tight, wet cunt. Channeling the same roughness, I feel her nails digging into my skin as they scratch down.

"More, Agatha. Make me hurt too," I whisper.

Her nails scrape my skin deeper that I feel blood is drawing out of my skin. But I don't care.

I need it just like she does.

Lowering my hand, I pull out the cross by the chain a bit and using the lower part, I fuck her ass at the same with my cock destroying her cunt.

Her eyes roll back in ecstasy that is giving her an

unimaginable and irresistible pleasure she never dreamt of. Her mouth turns slack like her mind can't function anymore to form any words to speak.

She is being driven insane and my God it's a sight to behold. But I want her to witness it…to feel more. I lean back a bit, raising her body by her throat so that we stay face to face. I pull out the chain and my cock, making both her holes empty.

"No, please," she protests but that doesn't last long when I put the cross inside her cunt and then my cock, making her pussy feel fuller.

"Fuck! Fuck! Fuck!" she yelps throwing her head back but I drag her face back towards me.

"Watch me, watch us joining together, little girl," I ordered.

Her eyes go down to my cock and the pendant penetrates her with the chain clinking against the wooden bed along with our skins slapping together.

Her cunt starts to twitch along with my cock that is moving along with the cross feeling her warmth and wetness

"I'm…I'm coming…" she mutters under her breath as if expressing her words openly that was roaming in her mind.

"Yes," I hiss, increasing my speed. "Come for me and milk my cock. I will spill deep inside your cunt that you will feel it the whole day tomorrow."

"Yes, yes. Come inside me," she pleads.

My cock aches for release as I feel myself coming anytime now. She raises her face and kisses me, highlighting both of our releases as we come together with a muffled moan. My body shudders as I spill my come inside her with a grunt.

Her body trembles from her orgasm as her nails sink into my skin. For a moment my vision darkens but when I let her lie down, I try to breathe evenly.

She is my dark paradise…my nirvana.

Her fingers had a bit of blood smeared from the scars she gave me but I wanted those to stay on my back as a reminder of her touch upon me.

I look down and slowly pull out of her, watching my come oozing out of her cunt along with my cross chain dropping down.

Fuck. How can she be so fucking addictive?

But I scoop up some of the come around her pussy and push it inside her, wanting it to stay there. Her cunt twitches slightly with her body giving a light shiver.

"You better keep it inside and don't clean yourself. I will be giving you more tonight," I whisper, kissing her lips.

"More?" she questions.

I chuckle lightly, kissing her lips. "When I said I want you to feel my come till tomorrow, then I meant it, little girl. And it will only be possible when I give you more."

I turn her over on her hands and knees making her yelp

in surprise as I let myself drown in her beauty and attraction.

Now that I have a taste of her, this one time won't be enough.

I will never get enough of her.
Never.
She is only mine.

Chapter Twenty Three

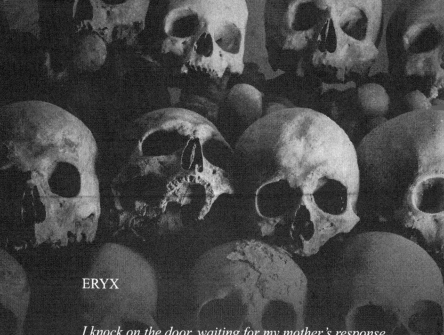

ERYX

I knock on the door, waiting for my mother's response.

"Come in," I hear her soft, muffled voice from the other side. Opening the door I step inside her room, finding her sitting on her bed and applying lotion on her arms.

She meets my gaze with a smile on her lips.

"Come here, sweetie," she murmurs, gesturing towards me and patting the bed to sit beside her.

Trying to control my racing heart, I slowly reach her and take a seat with my eyes casted down. She raises her hand and on instinct I flinch away, but when I feel her fingertips running along my hair I try to relax.

"Don't be like this around me, you know your mother will never hurt you."

No. I stopped believing that after I got to know the dark secret that she and father have been hiding from us.

She keeps caressing my hair before leaning in to kiss my head and pulling me closer to hug. Before this I have always sought for comfort in her arms but now...I loath it.

"I just wanted to let you know how proud I am," she murmurs. "For following our footstep and being part of the Magdalene. And your father and I are sure you will continue this ritual when we both go to heaven."

Never. I will never do that no matter what. I want to be as far as possible away from this hellhole.

Suddenly, she leans towards my cheek and lightly plants a kiss while her hand caresses my other cheek as it lowers down to my chest.

I scowl, feeling an instant discomfort, trying to move back from her hold. But she keeps me close against her chest, planting kisses on my neck and ear.

"W-what are you doing?" I whisper, anxiety and tension glooming in my tone.

"Showing my son how much I love him, showing him my appreciation," she rasps against my ear. Her hand slides down to my pants.

Fear grips me by my throat, knocking away the air out of my lungs.

"No, please stop...this is wrong, mother," I protest, moving her hands away. But it feels futile as she uses her strength and starts to pull down my pants.

"This is right. You deserve a reward and you should

please your mother, too."

"No! Let me go!" I yell.

She keeps touching me everywhere, holding my jaw and I don't hesitate with the chance to bite down harshly into her hand.

"Ow!" *she yelps, pulling away and I don't hesitate to run away.*

"Don't forget what will happen to your brother if you disobey me!" *Her words halt my steps with my hand pausing against the door.*

She found a weak spot, knowing well I won't be able to say no to her when I know the things she or father will make my brother go through.

I swallow the lump in my throat and feel my ears drumming with my heart pounding against my chest. I can barely breathe evenly as I walk back to her at a slow pace, even though I know there is no escaping.

I sit down again as she smiles softly, putting on the fake mask of being a loving and caring mother. But underneath she is nothing but a monster who is ripping me away from innocence bit by bit...day by day.

"Lie down," *she murmurs, pushing me down by my shoulder. My eyes are strained on the ceiling with my hands gripping the bed sheet tightly.*

"You will enjoy this, sweetie. Tonight will be the first step for you to become a man."

She kneels between my legs and pulls down my pants, making me feel vulnerable like never before. I feel her hand wrapping about my privates, moving it up and down.

Disgust clouds upon me, inking my soul with shame. My sight starts to blur from the tears forming in my eyes while mother keeps touching me…kissing me…everything…until I have nothing left.

I jolt awake, breathing heavily from the memory that took place in my nightmare. Swallowing deeply, I try to calm down my racing heart, when I feel the softness and warmth of a hand placed on my chest.

Agatha.

Letting out a sigh, I try to move her arm which makes her shift in her sleep. But when I look at her, I just feel my heart stopping from being mesmerized by her beauty.

It was nearly dawn when Agatha fell asleep and I joined her too. She is on her front, showing off her smooth back with my blanket covering her from her waist.

Her angelic face is illuminated by the ignited candles on the side tables. I softly caress her cheek as I push back a loose strand of her hair and tuck it behind her ear. She carries the beauty of the rose that she takes care of.

Innocent. Blooming. Captivating.

But it even carries dangers like the thorn of the rose that will prick me until my skin is bleeding.

A dangerous beauty that this beast is willing to die for.

I will save her as promised but first I need to repent for the dangers I'm causing her. I slowly leave the bed and put on some clothes before leaving the room.

When I get to the main hall room where the prayers happen, I find it empty. Perhaps, Geryon is still taking care of the dead bodies of those six women.

This is my chance.

I make my way to the checkup room and quickly make a new list of medicines for Agatha. Then I head to the closet where boxes of medicines are piled with the name of the patients written on it.

I find Agatha's box and take it out, searching for the small glass bottle containing green pills. Thankfully, I find the bottle and put it inside my pocket. Placing the box back inside the closet where it previously was, I shut the door.

"What are you doing here?" I hear Agnes's voice from behind that turns my body still.

I try to breathe evenly and put on a serious face before I face her with a cold expression like I always did.

"It's my job to be here. I don't need to explain to you," I mutter.

She is in her usual nun getup. Her skin looks slightly pale from the sleeping pills Agatha must have put in her tea. But I made sure to give her an antidote in case the dose was too high and seems like it helped her recover.

Though the look on her face expresses that she knows

what must have happened to her last night and who might have done it.

"But you don't check the medicine boxes that much. You simply give me the list and I stack them for you. Having doubts about my ability?" she asks, crossing her arms and stalking towards me.

"Doesn't hurt to be double sure. I'm just doing what I'm supposed to do," I mutter. "Get some rest for today, you look weak."

I walk past her but she grabs my wrist, halting my steps.

"And being with Agatha is something you are *supposed* to do?" she retorts, looking at me over her shoulder with a hint of sadness painting in her eyes.

"That's none of your business," I warned her.

"Everything that happens at the Magdalene is part of my business. Geryon doesn't like you being so close to her. You should keep your distance with her."

I grin darkly. "Geryon doesn't like it or *you* don't like it?"

She remains quiet with her jaws clenching with a rising anger. "She doesn't deserve you. And since when have you been so connected with a patient?"

"What is your problem with it? You have Geryon to give you attention, so go after him like you always do."

Her nostrils flare with rage burning in her eyes as she stands in front of me. "When will you understand that I want nobody but you. I go to your brother to make you jealous but you don't care."

"Trust me, I don't give a single fuck what you do with him."

She grabs my collar, leaning closer with her eyes watering. "Then why did you save me and bring me here? You wouldn't have done it if you didn't care. I still remember our first night together and more nights after that. But since that whore came here, you don't care about me anymore."

Without thinking I grab her jaw with a threatening grip and loom over her with a dark, heartless gaze. "Call her a whore again and I will cut your tongue out. Stay the fuck away from her and mind your own business."

She snickers at my words. "So caring and possessive of her already. But what will you do when she knows what you did to her?"

My silence boosts her suspicion and arrogance. "Did you tell her how you are the one prescribing her drugs that make her hallucinate? Does she know how you are drugging her just for money?"

Rage empowers me and I hold her throat, choking her tightly. She starts to struggle breathing with her eyes wide open like she wasn't expecting me to do this.

She asked for it so she will surely get it.

"I will tell you this final time. Stay the fuck away from her and me. You didn't mean anything to me then and you still don't mean anything to me. You never will. Don't fuck with me in this situation, Agnes, or I swear you will regret ever meeting me in the first place," I sneer under my breath before pushing her away with disgust.

She coughs holding her neck as I leave the room without a single glance or care for her.

I first met Agnes in a brothel where her pimp was beating the shit out of her that at one point she was unconscious. But when her pimp ordered his men to kill her because she got pregnant from one of her customers, I decided to save her.

Her pimp didn't care if she lived a rotten life or died like nobody. I bought her from him and took her to a hospital to get treated. She survived but her child didn't from the beating.

She had nowhere else to go so when I told Geryon about her he agreed to let her live in the Magdalene. But if I knew she was going to repay me this way, I would have left her at the hospital.

But she isn't lying either. She merely told me the truth I have been hiding from Agatha. And the sin I have been acting towards her is something I won't even forgive myself for.

But at that time, I had no other choice when Geryon told me about Tristen's proposal.

I step inside Geryon's chamber, who is sitting on his chair, drinking a glass of bourbon.

"You wanted to see me?" I ask, taking a seat in front of him.

He nods, passing me another glass and pouring the bourbon on it.

"A new patient is coming. We have to get her from Vailburg Port. Her brother-in-law has paid a million for it."

Like I cared how much money we are getting.

I take a sip of the bourbon letting the golden umber burn down my throat. "Is he aware of who we are?"

"Not fully. But he was somewhat of an idea. But he wants something else out of this. And we need the money to get more of our supplies for the patients."

I nodded. "What does he want?" I ask.

"His name is Tristen Arthur, one of Vailburg's richest men. His wife died last year and his sister-in-law, Agatha, lives with him now. But before dying his wife made her sister the sole owner of their family property. And to have that inheritance on his own he wants to prove to their lawyers that Agatha is mentally unstable because of her sister's death. He has been telling everyone she hallucinates her sister but Agatha keeps protesting that she only has nightmares about her. So, you have to find a way to make it happen."

I take another sip, nodding in response.

After committing so many sins, this one feels nothing to all those. I stopped feeling pity for the women who unknowingly became victims of this dark world because their fate cursed them and there is nothing they can do but accept it.

Agatha is going to be no different.

She will end up like one of the patients here or be one of Geryon's sacrifices. Rest is up to her.

"Maybe use those new medicines we recently got from Julius."

I frown, meeting his gaze. "The one that causes hallucination? But we only tried that on one patient so far. And not much changes have been recorded. So, we don't know what the side effects-"

He raises his hand to pause my words which only makes me infuriated because he knows how much I hated being interrupted. But he is even aware I won't protest about it if he does it.

"It doesn't matter. She is emotionally vulnerable after her sister's death which makes her an easy prey. You can even later put it in the files that her sister's death triggered her mental problems."

I nod again and finish the rest of the drink before standing up. "It will be done. I will add the medicines to her list when she arrives here. A daily intake of it after lunch should do the work."

"Good. Make sure that happens."

And it did happen.

She took the pills every day. It was slow at the first few days but it worked it's dark magic when she started to hallucinate which was triggered by the guilt of Helena's death. And if she keeps on taking more the effects would have stayed permanently too with her until she completely loses herself. Tristen could easily take her to the lawyers and show proof that is mentally unstable, even though she isn't.

But today it all stops.

I won't be leading her to destruction by taking advantage of her trust she placed upon me.

The only thing I will do is protect her and get her the fuck out of here before it's too late, because nothing has ever hidden from Geryon. And when he finds out he won't hesitate to make her his prey.

I will save you, Agatha.
I swear on my last breath.

AGATHA

A few days have passed by since our first night together. Geryon didn't come to me the next day for interrogation which made me feel relieved. He didn't know it was me and Beth.

But however, Beth suddenly seems to be…distant.

During our chores and eating times, she won't even look at me. I thought to wait for her to come around thinking maybe that horrific night might have affected her too much. But after a few more days it's clear something is wrong.

"What are you thinking?" Eryx asks from behind me as we sit together beside the window, watching the usual rainfall.

"Just thinking about Beth. Something feels wrong with her, she isn't talking to me or even looking at me."

"Did you get the chance to talk with her?"

I shake my head, leaning my head on his chest while he tightens his hold around my waist. "If you are worried, I can get her to talk with you tomorrow. I have some work to do with Geryon so meanwhile you can talk with her."

"That would be good," I mutter before we indulge ourselves in the silence.

"The rose is in much better condition," he mutters, making me gaze on the rose that was resting inside the jar beside the window.

I smile softly looking at it. "It just needed love and care. Even in the darkest place innocence can bloom."

"You worked your magic on it, that's why," he mutters and kisses my temple as I feel him smiling, and when I look over my shoulder, he indeed is. He rarely smiles genuinely and when he does…he looks mesmerizing.

From our first meeting, I have taken Eryx to be my captor who wanted nothing but to ruin me deep to my soul. He promised it but something made him change his mind and he became my savior.

But after knowing he is like a prisoner like me in the

Magdalene, I can understand his feeling…I can understand *him*. He is suffering through this darkness for his brother, whom he loved and cared for with every last bit of his heart that he thinks doesn't exist within him. But knowing his truth showed me the path towards that lost heart…that lost part of him that I am falling for.

He keeps caressing my arms with the back of his hands, sending a pleasing warmth through my skin. Every time his fingers touch me it feels like magic healing the broken parts of my soul.

He is like a dark magic to whom I'm starting to give up my soul and possibly my heart too, but only time will tell if this magic will bring my freedom or downfall.

Few hours later, Eryx and I leave the room where I go to for my instructed chores, going about my day and spending my time by working and having meals. By the end of the day, we are instructed to go to the confession room, which I have now noticed happens every five days. It is either held by Geryon or Eryx, but it's mostly Eryx.

When my name is called, I enter the room, closing the heavy door behind me as I stalk towards the confession booth. There are candelabras at the four corners of the walls with a small table where a few books are stacked on top.

There are two doors on the confessional box and as always, I go to the left side. I take my seat on the bench and pull the curtain close. A wooden net-like wall separates me and Eryx, who is in his usual priest dress with a white collar and his cross chain on his neck.

Despite the barrier, I feel his intense, scorching gaze heating up my skin and making my nerves alive with the dark desire I always feel around him.

As if he can read my emotions, I see him smirk through the gaps of the net and I feel my cheeks flushing.

"So, what do you have to confess, little girl," he says.

Little girl. The only name he calls me every time he wants to be intimate with me. And just from those two words I feel the atmosphere around us turning fiery.

"Nothing much," I whisper, looking down at my lap.

"Nothing much? So, you have been a good girl then?" he asks.

I swallow heavily, licking my lips. "You could say that."

"Hmm. But then something tells me you have had sinful thoughts that you wished to do. Am I right, little girl?"

I can tell he is trying to play a game with me. A game where things feel more forbidden between us and to be honest, I wanted to be a part of it.

So, if he wants me to confess, then I will *confess.*

"What do you want me to say, Father Eryx?" I lean closer, "That every time I'm with you, I think of nothing but being close to you. That I wish to rip off your clothes and kiss every inch of your beautiful body that makes me yearn for you more than ever."

He lets out a shaky breath while I continue confessing.

"I have sinful thoughts about you all the time because you are turning into an addiction for me that I can't let go of."

I bite my lip, touching my neck and skimming my hands lower. And the way his eyes follows my movements makes the scenario more erotic for me.

"Here is my confession, Father Eryx," I rasp. My heart racing at high speed with my nerves pulse rapidly. I snake my hand to the hem of my dress, before hitching it up and showing him my dripping cunt that made my panties wet.

"I confess, that right now, in this moment, I wish you would come to me and fuck me senseless. I think of feeling your cock stretching my cunt, marking me as yours. It is a sin for sure but I'm willing to commit it again and again."

"Are you making a priest turn into a sinner like you, little girl?" he groans, leaning closer, meeting my gaze.

I smirk. "How can I make you a sinner when you already are one? And let's face it, you love to commit sinful acts with me, Father Eryx. So, the question is…who should get the penance, you or me?"

I hear him pulling down his zipper and see him taking his cock in his hand, stroking it up and down. Though my eyes are fixated on him, my hands start to have their own mind and move to my aching pussy, that is only throbbing for his touch.

"To know who deserves penance, it's only fair if I confess my sins as well, don't you think?"

"Yes, please," I whisper.

"Here is my confession, little girl. At this moment, I want nothing more but to bring you to me, make you sit on my lap and take my cock so deep inside your cunt that you will feel your whole-body aching."

I breathe heavily and move my panties aside, circling my clit with my juices coating my fingers.

"I want you to ride me until your cunt feels sore that you won't be able to take it anymore but you still would want to continue. You know why?"

He pauses as we both remain silent with our ragged breathing filling in the air. He leans to the curtain on his side, pushing it open and nodding towards the entrance to his side of the booth.

He doesn't need to elaborate furthermore and I get up, walking towards his side and standing in front of him. The lust and desire electrifies our bodies as we keep gazing upon each other with a dark, hungry look.

"Because you fucking love it when I'm inside you, when I claim you as mine," he rasps. Leaning his hand forward, he snakes his hand behind my neck and pulls me closer, making me bend down.

"But you are right about one thing. This is a sin for sure, but even I'm willing to commit it every time for you. I don't care if I go to hell for this but I do know this is worth it."

I can't take it anymore and lean forward to kiss him, but he pulls me back by my hair, gripping it so tightly that I feel the soothing burn throughout my scalp.

"Tsk tsk," he tsks, shaking his head slowly with a devilish smirk. "Time to pray for your sins, little girl."

He lands a deep and swift kiss, before looking at me with a dark gaze. "But I need to do the same. So, we both need to go through the penance."

"How?" I whisper against his lips.

He moves back and suddenly picks me up, making me astride his lap. He turns with his back resting against the net wall. As if I weigh nothing to him, he turns me the same way.

"Let's pray, little girl. And you better take your penance and fulfill it with everything you got."

Grabbing my waist he pushes my ass up, closer to his face and draws my dress up. Sliding my panties aside, the moment I feel his tongue on my aching clit, I can't help but let out a yelp of surprise that I instantly try to suppress by pressing my hand against my mouth.

Dear God.

I hold onto his thighs for support and when I see his cock bulging behind his pants, I understand the wicked idea he is implying.

I unzip the zipper, pull out his cock and take it in my hand as I give it a few strokes.

Hard. Long. Thick. Drooling and pulsing.

He groans against my cunt that I feel it vibrating against my clit, which only highlights my pleasure even more.

Returning my focus back on his cock, I give it a long lick with my tongue before taking the tip into my mouth and start sucking him, while his mouth is busy devouring my pussy.

"Mmm," I hum against his cock, tasting the salty and addictive taste of his pre-come.

"Fucking God," he groans for a moment before returning back to licking me. I feel my thighs trembling with pleasure coursing through my pulsing nerves.

Suddenly, he pushes three fingers inside my cunt, thrusting in and out along with his tongue working its magic on my clit.

I moan silently, worried others will hear us who are waiting on the other side of the room, but the thrill of getting caught just sends adrenaline rushing down my spine.

Eryx lightly chuckles and lightly nibbles my clit as I nearly shriek from his touch.

"You like this don't you, little girl?" he rasps. "You are suppressing your moans so that nobody will hear you but at the same time you do want them to hear."

With one last lick he shifts our position again and leans me backwards by my waist that my back is pressed against his chest and my head leaning on his shoulder.

Spreading my thighs, he circles my clit with his other

hand wrapped around my neck. He softly bites my cheek. And all these intense sensation makes me moan out loud that I'm sure my voice was echoing even outside.

"That's my girl. Moan for me, show them who is worshipping your body. Let them know that you are only mine," he rasps in his deep voice against my skin, making my body buckle against his while I'm flying high on pure pleasure.

"Oh God," I whimper.

"So, fucking good," he whispers.

"But let's make it better for you. Put my cock inside your wet cunt, right now," he orders.

I lower my hand, and position his cock before slowly sliding it in and feeling full and stretched already.

"Ah! Eryx," I whisper.

"I bet they can all hear you now but now they know the euphoria you are experiencing," he groans, thrusting his hips as I feel his cock pushing in and out. My body surrenders to him completely.

"Fuck, every time my cock is inside that tight, wet cunt, I never want to leave. The more I have you, the more I crave for you every passing second. Your body tells me you are getting addicted to this, but trust me, little girl, you are the one who is hypnotizing me with your beauty and controlling me to the depths of my soul."

"More, please," I beg.

He chuckles darkly. "You want more," he sits up and facing our body towards the entrance, "-then ride my cock and take your pleasure."

And I do.

I move to a squat position, balancing my legs on the bench and my hands resting on his thighs as I move up and down rapidly on his cock.

And my God from this position I feel him deeper inside me.

"Fuck, yeah. That's it, keep going. Take what you want, little girl," he moans and fists my hair, leaning my head back.

My hips continue to thrust while I feel his cock swelling inside my cunt. My juices and his pre-come coats him as my insides start to quiver.

I feel myself reaching the peak point but only wished for this moment to last longer.

"Fucking hell, I'm getting close. Are you ready for my come, little girl? Ready for your cunt to be oozing with my load while you walk out of here?"

I whimper as his words trigger me to the last stop of my orgasm.

"Take my come. Every last fucking drop."

"Ah!" I cry out loud as my body shudders with the intense orgasm hitting my body like an ocean wave, making my body and soul float in the world of pleasure. I feel Eryx coming as well feeling him squirt his come inside me, making me full despite a few drops already leaking out and onto the floor.

My body turns slack as I lose my hold but Eryx engulfs me in his arm while we both breathe heavily and try to return back to reality.

"Is my penance served, Father Eryx?" I ask with a hushed tone.

"For now, little girl. For this sin, you need to confess to me again later in our room and be ready for more."

Chapter Twenty Four

AGATHA

Later that night, there is a knock on the door and when I open it, I find Beth standing on the other side. She frowns slightly like she wasn't expecting me to be here, but she quickly masks her curiosity.

"I need to talk with you," I murmur and guide her inside before closing the door.

She faces her back to me with her arms wrapped around herself like she was shielding herself.

"Beth, what is wrong? Why are you avoiding me?" I ask with worry rising in my tone.

"I'm not," she mutters under her breath and shakes her head vigorously.

"Is it because of that night?" I stalk towards her, to face her and urge her to look at me while answering. "Because of what you saw?"

She keeps her eyes cast down like she can't bear to look at me.

I hold onto her shoulders, trying to get her attention. "Please, Beth. If you don't tell me then how will I help you?"

She remains silent for a few seconds before I notice a lone tear coursing down her cheek. "You can't. Nobody can help me with this...nobody..." her words trail away.

Cupping her face, I meet her bloodshot eyes that make my heart ping with pain for her misery.

"I will help you, Beth. I promised you and I will keep that promise. Believe me-"

Beth moves back and takes a few steps away, shaking her head. "You can't...it's better to leave me alone. I don't want you to save me."

I frown in confusion. "But why?"

"Because I want to be part of this place..."

"What?" Utter shock consumes me.

"I have never been accepted anywhere, but I believe this is where I belong...I belong in the Magdalene...with the angels."

I shake her by her shoulders. "Have you lost your mind? What are you even saying? You said you want to be free and leave-"

There is a sudden, wild smile stretching across her face as she nods frantically. "I can be free. I can be free with the angels. They exist, Agatha...believe me."

My heart drops listening to her as something tells me that Geryon must have done something with her. Maybe he has fed her with his lies and bullshit about the ritual. And now she is starting to fall for his trap…maybe she already has.

"Beth, it's not true. It's all part of Geryon's fucked up ritual."

"No!" she screams, nearly hurting my ears with her screeching tone. "He told me the truth…he showed me. I have seen heaven…it…it exists."

"No, Beth! It's all lies!" I yell at her face, pleading to her with my eyes and now streaming tears to come back to reality.

"It's not. I see them now…" she whispers. Her eyes rapidly move in all directions like she can actually sense the presence of angels.

My heart thuds against my chest that I can feel it aching everywhere. My nerves racing faster as I look over my shoulder, following her gaze. There is nothing but the walls and yet Beth looks at them with a smile that sends shivers down my spine.

"Don't let him control you, Beth. Don't do this to yourself. You can fight this."

A frown exchanges with her smile with a raging look shadowing upon her face. "I am an angel. I am part of heaven and I will show you."

She puts her hand inside her pocket and retrieves a red

pill from her pocket. Suddenly she grips my jaw trying to make me have the pill but I catch her wrists, giving it all to push her away.

She struggles against my hold but doesn't give up. Using her leg, she kicks me and losing my balance I fall on the ground. Her hair curtaining around her as she continues to force me.

"Beth! Stop this madness!" I screamed but it's futile.

I try to push her body on the side table, hitting her back hard against it with the candelabra falling on the ground.

"You have to see this! You must!" she protests and holds onto my neck with a harsh grip that's hurting my windpipe.

I struggle to breath but she keeps choking me tightly. Panic consumes me as I start to lose the ability to think through this situation. I try to pry off her hand but it's no use.

But from the corner of my eye, I spot the candelabra and stretch out my hand to grab it. Just then she puts the pill close to my mouth, shoving it inside.

I hold the handle and in the next second I hit her temple with it just when the pill passes down my throat. Beth cries in pain and falls on the other side holding her now bleeding temple.

Fuck.

I start to choke from the aftermath of her suffocation but I quickly compose myself to look over Beth. Her eyes are slowly fluttering close with the blood pooling around her head.

Oh God. What have I done?

Horror shadows upon me with the fear that I might have hurt Beth so much that her life is at risk. I lean over her, lightly tapping her cheek.

"Beth, look at me. Can you hear me?" The agitation is crystal clear in my tone.

Her eyes are merely open but she still gives me that bone-shivering smile when I feel my vision blurry all of a sudden.

I shake my head but it instead triggers the ache in my head.

What is happening- shit. It's the pill.

"You will see it…It's real," I can only hear Beth's hushed voice but I can no longer see her. It's nothing but darkness engulfing me while my body starts to shiver vigorously like I'm having a seizure as my body falls on the ground. My blood turns cold as ice with my lungs begging for air.

A sudden white flash takes over the darkness and I see myself standing outside the Magdalene, instead of the bedroom. I frown in confusion and look around, finding nothing but the building and the forest. Everything looked dark and green. Even the sky had green instead of the usual grey shade.

I try to take a step forward but I can't move all of a sudden. My feet are rooted on the ground and I see dirty, burnt and bleeding hands growing out from the soil and grabbing my feet.

"Ah!" I scream out loud trying to push those horrific hands away. But their grip was so tight that I can feel it aching my muscles already. I look up when at the rooftop of the Magdalene I find a familiar face looking down at me.

Helena.

She is looking down at me with the same miserable, distant and cold expression she carried the last time I saw her.

"Save me." I can hear her voice even from this distance.

Desperation consumes me and I try to move away from the hands bounding me against my will.

"Helena! Don't move! I'm coming!" I scream while struggling to get away from the hands. But nothing is working.

Suddenly, I feel a dark shadow looming behind me. And it's truly a shadow that I find over my shoulder. A dark hand reaches out from it and cups my face.

"I will save her…" the voice is so deep and groggy that it sounds like a monster.

"No! I will!" I protest but it guides my face towards the roof where Helena is taking a step forward to her downfall.

"Helena no!"

But she doesn't stop.

"I will save her. Say yes…accept this darkness."

My throat feels clogged as I'm unable to speak, looking

back and forth from Helena to the shadow again and again. My ears start to tear up with fear of losing her but also feeling myself surrendering to darkness with no way of coming back.

But when I see her taking another step, I yell my answer. "Save her! Please!"

I witness Helena falling down again and unable to see her death again I shut my eyes, breathing heavily and sobbing at the same time.

I lost her…I lost her…

"Agatha," the soft voice of my sister fills my ears that it feels unbelievable.

My eyes slowly open and I see her…she is alive.

"Helena," I whisper as emotions overwhelm me beyond anything else with my heart pumping fast against my chest.

She is alive and smiling brightly…a smile I have long forgotten about.

"You are here…" my voice trails off. I look down and see my feet are free and without any further delay I wrap my arms around her in a tight hugging while I let my emotions flow out.

The caged sorrows and guilt I have been carrying for so long.

"You saved me, Agatha," she murmurs, running her hand along my hair. She feels so real like she never left me in the first place.

"You are my savior, my angel", she kisses my temple

and leans my face back, "I knew you would be there for me."

I cry harder, kissing her palms. "I'm so sorry for what I did…I'm so sorry, Helena. I should have told you everything…I should have done something before it was too late."

She shakes her head and kisses my forehead. I close my eyes, relishing in her feeling…her touch…her love.

I miss her so much that I'm willing to do anything to see her like this for the rest of my life.

"I can't believe you are here." My voice is choked and heavy from sobbing for so long.

"I'm here because of you…because you are my angel. *You are an angel,* Agatha."

I frown. "I am?"

She nods with a soft smile making my heart pang. "You truly are. And soon you will realize it."

"But I don't want to lose you," I grab her hands tightly, afraid she will disappear again, "please, stay. Don't go away, Helena," I beg her.

"You can see me all you want. Anytime…anywhere."

"How?" I immediately ask.

"Just like the way you came here right now."

The pill.

I have to take it and I will be able to see my sister as much as I want. I don't care if I need to surrender myself to darkness and make a deal with the devil because for Helena,

I'm willing to do anything.

    Even to get tainted by the devil.

Chapter Twenty Five

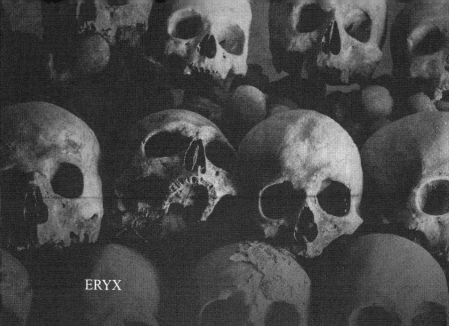

ERYX

Holding the lantern, I walk through the dark forest with my feet making scrunching sounds against the fallen leaves.

I have left Agatha with Beth so that they can talk with each other. For the past few days, she has been worried about Beth, so I don't hesitate to let her speak with Beth and resolve any issues they are having.

Meanwhile, I'm going deep inside the forest where Geryon called me to come to the usual spot.

Few minutes later I reach the graveyard side of Merry Heights where the dead bodies of several women that Geryon has sacrificed in the ritual are buried.

Using various tree branches I made cross signs over the dead bodies to keep the marks. And among those lines of crosses, I find Geryon at the corner side, digging a hole with a shovel.

When I get closer to him his grunts get louder before he stops his motion and looks over his shoulder.

"Took you long enough," he mutters, nodding towards another shovel, gesturing to me to join him. A pile of rotten bodies and heads are located near the grave Geryon is digging. They are mostly covered in mud and few worms with a pungent smell filling my nostrils, but I'm used to the sight and smell.

Taking the shovel, I plunge it into the ground and scope out the few grasses along with the soil before throwing it behind me.

"It's been more than a month now, but I don't see the effects on Agatha that you promised to do," Geryon murmurs while continuing digging.

I control my hesitation and avoid looking at him.

"It will take time."

"How much longer? I have to answer to Tristen. Just because you tortured him doesn't mean we won't finish the work he paid us for."

I remain silent and start moving to the other side to dig. Geryon doesn't speak for a while as we dig a deep hole until we are below the ground.

"I will get the bodies," he mutters before leaving me to finish digging.

I hear the dragging sound of the bodies and after a few more shoves I'm done. I turn to leave the hole, putting my hands on the ground and raising myself up when suddenly Geryon hits me with the shovel, pushing me inside the empty grave.

"Fuck," I grunt from the pain buzzing in my head and cheek.

"What the fuck is your problem?" I sneer at him, holding onto my aching skin as I lie on the soil.

Geryon stands tall on the other side rooting the shovel on the ground. "You are becoming my problem. I gave you one fucking thing to do and suddenly you are hesitating to do it all because of a cunt."

My jaw clenches as rage starts to darken my soul. I balance on my elbows while he continues to speak.

He kneels, resting his hands on his knees. "You have done this thousands of times, so, why are you changing your actions for a random girl?"

"I don't owe you any explanation and-"

He tsks, interrupting my words. "I own your ass, you asshole. Don't forget what I've got against you and I won't hesitate to-"

"I fucking know!" I yell with vexation setting my blood on fire. I stand up giving him a death glare.

"Your mere presence reminds me that you've got my own brother hidden in some place. Every fucking time I look at you, I remember how because of you I can't fucking see him!" I seethe through my clenched teeth, pointing a finger at him.

"You don't have to remind me every fucking day that you have turned my life into a living hell the day you found us in jail and to get us bailed you got me to agree to your fucked up arrangement. The same arrangement we both were escaping from!"

I snicker. "I curse your wretched life every fucking day but God must hate me for still keeping you alive."

He lets out a dark laugh, throwing his head back as if my words were hysterical for him.

"There is a God and he saves me because of the angels I have sent to Him. They protect me because of what I have given them."

I shake my head in disappointment. "Only if you could see the reality then you would feel nothing but disgust about yourself."

"Not me, brother. *You* are not seeing reality. This dark world is trying to blind you from it and the barrier is that fucking bitch," he spits out his words.

"Don't you fucking dare say a word about her. Keep her out of this or else I'll cut your tongue out."

"She is using you and you know it but you are a fucking pussy to see through it. But you have to finish your work. We need the money for our supplies and other necessities. You have to prove by next week that she is mentally unstable with proof. If you fail then I will kill your brother."

Ferocity and rage blinds my heart and soul as I feel the deepest urge to bury Geryon in this very graveyard alive.

"When will you stop with your sins, Geryon? When will all this end?" I ask.

"This is a never-ending chain, Eryx. And even if you kill me this will still continue. Cut off one tree to clear the field but the roots will still remain in the soil to bloom out more of them. It's the law of nature, brother."

"Just let her go. She doesn't deserve to be part of your fucked up plans. If you need money then we can get it from any other rich fucker. Vailburg has many of those assholes."

He raises his eyebrows, faking a surprised expression. "Who knew Eryx was capable of feeling so connected to a girl?"

He bites his lip and takes the shovel in his hands. "When was the last time you felt emotional for a woman? Your mother when she made you fuck her? Or your father when he made you suck his-"

"Shut the fuck up before I bury you in this grave instead of those bodies!" I threaten him, not wanting to recall those moments when my own parents raped me and my brother.

One of their another fucked up part of the ritual that we were bound to do to protect each other. Our childhood was the most terrible stage of our lives that no child should ever go through.

Just listening to Geryon mentioning those moments

makes my blood boil that I wish I could kill my parents all over again.

Geryon laughs at my outburst and stands up.

"You have always been a target, Eryx. First by your parents then by me and now by that whore. But if you don't do what I've told you then don't forget what will happen to your brother. Don't lose him for your stupid love for a nobody."

He roots the shovel on the ground to give me a leverage to climb with before he starts to walk away.

"Put the dead bodies in the grave and come back to my chamber. And stop protecting Agatha when you know well you can't do it. Otherwise, you will be in that grave."

His scrunched footsteps echo away when I get off the hole and dust away the dirt from my clothes.

Every time I try to go against him, he uses my brother as a weapon to lower my ambition, turning me into his slave again.

Every time he mentions what he holds against me, I remember the moment Geryon came into my life whom I expected to be my savior but he was like a fucking fox in a sheep's skin, waiting for the right time to make me his prey.

My gaze returns to the piled up, half cut rotten bodies and I start to put them inside the grave. He always made me do this, indirectly making me part of his fucked-up ritual where I cover his sins.

After putting all the bodies in place, I start to cover it with the soil by using the shovel. And with each fill the memories of Geryon's first step in my life comes alive.

"You have a visitor," the guard says, opening the cell. I frown in confusion as I stand up and follow him outside to the visitor's room.

Few of the booths were already filled with the prisoners talking with the innocent ones on the other side.

"Booth seven," the guard mutters, nodding towards the right corner of the booth.

I take a seat where a man is already sitting with the phone held against his ear.

He looked a few years older than me with his dark hair pushed back. Five o'clock shadows filled around his sharp jawline. His pale skin being illuminated by the ceiling light falling upon him. He was dressed in a priest's clothes with a cross chain around his neck. But there was something about him that made me feel like I knew him...like he knows me as well.

He grins when I take a seat and follow suit, holding the phone on my side against my ear with the mirror separating us.

"Finally glad to meet you, brother," his deep, vibrant voice speaks from the phone while I watch his lips moving.

"Who are you?" I ask.

He leans forward, remaining silent for a few seconds

before he looks at me with his eyes raking up and down like he was analyzing me.

"Years of being part of a royal life, getting all the privileges and opportunities...going to the best medical college Vailburg could offer, and all lead to what? Living a rotten life behind bars."

I snicker darkly. "It's way better than the prison I was in since the day I was born. Don't act like you know shit about me."

"I know a lot more about you than you do. After all, you are my step-brother."

Confusion and shock overwhelm me as my mind races with questions after questions. But as if he can read my mind, he resolves my curiosity by giving me answers.

"Your parents were part of the Magdalene before they were even married. In that group our father met my mother and they fucked." He didn't flinch while revealing the secret about his mother being fucked by my father.

"When she got pregnant our father refused to support her because she wasn't part of a rich family. Even after giving birth to me, he refused and told her to die if she can't carry the burden of my responsibility. Like a weak soul, she killed herself and I was sent to an orphanage."

Despite knowing my father was the reason his mother died, he still sounded like he was in favor of my father's side.

"But I soon got to know about all this a few years ago.

And I was going to come to meet you and your family. But when I arrived in Vailburg last week, I found through the news that you and your brother killed them."

I grin. "If you want me to apologize for ruining your plans for a family reunion then you are wasting your time. I have got no remorse for killing them after what they did."

"I know what they did and you two killed them for ruining your life. But if you work with me, continuing on the path that you left, then I can help you with something."

His words caught my attention, making my body still alert. "What do you mean?"

"I want to resume the rituals of the Magdalene. You will be joining me in that journey and never return here. In exchange I will give you something precious."

"Take your deal and shove it up your ass you fuck face. I am never returning to that fucked up world and no amount of money will make me agree to it." I was ready to get up and leave without a second thought, when his offer caught me off guard.

"I will help you and your brother be free from here. Even the death sentence will be lifted off."

I remain still, unable to think or speak for several seconds while he continues.

"He won't get involved in the Magdalene, that I guarantee you. It's you that I need because your parents started with you first. You are the first thorn of the blooming flower. All

you have to do is agree to my deal and you both will be free."

My breathing turns ragged with my throat turning dry as words vanish from my mind.

My brother never should have been part of my parent's dark world that they sincerely believed in. After killing them we didn't hesitate to accept our fate that will be set by the law of Vailburg.

We are no longer the heirs of one of the richest families in Vailburg. We are nothing but murderers who killed their own parents...we are psychotic and mentally ill for committing such a crime.

Some are calling us the devil's spawn.

But none of it bothered us...though I didn't want my brother to suffer death at such a young age when he is getting the chance for a better life.

It required me to sacrifice myself again for him...but if I had to walk down the path of fire again, then so be it. Because I wanted him to have a second chance in life where he will be miles away from the shadow of the Magdalene. I was unable to protect him then, but I won't let this chance go away.

"But if he won't be part of the Magdalene then where will he stay with me?" I ask.

He shakes his head. "He won't be staying with you. When he is set free then he is the controller of his own fate, wherever he wants to go, it's all up to him."

My brows furrow together. "Then how will I meet him?"

"You won't ever meet him again. He has already been through so much by staying with you, don't you think for once if you let him go then he can finally have a chance towards a better life?"

He leans back with a sigh. "Afterall what did he do with you?"

His question reminded me of the times he was forced along with me into those rituals...killing those innocent women... sometimes getting touched and fucked by strangers...even our own parents.

He was right. What did my brother get with me?

Misery. Darkness. Pain.

I still remember how lost and lonely he looked every night after a random man or woman would touch him or take him to a room. He never shared his agony with me, suppressing every ounce of horrific moment he faced.

He was better off without me...he will be alright without me...

Swallowing the lump in my throat I looked back at the stranger who was going to be our savior and destroyer. His eyes reflected his thoughts like he knew what my answer was going to be but he remained silent to hear it himself.

"I agree with your deal."

I let out a soft grunt when the final dirt is thrown, covering the entire grave. Sweat droplets form on my forehead that I wipe away with the back of my hand. Going to a nearby tree,

I take off two branches and use the dangling vines, tying it into a cross. Going back to the grave I stab the ground with the cross and say my prayers for the innocent souls to be free from the shadow of sins and darkness.

I let out a shaky breath and made my way back to the Magdalene where now I had someone worth waiting for.

Agatha.

There is no way Geryon is going to give up his motives for Agatha, so the only way I can save her is through Julius. All I have to do is contact him with the help of the radio and she should be free from here.

And me?

I will stay behind to pay for my acts of going against Geryon and for Agatha I'm willing to accept those with open arms.

Geryon told me to come to his chamber after I'm done with my task but I have no interest in seeing his face, so I make my way back to my chamber. I open the door, expecting to see the soft, angelic smile of Agatha while she greets me with a kiss like she did nowadays. But instead, I find Agath lying on the ground, unconscious, and Beth right beside her with blood pooling around her head. And the sight made my blood turn cold and my heart pang instantly.

I quickly check on Agatha, feeling her body being suddenly so warm like she has high fever. I hold her, resting it against my chest as I check her pulse. It's normal but her suddenly pale skin told a different story.

"Agatha," I mutter her name, lightly tapping her cheek, but she is unresponsive. Even her lips are turning into an ash shade like she is dehydrated.

Her temperature needs to cool down first. I put her to bed first and quickly rush to the bathroom, turning on the tap at high speed as it fills with cold water.

I return back to check on Beth as well. I kneel beside her, carefully lifting her head and checking her pulse but unfortunately there is none. She lost too much blood and she was already physically weak for the past few days.

Thinking of dealing with her later, I place her head down and pick up Agatha in my arms and I carry her to the bathroom, slowly descending her onto the cold water. The bathtub is half full but I keep it running until it reaches up-to her chin.

I tap her cheeks again but she remains still which only made my hidden fear come out in light, along with agitation setting my nerves on fire.

But she suddenly jolts awake with her eyes wide open and inhaling a deep breath. She looks frantically around like a scared child, gripping tightly onto the sides of the bathtub.

"Hey, look at me," I cup her face, noticing her teeth clattering like she is no longer feeling warm, but I can still feel her skin being boiling hot, "it's okay. I'm here. I'm here."

She swats away my hands and I notice the redness

forming in her eyes.

"No! You can't be here! Leave!" she screams and starts to push me away, splashing the cold water at me as she keeps hitting after hits against my chest.

"Agatha, stop! It's me."

But my words go unheard as she screams and writhes like I'm a monster from her nightmare she is trying to get rid of. "I won't let you take me away! I'm not leaving! Don't fucking touch me," she threatens.

"Agatha, get a hold of yourself."

"No! No! She is fading away...no! Let me go!" she screeches at the top of her lungs that I can see her veins popping out on her throat and forehead.

"It's me, Agatha. Come back. Focus on my voice," I mutter, begging her to find her way back to me. "Follow my voice."

I hold her hands tightly, bringing her closer so she has no way of escaping. Suddenly, she blinks rapidly as if my sound is her anchor and is returning back to reality. Her body starts to calm down as she meets my gaze.

"Eryx?" she asks.

I nod, both our breathing turns harsh and ragged. "It's me. I'm here, Agatha. I'm here for you."

She frowns, shutting her eyes close for a moment before she reopens them and this time it turns blank like all those previous rage and madness vanished into thin air. I loosen my grasp on her and she leans back, facing away from me.

She is silent for a long time, looking down at the water surrounding her and seeming to be pondering deeply about something. Her breathing is ragged but soon it evens out.

"What happened, Agatha?" I ask her, running my hand along her hair to her back as a gesture of comfort.

"I want to be alone…" Her words fade away.

"But-"

"Please, Eryx. I need a moment to myself." The desperation in her tone is crystal clear and I don't argue furthermore as I leave the bathroom.

I look at Beth's lifeless body and decide to take care of the situation. Picking up her body, I carry her to the checkup room, laying her body into the bed before I go back to my room and quickly clean the blood.

When returning back to the checkup room again, Agnes crosses my path.

"Agnes, go to the checkup room and clean a dead body. Make sure there is not a spot of blood left."

She frowns in confusion. "Whose dead body?"

"Bethany's."

"But how did she-"

I raise my hand, halting her question. "That's not the issue. Do as you are told and I will take care of the rest later."

I don't let her argue and leave her to deal with it as I head back to the bathroom.

Agatha is still in the same position I left her in and the stillness of her body says she hasn't moved for a second after I left.

I kneel beside her again and touch her arm lightly which is covered with goosebumps because of the cold water. "Agatha, you have to tell me what happened, otherwise I can't help you. Please tell me. The worry and fear is eating me alive."

Her bottom lip wobbles while her eyes are fixated on the water. "I was with Beth...asking if something was bothering her and she was ignorant at first. But she then started to speak about being...an angel."

I immediately understand where this is leading to and who is behind it.

Geryon.

Agatha told me later that Beth was with her that night and perhaps Geryon knew about Beth's presence, taking advantage of the situation he must have manipulated her into thinking she is an angel. He must have fed her the green pills too in order to control the strings of her mind more. No wonder she was suddenly weak and acting off.

"We both started to argue and she said..." her voice trails away.

"She said what?" I ask, leaning closer.

"She wanted to show me that angels exist and she forced me to have a pill."

I feel my heart stop.

"We fought against each other and while defending myself I hit her with the candelabra."

"Did you take the pill?" *Please say no. Please say no.*

She nods, making my worst fear come to reality.

"I saw her…"

"Saw who?"

"Helena…I saw Helena. She was with me and I was her angel."

I cup her face, urging her to look at me but when I notice the loss of emotions in her eyes, the dread of losing her started to shadow upon me.

"Agatha, it wasn't real. You didn't see Helena. She is dead and what you saw was a hallucination. The pill-"

"No. It was *real*." Determination and an unknown insanity are oozing in her tone. "I could feel her and she forgave me. She said she forgives me because I saved her. I was able to repent for my sin, Eryx. I was finally free from the guilt."

Fuck. This is already getting out of control. I'm well aware how strong the pill is, that only one is enough to ruin anyone's mind.

I shake my head. "Agatha, I'm begging you. Please listen to me. None of it was real-"

She abruptly stands up, sloshing the water on the ground before she gets off the bathtub and pushes away from my touch. "Stop saying that! You don't know what I saw!"

She leaves the bathroom, making me follow her but as she is about to leave the room, I pull her back by her arm feeling a sudden rage coursing through me like lava.

"Where are you going?"

She squirms against my hold like she suddenly loathed my touch. "Away from you! It's pointless to tell you what I saw."

I snicker under my breath unsarcastically. "I know what it is like, Agatha. Don't forget how my parents forced me into the ritual of the Magdalene. So, I know what you saw and felt. Everything would feel real but in reality, those are nothing but hallucinations."

She shakes her head frantically with a familiar wildness taking over her. The pill is still in her system and fucking up with her mind.

Bringing her closer to me, I press her back against the wall and cup her cheeks, urging her to look at me…to guide her way back to reality.

"Agatha, please. I beg you to listen to me. I know everything is like a haze of confusion in your head," I mutter in a calm, soft voice, caressing her skin with my thumb, "I know you can barely see anything clearly. But give it some time, take control over it. The Agatha I know is way stronger than the darkness she is going through. Please."

I rest my forehead against her, feeling her body shivering.

But she isn't getting away from my hold either.

"Find your way back to reality…find your will, Agatha. Come back to me…please," I plead in a hoarse tone, looking into her eyes.

Her eyelids close gradually like she is taking my advice and finding her way back. She is stronger than the trap Geryon laid on her and I know she will come back.

She is Agatha.

My Agatha.

"Take deep breaths with me," I guide her, as we start to synchronize our breathing, inhaling and exhaling deeply. Eventually I sense her body relaxing against mine as her hands curl around mine.

"That's it…deep breaths," I whisper.

I lose track of time as we remain in that position for a long time. But it is worth the wait, seeing that innocence and purity returning back in her eyes followed by the glimmers of her tears.

"It's okay. I got you," I mutter, lightly kissing her lips, tasting her addictive sweetness.

I see the goosebumps on her body that are still wet from the cold water. I help her change clothes, dry up her skin and let her have my T-shirt and pants. She remains silent when I guide her to the bed and make her lie down to rest. But a look of realization crosses her face as she looks on the ground and then back at me with a frown.

"Beth? Where is she?" she asks in a croaked voice.

My throat tightens as I know this will affect her in a bad way but none of it was her fault.

"She lost a lot of blood..." my voice trails off as I'm unable to put it in the right words that will reveal the truth but at the same time won't hurt her.

But Agatha understands the hesitation behind my words and closes her eyes in remorse.

I hold her hand immediately for comfort, leaning closer to her. "It was not your fault-"

"I hit her with the candelabra. Of course, it's my fault that she died-"

"You acted on defense. If you didn't try to save yourself then she might have killed you. It is not your fault. She was already physically weak and seems like she even took the pill that made her mentally weak as well."

But she still cries silently with her nose sniffling, letting sorrow control over her emotions.

"Don't let yourself drown in guilt, Agatha. It has already made your life very miserable. But I will save you from it very soon. All I ask is for you to give me some time and have faith in me," I mutter, tucking a loose strand behind her ear.

"I don't know what else to do, Eryx. I see things that I haven't in real life...things that have existed in my nightmares but now...all of it feels real. I swear I saw Helena and she forgave me." The desperation in her voice made my heart shatter for her.

She feels so lost…so alone, despite my presence. I have rooted the seed of despair in her life the day she got here, but Geryon poisoned her more with the green pill. I'm sure he even convinced Bethany to force Agatha to have the pill when he realized I might not be able to do his task.

But now things are getting out of hand. The only way to save Agatha is to get her the fuck out of here.

"It was all a hallucination. None of that exists…" my voice trails off.

She rubs her eyes before dragging her hands along her face. "I don't know what's real and what's hallucination."

She pauses looking at me with a suspicious look.

"A-are you real?" she asks, leaning away from me like she was afraid I would turn into one of the monsters she has nightmares of.

I cup her cheek, feeling myself on the verge of shedding tears for her. "No, Agatha. I'm real. The pill is just messing with your mind. But it will all be okay. Trust me."

I press my forehead against hers.

"Please have faith in me, Agatha. I have already lost so much in life…I'm not willing to lose you because of my darkness. I won't let it happen."

I lightly kiss her lips as she returns the favor like she is aching for a gentle touch.

"This is real, Agatha," I whisper against her lips.

She nods slowly but I can still sense the cloud of hesitation looming over her.

"This is real," she whispers.

I bring some water for her to drink along with some medicine for her aching head and it will help her sleep. I quickly changed out of my wet clothes before joining her again. Few moments later, her eyes gradually close as she falls asleep while my eyes never leave her face.

Even when sleeping she looks so beautiful and innocent that it hurts. I have never felt something like this before for a girl and I never expected to feel this protectiveness for Agatha.

She is starting to make me feel those dead emotions that I buried in the depths of my dark heart.

Calmness. Passion. Love.

I have given up on happiness and love ages ago. Letting it die like a dead flower without being nurtured by light. But something about Agatha, brings that hope alive, making a part of me think there could be happiness…there could be love.

CHAPTER TWENTY SIX

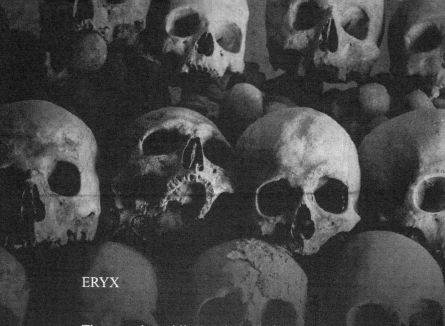

ERYX

The next day while Agatha rests in my room, I head to Geryon's chamber, knowing he won't be there at the moment. During this time, he is checking all the chores the patients are doing throughout the building.

So, I have enough time to contact Julius through the radio. This is the only communication device in Geryon's chamber but sometimes due to the weather it's tough to send messages.

Finding the table at the corner of the room beside his bookshelf, I close the door behind me before I take a seat. There is an attached small shelf where a pen stand is resting. I turn it around, letting the shelf shift up and revealing the radio that is hidden behind. Geryon had this mechanism built to avoid the patients from contacting anyone. Just as I'm about to switch on the radio and connect the wirings, Agnes enters the room.

I meet her gaze over my shoulder, seeing the suspicious expression frowning on her face. She saunters towards me with her arms crossed while she remains quiet.

"What are you doing here?" I ask, ignoring her and finishing setting up the radio. But then I remember I can't give any direct message to Julius because she will know why I'm here and inform Geryon.

So, I think of another way. Morse code.

I pull out the telegraph key that Agnes has no idea of and connect it with the radio's signal wire before placing it on the table.

"I wanted to ask about what happened with Bethany?" she questions, standing right beside me.

"I told you to stay out of it. Your work was to take care of the body and you did. No need to put your nose into businesses that don't concern you," I retort and bring my focus back on the radio.

After Agatha fell asleep, I took care of Bethany's body and buried her in the grave among the others with Agnes's help. I later told her about it before coming here but she didn't react much to it as she was still recovering back to reality. Though later she started to sob from guilt in my arms. And the only way I helped her was through my words and touch of comfort.

"You are hiding something for sure but when I find out, I

will surely tell Father Geryon about it. That time we will see who is more controlling, you or him," she seethes through her clenched teeth with anger painting her tone.

But at the moment I wanted her gone before Geryon came back.

"Do whatever the fuck you want, Agnes. Get the fuck out of here before I smash your head against the bookshelf," I threaten her and after making sure the telegraph key is connected, I start to tap on the knob that made the continuous clack sound of every dit and dah signal I started to send.

Thankfully Agnes gets the message and while feeling her scorching glare upon me, she finally leaves the room. I tap quickly on the knob and send out the message to Julius, where I'm hoping he must be receiving it.

Need your help to save her. Bring a boat on the back side of the island by tomorrow. Hide it beside the vast palm tree and wait at the Vailburg dock. I will be arriving with her in three days.

He will understand whom I'm referring to and I hope he gets my message on time. I pull back the connections and put everything back in place, deciding to leave quickly. But as I pass by the table, a name catches my sight, making me halt instantly along with my heart racing.

Eros.

My brother.

The one whom I gave up my life for to Geryon.

I swipe away the other papers resting on top of his name before bringing the piece of slightly brown, crumpled paper.

Without wasting time, I start to read every line, every word written on the paper. But the more I read the more I feel my heart crumbling into uncountable pieces as my soul darkens with sorrow and loss.

It's a letter that was sent a few weeks ago, giving the overall update about Eros's condition. He was living under the basement of some shitty house and doing odd jobs as a garbage boy in Brinecliff, another island which is a few miles away from Vailburg but the state of it has a more miserable scenario.

But when I read the part that he is physically not doing well and had no means to treat himself, it took everything in me to control myself from fleeing this place and going after my brother.

"Fuck," I curse under my breath, feeling my hands tremble as I put back the paper. But then I find an open book with a rough drawing on it. I take it and go through the pages but I can't understand anything as the language seems to be from ancient times. With the brown and torn edges of the paper it's clear this was written a long time ago. I see the rough drawing of a circle similar to the one Geryon performs on but at the center there was a human like figure instead of the skulls. This seems to be a different ritual and I'm not sure if it's part of the Magdalene or not.

I quickly put all the things back to its original place and made my way out of the room. Now that I know where Eros is, I can go after him...I can finally save him.

But Agatha's safety is in my mind too because she is important as well. Now all I can do for now is wait for Julius to send the boat so that I can take the chance and take Agatha far away from this place so she will no longer be in the shadows of the Magdalene.

This time I won't let fate defeat me. This time I will take the leash and control it to mend my past and present in order to lean towards my future. All I hope is it doesn't get too late.

AGATHA

I suddenly jolt awake from deep sleep, unaware what awakened me. I look at my side, finding it empty.

The moonlight streams through the window with the fog covering the view outside. The candelabras on either side of the bed illuminates the room furthermore. Reaching for the glass of water on the left table side, I finish it in a few sips.

I feel slightly weak from what happened the day before yesterday but I'm trying to recover as much as possible. Though a part of me couldn't stop thinking about Helena again and again. Eryx told me to trust him on this and realize that it was all fake...a hallucination.

But it felt too real to be denied.

Later Eryx informed me about the boat that must have arrived already and soon we will be out of here. We were both going to be free, but I couldn't stop thinking that even if we left then Geryon won't stop to hunt us down.

He won't accept such betrayal from Eryx.

I think to look for Eryx and step out of the room. It's dead silent in the main room. I wrap my arms around myself as I continue to walk when I hear muffled screaming from the upper floor.

I follow the sound and reach the floor, seeing the balcony doors opened where I'm assuming Agnes to be standing. Her body is shivering with her shoulders trembling like she is crying.

I slowly walk towards her while looking over my shoulder to see if someone else is there too. But it's only Agnes.

But when I reach almost to the doorway, I find another shadow beside her and move back, hiding in the darkness.

"And you couldn't tell me this before!" I hear Geryon's vengeful tone as he yells at Agnes. I try to take a peek and see him holding her face by her jaw tightly, and it is clear she is hurting from the look of agony floating in her eyes.

"You were useless when you first came here and you are still useless now," he seethes through his clenched teeth, looking like a monster who was about to pounce on Agnes to hurt her more.

He lets her go like he feels disgusted while she continues sobbing and trembling. "I warned that asshole...I warned him if he didn't do his work then he would face consequences. And yet that fucker went behind my back," he sneers.

He breathes heavily and closes his eyes like he is trying to calm himself but is failing miserably.

"At first Eryx fed those pills to Agatha and fucked up her mind according to the plan. I even told him to increase the dose so that he can gather the evidence quickly to send it back to Tristen. He didn't pay us for nothing. He said the lawyers will make Agatha the permanent owner of her inheritance if the evidence of her unstable mentality wasn't shown soon enough. But fuck knows what happened to that asshole that now he is willing to risk everything."

The moment Geryon finishes his words I feel my world stopping...my heart freezing.

This can't be true...he must be lying.

But there isn't an ounce of hesitation in Geryon's tone which only gives the proof that he is telling the truth...a truth that was hidden by Eryx who is my destroyer after all.

And this truth has shattered my trust in him in the blink of an eye.

"I-I told him that you won't spare him when you will know what he was doing but he kept ignoring-"

"I didn't fucking ask for your commentary on your weak ass threats."

Agnes shrinks back while her cheeks are glistening from the tears she shed. But she still leans towards him and holds his hand like it was her way to show and feel comfort.

"I will never go against you. I am always loyal to you Father Geryon. My heart and soul only belong to you-"

He pries away from her hold and pushes her away.

"Keep your nonsense to yourself. Get the fuck out of my sight," he warns before looking ahead at the forest.

"But-" Her words are left incomplete when Geryon slaps her right across her cheek so harshly that she falls on the ground, holding her face and sobbing harder.

"One more word and I will throw you off this balcony. Leave!" he orders.

This time she listens and stands up to leave. I quickly hide back as she runs away down the hallway and reaches her room before shutting the door.

"I've had enough of his bullshit. No more chances for you, Eryx," Geryon mutters to himself.

"You have signed your soul to me, so, you bet your ass I will own it until your last breath. Even your death will be controlled by me," he snickers under his breath, "-you are more interested in saving people's lives huh? Let's see who saves you tomorrow. It all ends tomorrow."

He lets out a shaky breath before arching his head back and looking at the sky.

"Everything ends tomorrow," he promises.

My heart hammers against my chest as I swallow the lump in my throat. I could barely think through after finding how Eryx was keeping me in the dark from his truth.

Every time I saw a hint of uncertainty and distrust, I tried to ignore it. But I should have seen those as signs of the lies he was telling me.

I look at Geryon who is unaware of my presence and I take that chance to escape and return to our- *Eryx's* chamber. As I close the door behind me, I walk like a lifeless person to the bed and sit down while trying to look for a way to mend back my broken heart.

But I let Eryx destroy it.

I defy myself to shed a tear for him after what he did to me. He made me fall into his trap…and he even made my heart his victim as well.

I don't know for how long I stay seated on the bed, thinking mindlessly about the betrayal I have faced. But when the door unlocks with the person who ruined me entering the room, do I return back to reality.

When his gaze meets mine, he senses the sudden emptiness in my eyes and frowns with a look of fret crossing his face. He comes towards me, kneeling in front of me and holding my hand like he cares about me.

"Agatha, what happened?" he asks. But none of his concerns mean anything to me. I pull away my hands and keep looking at those same eyes that trapped me.

Silence is my only response, but in that quietness, he is able to put the missing puzzles together and is starting to understand my ignorance.

"Agatha…I…" His words fade away like he is unable to put the right words to explain himself. But even he is aware that I'm no longer going to believe him.

"How could you?" I whisper. "You saw me struggle and cry in distress so many times. You pretended to care for and I fell for them like a fucking moron."

His eyes close like he is truly in pain but I don't help to soothe his pain because he deserves it.

"I didn't have a choice. I have been a prisoner of Geryon's orders for years just to protect my brother." He tightens his hold on my hands, silently begging to listen to his side of the story.

"I have done this before with other patients and I thought I wouldn't care about doing the same with you. But when I saw you shared the same darkness as me, my dead heart refused to make you suffer."

Yeah, fucking right.

"And if you didn't change your mind, then what? You would have let me suffer while pretending you are my savior?" I retorted.

His face grimaces in agony as he shakes his head. "No. I don't know what I would have done, but I swear I don't want to know anymore because I truly care about you-"

"Don't," I hissed. "Don't you even dare say something you don't hold value for."

He leans up until our faces are closer as he cups my cheeks. Before his touch always felt like a soothing balm to my wounds but now, they feel like the thorns of the rose that is starting to wither nearby the window.

"How much did Tristen pay you?" I ask grimly.

"Agatha, you don't-"

"How much?" I interrupt him while my eyes glare at him.

He is silent for a few seconds but when he realizes I will seek that answer one way or another, he finally gives in.

"A million."

I snicker coldly under my breath. "At least I know my value now."

He shakes his head, looking heartbroken like my words are like daggers that keep stabbing him again and again.

"I never cared about the money. It was about saving my brother but now you matter to me as well. I swore to save you and I will do that."

"I am not going to repeat my mistakes and trust you again," I mutter with a cold tone.

"Please, Agatha. All I want is you to be safe and get the fuck out of here before things get out of control. The boat is here and we can leave by tomorrow. Just let me help you and then later if you wish then I will never show you my face again."

"And I am supposed to trust you in that? Why should I believe that you want to truly help me? Why shouldn't I think that this isn't one of your conspiracies?" I ask.

My nerves are burning with rage and pain, wishing I could channel it all onto him so he would know how much it's hurting me deep inside.

"Because I want you to trust me with my truth this one final time...please," he whispers, looking right into my eyes with honesty and determination clouding in his gaze.

"Please, Agatha..."

"Leave me alone," I mutter, pulling away from his grasp and looking towards the window.

I hear his breathing turning ragged but he doesn't protest at my words. "I know you must hate me now and if I have to spend my whole life repenting for it, I will do it. But I won't be leaving tomorrow without you."

He sounds serious and truthful but I no longer care.

"I will wait for you at the back door tomorrow. If you come then I will take away from this living hell. If not, I will still wait for you until you are ready to leave with me," he mutters and gets up.

He leans down and kisses the top of my head. "Trust me with my truth like I trusted yours," he murmurs and leaves the room.

I don't bother warning him about Geryon and what he

might do to him tomorrow. All I know I'm on my own in this journey. I'm my own protector now and I have to get out of here quickly.

I don't know where he has got the boat located and I can't waste time looking for it and risking either Eryx or Geryon finding me. So, following Eryx tomorrow is the only way. He said we will leave in the morning before anyone wakes up. When he will take me to the boat I will attack him and escape using the boat, leaving him to be punished by Geryon.

He will be the bridge to my freedom tomorrow, that I will be burning down when the time comes.

My eyes move towards the rose as I stalk towards it. It looks dull and dark with the top bent lower. I take it in my hand, feeling the loss and pain the rose must be feeling like my broken heart.

"Love has never been written in our destiny," I say to the rose, lightly touching the petals.

"If darkness and sin is what our fate wants from us, then so be it."

I hold the rose by the stem in one hand in a tight fist, feeling the thorns piercing my skin. But the pain no longer matches the agony my heart is feeling, as I keep gazing towards the dark sky…hoping tomorrow I will finally have my freedom.

CHAPTER TWENTY SEVEN

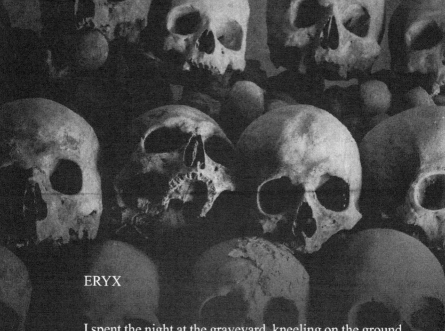

ERYX

I spent the night at the graveyard, kneeling on the ground and looking over the lives I've buried here.

I have committed several sins in life that have always drowned me in the sea of guilt, and I have always felt the pain of those sins so many times that at one point I no longer felt it.

But after seeing the way Agatha's trust for me was shattered, I felt that pain all over again. Nothing felt more painful than seeing her eyes glimmering with betrayal and heartache.

And the reason was none other but me.

She no longer has faith in me and doesn't want to be saved by me. But I have to do everything possible to help her. And if afterwards she doesn't forgive me and wants me gone then I will walk away from her life without any hesitation.

After the things I have put her through, I don't deserve her. Fuck, I never deserved in the first place. But this fucking heart of mine that she revived back to life didn't want to let her go.

It only wanted her.

I swore to destroy her since the day she arrived here but that notion changed into something else very soon.

The destroyer became destroyed.

I was willing to wait for her as long as it would take. But she needs my help in this, and this time I won't betray her. I will be the path towards her freedom no matter what.

I will even make sure Tristen's shadow remains miles away from her. Even when she isn't willing to face me, I will still be there for her…to protect her…to love her.

By the time night descends, I decide to get up and leave. I go to the area first where I hid the boat to check everything was ready. I made sure to hide the boat using leaves and scattered branches. Luckily, Julius even packed a few essentials in a sack bag that is inside the boat.

After making sure everything is ready, I return back to the Magdalene and wait at the back entrance.

Every now and then I look over my shoulder, telling myself that she will come. She has to.

But every time my gaze returns on the door, finding it closed, I feel the hope of her coming to me fading away.

I feel hours passing by as I wait there. The clouds start

to grumble, foreshadowing a stormy weather as always and the crows start to caw louder than ever. The crashing waves echo along with the cawing, but I am used to this ominous scenario.

But I won't give up. I keep waiting.

Though when I hear the creak of the heavy wooden door opening after a few more hours, I feel my heart racing.

She came.

I try to control my breathing and relax my nerves, while the urge to take her in my arms feels too strong. But when I'm about to turn, I feel a needle pricking into my neck as I feel something being injected into my nerves. Awareness and sudden weakness overcome me as I turn around while my legs start to turn weak, making me kneel on the ground.

My vision starts to blur along with my nerves suddenly turning weak as well, and shaking my head turns out to be a bad idea as it makes my temple ache. But when I fall back with a loud thud, the voice I hear doesn't belong to Agatha.

"This is for your own good," Agnes whispers as I see her blurry face floating in front of me. But using my leftover strength I grab her neck tightly as she struggles slightly.

"What the fuck have you done to me?" I groan weakly.

She lets out a choked voice and I shake her by her neck. "Answer me!" I demand.

"Geryon t-told me to d-drug you," she answers with a croaked voice. "T-to take you for…"

I barely make-out the rest of her words as the drug controls my mind and makes my hold on her neck slump down before it blankets me into darkness.

The roaring thunder and heavy spattering of the rain is the first thing that reaches my ears when consciousness returns to me. I slowly open my eyes as my vision steadily becomes normal. But what I see in front of me only makes my heart stop in fear.

I was inside the main hall, the prayers room, with my hands tied behind a bench with wires that were digging into my skin. I can already feel the blood trickling down from my hands whenever I twist my wrists. Even my ankles are tied with more wires.

I look in front of me where Agatha is in the same condition but she is in a white nightdress. Her hair curtains around her face with her head casted down, signaling she must be unconscious.

When my gaze shifts to the other side of the room I see one of my worst nightmares.

It is the final ritual of the Magdalene.

The circle with a star in the center is drawn with a white color on the floor. Candles around it were positioned along with all the women and other nuns of this place around it, holding each other's hands. They all look at Geryon who is standing at the center and looking at the ceiling. His vast shadow falling upon the wall behind him, but only I know that is the shadow of a monster. The hall doesn't have any of the other benches, except for the Mary statue that is behind Geryon, surrounded with more candles. The tapestry is brought lower that it touches the floor, acting like a curtain that holds the story of the final ritual of the Magdalene.

He is chanting verses and the women hum along with him. I look back at Agatha who is starting to stir awake. Her eyes gradually open as she takes in her surroundings before her gaze falls on me, filled with concern and confusion.

"Eryx…" she whispers with a hoarse tone.

"W-what is going on?" She looks at the final ritual that Geryon is doing with the women and when realization hits her, her eyes wide open in shock and terror.

"Hey, hey, look at me," I mutter to her, making sure Geryon can't hear us as she returns her gaze back at me. "I swear I will save you and get you out of here."

She swallows, remaining silent while breathing heavily.

"Good to know you are awake, brother," Geryon's voice echoes through the hall.

He smiles darkly like the monster he is and stalks towards us. I try to get free from the wires but the more my wrists move the more I feel my skin bleeding and aching so badly that I feel like my hands will get cut off from my arms.

But I don't quit trying.

He stands beside Agatha and kneels in front of her. Agatha doesn't let her fear get reflected in her eyes or face, being the brave soul she was born to be. I know she once let her walls down because of the torture Geryon put her through, but she refuses to give him that satisfaction again.

"I will never know why God sent you to become a barrier between me and my brother, but I will make sure to send you back where you came from because you deserve to be in hell," he sneers. He leans closer to her, running his fingertip lightly along her cheek as Agatha instantly shifts her head to the other side. My blood boils that I want to cut his hands into pieces right away.

"You could have been an angel…I would have pleased you and made sure you were happy with me. But you'd rather get tainted by the devil."

"Don't you fucking dare touch her! Stay away from her before I cut your hands off and feed them to you!" I threaten him.

He only smirks and grabs her by her jaw, forcing her to face me as he keeps staring at me. "You choose her over your brother! Her!"

"You were never my brother and you never will be!"

Out of nowhere, he charges at me and lands a hard punch across my face that blood splatters from my mouth. Another punch lands on my other cheek with my drool coated in blood dripping down my chin.

"We have been connected by the Magdalene, Eryx. But you never accepted that. I lost my mother and father, but I still hoped that you would understand me…accept me as your brother." I witness a cloud of misery in his eyes that I have never seen before, telling me he means what he was saying.

"I thought the place that took away our family, will unite us into a new family. But you have refused to accept this place…you defy to see the beauty it holds, Eryx."

I shake my head. "You defy to see through your sins, Geryon. Darkness has blinded you so much that even goodness has faded away from your life with no hope of returning."

He hits me again and this time I feel it through my bones. The ache starts to spread through my face, reaching my skull that my temple starts to hurt.

"It's all bullshit. And she," he points towards Agatha, "-she put more nonsense in your mind. But I will get rid of her right in front of your eyes, just to remind you that you can never cross me again."

He goes to her and frees her from her bindings but he grabs her by her hair, dragging her to the circle.

"Let me go, you fucking monster!" she screams, writhing against his grasp with her face flinching in pain. Meanwhile I try to be free but the pain starts to get unbearable with the wires digging deeper into my skin.

"Stop! No!" she yells when Geryon gestures to the women to hold down Agatha. Without hesitation they follow his instruction as he starts to chant the verses again.

"Lord, hear our pleas. Hear our prayers and help us make your world better again by sacrificing this tainted soul," he mutters looking up with his arms spread.

Fuck.

"And accept our angels in your heaven and let this tainted soul rot in hell for ruining your beautiful world. Accept it, Lord. Accept it!" he begs. "Let me be part of your heaven."

Adrenaline rushes through me as I give it all to loosen the wire, not caring if my hands bleed to death. I have to save Agatha no matter what.

Please, God. Please give me strength. Please God... Please.

But as if God has truly heard my silent prayers, a miracle happens. I see Agnes hiding behind a pillar with a knife in her hand. She looks back and forth from Geryon to me and when she notices Geryon being lost in his chanting, she takes the chance and rushes towards me.

Using the knife, she cuts off the wires, freeing my blood coated hands and hugging me. "You are safe now; I will save you..."

Leaning back, she touches my face looking hurt from seeing the bruises on my face. "Let's get out of here...we will escape. Just you and me," she murmurs with a madness that has possessed her heart and soul. An addiction of possessiveness that made her wide eyes seem like she was losing her mind. She helped me to get me out of here, not to give me a hand to let Agatha escape as well.

But even now she doesn't understand that she and I can never be together when my heart belongs to Agatha.

She grabs my hands and urges me to go along with her while Geryon is distracted. But when she sees me remaining still with no intention of leaving with her, she frowns in confusion along with her eyes watering up.

"B-but I-I saved you…I…" she rasps.

"And I will always remember this moment, thanking you for saving me from this dangerous situation, but I have to save Agatha," I mutter.

Her lips press together in a thin line like she is controlling herself from shedding tears, but rage is taking over her as she looks at Agatha.

"It will always be her, won't it?" she asks.

I nod. "Only she will ever rule over my heart."

She gets up with her eyes strained on Agatha with her grip tightening on the knife. An unsettling feeling crosses my heart seeing her like this.

Broken. Enraged. Distant.

"She is ruling over your heart now because she is alive. I'm sure she won't be a problem once she is dead."

Before I can stop her, she strides towards Geryon, breaking the circle. I try to get up despite weakness making me it's prisoner but after that drug and losing blood it is proving to be difficult to stand straight.

Holding onto the bench for support, I try to get up but when I see Agnes getting closer to Agatha, I feel my heart freezing from a fear I have never felt before.

THE DEVIL TAINTED US

Chapter Twenty Eight

AGATHA

Each and every hand that was pinning me down on the ground feels like vice grips, digging the wires deeper into my skin while a pool of blood starts to form around my legs and hands.

But I don't give up to get away from their grasps. "Let me go!" I scream.

"You will be sent to hell," one of them mutters in a monotonous tone, talking with me for the first time.

"You don't belong here," another speaks.

"You are tainted by the devil," the third one murmurs.

"We won't let you darken us with your sins."

They all start to speak these lines over and over again while Geryon keeps chanting some prayers. The more they speak the more my ears start to hurt, along with my head aching.

But suddenly I hear thudding footsteps approaching and I look at my feet side where Agnes was approaching me with a knife in her hand. And the look on her face is enough evidence to tell me she is blinded with an unknown rage that she is going to take out on me.

She pushes away the two women holding my legs and swiftly slashes the knife along the cheeks of the two women holding my arms, making them falter back.

"This ends today! He is only mine!" she yells, drawing the knife back to stab me and I almost accept my fate. But then I hear Eryx's loud roar as he pushes down Agnes so hard that she hits her head with a loud thud against the nearest pillar.

"Eryx," I whisper, trying to get up.

He is about to kneel down to help me up but Geryon comes in and kicks him on his chest as he falls back.

"Not today, Eryx. I won't let you save her today," he promises. As Eryx leans up, Geryon doesn't waste another second, kicking him right across his face. I take my chance to move up when the other women suddenly come to me and pins me down like I was previously. My legs and arms are trapped before I am aware, but I don't care this time and endure the pain.

"Fuck!" I grunt, twisting my arms. Because of the blood covering my wrists, their grips slightly off. I raise my hands and strike them in their eyes with the pointed ends of the wire.

"Ah! God! Ah!" They both scream at the top of their lungs as they back away with blood spurting out of their eye sockets. They hold their hands against their eyes, yelling in agony with the blood smearing their palms and leaking through the gaps of their fingers.

Reaching for the nearest candle, I use that and plunge the end of the fire side against the neck of one of the women holding my left leg.

"Ah!" She screams the same way and falls back. With my one leg free I kick the other woman. The others go towards the injured ones, to help them like they start to care for the first time.

I get up and carefully get the wires from my wrists and ankles. Looking at Eryx, when I see his face coated with blood and bruises, my heart falters with fret and fright. But he gets up, even though he is broken from the hits and punches delivered by Geryon, fighting with his weak muscles.

I make a move to help him in his battle but then from the corner of my eyes I see Agnes's figure approaching me in stealth mode.

But luckily, I find a knife that Geryon must have dropped and pick it up to defend myself from Agnes. With a sly grin, she walks slowly towards me, holding the knife forward with her eyes wild and wide open.

"He can never be yours, you cunt," she mutters through

her clenched teeth. With every step she takes forward, I take one back.

"There is nothing to love about you," she eyes me from top to bottom with a disgusted look, "never loved by anyone. Your parents left you, your sister killed herself because of you and your brother-in-law used you for who you truly are…a fucking whore."

"Agnes…you don't have to do this," I mutter.

"Nothing will stop me today, you whore. Not you, not Eryx and not even God Himself."

She was getting closer but this time I have nowhere else to go when I hit my back against the statue. I look around for a way to escape and then I find a small bowl containing white paint. When I see Agnes about to pounce at me, I throw the paint on her face.

"Oh God!" she shrieks and closes her eyes tightly and loosens her grip on the knife while trying to get the paint away. But she still tries to bridge the gap between us on her instinct. Without hesitation I plunge the knife into her belly, twisting it deeper.

She grunts in utter agony as I see blood oozing out of her stomach followed by a squelching sound. In a few seconds her body starts to turn limp with her hands guiding forward for support. But I move away as she stumbles against the statue and falls lower, making the candles fall over one another like dominoes.

Before I am aware of it, I witness the tapestry catching fire and soon spreading all over it, looking like a curtain of hell fire.

"No! No! No!" I hear Geryon yell with a venomous rage, making me turn around. He looks at the burning tapestry and then at the circle which is now ruined. He looks utterly shattered while witnessing the sight like he is broken deep down to his soul. Behind him Eryx is coughing and trembling on the ground.

"No! Please Lord, no!" The other women scream as well and as if they think they can save it from burning, they don't hesitate to jump into the fire and get trapped by it.

"Ah! Ah!" their screams of pain as their bodies catch fire echo through the Magdalene. Their skin burns as they rush blindly at all places, spreading more fire around.

"What have you done?!" Geryon spits out his words so loud that I can see his veins popping against his neck and forehead with his eyes turning red. "Y-you...you have ruined my path to heaven...you did what the devil sent you here for..."

He looks around the disaster that he has no control over before his gaze meets mine with an insanity that shares the uncontrollable rage he is carrying.

"But this won't stop me from sending you back to hell, you fucking cunt!"

He charges at me and I prepare myself to use the knife

but as I take a step back, I slip on the puddle of blood, falling hard on my back.

He kicks the knife away from my hold, and as I try to get up, he wraps his hand around my throat so tightly that in a few seconds I am struggling to breath. He beckons my body up by his hold while I can't do anything but surrender to his strength.

"I should have sacrificed you the day you arrived here. I knew you were nothing but a devil's creation who came to ruin us. And today you have…" he gestures around us as the fire spreads more and more, turning the room hot and smoky that makes me struggle even more.

"But today it ends for you," he squeezes my throat tighter that my vision starts to blur, "return back to hell because I won't let you ruin my journey to heaven."

My nerves race faster with my heart pumping vigorously. With my unfocused sight, I see Geryon's face turning hazy but I don't miss his other hand raising the knife in his grasp before he strikes his move at me, while my consciousness takes me to a darker place where I know I will never be returning from.

But even in these final moments my mind reflects the moments I have spent with Eryx, making me wish I could tell him that I have forgiven him…that I should have trusted him…that I love him.

But it was too late now…too late.

THE DEVIL TAINTED US

CHAPTER TWENTY NINE

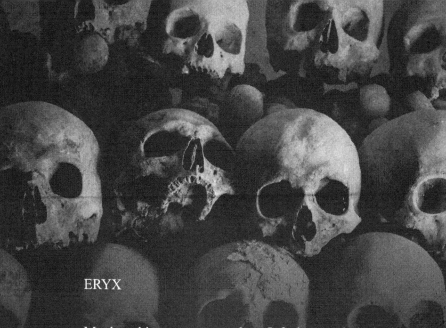

ERYX

My breathing turns ragged as I feel my whole body turning weak. There is nothing but fire everywhere, burning down the Magdalene with every passing second.

I cough up my blood and let it drool on the floor. The bruises on my skin and wounds on my wrists make my entire body ache so badly. But my mind only races with thoughts of Agatha as I lay on my back on the ground.

"But today it ends for you," I hear Geryon's rough voice as I see him choking Agatha to her death.

No. I won't lose her.

Not now. Not ever.

I won't let Geryon take her away from me. With every ounce of energy I have left with determination and rage fueling my nerves, I get up and rush towards Geryon as he raises the knife in his hand.

But before he can plunge into Agatha's body, I hold him by his waist and pick him up, throwing him over my shoulder. The knife clanks away from his hold.

"You have taken everything from me, Geryon. But not her," I murmur, breathing heavily.

He smirks and gets up. "You won't be able to save her when I kill you."

"Not before I kill you first, *brother*" I threaten him, spitting out blood. "You are returning back from where you came and that is surely not heaven."

With a roar he charges at me and raises his hand to hit me, but using my arm I dodge his attack and knee him on his stomach. He grunts back but I don't give him time to recover and rain punch after punch across his face, that with every hit he staggers back with bruises already forming on his cheeks.

I hold him by his collar and hit his forehead with mine as hard as possible twice in a row. Ignoring the ache in my temple, I hold his shirt and belt before swinging him behind me, watching his body slide on the floor until his body hits the statue, making him stop.

Adrenaline pumps through my body, awakening up my nerves. I stalk towards him and as he is getting up, I kick him on his face, stomping his nose and chin as hard as possible with my feet.

"Urgh! Fuck!" he growls in pain, holding onto his aching face.

But I don't let him compose himself. I grab his collar with one hand, making him lie on his back and astride him. With my other hand I punch him blindly without any pause, pouring every ounce of locked up anger, guilt, agony and heartache I feel because of him.

Every hit that I land reflects all those miseries he cost me and today nothing will stop me from repaying him back. His grunts of agony and breathy curses are like music to my ears.

But none of it feels enough.

He deserves to suffer endlessly.

His blood coats my knuckles and I relish the bruises and cuts that are forming on his face already. But I crave to hurt him more.

I grip his hair tightly and smack his head continuously against the statue until more blood pours out. His body is turning limp and weak like he has no ounce of energy left to fight me. His face is starting to swell with his eyes half closed.

I lean him away, making him look at me while my hand grips his bruised jaw.

But he still grins with a blood coated smile. "What are you waiting for, brother? End me. But you know well that your sins will always lurk behind you like a shadow for the rest of your life. You will always carry the burden of your sins no matter where you go," he nods weakly at Agatha who is unconscious on the floor, "-even she won't be able to get you out of it."

He chuckles under his breath. "The Magdalene will always be a part of your life."

I look right into his eyes, fearless and unbothered by his words.

"I know the shadow of the Magdalene will never leave me, but unlike you, I will repent for my sins. I don't care if I will be in heaven or hell, but will make sure to give myself the life I deserved that was taken away from me. And Agatha brought me out of that darkness the day she got here and nothing will ever change that."

"You will rot in hell, Eryx. You and I both know that."

I shrug with a dark grin. "Maybe, but I do know that you will be burning here and even in hell, because the devil tainted you, *brother*. Die and never come back."

I hold his neck, guiding him towards the burning tapestry.

"May your soul rot for eternity," I curse him, pushing him into his death, hearing him screaming and crying in endless agony. And in a few seconds when his voice is no longer heard, I feel the cloud of darkness escaping from my heart. I grab the cross necklace that he gave me when I first came here and throw it into the fire, erasing his last remaining presence from my life.

I turn to Agatha and quickly take her in my arms.

"Agatha," I call her name, lightly tapping her cheek. I check for her pulse and it is steady. I look around, seeing the fire reaching the rooftop and pillars. The ceiling makes a loud cracking noise, giving the sign it is about to fall down anytime.

I pick up Agatha, ignoring the excruciating pain throughout my body, and stagger towards the door. The second I step out of the building I hear the loud thud of the ceiling falling, spreading the fire even more.

Going around the Magdalene, I give it all to get Agatha to the back of the island where the boat is ready. Every step I take feels like thorns spiking my nerves again and again, making me bleed more.

But I don't give up.

I have to save her even if it means sacrificing my own life. The distance feels like a forever journey but when I hear the crashing sounds of the waves with the wind howling, I feel a surge of calmness going through my nerves.

I start to walk towards the spot where the boat is hidden and soon, I find it. Lowering Agatha on the ground, I get the boat ready, dragging it to the shore side, before returning to get Agatha and place her inside the boat. Taking the oars, I begin rowing the boat and turn it around the island.

When I notice Agatha's wounded wrists, I find a wooden box that I told Julius to send along with the boat, containing essentials. Thankfully there is a small first aid box with bandages and antiseptics inside. I disinfect her wounds and wrap the bandage around her hands to stop the bleeding until we reach Vailburg, where she will get proper treatment. I even treat my scars on my wrists but weakness still lurks upon my body.

I resume rowing and look over my shoulder, seeing the Magdalene burning…the place that turned my life into a living nightmare every single day, is finally being destroyed into ashes.

And with one final look at Mery Heights, I bid farewell to this cursed island, vowing to myself to never return back here.

The darkness ends today.
It ends now.

THE DEVIL TAINTED US

Chapter Thirty

AGATHA

I expect the cold and gloomy atmosphere to welcome me but when my eyes open gradually, it is the streaming sunlight through the window that greets me.

I blink a few times as my vision focuses clearly and I find myself in a different room that is nowhere near the rooms Magdalene has.

A heavy blanket covers me down from my waist as I lay in a comfortable and soft bed. The walls have striped light blue and white wallpaper with a wardrobe, a dressing table and a small sitting space, filling the room.

I frown in confusion but hesitancy and worry are present as well as I sit up slowly. I lightly hiss in pain and look down at my wrists that are bandaged. I drag up the blanket lightly and find my ankles bandaged too.

And that's when the horrific memory of Geryon nearly

choking me to death fills my mind- the Magdalene being set on fire…Agnes dying…the women burning…Eryx…

Eryx.

Where is he?

I vaguely remember him coming to save me from Geryon despite his injuries. And finding myself in a different place and alive can only mean he not only saved me but also helped me get free from that living hell.

I remember planning to kill him with a knife after he would take me to the boat. I had it all arranged where after killing him I would take the boat and escape the place but when I was about to leave my room, one of the nuns came into the room and out of nowhere injected me with something. Before I could fight her off, I fell unconscious and next thing I knew I was tied down and supposed to be sacrificed.

But Eryx saved me. He saved me even though he knew I hated him for what he did to me, and yet he did everything possible to set me free…even endangering his life and the chances of saving his own brother.

Just then the front door opens with a man I have never met before entering with a small wooden box in his hand. When he sees me sitting upright there is a slight surprise in his face before it gets exchanged with a casual smile.

"Finally, you are awake," he mutters with a deep, rough voice before sauntering towards me and placing the box beside me.

"Who are you and where am I?" I ask.

He snickers. "The bastard didn't even mention me to you and yet he asked for a favor."

He sits at the end of the bed keeping a respectable space between me and him. "I'm Julius, a friend of Eryx. You are in Vailburg and this is my house. And before you ask how you got here, Eryx got you here with the boat I sent to Mery Heights and from there we took you to the hospital. But you went through a lot of fucked up shit so you kept coming back and forth for a couple of days."

"How many days?"

"It's been six days now. But it seems like you are finally awake."

"Where is Eryx?" I ask.

He is silent for a few seconds which only makes my heart plummet with tension and dread because last time I saw Eryx he was badly injured and lost a lot of blood.

"Please don't tell me he…" I can't even say the words, "i-is he…"

His expression softens as he offers me a small smile.

"He is safe and alive but he isn't here in Vailburg."

I frown in confusion. "What do you mean? Where is he then?"

"He left for Brinecliff yesterday to find his brother, Eros."

"When is he coming back?"

He shakes his head looking down with a sigh. "He isn't.

He said to inform you after he finds his brother he will move to a different place."

My breathing turns shallow as I feel my throat clogging with emotions. "W-What?"

He nods at the box before speaking, "He left this for you and said it has everything you will need."

I immediately get the box and open it, and find some papers inside it. I pick up the first one and unfold it, reading what's typed and find it's a statement letter from Eryx proving that I have no mental illness and I'm absolutely normal and sane to be the holder of my family's inheritance. The second letter contained the death certificate of Tristen that stated he died in a car accident.

Tristen is dead?

Did Eryx have something to do with it?

As if Julius can read what I am thinking from my expression he answers my question. "Eryx didn't do anything. Sometimes fate punishes the sinners and your brother-in-law got what he deserved."

My gaze returns back to the box where the final paper sits and it is a letter from Eryx.

Agatha,

The day you came into my life I swore to be the villain of your story and I did become one, putting you in misery, suffering and heartache. But I no longer want to be the reason for all your agony anymore.

You are free from me…from this sinner who fell in love with his angel.

And just for that love I don't deserve you because my angel deserves to have a life where it's filled with happiness, hope and beauty. And in that life a monster like me can never be a part of it.

But nobody will ever replace your place in my heart and soul. Nobody.

I have submitted a copy of your medical statement to one of your lawyers and he will be dealing with your family house and wealth that will soon be yours. You are even free from Tristen…you are free from Geryon and the Magdalene.

You finally have what you have been yearning for, my little girl. It's all yours now.

It's time for you to have a life that was taken away from you but I know how brave and strong my Agatha is, and in no time, she will be living a blissful life. And just that thought is enough to make me happy for eternity. Our paths may have crossed but it didn't lead to one journey. We are different and so are our paths.

I know you will never forgive me for what I have done to you and I don't deserve your forgiveness. But if you ever need me then I will be willing to lay my life for you in a heartbeat.

Just like I trusted you with my truth, I hope one day you can trust me again with my truth…and the truth is I love you, Agatha.

I love you with every living being within me and even in the afterlife you will be the only one that will be inked in my heart.

Forever yours,

Eryx.

He left...he has left me forever.

I feel my cheeks getting wet from my streaming tears. My gaze returns to Julius who wears a sympathetic expression.

"He left without telling me goodbye," I whisper as my hands tremble while I lower the letter.

"He wanted to stay but he said if he saw those tears in your eyes then he wouldn't have the heart to leave you. He was absolutely miserable when he left and his eyes carried nothing but pain. I saw him, Agatha, and I could tell he was heartbroken to leave you. He truly cares about you and that's why he took this step."

I shake my head, breathing shakily. "I can tell but he didn't care enough to give our love a second chance. He made the decision for both of us, without knowing what I wanted."

I wipe away the tears with my palm and look at the letter in my hand. "What he did was unforgivable and he had no other choice at the time. He promised to save me and help me get free from the Magdalene, and when the time came, he kept that promise."

I swallow the lump in my throat and lick my dry lips.

"Even I vowed to be there for him and I won't break my promise."

"What do you mean?"

"I want you to take me to Brinecliff. I have to meet him."

"You can't leave Vailburg until you fully recover, Agatha. And it was strictly instructed by the doctors," Julius mutters and gets up, going for the side table and grabbing some pills and a glass of water.

"And you have to let him be for now because he finally found his brother after a long time. So, he needs to figure things out with him first. But I don't think he would want to meet you anyway. He knows what you feel…he knows you hate him."

My eyes look at the words Eryx wrote for me and I can't help but snicker sadly.

"That's the thing about feelings…it can fuck you up in every scenario. When you feel love for someone, you don't see the darkness they carry. And when you hate that person, then you don't see the goodness that was hiding within them."

CHAPTER THIRTY ONE

ERYX

After getting off the port along with other people from Vailburg, I don't bother searching for a motel. The first thing I want to do is look for my brother, Eros. With my bag over my shoulder, I start walking ahead in the unknown place.

The place is dark and gloomy that it almost reminds me of Mery Heights. Most of the buildings look rustic with the wall paints mostly peeling off or the windows and doors being half broken.

The locals mostly wear dark and shabby clothes, with some of them looking at me with a constant stare. Exiting the port area, I walk along the sidewalk as I take out the piece of paper with an address written on it.

Brinecliff Medical Center.

A man with unsteady steps was passing by my side when he suddenly bumps into me.

"Watch it," he mutters with a slur, looking up at me with a glare filled look.

"I apologize. Do you know where the Brinecliff Medical Center is?" I ask him.

"Why? You want to get admitted there?" He jokes and chuckles like he is loving his own pathetic joke.

Shaking my head, I ignore him and continue walking when I ask another passerby the same question only for him to ignore and walk away.

But accidentally, I stumble into a little boy who hits his body against my waist so hard that he falls on his ass.

"Hey, you okay?" I ask him, kneeling down and helping him stand up.

He simply nods and looks down. Leaning his hand down he picks up my paper before passing it to me.

"I'm sorry, I didn't see you," I mutter and stand up.

He remains silent and keeps looking at the paper in my hand.

I frown following his gaze and ask him. "Do you know where this place is?" I tap on the address.

He nods slowly and gestures to me to follow him. He titters away with his small feet while I am right behind him. He seems to be six or seven probably and already seems to know this place very well. But unlike others, he is in a somewhat decent dress, wearing a gray shirt with blue pants. We continue our journey for several miles before he stops before an old, three-story building.

I take in my surroundings, feeling my heart racing just from thinking about my brother living in this disastrous place for years. It only makes me want to kill Geryon all over again.

The kid runs ahead, getting inside and I follow him in. A pungent smell right away greets me making me scrunch my nose in disgust. As I step inside furthermore, I get the strong fragrance of medicines mixed with the disgusting smell of pee and vomit probably.

Fucking hell.

Water leaks from the ceiling and the walls look like they haven't been fixed for centuries.

The kid runs to the reception desk and stands beside a woman who I'm guessing to be the receptionist. She looks down at him with a frown.

"What are you doing here? I told you to go back to-"

When the kid points at me she stops talking and stands straight. "Can I help you with something?"

I nod and stalk towards her. "I'm here to look for a patient. Eros. He was brought here from Vailburg a few years ago."

She nods. "Let me check the register."

She gets a thick, long register that is so dusty that when she places it on the table, I feel some of the dust coating my face. I give a quick rub and my eyes fall on the kid who is looking at me with innocent eyes, hiding behind the woman's dress, feeling shy.

Only if I had such innocence left within me when I was his age. The only time I felt that purity back in life was when I was with Agatha.

It was the toughest decision for me to walk out of her life, but I'd rather be away from her and know she is happy and safe, rather than be with her and cloud her life with my darkness again.

"Yes. He is in room 215 but he must be on the balcony side as usual. But you are...?" she asks.

"His brother."

She simply nods and gives me a paper. "This is a pass to meet the patients. The balcony is on the third floor, left corridor and goes straight."

"Thank you."

I walk ahead and the more steps I take, the more horrible the scenario of this place I witnessed. There is no doubt this place hasn't been cleaned for ages and it's a surprise the woman at the reception was not puking every second from the gut-wrenching smell. I hear a few faint screams coming from some rooms I pass by like it was screams of agony and sufferings.

But I won't stop.

Few wards are standing at the hallways for protection and looking over the patients of this place and even they look quite miserable. Reaching the third floor, I feel my pulse racing all of a sudden as the distance between me and my brother is starting to become minimal.

I am finally going to see him…after such a long time that it feels like several eternities have passed. I try to take deep breaths to calm myself down, but the questions in my head make my throat feel clogged with nervousness and doubt.

Will he recognize me?

Does he remember me at all?

How will he react?

Confused? Angry? Broken?

I see a door open at the end of the hallway and continue my steps. There is a ward standing there and when he looks at me, he frowns with a questioning look.

"Who are you?" he asks, standing in front of the door.

"I'm here to see Eros." I show him the pass. "Is he here?"

He nods, gesturing at the balcony. "He is sitting on the bench. You can go and see him."

Gulping the lump in my throat I enter the balcony, greeted by the cold wind blowing and few worn out leaves falling from the nearby tree are scrunching underneath my steps.

When I look to my right, I find the bench and someone sitting there with his back facing me.

My heart beats so fast I can hear it drumming in my ears. The man was lost in his thoughts so much that he doesn't notice my presence, even when I halt by his side. And when e his face, a wave of relief washes over me that I yond overwhelmed.

"Eros," I whisper his name. But he keeps looking at the ground like I don't exist for him.

I kneel beside him, touching his shoulder. "Eros...it's me."

He blinks a few times like he has returned to reality and turns to face me. He looks just like I remember him but slightly older and physically weak. His dark brown hair moving along with the wind. His raven black eyes are filled with emptiness and misery as the dark circles indicate the sleepless nights he has been through. His skin is pale and while along with his cheekbones looking thin from weakness.

He frowns as if his mind is processing with thoughts about who I am which only makes my heart and soul start to crack with agony like a fragile glass.

"It's me, Eros. Eryx...your brother," I mutter with a pleading tone.

His silence only wrecks me furthermore as I hold his face. "Eros...do you remember me?" I ask the question that has been dreading in my mind since I got here.

No words.

Please, God. Don't punish me this way.

"Please, Eros, try to remember. We are brothers," my tone turns frantic. "Remember when as kids we would fight over toy cars but then seeing you make that sad face, I would give it to you. And that time when you were flirting with a girl and his boyfriend came to beat you up, but instead of saving you we both got our asses kicked."

I chuckle at the memory, silently begging him to remember those moments…the times when the shadow of the Magdalene and our parents were miles away from us.

He finally responds but instead of nodding he shakes his head, prying away from my hold.

"You can't be my brother," he mutters in a groggy, deep voice. The same voice I have been dying to hear for such a long time.

But his words are like daggers to my already shattering heart.

"What?" I frown.

"My brother has always sworn to protect me but you left…you left me," his voice starts to tremble with tears forming in his eyes.

"You can't be Eryx. Because the Eryx I remember, promised the day we both left the prison that he will be with me…be my only true family. But you never came back."

I nodded, looking down in shame and guilt. "I did promise, Eros. But fate was cruel to both of us, it tested us and our bond day after day. It has ruined us since the day we were born."

I hold his hand tightly, holding determination and promise in my voice. "But no more, Eros. It all ends now."

...n never end for us, Eryx. The Magdalene will follow us."

I shake my head curtly. "Not anymore. It has been burned down to hell. The shadow of the Magdalene will no longer be in our life."

He frowns. "What do you mean? You were at the Magdalene?"

"Yes. All this time I was there, serving for the devil who tainted us. The sins…the darkness…the deaths," I let out a shaky breath, "I have seen it all and done it too. And it was all so that I could protect you. But if I knew this is how your life was going to turn out, I wouldn't have sacrificed myself."

I sniffle, seeing my brother shedding tears while he tries to reason with my scenario.

"But it's all over now. I give you my word that from now on, we will have a better life…a life where our pasts won't be part of our future."

"Do you think we can do that?" he whispers.

"As long as we both have each other, we can do anything."

Suddenly, he lets go of my hands and engulfs me in his arms, hugging me tightly. I return the gesture, feeling that soothing calmness settle in my heart that I lost the day I left my brother.

"Always together?" he asks.

"Always, brother. Always together."

THE DEVIL TAINTED US

A few days pass by at Brinecliff. After finding Eros, I do everything possible to get him the fuck out of that rotten place.

But I also find out, due to lack of food and proper care for such a long time, Eros is physically weak. He can barely walk on his own. But I know my brother, he is strong enough to regain himself and I will help him in that path.

I rented a small room in an apartment to help Eros get physically and mentally better.

But there is also someone who keeps crossing my mind every minute of my day. A person who is the missing piece of my heart that I have left at Vailburg.

Agatha.

By now she must be all healed up and ready to take over her father's inheritance. Perhaps soon she will also find someone who will make her happy and get married to him, having her own little family.

The mere picture makes me wish to go back to her, as the thought of her being with another man is tempting me to kill the fucker. But after what I have put her through, I know I wasn't the man for her with whom she will have her happily ever after. Before I know it a memory of us being together crosses my mind.

Agatha lets out a deep sigh with her head resting on

my shoulder. Her naked body pressing against mine as her fingertips draw lazy circles on my chest. My one hand is wrapped around her waist, feeling the curves of her hips while my other hand touches her arm.

Our eyes never leave each other's gaze as we relish in the closeness while it's raining heavily outside.

"Can I ask you something?" she whispers.

I simply nod, feeling my heart somersaults just from witnessing how beautiful she looks.

"I just wonder, despite this darkness in your life, if you ever had a good memory?" she asks.

I'm silent for a moment because no matter how many memory lanes I cross by I can never find a single moment that has not been tainted by my sins. I let out a shaky breath, moving my hand upwards to cup her cheek.

"I wouldn't have bothered about making memories before because deep down I knew it wasn't written in my fate. But with you...I wish to have as many memories as possible. With you my moments are never tainted by darkness, they are bloomed by your presence."

She gifts me with her soft smile, leaning closer and planting a kiss on my lips.

"I believe that because with you...I feel the same," she whispers.

"I'm sure you will poke a hole in the glass the way you are staring at it," Eros mutters with a grunt as he is doing his leg exercise on the floor.

I blink a few times as I return back to reality…a reality where Agatha is no longer present. I gulp down the rest of the bourbon, setting the glass on the table before walking towards him. I kneel down and hold his legs and nod at him.

Understanding my sign, he only raises his half top of his body before leaning back and repeating the same motions.

"You were thinking about her, weren't you?" he asks.

I shake my head. "I wasn't thinking about anything."

"Eryx, don't bullshit with me. You have been in this same Romeo pose for days now. If you miss her so much then go back to her."

I sigh. "I can't. It's not that easy. After the things she has been through…"

Eros breathes heavily but doesn't stop exercising as perspiration coats his forehead. "The way you described her to me a few days ago, I can tell she is stronger than you are and has a heart of an innocent soul."

He stops and sits up, meeting my gaze while he breathes heavily. "I know you want to protect her and I know you love her like nobody else."

He shakes his head with a light chuckle. "Fuck, I don't think I've ever seen you so protective towards a girl ever before. Even when you dated back in college, it was just for sex. But with her I can see in your eyes that she is your forever."

"But I am not her forever."

"Is it just to protect her or are you punishing yourself for the sins you committed against her, Eryx?"

I frown from his question, unable to find an answer for it.

"Ask yourself if you are protecting her from you or are you protecting her from the Eryx who was tainted by the devil that our parents brought upon us? Because deep down I feel like no matter what you are, she will accept you the way you are and even accept your flaws."

"I have already said goodbye to her and if I go back and see her, I know I won't be able to leave her ever again." I run a hand through my hair. "Every time I see her beautiful face…every time I think about her beauty, I swear it hurts so much it's unbearable."

"Go after her, Eryx. You deserve to be happy and she is your happiness."

I shake my head slowly, looking away. "What's done is done. Some things can't be changed."

THE DEVIL TAINTED US

Chapter Thirty Two

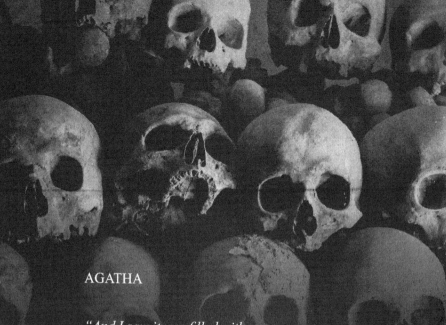

AGATHA

*"And I saw it was filled with graves,
And tomb-stones where flowers should be:
And Priests in black gowns, were walking their rounds,
And binding with briars, my joys & desires."*

Eryx recites one of my favorite poem by William Blake for me as I sit on his lap while the clouds grumble with the rain pouring heavily outside. The candelabra on the table and two hanging on the walls are the only source of light and warmth for us. But for me, Eryx's body is more than enough to keep me warm in this cold weather. After he finishes reciting, he looks down at me and places a soft kiss on my forehead making my heart melt.

"I will get another book," he mutters and starts to get up, but I wrap my arms around him tightly and shake my head.

"No. Stay."

He lets out a light chuckle which I get to witness rarely, but when he does it always makes me wish he would smile or laugh often.

"You were the one who wanted to hear his poetries. This book is finished so I have to get another copy from the shelf."

I shift my body and face him forward, pressing my front against his and wrap my legs around his waist. His hand caresses my back as he kisses my temple.

"I said stay so you stay."

"Getting bossy are we? But I can still get up this way because I want to read more," he murmurs with a teasing tone. Before I know it, he stands up and I tighten my hold around me, letting a screech in surprise and giggle at the same time. He goes to the shelf and gets another book, but instead of returning back he keeps my back pressed against the shelf. Forgetting about the book he puts his hands underneath my ass giving them a rough squeeze.

His eyes darken with a familiar look of desire and lust gazing upon me which always makes my nerves rush faster than ever.

"I thought you wanted to read more," I taunt him, lightly circling my hips as I feel his erection digging against my pussy.

Keeping one hand on my ass, he snakes up the other holding me by my throat while his chest rumbles with a groan. "I'd rather stretch your tight cunt with my cock and fuck you until my come is oozing out."

My God. His words...his words are always more than enough to make me surrender to the desire we both feel and crave for.

"I was controlling myself before but I can't anymore," he whispers against my cheek, giving a tight squeeze to my neck.

I chuckle lightly and kiss his lips.

"I always want you so much, little girl. My soul will crave for you for eternity."

He returns my kiss with a possessive and rough touch as his tongue mingles with mine.

"Only you, little girl. It will always be you."

I close the book with a light snap before placing it on my small shelf.

A week.

It has been seven days since Eryx left Vailburg. Seven days since he disappeared from my life like he never existed.

Seven fucking days where every second was filled with the memories and thoughts about Eryx. Every time I would ask Julius about him, he would have no response.

I am fully recovered now and recently got to meet my lawyer, signing the papers of the inheritance I got. Two days back I moved into the house and tried to do everything possible to feel settled back. But despite the millions I have in my account now, along with a luxurious mansion, I still feel lonely…unhappy…broken.

I am back at my father's house and unpacking some of the new clothes I got for myself in my old bedroom. It is just how it was when I left, like nothing has moved even an inch.

Placing my clothes neatly inside my wardrobe, I shut the door with a sigh when my gaze falls on the table at the corner of my room, filled with paint brushes and box sets of acrylic paints. There are a few old canvases, sitting beside the table with dust resting on them, along the wooden easel laying on the ground.

I stalk towards the spot and run my fingertips along the brushes that are dry and stiff from not being used for years. I remember when Helena got me this expensive brush set for my birthday. She woke me up at midnight just to gift them to me.

"Agatha, come on, wake up," Helena's hushed voice starts to break my peaceful sleep.

"Mmm…no. There is no school today. I want to sleep longer," I mumble with a groan.

"School never happens at midnight, silly. Now get up. I want to show you something." She shakes my body so that I have no other choice but to blink open my eyes.

With a yawn, I sit up, rubbing my eyes while I try to look at Helena with sleep weighing my eyelids.

"Look what I got you as your present."

That gets my attention and I fully open my eyes, seeing Helena sitting in front of me in her usually white nightgown with a box in purple wrapping paper.

She passes it to me and I don't waste a second, tearing the wrapping and opening the box inside.

It is a set of twenty-four brushes. The ones I have been asking for months but mommy and dad refused as I already have brushes.

But Helena got them for me.

I shriek in excitement and immediately embrace her tightly. "Thank you. Thank you so much. This is so amazing," I lean back, smiling brightly, "I didn't know mommy and dad would agree-"

She shakes her head. "They didn't. But I used some of my saved money to get my sister something she has been wanting for so long."

I frown. "But what if they get mad at you…"

She lightly chuckles, tucking a loose strand of my hair behind my ear. "They won't. And I want nothing but for my sister to be happy and have something that is part of her dream."

I feel emotional from her words and hug her again, feeling the warmth and calmness that I always feel being in her arms.

"Are you sure you want to be an artist when you grow up?" she asks.

I nod frantically. "I really do. But I don't think mommy and dad would agree, especially father."

This time she moves back with a softening gaze but it still holds a determined look as she cups my face. "Agatha… no matter what path you choose in this world, on your own, there will always be people who will be against it. But never let them steal your dream from you."

I listen to her intently.

"You want to be an artist, then be an artist who would prove to those people that are objecting now, that the dream you choose for yourself gave you the ultimate happiness they were stopping you from. And I know my sister very well, once she puts her mind into something, she always gets it."

My dreams were stolen from me and my guilt weakened me. But deep down I know Helena would have wanted me to follow the journey I had to leave midway.

But not this time.

This time it will be different.

I tie my hair in a messy bun and remove the scarf from my neck. Shedding the coat I place it on the bed, smoothening down my peach-colored dress, I grab a stool and place it beside the window. I start to set up the easel and put the canvas on it. I drag the table close to the easel before I sit out, letting a deep breath.

Swallowing the lump in my throat, I lick my dry lips and pick up a pencil from the table. Placing the sharp graphite tip against the rough paper, I pause for a moment.

I will follow my dreams...it will be different this time.
No more darkness. No more guilt.
A new step to my new journey.

I straighten, leaning closer to the paper and let my hand move as I start to outline a rough sketch.

A few more days pass by and I leave my house to visit a place that I have avoided for a long time now. But now I am ready to finally let myself be free from the cage of guilt.

The driver stops the car at Vailburg Graveyard, parking close to the entrance door. Opening the door, I carry the bouquet of red roses in my hand before walking out.

I pass through the rustic iron gate and step inside the vast area where uncountable bodies lie underneath the ground but several wild flowers bloom around their tombstones. Further away there is an enormous field of roses with the natural fragrance wafting around my nose even from here. I move forward until I stop at the spot where my sister was.

Helena Arthur
1957-1982
A daughter. A sister. A wife.

I kneel down and place the flowers on her grave. My eyes instantly glimmer with tears with my throat clogging with overwhelming emotions.

Loss. Heartache. Sadness.

I touch the stone, feeling the roughness against my palm. But despite it being just a piece of stone, I feel like I am closer to Helena…as if she is right in front of me, giving me her soft smile that she always gave when seeing me, filled with love and adoration.

I let out a raspy breath, trying to find the words to express my feelings to her. But it is difficult.

It always will be.

"No matter what I say or do, nothing will bring you back." I bite my lip as the tears stream down my cheeks and drop on her grave.

"I could only wish to go back in time and do things differently. I will always be sorry for what happened, Helena. I would sacrifice anything just to have you in my arms even for a moment. I just hope that you will forgive me and you find peace and eternal happiness in a place you deserve to be in."

My heart aches just from missing my sister so much. The emptiness I am feeling feels unmendable. I don't know if this is my start to picking up the broken pieces of my heart but I know I have to begin somewhere.

I feel the howling wind caressing my face and lightly grazing my hands. But it doesn't feel cold…it was warm and soothing that it almost feels like someone's touch.

A familiar sensation that always left a peaceful feeling within me is running through my skin…something that I felt whenever I was with Helena.

Maybe it is her. A spiritual gesture she is sending me that was wordless and yet holds a deep meaning.

"I will always miss you, Helena. I love you so much." I lean down and lightly kiss her name. For the next few moments, I share with Helena what I have been through, sharing every horror and misery I went through. I pour out all my guilt and shame that I carried since the day my innocence was clouded with darkness.

I confess it all to her, finally feeling the burden weighing off my shoulders.

"I just wish you could be here to guide me in this unknown journey. I did have someone who helped me find my path to freedom and I hoped maybe he will be by my side when I wake up. But he was gone."

I sniffle. "He left me alone…h-he didn't give us a second chance. I guess he didn't love me enough."

"Wrong. I love you so much that I was willing to let you go."

I jolt from the familiar dark, deep and intense voice that has made my heart pace up every single time I hear it. But I don't turn to look.

It was maybe a dream. He couldn't be here.

"No…this isn't real," I whisper, shaking my head and

shutting my eyes closed.

This isn't real. It's a hallucination.

"Agatha," he whispers my name but I only shake my head in response as I stand up and start to run away. I want to be away from this as far as possible. But I hear thudding footsteps following me as I flee towards the rose field.

The heavy footsteps get louder and closer. I feel strong, calloused hands holding my shoulders and bringing me close to a hard, muscular chest. Heavy and warm breathing fans my hair but I don't dare to look over my shoulder, until I am turned around. But when I feel his warmth against my cheeks, I gradually open my eyes, gathering all my courage to know if it's reality or dream.

"It's real, Agatha," he whispers. Leaning closer he lightly kisses my lips, letting me savor his taste that I have missed so much.

"You are here…"

He nods, looking at me with a softening gaze that I have rarely witnessed in his steel cold eyes. He always keeps his emotions guarded inside his walls but not today.

He let it all out…for me.

But when the memories of him leaving me alone hits me, I stagger back, prying his hands away from my cheeks. He frowns as if the distance truly hurts him.

"Why are you back?" I ask. My voice breaks slightly from being emotional but I refuse to break down in front of him. I won't give him that satisfaction.

"I came back for you," he answers, taking a step closer while I take one back.

"You left me once without hesitation," I snort. "I'm sure you can do that again easily. So, don't waste your time on keeping promises you break and leave."

"It wasn't easy, Agatha. It was never easy," he mutters honestly. "You never escaped from my mind even for a second. I would even dream about you every night, only to be greeted with loneliness when my eyes opened."

"If it wasn't easy for you then you would at least have had the guts to say goodbye to me."

He shakes his head. "I wasn't brave enough to do that." He looks down letting out a sigh. "I knew the moment I would see those innocent eyes…that pure soul who bloomed my life with her love and care, then I wouldn't have been able to leave."

"Then what made you come back?" I ask, crossing my arms.

"Because I love you, Agatha and you are my forever. I have given it all to ignore that feeling because I feared once I let that in, there would be no turning back and if I get hurt then I won't be the same again. But I'm not afraid anymore."

He comes closer, touching my arms and leaning his forehead against mine.

This closeness…this touch…this calmness.

I only felt it with him and I always will. It was a truth that I couldn't run away from no matter how hard I try.

I close my eyes, letting myself relish in his touch, unable to help myself from holding his strong, muscular arms.

"I want to feel the love I have caged in my ice-cold heart for years. But there is no point in letting it be free if you aren't in my life because that love only belongs to you, Agatha."

I let out a shaky breath while my heart pounds against my chest.

"But how will I trust you with not leaving me again? You said our paths are different."

"Just like I trusted you with my truth, you can trust me with mine."

My heart swells from his words...the same words that have always been my anchor in those dark times at the Magdalene. The same words that assured me he will always be there for me.

"I was wrong to think we have different paths because *you* are my path, Agatha. You always will be. And I know you shouldn't trust me after what I did...after what we have been through. But I'm tired of escaping again and again. I want to be with you...my home. I won't leave you ever again, Agatha. All I ask is for you to give me a chance to be your forever. Will you give me that chance?" he asks.

Letting out a raspy breath I cup his face, bringing his face close to mine and touching our lips together in a deep and passionate kiss that set my nerves on fire like always. He groans softly before pulling me closer and wrapping his arms around me.

"Only if you let me be your forever," I whisper against his lips.

He lightly chuckles. "You have been my forever since the day I saw you, Agatha."

"And now you are mine."

"Only yours."

He puts his hand inside his pocket to find something and when he retrieves a rose I recognize, I gasp in surprise.

"How did you…"

"It was in your dress pocket. When you were at the hospital, one of the nurses gave it to me. I thought to take it with me as a memento because it always reminded me of you. Innocent, pure and beautiful."

I remember…that night I wanted to destroy this rose after feeling betrayed by Eryx. But I didn't have it in my heart to ruin it, so I kept it inside my pocket. I take the rose in my hand, lightly caressing the petals that are a bit dry. But I know just like me, it will be getting love and care, and in no time, it will be blooming again.

Just then I remember about his brother and lean back with a scowl. "What about your brother? Did you find him?"

He nods with a pleasant smile. "I finally have my brother back and he is eager to meet you."

"He knows about me?" I ask.

"According to him, I've been acting like Romeo who can't stop thinking or talking about his Juliet."

I giggle, tangling my arms around his neck, lightly stroking his hair. "Thank you for bringing me out of my darkness."

"No, little girl. Thank *you* for accepting mine despite the consequences."

"It was all worth it to get this ending," I murmur.

"We were afraid to be tainted by the devil in the beginning but now, we are tainted by each other for the rest of our lives."

THE DEVIL TAINTED US

EPILOGUE

AGATHA

2 YEARS LATER

The crashing of the waves and howling wind fill the atmosphere, with the earthy fragrance of the wet sand and sea wafting around my nostrils.

My gaze falls upon the horizon where unknown lands lie miles away, with the view mingling with the crystal blue sky where the bird flies free. My white dress moves along with the strength of the wind but my legs keep it caged in its place.

This is what peace feels like.

Freedom. Calmness. Heavenly.

For years I have hoped for this peace but the darkness that shadowed my life made me hopeless about this moment. At one point, I told myself this moment doesn't exist in reality.

But now…being with Eryx, I know what peace truly

feels like.

He kept his promise and didn't leave me. Every single day he showed how much I mean to him and that I am his whole world.

I even got to meet his brother, who treats me like his own sister. Eros soon recovered and started to work in a small pharmacy in Vailburg. Eryx on the other hand, wanted to do something simple and started to work in a library. While I followed my dream and opened my own art gallery and school. We soon realized that a life of luxury wasn't meant for us, so I sold my parents house and shifted to a one-story house, near the shore side.

I look down at the ink on my ring finger, a reminder that I'm a part of Eryx. He also has a ring tattooed on his finger like mine as we both wanted to mark each other forever. It has been two years and each day feels like a new day with him that leads to the path of love and happiness.

"I knew you would be here," Eryx murmurs from behind, breaking me free from the trance of thoughts.

I smile over my shoulder as he stalks towards me with a smirk. No matter how many times I look at him, I always feel alive being with him.

He sits beside me. His arms and chest stretching against his black shirt that I can;t help but stare. He puts one hand over my shoulder and I lean my head against his chest.

"How are you feeling today?" he asks, his other hand

caressing my swelled-up belly where our baby is growing day after day.

"Slightly tired."

He lets out a breathy chuckle as I feel the vibration of his chest against my back. He leans forward and kisses my temple.

"Just a few more weeks and she will be here."

I frown. "How do you know it's a she? The baby could be a boy too."

"I just have this strong feeling it will be a girl and if it is a boy even then I have no problem. Because no matter what, I will love our child with all my heart, just like their mother."

"Now don't get too sentimental with your lines when you know my hormones can fuck me up anytime and make me cry."

He lets out a hearty laugh that always makes me swoon.

"Well, other than fucking you up, I know your hormones do something else too that I have no objection about."

I try to hide my smile, feeling my cheeks flushed. "I don't know what you are talking about."

He grabs my hair, leaning my head back with a dark smirk that holds a dark promise as always. "You know well what I'm talking about, little girl. I'm talking about the times you would ride my cock like you can't get enough. And trust me when I say, just the thought of your belly swelling because me makes me want to fuck you harder."

I bite my lip, feeling my heart race against my chest as my hormones kick in and clench my thighs. As if he knows his words are already affecting me, his eyes gloom with the dark desire that sets every inch of my skin of fire.

"Does my little girl want to be fucked now?"

I nod with a whimper.

He tightens his hold on my hair making me ache for him more as I let out a moan.

"Use your words, little girl. Say what you want," his lightly nibbles my cheek as I yelp, "and I will give it to you happily. Do you want my cock in your aching, wet cunt?"

"Yes, please! Yes."

"Please what?" he teases me.

"I want you, Eryx. I want you inside me and fuck me like there is no tomorrow," I beg. "Please. I'm burning for you."

"That's my good little girl," he whispers, gifting me with a sinister smile before he scoops me in his arms and carries me inside our house.

Taking me back to our world where it is just the two of us.

No sins.

No darkness.

No emptiness.

We bid farewell to that darkness forever and let happiness and love rule over our world…letting us be far away from the Magdalene and its darkness. As Eryx carries me inside our house, my eyes spot the vase where the rose which was on the verge of dying back in the Magdalene, is now fully blooming along with the other roses surrounding it.

Just like us, it got a second chance in life where no longer...*the devil tainted us*.

THE END

MORE BOOKS

Shanjida Nusrath Ali is an English major student by day and an aspiring independent author by night. Known for her mafia romance book, Cross My Heart, she loves to write about characters going through a dark and heartbreaking path to love with consequences at every turn and coming out stronger in time.

Books
Destroyed (Dark Love Duet #1)
Freed (Dark Love Duet #2)
Cross My Heart
Kingdom of Sinners (Bitter Love Duet #1)
Deviant Vows (The Quarter Chronicles #1)
Omerta Anthology

ACKNOWLEDGMENT

Wow! I still can't believe I wrote my first ever Gothic romance book. A genre I never read before and never felt interested in but here I am xD Finally writing one. But in this unique journey I had the love and support of my readers and authors friends, without whom none of this would have been possible.

Firstly, thank you to my beta readers: Zavi James, Claris Jade, V. Domino, Valentina and Emma Louise. I felt pretty much lost in this genre but you guys really guided me through this. Everyday I doubted myself thinking this book isn't enough but can't thank you guys enough for your help and support.

Secondly, thank you to my PR, Givemebookspr. You guys really helped me a lot with spreading the word about my book. I was very surprised myself to see so many readers being excited about TDTU but wouldn't have been possible without your magic.

Thirdly, thanks to my aunt and mom. You guys kept supporting me and pushing me to try something out of my comfort zone. And you were right mom, I wouldn't have known if I'm able to write Gothic romance or not unless I tried it. Thank you for always believing in me.

Lastly, thank you to my readers. The reason I write my books for. Always appreciate your love and support for my books.

Printed in Great Britain
by Amazon